As Kane stood there, I was guessing he could effc [was exactly what it felt h... Kane responded with a lazy drawl, "I was just having a little fun checking out my new charge. I hadn't planned on shifting back in front of her, but you had to come thundering in."

Alec slid his gaze back to Lucas. "What does he mean *new charge?*"

Lucas cleared his throat a bit uncomfortably. "Kane told me just before class," Lucas replied. "He's been assigned to our team."

"No he hasn't!" Alec snapped sharply. Evidently, there was no love lost between the two men. Kane crossed his arms over his broad chest in challenge, his wavy, dark locks falling loose over his forehead, that only added to his naughtiness.

"I have," Kane reiterated. "Assigned by your uncle, in fact. It seems he appreciates my rather obvious talents."

Alec's literally snarled. "Don't get comfortable. It won't stick."

But I was surprised to see Lucas's eyes glittering with amusement, almost as if he found the whole situation entertaining. "Now, now, boys. Fu—" Lucas began, then restarted himself after slicing me a quick glance. "Forget the past. There's no reason we can't all work together."

"This has to be a joke!" Alec pressed. "He can't be assigned to her. He can't even keep his hands to himself with normal women."

I inhaled quickly, instinctively taking issue with the implication that I was not normal.

"Sorry," Alec whispered over his shoulder.

I stepped around Alec, surprised to see the extreme tension and hardness in his jaw. He clenched his fist at his sides and cast a gaze of fire at Lucas. Lucas just shrugged his shoulders. "Don't look at me, man. I've got my own problems."

"OK, enough!" I grumbled, pushing in front of Alec and stepping before the hedonistic, shape-shifting force known as Kane, positive I heard mumbled curses behind me. "Hello, I'm Olivia. It's nice to meet you . . . I think. But if you ever shift back naked in front of me again, you'll find yourself crumbling from a hard knee to those very private parts."

His scorching gaze slid over me from head to toe. Under that gaze, my clothing seemed pointless. "I'll consider myself warned," he replied lazily, then added, "But what if I'm not shifting? What if I'm just walking around naked?"

Oh yeah . . . A very naughty boy.

Book's by Christine Wenrick

Book One: The Charmed
Book Two: The Charmed Souls
Book Three: The Charmed Fates

the CHARMED SOULS

Book Three of The Charmed Trilogy

CHRISTINE WENRICK

PRINT - ISBN 13: 978-0-9882069-3-9

E-BOOK - ISBN 13: 978-0-9882069-2-2

For information, please e-mail Red Tree House Publishing, Seattle, Washington
at: christinewenrick@redtreehouse-publishing.com

Cover design by Samantha T. Davis, Mill Creek, Washington
Contact e-mail: Samantha.T.Davis@gmail.com

Editorial and interior design by OPA Author Services, Scottsdale, Arizona
Contact e-mail: Info@OPAAuthorServices.com

Printed in United States of America

June of 2013

Dedication

To all of the fans of *The Charmed* who are so invested in sharing the next chapter in Olivia and Caleb's story. You make all of this possible.

Prologue

"I don't care, Christian—just fix it!" Gemma May barked, uncharacteristically, then muttered to herself, "*Good God*, it has to be a Monday." She knew she was being unreasonable, but today she didn't care. She wasn't in the mood to care. Her coven leader, Jax Walker, had set her off yet again this morning with his growly *I'm in charge* tone. Well she would show him . . . at least she was plotting how to show him when the high-pitched chime of the entry bells drew her attention to the front of the Walker Foundation Blood Clinic where she worked.

Her attention was drawn straight to the striking, ebony-haired young woman entering the clinic's doors at that moment. Of less than average height, the slim beauty in a brilliant, cobalt-colored coat that perfectly matched her wide, blinking eyes appeared incapable of hurting a fly. But Gemma's senses told her differently. If provoked, this woman had the potential to be very dangerous. She was a Dhampir, part human/part vampire—a hybrid with speed, strength, and senses far superior to that of any human . . . just like Gemma.

Just as quickly, the brunette locked her gaze on Gemma, appraising her from head to toe, as though she was a possible adversary, before turning to the receptionist and saying in a soft, melodious voice, "I would like to donate today."

The older woman handed her a clipboard and pen. "Fill these out and I'll have someone take you back. We're a little busy today, so it might be—"

"That's all right," Gemma interjected as she came forward, "I'll take care of . . . ?"

"Maya."

"Maya," Gemma echoed, knowing there was little point to paperwork. All of the information would be false. The simple truth was, a Dhampir's blood couldn't be mixed with a human's, so this woman obviously had no intention of donating. She was here for another purpose, and Gemma was determined to find out exactly what that purpose was. *Or,* at least stall her until growly Jax and her other coven brother, Caleb, could arrive. Luckily, the vampires were close and would have sensed by now her considerable unease with this situation.

Gemma led Maya to the donation chair farthest from the room's entrance, the best location for assuring privacy for their conversation. "Have a seat," she instructed coolly, rolling a nearby stool for herself over to the donation station. "So, Maya . . . How did you hear about our little clinic?"

Maya chewed fitfully at her bottom lip, watching closely as Gemma examined her arm with exaggerated slowness, finally pressing two fingers over the most accessible vein just under the surface. After a long moment she replied, nervously, her voice almost breaking, "A friend suggested that I come."

"A friend . . . ?" Gemma feigned only mild interest, but inwardly she wondered if a message was being sent from another nearby coven. It was unusual that they would approach her here at the clinic—but not unheard of. "Do I *know* your friend?"

"I'm not sure," Maya blinked, her eyes finally reflecting some honesty. "That's what I'd like to find out."

Gemma's brows wrinkled at her answer. "Does this friend have a name?"

"Of course . . . but I can't say."

Gemma tightened the latex band over Maya's arm and tapped her index finger above the selected vein, knowing full well the woman was becoming more anxious by the second. "I don't understand. If you won't give me a name, how can I tell you if I know her—or him?"

Maya again chewed at her bottom lip. "By answering a question for me."

Gemma's olive-green gaze brushed over Maya with careful consideration. This whole exchange was quite odd, but she sensed that Jax and Caleb were close to the clinic, so she would play this woman's game as long as it kept her distracted from the two vampires nearly on top of them.

"My friend wants to know if the over-protective sods have eased up on you at all."

Gemma froze in mid-breath, though outwardly she tried to show no reaction. Her mind raced with a thousand different thoughts as she licked her lips and tried to decide what to say next. She realized in that moment that she couldn't afford to have this "donor" panic and run on her. Unfortunately, reaching for the thin needle on the tray beside them was exactly the wrong thing to do to keep the woman calm.

Maya pulled her arm back, removed the latex band, dropped it onto the surgical tray beneath her hand, and said, "Perhaps another time."

She then virtually leapt to her feet and headed straight for the exit.

"Maya!" Gemma called, a somewhat frantic edge in her voice that she just couldn't hold back. Luckily, Maya stopped and looked back over her shoulder. "Tell me more about your friend? Is *she* all right?"

The Dhampir smiled gently, as if that were the response she had been waiting for. But then her head swung forward again and in the next moment she strode out of the collection room and through the clinic entrance.

"Wait! Please!" Gemma cried as she followed the other woman outside. "Has he hurt her?"

Maya didn't answer right away, instead reaching into her pocket and pulling out a spectacular sapphire necklace, the color dark—like the deepest ocean. The moment it came to rest around her throat, Gemma's eyes widened in shock as she immediately lost all touch with the supernatural energy of the Dhampir standing right in front of her.

"He's hunting her . . . ," Maya finally answered just before she rushed forward on the sidewalk, but her escape was halted by two giant male figures who stepped into her direct path. The vampires were here, the taller one's cool, gray stare freezing her like ice before fixing on the ridiculously large gem around her throat.

"Oh, dear," Gemma heard Maya whisper once she realized she was trapped.

Chapter One

*If a man loses his soul, does he lose the essence of the man?
Is he able to weigh the value of what he has lost? Does it negate
a life built with strength and character? Or perhaps . . . does it
just give the man a part of himself worth fighting for?*

***

"Stop it, Caleb Wolfe! I mean it." My giggled cry echoed off
the high, forested peaks around us. Caleb responded by rolling
us over on the plaid blanket, his long arms trapping me beneath
him as his eyes, the liveliest mix of grays I had ever seen,
sparkled with equal parts curiosity and mischief, just before he
lightly speared his wiggling fingers once again into my side.
"Caleb!" I was doing my best to hold back the laughter.

"Ticklish here, are we?" he said with a deep, husky chuckle
that warmed my stomach from the inside. His fingers stopped
their motion as he drew me even closer. "I've learned something
new about my sweet girl today. I like that. I want to learn
something new every day."

I smiled at him. "Well, considering one of us is immortal and
the other partly immortal, that could add up to a lot of new
discoveries. Are you sure you're up for that?"

"Yes," he replied without hesitation, reaching above my head
for a juicy, red grape from a bunch in a bowl, which he
summarily plopped onto my tongue. "I want you with me. I
don't care that you're a Charmer or that I'm a vampire . . . or
that the Supernatural World says we can't be together. They
can all be damned. I want you with me—like this. Just you and
me."

Brushing my fingers downward along his cheeks, I slowly
moved lower to caress the masculine bristles that shadowed his

jaw as I stared back up at him and smiled. "Don't get greedy. You'll jinx us."

"Never, my sweet. You and I are meant to be together. No one can break that, no matter what occurs." He said it with immense confidence as he weaved his fingers through my hair and lifted the strands towards the light. "I love how the light catches the red."

"Really?" I smiled, suddenly more intrigued as I wriggled a little closer to him. "What else do you love?"

His dark brows shot up. "Fishing for compliments now, are we?"

"It never hurts for a man to acknowledge how lucky he is."

"Ah, yes, lucky . . . very well." He lowered his head and brushed his lips ever so lightly over my cheek, trailing them toward my lips. "Your skin—I love your skin," he murmured. "It's soft as a newborn's."

I sighed softly in reply. "That's a good start, but a bit uninspired, don't you think?" I was baiting him, of course, but he seemed to be in good spirits about the whole thing. "I think you can do better."

"I see," he smirked, kissing me just once, so lightly that he just tickled my lips before moving behind my ear. "Your scent . . . How I love your scent . . . vanilla and oranges. It makes me want to just lick you—"

"That's much better," I laughed out in a rush of breath right before his lips caught it and locked over mine, causing an indescribable shiver down to my toes as he kissed me.

"You're all mine now, Olivia," he whispered low. "And I'll never let you go . . . not ever again."

My heart was pounding as he said the words. I wondered if he had any idea how he truly affected me. "Do you mean that, Caleb? Because I just want to stay here with you . . . be lost with you on this mountain."

He settled comfortably between my thighs, curling my legs around his hips so his body was cradled within mine. A slow, heavenly sigh escaped me as I arched to him, my hands sliding over the taut muscles in his back. "All mine," he repeated with roughening breaths, his kisses deepening until his tongue pushed past my parted lips.

God, his kisses were powerful. It was like playing spin the bottle with Cupid himself. But a sudden chill in the air swept over me, and Caleb froze, his body now rigidly alert to everything around him as if sensing something he didn't like.

"Caleb . . . ?" I questioned.

His expression remained even, but the playfulness that had been between us only moments before was gone. "Wait here," he instructed. "I need to check something out. I won't be long."

"Tell me what's wrong?"

He smoothed a large hand over my cheek. "Everything's fine, I promise. I'll be right back."

Before I could question him further, he disappeared into the tree line, and all of a sudden it was much too quiet. Lying back on the blanket, I closed my eyes and waited for the familiar sounds of the forest to return. Where was the brushing sway of the trees or the knocking of the woodpeckers? Even the scent in the air had changed. No longer could I smell the freshness of the grass or the fragrant wildflowers. Everything in the atmosphere around us had seem to dull.

"Don't worry . . . He'll be back," came a familiar and unsettling voice just above me.

My eyes popped open to see the face of a man I hoped to never see again—Luther Davin.

I jumped to my feet, only to be quickly seized from behind by unyielding arms. "No! This isn't possible," I cried, trying to yank myself free from one of the more than a dozen vampire soldiers that now surrounded me. "You can't be outside like this during the day. You're cursed to walk the night."

The Nightwalker's responding laugh sounded amused. "There are no rules for me. I control them all. And I can get to you whenever and wherever I want—day or night."

That didn't make any sense, but there was no time to question it. Determined to not be a prisoner to this man again, I tried to reach my hands toward him, hoping to catch him in my painful Charmer touch, but a vampire soldier caught me and forced my covered arms behind my back. Davin waved his finger back and forth in mocking dismissal. "No, no, little Charmer. You'll not use your gift of touch on me. Save it for those bloodthirsty Lycans who are so drawn to you."

"Never! I won't let you use me as a weapon to fight the Lycans—no matter what you do to me."

"Yes," he sighed. "Unfortunately, I had a feeling you would see things that way. Disappointing, really. And completely wrong, of course . . ."

His eyes as black as the night, Davin glanced past me and commanded my captor with a simple flick of his blanched wrist. I continued to try and fight, but the soldier tightened his grip, releasing one of my arms as a second soldier took it, stretching me until my feet almost left the ground as they dragged me over to a nearby tree, chaining me to its base with heavy metal shackles.

"You see, I've given this a lot of thought," Davin continued as he paced in front of me. "I believe the problem is that you're too distracted. We need to remove that distraction so you can better focus on what you must do for me."

"You know what? You can just—"

"Ah, ah, ah. You don't want to finish that sentence."

"Oh, yes, I do."

"Fine . . . Have it your way," he drawled, motioning with his hand to one of the soldiers standing at the tree line. The vampire turned and nodded towards the thick forest beyond. Soon two more vampire soldiers emerged, dragging another with his head bent low over his chest. He was weak. Massive lengths of silver hung from his neck and burned into his skin like fire. Then I realized I knew who the man was. "Caleb!"

Davin tossed his hand lightly through the air as if dismissing the severity of the situation. "Oh, don't worry, child. His death will be quick, I promise."

"Davin, you don't have to do this—"

His face was suddenly within a hair's breadth of mine, his voice dripping with venom. "Oh, but I do. Do you remember how you so fearlessly challenged me at the prison? Demanded, in fact, that I choose between his life and your service to me?" He sucked in a sharp breath between his protruding fangs. "This is to remind you of your place, child. You'll bow before me and do as I command, or those closest to you will meet their death, just as he will now."

"No! Stop this—please! I'll do whatever you want. I swear. Just let him go and I'll do it."

Davin's long nails dragged along his jaw as his chin lifted with an arrogant tilt. "I don't believe you."

The soldiers chained Caleb to a tree, stacking dry sticks and branches at his feet. Even against the punishing silver, the unrelenting warrior inside him fought against the chains, but it wasn't enough. One of Davin's soldier's then drove a wooden stake straight through his heart.

"Oh, God! No! Please! I'll do whatever you want," I shouted this with true misery, even though I knew the stake through his heart would not kill Caleb, only immobilize him against the tree. "I'll give my life for him. Please, just stop!"

"There's no God here, Olivia. Only me."

The sticks were lit and the thirsty kindling wood went alight around Caleb's feet.

I screamed until my throat was raw, but they didn't stop.

"As long as he's alive you'll continue to fight me," Davin hissed. "So I've decided to remove him from the equation. And, lucky for you, I'm giving you a front row seat."

"No! I won't fight. Please, I won't fight!"

My pleas were ignored as flames began to whip all around Caleb's body, which was paralyzed by the stake in his heart. I had been yanking so fiercely to free myself from the chains that my wrists were now covered in blood. "I'm sorry, Caleb. The chains are too strong. I can't get free."

My lover then spoke to me, clear as day, even though he shouldn't be able to. "It's all right, my sweet," he said, his agonized voice barely above a whisper.

"No," I sobbed, cursing my own lack of strength as I watched the flames blacken his skin, burning it away from his beautiful face, which writhed in agony.

"No! I'm sorry! I'm sorry!"

The vampire finally couldn't hold in the sounds of his pain any longer. He called out in the shrill cries of a man being tortured, then calmly focused his gray eyes on me. "You were always too weak, Olivia," he said.

***

"Nooo!" I swung upright to the sound of my own screams and was instantly thrust into a completely different setting. Bright sunlight jarred my eyes as it streamed through double sliding glass doors that looked out to a grassy setting and large lake beyond.

"Oh, God, it was just a dream," I gasped aloud, clutching my hand over my pounding heart. "It's OK, it was just a dream. He's all right. He has to be!" I could feel the cold sweat under the wrinkled clothes I had slept in. I blinked several times, re-adjusting to the unfamiliar bedroom setting around me. Then I remembered; I was a long way from Caleb—and from home.

Chapter Two

I was no longer in Seattle, no longer in the Cascade Mountains, and no longer with Caleb, the vampire I believed with my whole heart to be my one true love. The beautiful images of him in my dream were just that—images. Memories of a man my soul deeply missed.

As my heart began to slow to a more normal pace, I recollected the final hours of the long drive here . . . wherever 'here' was. Alec Lambert, the Guardian assigned to protect me by the secretive group known as The Brethren, had continued to drive us northeast toward this place he felt sure would keep me safe from the clutches of Davin and his evil vampire soldiers. But in choosing to leave Seattle with Alec right away, I had left Caleb behind without even a chance to say goodbye.

Still, I hoped that our separation would give him the time and space he needed to realize that our love for each other was real and not an illusion created by my Charmer gifts. Until then, I planned to train with The Brethren to learn how to use my new gifts and defend myself in a supernatural world that I just discovered existed all around us.

It was a solid plan . . . or at least I thought so, until my nightmare. Had Davin stayed behind to hunt Caleb, knowing he was his best chance at drawing me back out?

A light rap sounded at my door. "Come in," I called, but there was no response.

I pushed from the bed, rumpling the lovely, hand-stitched comforter I was resting on, and crossed the room to answer the door. Opening it, I discovered a long corridor, but there was no one standing on the other side of my door. Instead, a tray containing several hand towels, neatly folded, and a tall porcelain water pitcher that had steam rising from the spout had been carefully placed on the floor of the corridor, in the very center of my doorway. Then a rhythmic scraping and squeaking from somewhere down the hall caught my attention, the sound, strangely enough, seeming to send out the same sound pattern—scrape, scrape, *squeak* . . . scrape, scrape, *squeak*—as the opening chords of Tchaikovsky's piano concerto #1, a piece that always seemed to be stuck in my head in some way or other simply because in all my years of playing I had not mastered it yet. I poked my head further out into the hallway and saw a woman dressed in a maid's uniform, slowly pushing a service cart down the hall, placing the same trays in front of each door.

It seemed I was in some sort of hotel.

I glanced back into my room, which was about the size of a standard hotel accommodation, and observed—for the first time—that it had a quaint, mountainous retreat sort of feel to it. Clean and bright throughout, the room's furniture was knotty pine, upholstered in soft neutral touches, and cushy carpeting flowed beneath my feet. A small desk and chair flanked the bed on the right, and against the opposite wall was a conversation area that consisted of a two-seater sofa—a love seat—in lush green velvet, with a coordinating print lounge chair. A cast-iron stove served as the room's heat source. It was the perfect setting in which to take shelter from the weather on a cold day.

Picking up the tray, I turned inside once more, noticing that there was no bathroom or cooking area, just a thick, pine countertop on which was a large marble wash basin and a wood-framed mirror that leaned against the wall. This space was divided from the rest of the room by an ornate wooden panel that was secured at the ceiling and floor. Setting the tray down on the spacious counter beside the basin, I realized the water and towels were meant to wash with and that there must be some sort of shared bathroom facility somewhere on the floor. Though that idea seemed a bit inconvenient compared to what I was used to, the old-world charm of it seemed to fit the style of the room.

When I was finished washing up I returned to the bed.

There was a handwritten note waiting for me on the bedside table.

Breakfast is at 8:00—downstairs on the third floor. I'll meet you there.
Alec

Glancing at the clock, I saw that it was already 8:10. I was late!

I stumbled around the room, muttering fiercely to myself. "Great start, Olivia. How will they take you seriously if you're late on your first day?"

Having no time for a full shower, I searched the room for the bags I was sure Alec would have brought up for me. It didn't take long to find them; they were neatly stacked in a small closet just off the entry. I grabbed a comfortable pair of knit yoga pants, a scoop-necked tee, and some running shoes. *Best I can do,* I thought; after all, I had no idea what was appropriate for the first day of learning how to defend myself against vampires.

I found my way down the noticeably new elevators to the third floor, then followed some people into a giant, high-ceilinged room that appeared as if it had once been a formal hotel dining room. The walls were lined with elegant wood panels, and from the ceiling hung several huge, glass-lantern chandeliers that continued the old world charm. A massive stone fireplace dominated the entire south wall of the room, and on the opposite end, several large tables were set up, buffet style, draped in formal linens and covered with dozens of large trays of food. Servers bustled back and forth from the kitchen beyond, bringing fresh trays as the previous ones were emptied.

There must have been at least fifty people already seated in the room, and the large crowd of unfamiliar faces felt intimidating, as I imagined they seemed to sense someone new had entered the room and all seemed to have turned—practically in unison—towards me.

"Go ahead," came a soft voice from beside me to break up the awkward moment. "Pick up a tray and help yourself." I turned to see a striking young woman with long black hair, straight and shiny as silk, and eyes as wide and blue as the sea; she was giving me that '*you're the new kid in school*' sort of weak smile.

I nodded at her and picked up a tray, stepping forward to work my way around the buffet, which included everything one could possibly think of to eat for breakfast: omelets, ham, crepes, French toast, and much more.

Then I heard something confirming my suspicion that I was being observed in some way. "She's a Dhampir?" one woman questioned another—in low tones but loud enough for me to hear—behind me, closer to the end of the table. "She seems so . . . so meek."

Turning my head just enough to see the two women with my peripheral vision, I saw the other woman shake her head in definite disapproval. "Last night I saw Alec carrying her up to her room like she was a child. It was embarrassing."

Her friend snorted. "You're just jealous you didn't think of the idea first."

"Well, that's certainly true. But this ought to be fun . . . watching her learn to fight."

Suddenly feeling a bit self conscious, I turned my head straight forward once more and lowered my gaze to my still empty plate. I'd been in such a rush this morning that I'd not considered how I got from Alec's SUV to the bed I woke up in. I hated feeling like the new kid in school. *At twenty-six,* I thought, *I should be well past all this petty, gossipy crap.*

Setting the tray down, I reached for a plain bagel on a napkin and picked up a glass of milk, hoping that the bland combination might somehow settle my stomach. I then discreetly watched the two women as they walked toward a table full of other females, all of them staring at me with interest. The friendly thing to do would be to go over there and introduce myself, ask to join them. But I quickly lost my courage when I saw there was no empty seat for them to offer me.

Instead, I moved to one of the vacant tables by the wall. I felt a bit ridiculous sitting alone at a round-top table large enough to seat eight people, but soon most of the other diners seemed to forget I was there, nibbling at my bagel and strumming my fingers against the tabletop in rhythm with that blasted concerto I couldn't get out of my head.

That's when I noticed Alec and fellow Guardian, Lucas Rayner, enter the dining hall. The testosterone-amped duo crossed the room with purpose, brimming with self confidence, their strides long and easy, both of these handsome men seeming completely oblivious to the multitude of female gazes that followed them. Especially Alec, who had this effortless California-golden-boy look about him.

There did seem to be quite a few gazes directed at how Lucas's backside filled out his jeans, though.

Watching all of this, I was sure I was scowling as I remembered my few abrupt conversations with the crusty Lucas. He and Alec were best friends, but that certainly didn't endear him to me. The man was a walking cuss word waiting to erupt. He certainly looked like Alec, though. In fact, he looked as if he could be Alec's older brother, somewhere in his early thirties. He was fair-haired, fit, and handsome in his own way, but definitely rougher around the edges. This point was emphasized by the large scar that extended from his right temple to the middle of his right cheek.

From what I knew of him, on his best day he could be blunt, and on his worst he could be downright rude. Lucas was flawed in more ways than I could count, but there was no denying how important he was to Alec, so I left it alone . . . most of the time.

With a full plate, Alec moved away from the buffet table and stopped to scan the room. His gaze soon landed on me and he flashed a smile that caused me to swallow, a little too fast, the current piece of bagel I was aggressively chewing in my frustration—and I nearly choked. He made his way straight toward my table, and Lucas followed while at least a dozen women tracked their movement across the room.

Great! This certainly wouldn't help me make friends.

Alec sat to my right and Lucas settled in beside him, the

grumbling snarl already returning to his lips after he had just been laughing with Alec a moment before.

"Good morning," Alec offered sincerely.

I smiled. "Good morn—"

"Fuck!" Lucas snapped just then as juice spilled all over his plate from his tumbled glass. Within seconds of being seated with me, the rude, brash man I knew was back. And like a bee drawn to honey, I couldn't resist the temptation. "Don't worry, Lucas," I smiled insincerely, "all breakfast foods taste better soaked in orange juice . . . especially French toast and eggs."

Alec choked back a laugh, nearly spitting out his own juice.

Lucas narrowed his gaze at me in warning—but not a lethal warning; more like a '*leave me the hell alone because I got up on the wrong side of the bed*' kind of warning.

He rose to his feet, grumbled a couple of curse words under his breath—mixed with some derogatory comment about women being nothing but trouble—and then proceeded to toss his tray into a nearby garbage can. *The entire tray!* Plates, silverware and glasses, all went flying in one giant heap. I stared at him in wordless disbelief as he simply turned and stalked back towards the buffet tables.

"What? Did he fall out of bed alone this morning?" Hunter Phin Daniels laughed as he sat down in the open chair beside me. "Is Amy finally fed up with him?"

Evidently, if this Amy was fed up, there were many willing volunteers to replace her, as once again several sets of female eyes followed Lucas—or, more accurately, his tight, jean-clad ass—as he sauntered back to the serving tables.

"I wouldn't bring up Amy if I were you," Alec chuckled.

"Well, now I can't resist," Phin laughed as he rubbed his hand over his recently shaved head. "The appeal of giving him shit is just too great." Though he was being talkative in our small group, Phin, short for Phinneas, was very different from Alec or Lucas. If Lucas was the rebel and Alec the star jock, then Phin would be the loyal best friend. A generally more reserved and quiet man, his striking blue-gray eyes did most of the talking for him, popping out against the most beautiful light chocolate skin I had ever seen, and holding you glued to him whenever he spoke.

"How did you sleep?" Alec asked me.

"Good. Maybe too well, actually. I never even made it under the covers." Alec watched me as I toyed with a piece of my bagel. "Thank you for bringing me up to the room last night. But you could've wakened me."

His smile then turned into a frown, as if he was considering why he would do that. "You were dead to the world. Besides, I didn't mind bringing you up."

"You needed rest," Phin joined in. "You've been through a lot in the last week."

I had been through a lot—being kidnapped by Davin and held hostage at a prison just before he tried to practically feed me to a giant and angry Lycan. But I couldn't afford the time to dwell on it. I had to stay focused on getting stronger, and learn how to defend myself against the vampires, demons and Lycans my Charmer gifts would undoubtedly attract. Then I would be able to return home to Caleb.

Leaning back in my chair, my hand touched a crude-looking necklace around my throat that I had awakened with that morning. "Alec, what's this?"

Alec glanced up for a moment and then continued to dive into his food. "It's a necklace. I put it on last night while you were sleeping in the car."

That answer didn't really help. The tacky glass vial that served as the "jewel" for the necklace was hardly decorative, definitely not a fashion statement. "Yes, I know it's a necklace, but why did you buy me a necklace full of dirt?"

Alec swallowed his food quickly as Phin laughed quietly across the table from him. "I didn't buy it. I *made* you a necklace filled with sacred ground. When you wear it, you become blurred to vampires—they lose your energy. They can't track your location."

"Oh . . . ," I replied quietly, realizing what that meant. "So Caleb can't sense me."

Alec responded to that with a deep frown. "Don't give me that sad look, Olivia. You needed to wear this. You and I both know Caleb can track you easily. I couldn't allow him to follow us here."

"But Caleb doesn't like it when he can't sense me. He worries about me."

Predictably, I received a scolding glare in return. "Olivia, you can't think of everything you're about to learn of the supernatural world only in terms of Caleb. There are vampires and demons out there that you need to protect yourself from. Besides, we've talked about this. Caleb will forget you as soon as your power over him wears off. There'll be no need for him to sense you anymore."

"If you're so sure of that, then why do I have to wear it?" I challenged.

Alec blew out a flustered breath. "My, you're stubborn this morning." He reached to remove the necklace. "You don't have to wear it while you're here."

"And why's that?"

Alec didn't answer, instead glancing at the bagel fragment remaining in my hand. "Is that all you're eating?"

"I'm not really hungry this morning."

Alec grabbed an extra clean plate from a nearby table and plopped it in front of me, moving a piece of ham and some fruit from his own plate, motioning for me to eat it. "You need to eat more before you can begin training, especially protein."

"Am I not starting my training today?" Alec shook his head as he finished his bite. "But I'm ready to learn now. I want to know how to defend myself against Davin. I promise I'll work very hard."

Alec smiled at that, seemingly pleased by my eagerness to get started. "No, not today. Gideon's going to get you settled and take you on a tour of the grounds after lunch. Then tomorrow you'll see the doctor. Once Dr. Li gives the all clear on his end, you can begin your training."

Now I knew my face was scowling. *I hated going to the*

doctor.

"Wipe off that scowl, Olivia. This isn't an option. We all had to pass physicals before we could start training. What's with this aversion to seeing the doctor, anyway? Didn't the Greysons ever take you?"

The Greysons were the couple who raised me—the people I believed were my parents until I recently learned the truth that my real mother and father had died when I was just a child. I shrugged. "No."

Alec glanced up in surprise.

"I was never sick," I added.

"They knew who she was," Phin interjected. "They knew as a Dhampir she wouldn't get sick, and they couldn't very well have them testing her hybrid blood. They would've had to find a physician they could trust."

"You're right. Sometimes I forget how difficult it must have been for them to hide her in plain sight."

Alec then gave me a reassuring glance. "It won't be bad, I promise"

At that point, Lucas stalked back to the table, his tray even fuller than the first time—if possible—although noticeably lacking any beverages. He dropped the tray on the table with a loud clap. Phin looked as if he was about to make a smart-ass comment, but Lucas stopped him with a single, sharp finger. "Don't start with me today."

Phin's bright eyes seemed to widen at the challenge. "Then I guess I shouldn't ask how your apology dinner went with Amy last night."

Oh boy . . . Now something was about to explode.

"Dammit, Phin—" Lucas growled, just as he was cut off by the approach of Gideon Janes—a very '*British*' Englishmen with an unfortunate case of horribly bad fashion sense. The faded pattern of the man's jacket was even worse than anything I'd ever seen him wear in Seattle.

"Gideon!" I cried, jumping from my seat. He appeared startled by my over-exuberant greeting. "Perfect timing. Let's go."

"You haven't even touched your food," Alec called after me, obvious concern in his voice.

"I promise I'll eat more tomorrow. I'm a bit nervous today . . . first day and all. But thanks for sitting with me."

Then, as I continued forward with Gideon, I tossed back over my shoulder, "Even you, Lucas."

To which he grumbled, "Women."

Chapter Three

Gideon and I stepped from the lobby of the chalet-style hotel, and in every direction it seemed there was something amazing to behold. To my right were thick pine trees, with the jagged peaks of the Canadian Rockies above. And about a hundred yards ahead the pristine grass meadow we were meandering through rolled downward in a not so gentle slope 'til it hit the shore of a crisp, glacial lake that was surrounded by more mountainous terrain. Aside from the hotel itself, the whole area looked completely untouched by man. It was truly amazing. "It certainly is beautiful here. I understand now why Alec couldn't stop talking about this place on the drive over. But why's he so confident I'll be safe here?"

"Because we're on sacred ground," Gideon answered as he splayed his hands out in front of him. "The Brethren purchased the property and hotel nearly a century ago. All of this land, for two square miles, has been consecrated by a bishop. You're safe because vampires and Lycans can't sense you here, and they can't cross onto it. They are literally stopped by an invisible wall. In fact, this is probably the safest place to be while you're training."

My heart did a big thump when I realized *that* was why Alec said I didn't have to wear the necklace anymore. He knew Caleb could no longer sense me—and hadn't been able to, practically since we'd left Seattle, thanks to his makeshift necklace.

"There are twelve of these Brethren sites around the world," Gideon continued. "Each site is referred to by its own name, and each of the twelve Elders is primarily responsible for a site. Meaning, they spend most of their time at their home locations when they aren't gathered together in council. This site is referred to as The Oracle. It is one of the oldest and largest sites, comparable with the one outside of London, The Hallow, which was the original site. It's home base, so to speak."

"So which Elder is in charge of The Oracle?"

Gideon motioned for us to proceed to the right, taking us north, away from the hotel and lake towards the base of the mountains. "Alec's uncle, Reese Lambert."

I blinked up at him in surprise. "His uncle? Does that mean . . . ?"

Gideon nodded. "Reese and Alec are direct descendants to one of the original twelve men who formed The Brethren two centuries ago. Reese will hold their family's seat until it will one day be passed down to Alec."

I was shocked. Alec had never mentioned that he would someday be an Elder. No wonder people always seemed to watch him with such fascination. "But if Alec's so important to The Brethren, why's he risking his life being my Guardian?"

Gideon responded with a measured smile. "Each future Elder must find his own way. Each must know the strength within himself before becoming worthy of leading others . . . even if that means facing their own mortality. I've known Alec all his life. At times, preparing for the responsibility ahead of him has been difficult. He lost his father, Gerard, when he was thirteen, so he has only had Reese to guide him as he grew up. In fact, Gerard's seat was intended to pass straight to Alec, but Reese stepped in when the Elders, in council, deemed that Alec was too young and inexperienced in life to take the seat."

We continued to walk for a while as I processed what Gideon was telling me. "That seems like a lot to place on his shoulders. How does he feel about becoming an Elder some day?"

"He's been raised in this world," Gideon assured me, "prepared for it, as you were meant to be. It's all he's ever known. He will be ready when the time comes."

Gideon then nodded towards a small building nestled in the trees about a hundred yards ahead of us. "This way. I have something I want to show you."

"Gideon, can I ask you something?"

"Of course."

"I noticed at breakfast that people seemed to be clustered together."

He nodded. "That doesn't surprise me. The Guardians and Hunters are divided into different teams. They tend to socialize a lot within their own teams and groups. Alec's team, of course, is responsible for protecting you."

"Why would I need protection here if this place is on sacred ground?"

He hesitated before answering, as if choosing his words carefully. "Until you better understand your gifts, and as long as Davin's still out there, The Brethren believe it's important for you to have protection. Luther Davin was once Sovereign Elder of The Hallow, meaning that his family holds the highest seat on the council and so is intimately familiar with how The Brethren operate—their locations, personnel—and defenses."

I fell silent for a long while, trying—without much success —*not* to think about the madman who so desperately wanted to use my gifts for his own purpose—drawing in and trapping his enemy, the Lycans. My experience with him on Vancouver Island had shaken me. And to know he was still alive and possibly still searching for me had made for several sleepless nights since then. I tried to reassure myself that he would give up after seeing the lengths The Brethren and Caleb would go to protect me. But deep down, I knew the truth. Luther Davin would never give up.

I then thought about Ryan, the member of Alec's team who was lost while trying to save me from Davin on Vancouver Island. "Will Reese assign someone new to Alec's team after . . . after?" I didn't want to say it. Even now, nearly a week later, I hated even thinking about it. Luckily, I didn't have to. Gideon knew immediately who I meant.

"He already has, though I don't believe he's had a chance to tell Alec yet. Alec may have a few concerns about his uncle's choice, but the Shifter was hand-picked by Reese himself."

"Concerns . . . ?"

"Nothing for you to worry about . . . He's quite a capable

fellow."

We approached a heavy thicket of pine trees that concealed the small building just beyond, and I glanced back to verify that we had come quite a distance from the main building.

"You'll need to make yourself familiar with all the natural markers of the property," Gideon began. "I assure you, behind these lines you're very safe, but you should be aware that the sensing goes both ways. While on these grounds the Dhampirs —including yourself—have trouble sensing vampires outside of sacred ground—as well as each other within the property, unless they are close to them in proximity."

The building we approached was now completely visible. It was a chapel, almost completely hidden within the trees. Small and lovely, the little building looked as if it had been built long ago but had recently been restored. The stone structure seemed freshly cleaned, the stained glass newer, brighter than it should be for a building this age, and the thick wood doors at its entry looked barely used.

I began heading inside when Gideon gently stopped me. "This way," he said, directing us instead toward the back.

We crossed into a large graveyard, the numerous headstones very real reminders of all those who had lost their lives for this group's cause.

Gideon stopped before two gravestones, one marked Evelyn Moreau and the other James Moreau, and I suddenly felt a shiver run through me, as if some instinct deep inside me knew exactly what Gideon was about to say. "Eve and James Moreau were your parents."

Unexpectedly, I fought off watery eyes as I knelt before the two markers. "My parents . . . ," I whispered, inhaling a slow, steady breath. Since discovering the family who raised me—the Greysons—had not been my birth parents, I had known nothing of my biological parents. Now, seeing the place where they were laid to rest, I experienced a painful reminder that I would never meet them, never know them, which made me wonder if I would ever truly know myself.

"I want to apologize to you, Olivia," Gideon began sincerely, staring at my mother's grave as he spoke. "For pushing you so hard in Seattle. I knew your mother well, and just before she died I promised her that I'd look after you. When the Greysons disappeared with you, I felt as if I had broken my promise to her. That's why it has been so important to me to see you come home."

I frowned as I kept my back to Gideon. The Oracle wasn't my home, Seattle was. But I saw no reason to dash the man's illusions. "You cared about my mother, didn't you?"

He stepped forward, slow to answer, as if taking time to reflect first. "To me, there was no more beautiful creature. I loved your mother for a very long time." Sighing with a smile, he shook his head. "She never felt the same way about me. Her heart was lost the day she met your father, James, and remained so even after he was gone."

"My father . . . James," I echoed quietly as I turned to his gravestone. "His gravestone shows he died nearly two years before Eve. How did it happen?"

"He died in a battle with the Lycans. But he didn't go down easily. He was an exceptionally brave man, especially considering that he was human."

Sadness filled me at wishing I could've met him—both of them—just once. How would I ever know if I was anything like either one of them? "How was he strong enough to be a Hunter? The ones I've met so far have been male Dhampirs like Phin."

"He trained relentlessly, strengthened his body . . . Not unlike Alec and Lucas. Your father was an inspiration to a lot of the human males who've come after him and are just trying to measure up in a supernatural world."

An inspiration? That was ironic. Perhaps those who admired him forgot that he died so young, leaving behind a distraught wife and a daughter who would never know him.

"He wanted always to be at your mother's side, protecting her. That, unfortunately, was how he died. Your mother's gifts, unlike your own, didn't work on the Lycans. He died saving her from the beast that eventually killed him."

Closing my eyes in horror, I tried to brush away the images

that were filtering in. I didn't want to think about how he must have suffered right before his death. I couldn't understand why either of my parents would choose this life. "So my mother had to raise me by herself?"

He nodded, a melancholy smile slowly crossing his features. "She was a dutiful mother but never quite the same after your father died. I helped her as much as I could with taking care of you, but . . ." Gideon paused, almost as if his next words were stuck at the back of his throat, " . . . somehow I think she sensed she wouldn't live to see you grow up. I believe that's why she asked for my help. Her broken heart consumed her, and she wasn't focusing as she should've been when fighting the Immortals."

Responding to the look on my worried face, he placed a reassuring hand on my shoulder. "Her death was quick."

I realized just then that this rather formal, and at times awkward man, was a connection to the past, a connection to my mother and father. I had first seen Gideon as representing *the hammer*—a man who pressured me relentlessly to come here, to a place I didn't know. I had been resistant to that pressure, but as he continued to tell me stories of both my parents, my perception of him began to change. He had loved my mother, and his life since her passing had been committed to promises he made to her in the name of that love. As I watched him now, his fidgety movements and outdated dress became the indentifying marks of a kind and gentle man who wanted nothing more than to fulfill the promise he made to my mother nearly twenty years ago. And if my mother had trusted Gideon enough to guard with my future, then I believed I could trust him, as well.

"Olivia, may I now ask you something? Something rather important?" Gideon asked as he stepped closer. I nodded in reply. "Alec and Lucas talked to me of the day they came to get you on the mountain. The vampires that you were staying with —"

"Daywalkers," I corrected.

"Pardon me?" Gideon asked with a questioning expression

showing suddenly on his otherwise furrow-free face.

"That's what you were going to ask me about isn't it? The vampires the Guardians saw were outside during the day. They're Daywalkers."

Gideon's gaze swept back and forth as if he were trying to open up his mind to the possibility. "Remarkable . . . We've never seen such a thing. I mean, I guess there are remote references that can be interpreted in old text . . . I just don't understand how—"

"Because their soul is still with them," I answered, not quite sure why I felt so confident about it.

Gideon immediately shook his head. "That's not possible, Olivia. Vampires don't have souls. They possess no moral compass to permit them to distinguish between right and wrong."

"That's not true," I insisted, rising back to my feet and feeling somehow taller for it. "I don't know what all your text books tell you about vampires, but I know what I felt when I mirrored Caleb. He has a soul. I'm sure of it." I was becoming more and more emphatic as I talked. "There was light inside of him. I touched it. When I mirrored Isaac, I felt only darkness. And Davin . . . there was something underneath, a sliver of his humanity that was left, but it was trapped—infected."

Gideon's pale brown eyes were wide with shock, as if I had just tried to proclaim that the earth was not round. "You're suggesting that these Daywalkers have somehow reclaimed a part of their soul . . . and that is what allows them to be out during the day?"

"Reclaiming it or holding onto it. Don't you see? There has to be something left of their soul that allows them to be more controlled—more human."

Gideon stared at me doubtfully but I continued to press him. "Just consider this. What if the soul isn't lost when they're turned? What if it's taken over . . . suppressed . . . or infected by darkness—a darkness that slowly destroys it? That's what I felt in Davin. I didn't feel it in Isaac, but he had already been consumed by evil for a long time."

"Olivia, I . . . It's just that your gift is so new. I'm just not sure you recognize yet what you're touching, what you're feeling."

I lowered my head with a disapproving sigh. "I wish there was a way I could prove it to you—to show you."

"It's all right," he replied, though he appeared lost in thought. "It's curious, though. Your mother used to say to me that the evil she touched was similar in both humans and vampires. I took it more metaphorically at the time, but . . ."

"What if there's something to that? What if it's the same as the darkness that invades a serial killer's mind?"

Gideon furrowed his brow. "I suppose there's something to that. "I'm not sure we really understand what happens to a soul that has no remorse, no concept of the wrong it has committed."

That idea led us to speak of many more theories, and next thing we knew, the entire afternoon had disappeared. "Oh, dear, we've missed dinner," Gideon announced. "You must be hungry. Let's get inside and see if we can track down some leftovers from the kitchen."

As we stood up, I reached out and grasped Gideon's arm midway between his shoulder and elbow. I put just a little pressure on my grip and said, "Thank you—for sharing stories of my mother. It's so hard not to know anything about her."

"You will," he reassured me. "Since I was close with your mother, I know a lot about both her and your father. I'll share with you what I know, as well as teach you about your gift. I don't want you to be afraid of it. Your mother would've never —"

"I can teach the child of her mother," interjected a familiar voice.

Startled, Gideon and I both swung around to see Luther Davin standing not ten yards from us beneath the evening shadows of the mountain.

Chapter Four

Vampire soldiers flanked Davin on each side as he stood there in a long, ceremonial coat, those evil, black eyes of his fixed on me. "I knew your mother well. She was a beauty just like you. I'll teach you of her. That's what you want, isn't it?"

I just stood there in stunned silence until he broke my wordless trance by slamming his palms against the invisible barrier that separated us, and it suddenly became very clear how important that invisible wall was between us. "Isn't it?" he barked.

Gideon gave me no time to respond; grabbing my arm and swinging us both back around towards the hotel. "It's all right," he reassured. "They can't cross onto sacred ground." But I could see in the pinched features of his face that he didn't like having to rely on an invisible wall any more than I did.

"I'll kill him, Olivia!" Davin warned, halting me in my tracks and fearing I knew exactly who '*him*' was.

I yanked my arm from Gideon's firm grip, my feet barely touching the ground as I swung around to race back to Davin.

"Olivia, don't!" Gideon called.

I stopped just a few feet before the edge of the invisible wall, then jerked back suddenly when Davin swiped his arms out as if expecting to grab me, but he still couldn't cross the plane.

"I'm not with the vampire anymore," I said, as evenly as I could—considering my heart was trying to pound its way out of my chest. "He doesn't remember me. My home is here now."

"Nice try, child. I don't have to hear your heartbeat to know you still care deeply for the vampire. I can see it in those fear-filled eyes of yours. If you won't come to me freely, then I'll go to him. And I promise you, I will take my time in torturing him."

His tongue licked slowly over his lips, capturing every bit of my attention. The vampires beside him laughed as if looking forward to the entire, sickening event. "Perhaps stakes and silver," he continued, "or I could just roast him slowly over high —"

"No!" I yelled as if I could will it to be so, inching dangerously closer to the barrier until a jarring hand ripped me back with a force that stunned me. This time Gideon refused to let go, even as I fought to stay right where I was. "If you hurt him, I'll never give what you want. Not as long as I live."

"Oh, come, child. You think he's the only way I can cause you pain? After I've disposed of him, I can always move on to the next." His coal black gaze almost lit up with delight. "Aren't you wondering how I knew you were here?"

He didn't wait for me to answer.

"Your Guardian, Alec. I know him well. He'll always keep you close to him. You'd better make sure he stays behind this wall."

"No! No!" I tried to go back to him, but Gideon roughly lifted me off my feet, his arm snatching around my waist to drag me upward and against his side and away from Davin. "No, Gideon! We can't let him hurt them. We have to go back! I have to stop him!"

Gideon didn't respond, only continued to drag me farther and farther away. "Gideon, please!" My entire body was shaking as my breaths wheezed in and out, like painful waves engulfing my lungs. Gideon continued to carry me all the way back to the hotel.

Once we were close to the hotel building, a group of trainees that had been hauling in equipment for the night had stopped their work, not quite sure what to make of the odd sight in front of them. "Lambert!" one of the men called into the lobby.

Alongside Lucas, Alec came walking out to witness Gideon dragging me up toward him, head first, with my feet kicking behind. "What the hell's going on?" he demanded in a definitely *Elder* tone.

Now out of breath, Gideon tried to pull me all the way over

to Alec, but I fought him the whole way. "It's Davin," he gasped.

The instant response on Alec's face was pure fury, but of course it was Lucas who cursed about ten different blasphemous words with barely a breath in between and then asked, "He's found her here already?"

"I need to go back!" I said firmly to Alec.

Alec now understood that I was trying to return to Davin, and he was having none of that idea. Suddenly, my knees were cinched between powerful arms before he hauled me clean off my feet and threw me over his right shoulder. "*What the—?* Alec, what're you doing?" I couldn't decide whether I was embarrassed—or just incredibly angry.

Alec ignored my protest and continued striding toward the front entry.

"Put me down, you giant oaf! I have to go back."

"You're not going anywhere," he growled. "Lucas! Get me details, and make sure Phin is on his trail with a couple of Hunters in five. Then meet me inside."

"You got it," Lucas called back.

Once inside the lobby, Alec deposited me by simply dropping me onto a leather sofa. He was caught off guard, though, when I pulled him down with me and wrapped my arms tight around him, burying my head into his shoulder. He must have realized how scared I was, because he didn't try to press me just then; instead, he chose to sit there and hold me quietly in his arms until my breathing became more even against his shoulder. "Olivia, tell me what happened?"

Before I could even answer, Lucas rushed up and answered for me. "The bastard cornered them at the graveyard. Gideon said he threatened to kill the vampire—and you—if she didn't go with him."

As Lucas spoke those awful words, I squeezed my arms tighter around Alec.

"Alec," Lucas warned. "She tried to cross the line and go to him. She fucking would've if Gideon hadn't been there to stop her."

"Olivia!" Alec snapped, pulling my head from his shoulder, using both hands and locking my face, vise-like, eye-to-eye and just inches apart. "You can't do that. Don't you ever try to sacrifice yourself again! Davin isn't going to hurt me, and he won't hurt Caleb. He's trying to scare you into giving him what he wants."

"You don't *know* that—"

"I *do!* I do *know* that. Use your head, Olivia! He needs you to have a reason to leave the safety of sacred ground. Caleb's that reason. He won't kill the only leverage he has over you."

Shaking my head in his hands, still in deep denial, I replied, "But Alec, what if he hurts them? I'd never forgive myself if he hurt either one of you, or Phin . . . or even Lucas."

"Gee, thanks," Lucas replied with a sour expression.

"That's not going to happen. Are you listening to me? It's not going to happen."

"He's right," Lucas added. "We're not about to let anything happen to Alec."

"What about Caleb?" I pressed. "His coven? Please, Alec. I need to know they're OK. You have to send somebody to check on them."

Alec was shaking his head before I even finished the words. "I can't do that. You know I can't do that. You're going to have to trust that I know what I'm talking about when it comes to Luther Davin. I know him. I know how he thinks."

At that I was silent. Alec's reasoning began to make sense. But the way I felt in that moment, I just couldn't bet Caleb's life on it.

Alec smoothed his hand over my cheek. "I want you to make me a promise . . ." he began, his gaze more intent than I had ever seen it before. " . . . that you won't step one foot off this land . . . not until we find Davin and destroy him."

"No, Alec—you can't go after him. He'll kill you!"

"Olivia, you're not getting what the job of a Guardian is. It's pretty basic . . . *I guard.* I'll always be between you and whatever threatens you, and I'll always come for you. There's no negotiating this."

I swung away from him, grinding my teeth. I was trying to understand why my stubborn Guardian was so willingly putting himself in danger like this. Alec seemed to sense my frustration and pulled me back around to face him, his expression now just as determined as my own. "If you set one foot off this land and sacrifice yourself to him, Lucas, Phin, and I will come after you. Then it will be war with Davin again in the outside world. Is that what you what?"

"No!"

"Then you need to do as I ask. Understand?"

When I didn't reply right away he shook me lightly to further his point. "Olivia?"

I finally nodded reluctantly, still worried that Caleb, Jax and Gemma were in great danger, but I was completely torn between my love for Caleb and the fact that I didn't want my protectors harmed if they had to come after me.

So, I would do as Alec asked . . . for now . . . until I found a better way.

❋❋❋

The next day, after a hard morning run on the grounds and a rather indulgent shower, I searched the third floor for Gideon, who was supposed to escort me to Dr. Li's office. As I approached the dining hall I heard his—and Alec's—hushed voices in conversation among other voices on the floor, but they were nowhere in sight. Using my superior Dhampir hearing to home in on just their voices, I soon found myself in a hiding place just outside a concealed back corridor. Neither man was aware of the Dhampir ears intruding on their conversation.

"You believe she'll try to sacrifice herself again?" Gideon asked.

"I know she will," Alec grumbled. "You saw the fear in her eyes. Her love for that damned vampire is her weakness—and Davin knows it. He's using it against her." Alec then sighed roughly. "But I'm not wrong. Davin won't destroy the only leverage he has with her in the outside world. I just need to find a way to make her understand that."

"You could send someone to check on the vampire. That would ease her mind."

For a moment my heart surged with hope that Alec might agree to the idea, but it was soon dashed. "Not a chance. It's only been a few days. He may not be out from under her illusion yet. If he even suspected our people were watching him, he'd track them back here like a bloodhound. I should know . . . I watched him tear over land and sea to get to her after Davin kidnapped her."

Gideon pursed his lips and let out a long breath. "Have you considered the possibility, Alec, that the Daywalker really does love her?"

"Don't be ridiculous," Alec snapped. "*Daywalker* . . . it's a load of crap. He's a vampire, pure and simple. He can't love her. Their union goes against everything she is—everything she was born to do. The vampire's just trapped under her illusion, that's all."

I leaned back against the wall and closed my eyes. Alec's words hurt me to my very core. He believed in what he was saying so fiercely that I couldn't help but wonder if he had any intention of ever allowing me to leave this place he considered his home.

"But it isn't *my* home," I thought, almost speaking the words aloud.

"And yet he never harmed her," Gideon countered, "never tried to possess her when she was with him. I find that very intriguing. Perhaps you need to make room for the possibility," he continued. "This would not be the first or only time that something has defied the laws of the supernatural world."

Alec's sharp snort of disgust stopped Gideon right there, and he didn't press the subject further. He just said, "What would you suggest we do?"

"I'm going to ask Phin to take a couple of the Hunters and track Davin's movements at night. If I can prove that he'll stay close to her and not go back to Seattle, I'm hoping she'll listen to reason and remain on sacred ground. At least until we can destroy him."

"Have you discussed this with Reese?"

Alec nodded. "He agrees with the idea. I wanted to go with Phin—"

"But Reese won't allow that," Gideon finished for him. "That shouldn't surprise you. You may be a Guardian, but Reese is still very protective of you."

"I know," he grumbled, as if it wasn't the first time the issue had come up.

More people entered the hall, and not wanting to be caught eavesdropping, I made my way into the dining room, where Lucas and Phin were already seated at a large table, each enjoying an enormous plateful of food that I was sure would send them both into a food coma.

How could they possibly work off that many calories?

As I approached the table, Phin gave me a welcoming smile, while at the same moment I was catching the remainder of Alec and Gideon's conversation, their voices now becoming louder in my mind. They were moving toward the dining room.

"You know she'd sacrifice herself for you, as well. I saw it in her eyes when Davin threatened her with your life."

"Gideon, that's not going to happen," Alec complained. "I won't allow it."

Gideon paused, disappointment filtering through his voice. "Why do you so easily dismiss your importance to The Brethren? Unlike Olivia, you've given your entire life to this cause. You were raised in it. Yet you diminish your own value to the future of it. Why?"

"She has a gift so powerful; we may never fully understand it. She alone could make a difference in the balance of this war. Her importance is immeasurable."

"Gifts are not the only thing that will win this war—leadership will. A committed belief to that which you are fighting for. Right now, Olivia doesn't . . ."

"Olivia," Phin called, interrupting my eavesdropping. "Join us."

"Good morning," I returned, surprised when Lucas pulled

out a chair beside him. He let out a small, grumbly sound, but there was no cursing.

This was progress.

"We brought you some food," Phin remarked, pointing to a full plate at a vacant seat.

"I can see that," I said, trying to hold back a sarcastic smile. "Thanks, but I'm not supposed to eat anything before my tests."

"Ah, today's the big day."

Alec walked up behind me then, squeezing his hands over my shoulders briefly before taking a seat. Even if I hadn't just overheard his conversation with Gideon, I would've been able to tell that something was bothering him. It was evident in the strained dimple on his chin. The way it pulled and moved was always the key to knowing Alec's moods.

"Phin, I need to speak with you after breakfast," Alec said quietly.

Phin shook his head in quick reply. "No, you don't. The answer's yes. We'll go tonight."

A self-scolding smirk crossed Alec's lips as if he should've known better than to try and have his conversation with Gideon anywhere on the floor. He then looked at me, his wrinkled brows asking a silent question.

I nodded to confirm his suspicion.

His expression grimaced and I took his hand under the table to give a reassuring squeeze. "If you can show me . . . I'll do as you ask."

Lucas sat back hard in his chair. "Does someone want to tell me what the hell's going on since I seemed to be the only one out of the loop? Damned vampire hearing . . ."

"I'll catch you up later," Alec replied.

Gideon walked up and I rolled my eyes in dread. "Gideon, do I have to—"

"Yes, you have to," he answered before I even finished. "And do you forget that you were injured in a brutal battle less than a week ago? You need to be examined to make sure you're completely healed."

"But I'm fine—"

"Olivia, stop being so stubborn and just go," Alec said, pushing me from the chair.

"Fine, I'm going."

***

After spending the afternoon being poked and prodded by Dr Li, I took some free time to organize my room and then wandered the property during the dinner hour. Soon, I discovered my favorite private spot along the hillside just above the lake—a large rock, big enough to seat several people, perfect for watching the last of the sun's rays roll off the water's glassy surface.

Thinking back on everything that had happened in the last week, I was still trying to take it all in. Only three days ago I was saying goodbye to Caleb, pouring my soul out through the keys of a piano, trying to let him know with each note how much I loved him—how much I needed him. And now here I was, in a strange land, far away from him, my fingers itching to play again, with several dozen new and curious eyes on me, being poked and tested while Davin just waited for me to step off sacred ground. It all seemed so unreal, far off, like it was happening to someone else, not me.

I ached for the vampire who was in my heart, and I worried for him, wondering what he was going through as he tried to determine if he was trapped under a Charmer's illusion. I wished he were here so I could wrap myself into his strong arms and listen to his deep, rumbly voice assure me that, despite everything that had happened, things were going to be all right. Yet, I knew every day I made it through was one day closer to returning to him. I reminded myself that I was doing all this for us. "I miss you," I whispered. "But I know I'll come back to you a stronger person." One that he wouldn't have to risk his life everyday to defend, because I would be able to defend myself in this new world I was only starting to understand.

This was for us.

"Rough day?" Alec asked, pulling me from my thoughts.

He perched himself beside me on the rock and almost immediately I caught a familiar scent on him. "You smell of apples."

He smiled and reached into his pocket to pull out a large Granny Smith and a small packet. "I brought this for you. There's some peanut butter in there. Protein."

"I've already had plenty to eat."

He scowled as if he didn't believe me. "While you're training, you—"

"—have to have more calories," I finished for him, with a grin. "Really, Alec . . . I haven't even started training yet, and you'd have me eating double the calories I normally do."

"Trust me," he winked, "you're going to need them."

He wrapped his arm around my back and surveyed the quiet darkness around us. "I'm surprised you're out here this close to the perimeter after what happened."

"I saw Phin before he left. I know he won't let Davin come near here. And I won't let Davin keep me locked up in fear."

"I'm glad to hear that," Alec said. "So, how did things go with Dr. Li today? You're still in one piece . . . no major organs missing?"

"Very funny." I shrugged my shoulders negligibly. "Fine, I guess."

"You should have your test results in the next couple of days. Once you're cleared, you can begin training." He reached back inside his pocket to pull out a folded sheet of paper. "I've a list of the classes you'll be doing."

"Really?" I grabbed the sheet of paper from his hand. "What are they?"

"All right, grabby," he laughed. "In the morning there's exercise—"

"Can I do the yoga class?"

"Sure, but this class focuses on testing your strength, as well as your running and jumping abilities. But you'll still need it. Yoga is great for focus and relaxation. You probably could've used a little of that today," he teased.

"You're just a regular stand-up comedian tonight, aren't you?"

He ignored the comment and continued, "Then you have defense training—which Lucas and I teach. And after that, weapons training. You'll spend your afternoons with Gideon. He's your assigned Guide and will work with you on your abilities specific to being a Charmer. And I believe he already mentioned that he would be giving you some family history, as well, right?"

I nodded eagerly. "I'm looking forward to that most of all."

"Good," he said, glancing off into the distance.

"This all sounds good. I should be kicking demon butt in no time. So why do you look so concerned?"

Alec glanced up with a start, surprised to realize that I could already read him so well. "Reese told me The Elders have requested that you take an Advanced Situations training course with one of the other Guardians here. His name is Jude. You've not met him yet, but he's nice enough. Basically, Jude will simulate hostile situations and teach you how to get out of danger using the tools at your disposal."

"Sounds good. So what's the problem?"

Shaking his head, he replied, "I just don't understand why they're having you do this so soon. Usually, these techniques are learned after someone has taken the defense class."

"I'm sure it'll be fine. I'm willing to work hard, Alec. I really want this."

His lips curved upward into an approving smile, his gaze softening as he stroked his index finger along my forearm from elbow to wrist. "I was worried when I didn't see you at dinner tonight."

I smiled inwardly. This man was born to be a Guardian—a protector of souls. "I needed some time. The changes in my life the last couple of weeks have been a lot to process."

His brow arched high. "Would you like me to leave?"

"No, of course not, you're fine."

As I said those words, he set the apple down beside me, his scent seeming to wrap around me as he leaned in. He smelled of the beach and sun. I had never noticed his scent before, and that made me aware of how close he was to me. He exhaled a heavy breath that crashed against my ear. "I want you to be happy here. I want this to be your—"

"Home?" I finished for him. "Alec, this isn't home to me. My home is—"

"—not with the vampire," Alec cut in.

I watched him for a long moment, trying to measure how much any talk of Caleb bothered him. Over time, I had thought his hard opinion of Caleb would soften, but it seemed to only be getting worse. I didn't understand why it was important to me that Caleb and Alec like each other. Of course, it was a completely ridiculous notion that they ever would see the world through the same eyes, let alone respect one another.

"I was going to say, in Seattle."

His finger slid back up my arm, all the way to my cheek. Leaning over me, his sunny scent grew stronger, while his warm breath brushed over my ear. "If you give it a chance, this can become a home to you. I can keep you safe here. I promise I'll keep you safe."

Suddenly, I became very aware of the tremendous heat radiating from his body. His hand curved to the shape of my cheek, drawing me closer to him. My lashes blinked back in surprise, realizing what was happening as his breathing deepened and his soft lips kissed my cheek and moved down towards my mouth.

There was no question Alec was a handsome man, probably already well experienced at pleasing a woman. I felt it in the kisses that explored my skin so gently. But he wasn't Caleb. He wasn't the man I was hopelessly in love with. His lips were too warm, and I missed the frosty tingling.

"Alec," I said, as calmly as I could, given that his warm breath had fallen right over my lips just before he had pressed them against his own. I pulled away gently, trying not to hurt his feelings. "Please stop. This isn't real for you."

Alec blinked and drew back from me, and I could see the realization beginning to reflect from his eyes. After a moment, he dropped his head, cursing under his breath before he quickly moved from the rock. "I'm sorry. I'll leave—"

"Wait." I grabbed the Granny Smith and slid off the rock to stand beside him. "It's OK, Alec. I'm sorry my mother's gift is making things so difficult for you."

He laughed, almost dismissively. "I don't think it's just your mother's gift," he began. "You're utterly charming in your own right. But I'll do better, Olivia."

Even in a situation that was potentially awkward and embarrassing for him, he always spoke with complete honesty. This man of truth never wavered from it. I admired that about him. "I know you're my Guardian, but I don't want you to worry so much about protecting me. I'm here to learn how to protect myself. I want that for myself."

"I understand that, but I think you're expecting too much, too soon. Give yourself time," he said. "Besides, it's in my nature to protect the people I care about. It's why I am who I am. That won't change because you become stronger."

I smiled, careful not to make contact with his skin, which would cause the illusion to become stronger for him. I didn't want to make things more difficult than they already were. "Will you walk me back to my room?"

Without saying another word he led us back toward the hotel.

I just hoped there would be no awkwardness with my Guardian tomorrow.

Chapter Five

For the next couple of days, I wandered around and familiarized myself with the boundaries of the property, just waiting for the green light from Dr. Li to begin my training.

Today it was warm and sunny outside, so I sat on a bench in a small garden just off the lobby and observed two groups training in the open field. One group was working on mastering proficiency with the crossbow. Each bow was loaded with silver-tipped arrows and the archers aimed with nail head precision. Alec and Lucas co-led the other group, which was concentrating on defensive maneuvers. But what was most noticeable to me about this group was the absence of any mats to soften their landing against the hard-packed ground.

Sometimes it was difficult for me to imagine that I would soon be a part of all this. To any casual observer The Oracle would seem to be some sort of private school with a lot of fun sports activities going on, but it was much more than that. These people were training for their lives. *I* would be training for my life. The question was, would I be able to handle the challenge?

"Can I sit with you?" a soft voice asked, pulling me from my thoughts. I looked up to see the same woman who had spoken to me at the buffet table that first day. Her bright blue eyes were wide with curiosity as she went ahead and took a seat beside me without waiting for me to answer. "My name is, Maya. Maya Brunetti."

Surprised that she was talking to me, I nodded at her slowly. Up to this point, she was the only woman who *had* talked to me. Unlike the men at The Oracle, the women seemed to prefer keeping a distinct and rather obvious distance, perhaps wanting no part of my mother's powerful gifts. But the friendly woman sitting beside me now had a genuine smile on her face that reached to her eyes, and that was nice. "My name is Olivia," I replied cheerfully.

"Yes, I know. You're the Charmer."

I sighed heavily. "Are you afraid of me . . . like the other women?"

She shook her head, her sleek, black trusses catching the sunlight as she did. "No. But that's probably because of my gift."

"Gift? Are you a Dhampir like me?"

"Yes . . . although my gift isn't as special as yours. I'm an Empath."

"Empath?"

"Yes," she nodded. "I take in the emotions other people are feeling, like joy or sadness. But I have to be close to them. Making contact with them is best."

"I have a friend who has a very similar gift . . . though he can feel a person's emotions from very far away."

Maya closed her eyes for a moment, then her head tilted upward and she opened them once more and returned her gaze to me. "You think of this friend—*him*—often, don't you?" Then she stated matter of factly, "You're in love with him."

I could only blink back at her in amazement.

"The other women here don't see what I see," she continued. "Being here is hard for you. And even though you're surrounded by your handsome Guardians and Hunters, their attentions go unnoticed. Your heart's breaking for this man."

"You're wrong, Maya. Your gift *is* special. How can you see all that? You just sat down next to me."

Her eyes slid away, shyly. "I've been close to you a couple of times without you noticing. I was curious."

"Oh." She watched me to see if I seemed weirded-out by that admission, which, of course, I wasn't. "Well, since you already know so much about me, why don't you tell me something about yourself?" Her expression brightened, and it seemed as though she wanted to be friends. That would be nice, what with me being away from home and not knowing many people here yet.

"OK. I'm twenty-one, and originally from British Columbia. I've been here at The Oracle since I was fourteen."

"Are your parents still in British Columbia?"

She shook her head. "My mother died when I was born. She was human . . . my birth was too much for her. And as for my father, I'm not sure where he is. He left me when I was young."

I couldn't believe it. It was the same story as Gemma's. No wonder all of these Dhampirs were fighting for The Brethren. Their vampire fathers kept abandoning the children they sired with human women. "So, did you stay with relatives in British Columbia before you ended up here?" Her expression seemed to go rigid for a moment, and I feared I was being a little too nosy. "I'm sorry. I didn't mean to pry."

She placed her hand over mine. "No, it's fine. It's a long story—maybe better for another time."

I glanced down at her hand as she touched me. "You . . . you have to be careful touching me. My gift . . ."

"I know," she replied gently, squeezing my hand in reassurance before pulling it back. "We were all warned of your gifts before you arrived."

"Oh," I said, uncomfortable again, glancing around and becoming aware of the many people watching us—some openly, some furtively—that I hadn't noticed before. One of those was Alec, who had been quite openly watching our conversation while he handled his training group, but he smiled as though pleased that I was making a new friend. "Do you like it here at The Oracle?"

She nodded. "It's become home for me—someplace where I don't have to hide who I am."

I nodded quietly and was gazing back out at Alec's group when I suddenly heard Maya gasp a hard in-breath and clasp her hand over her heart. "Olivia, I hope you don't think I'm prying, but I feel the overwhelming pain in your heart for this man you miss. If you love him so much, why are you not with him?"

All I could think at that moment was how nice it would be to talk with someone about Caleb, but I doubted a Dhampir who had been abandoned by her vampire father would have much sympathy for a woman in love with one. Yet I couldn't resist beginning the dialogue.

"I want nothing more than to be with him," I began, realizing suddenly that my tone of voice reflected my sadness. "His name is Caleb, and he's a vampire—a good vampire. You've been warned about my gifts—how painful my touch can be to a vampire and the illusion that I create around them? Those gifts make things, uh, complicated for us."

"Yes, I can feel how I'm drawn to you now—but it's nothing bad. I just feel like I want to stay here beside you—not leave you . . . like I'm floating in a nice dream."

"That's because you have a good nature about you. You can better handle the draw towards me. But if I touched your skin for any length of time, those feelings would magnify until it would become unnatural for you. Caleb . . . what he feels—how he responds—is much more intense, especially when I touch him. He doesn't know if what he feels for me is real. So, I'm giving him time and space he needs to figure it out. That's why I came here."

"That must be very hard for both of you."

I blinked back at her in surprise. "You don't dislike him because he's a vampire?"

"No," she replied simply. "I can feel him through you. He's a good man, regardless of whether he's a vampire."

My bottom lip quivered a little as I held back the emotion starting to well inside me. "Thank you, Maya. You've no idea how much that means to me."

She smiled, but just as quickly her attention was diverted over my shoulder. I turned back towards the lobby to see that Phin had stepped outside. His dark, shirtless torso glistened with a fine sweat he had obviously earned from vigorous training. He was wiping down his broad, muscular shoulders and rippled abdomen with a cloth when I heard the slightest catch in Maya's breath. She was staring up at him, her blues eyes seeming to grow in size with each blink. She was attracted to Phin. You didn't need to be an Empath to know that.

"Hello, Olivia," Phin nodded as he tugged his tee shirt over his chest and then pulled a chair across from our bench, the blue-gray of his eyes standing apart from the rest of his features and reminding me of a shadowed sea. He didn't look at all tired from spending his time training during the day and hunting Davin's trail at night. But, unfortunately, he seemed to be focused on me, giving almost no attention to Maya, who stiffened a bit in her seat beside me. Once I saw her brows furrow with something that was a cross between pain and frustration, I guessed that she could feel his attraction to me at that moment loud and clear.

And I wondered why I was having trouble making friends.

Maya raised her chin stiffly. "Hello, Phinneas."

Phin turned to her and smiled. "Maya," he acknowledged, as if he'd just noticed she was there, and then he turned back to me.

Oh, boy . . . I had to work quickly. "Phin, Maya was just telling me about her Dhampir gift. It really is quite remarkable."

He leaned back comfortably in his chair as he stretched his long legs out in front of him. "Yes, Maya's our resident little psychic," he teased, but I could tell that Maya didn't like the comparison. She held herself so stiff I thought she would get up and leave at any moment.

"Really?" I questioned. "I think it's a little more than that. Maya, I do believe you've been challenged."

She glanced up at me, startled, not sure where I was going with this.

"Phin, why don't we have a little fun? Think of a memory from your childhood—any memory. Think of how you were feeling at that moment . . . something no one else knows, and let's see if Maya can describe it." His eyes narrowed slightly, as if he was either suspicious or reluctant. He wasn't biting. "Please?" I added. "I'm curious."

That seemed to do it. He sat up straight in his chair, turning to face Maya. "All right. But I warn you, this isn't something you can just get lucky and guess."

Maya seemed suddenly flustered as she instantly became the

focus of his attention. Her big eyes widened and blinked back at him. "I—I will have to touch you."

He studied her carefully, as if taking in all the details of her face. Lazily, he reached his arm across her lap, his body language more open as he grinned and said, "I've no problem with that." Phin's attention was now definitely focused on her.

Slowly, Maya brought her fingertips up to graze over his wrist. The movement seemed to tickle him a bit, so she lingered for a moment before sliding them over the fine hairs of his forearm. The air between them suddenly felt charged as a visible shiver ran through her. "Your memory," she began. "It's very cold. The kind of cold you feel in your bones." She glanced up at him with surprise. "You're having trouble breathing—you're gasping for air when you can. And you're wet. Water. You're in fast moving water."

Phin pulled his arm away from her, rubbing the spot she had touched on his arm as if she had burned him. "Very good," he replied cautiously, obviously not having expected she would have guessed correctly.

"Where were you?" she asked quickly.

"You tell me. You're the psychic." He couldn't keep back the bitter snap in his voice.

Maya had unwittingly struck a nerve.

She shook her head. "I'm not sure. I couldn't see it . . . just feel what you felt. But you were young . . . no more than ten, I'd guess."

He stared at her in disbelief, his respect for her gift much more apparent. "It was a local river. That day, the current was too fast from all the mountain runoff. A friend and I tried to help a boy who had been swept down river and was trapped between some rocks. He was drowning."

Maya gasped. "Did you get him out?"

Phin pulled back in his seat. "It's a long story—"

"Please tell me. I'd like to know."

That was my cue.

"Excuse me," I said quickly as I got up and walked away,

hoping that any *drawing* I was doing to Phin was leaving with me. In about an hour I would peek back in on Maya and see how she was doing. Maybe she would even want to join me at dinner that evening.

That would be nice.

In the meantime, I stalled by walking around the grounds to the back side of the property. It was easy to explore during the day because I didn't have to worry about Davin making any surprise visits. Yet, I sensed something, something unfamiliar—someone watching me. I glanced back up towards the hotel. From this side of the hotel it was easier to see up to the twelfth floor, where The Elders stayed when they were here. That's where I sensed the prying eyes were coming from. I stopped momentarily, perching myself against a rock and pretending I was tightening my shoelace. But I was now in full concentration, listening for voices.

But it wasn't voices I heard.

I practically gulped when I heard a low guttural growl directly behind me. Trying to remain calm, I slowly lifted my head up and my breath caught at the sight of a *very, very* large black cat stalking towards me. Actually, it was a jaguar.

What on earth? Who knew they had black jaguars in Canada?

The cat's movements were slow, deliberate—almost sinful in their grace, in the animal's ease of sway. Before I could even think to respond, the cat leapt up, dropping his giant front paws on each side of me against the rock, trapping me beneath its huge body. Why, the animal's paws alone were larger than my hand.

My heart was racing beyond reasonable panic; I was convinced I was about to become a feline lunch. The jaguar's enormous body was so close I could see the rose-shaped spots that dotted its ebony coat. Its large eyes, a mesmerizing silver color, stared down at me with something akin to predatory hunger. A low purr rumbled endlessly inside its chest as I slowly brought my hands up to its coat, preparing to dissuade the animal with my touch.

And if that didn't work, I'd use whatever strength I had to fight the animal off.

"Knock it off, Kane!" I suddenly heard Alec bark.

My eyes blinked open and I was startled to see not a jaguar, but a man, leaning over me . . . the tall, dark, and definitely handsome kind of man that women lost all thoughts in their head over. He smiled down at me wickedly. "Sorry, just having a little fun. But you might want to keep your eyes north."

Of course, then I had to look south. He was also very definitely naked!

He moved back slowly, holding his palms high to signal he meant me no harm, but Alec hurried the process along, grabbing the man by the arm and whirling him back on his feet, throwing his coat at him. "Put it on!" he snarled.

"Fucking shape-shifter," Lucas growled.

Shape-shifter? I was speechless as Alec pulled me back up from the rock. "Are you all right?" All I could do was to nod in reply.

Alec then turned on Kane. "What the hell do you think you're doing?"

I stepped behind Alec, peeking from behind his shoulder. "Yeah, what the hell?" I added.

Even though Kane stood there clad only in Alec's coat, he was an impressive sight. He looked to be about the same age as Alec, maybe a little older, but not quite as tall. His hair, lashes and brows were all thick and coal black, just like the jaguar's coat. His features were sharply defined, his mouth seductively wide, and his eyes the same mesmerizing silver color.

As he stood there, I could sense a naughtiness about the man. I was guessing he could effortlessly visualize any woman naked . . . which was exactly what it felt to me he was doing at the moment. "Easy, man," Kane responded with a lazy drawl, "I was just having a little fun checking out my new charge. I hadn't planned on shifting back in front of her, but you had to come thundering in, as usual."

Alec slid his cool gaze back to Lucas. "What does he mean

new charge?"

Lucas cleared his throat a bit uncomfortably. "Kane told me just before class," Lucas replied. "He's been assigned to our team."

"No he hasn't!" Alec snapped sharply.

Evidently, there was no love lost between the two men. Kane crossed his arms over his broad chest in challenge, his wavy, dark locks falling loose over his forehead, an effect that seemed to only add to his naughtiness. *Oh, I would definitely have to stay away from this man. There probably wasn't a Dhampir he met that he didn't try to have beneath him in minutes.*

"I have," Kane reiterated. "Assigned by your uncle, in fact. It seems he appreciates my rather obvious talents."

Alec's lips literally snarled. "Don't get comfortable. It won't stick."

But I was surprised to see Lucas's eyes glittering with amusement behind him, almost as if he found the whole situation entertaining. "Now, now, boys. Fu—" Lucas began, then restarted himself after slicing a quick glance to me. "Forget the past. There's no reason we can't all work together."

"This has to be a joke, right," Alec pressed. "He can't be assigned to her. He can't even keep his hands to himself with normal women."

I inhaled quickly, instinctively taking issue with the implication that I was not normal.

"Sorry," Alec whispered over his shoulder.

"Alec, get over yourself," Kane snorted. "You aren't much better in that department."

I stepped around Alec, surprised to see the extreme tension and hardness in his jaw. He looked as if he was about to throw out a blistering response, but Lucas beat him to it. "He's got you there, buddy."

Alec stiffened. "Like hell!"

Kane didn't back down from Alec for a second. In fact, he seemed to be enjoying himself immensely. "Oh, really? Today's

Thursday. The last time I was with a woman was Tuesday night. Can you claim differently?"

Tuesday night? We'd only been back since Monday. There's no way—

"That's not the point!" Alec blasted back.

I swung my head up to him as a choked laugh escaped from Lucas's slack jaw. He wasn't denying it.

You've got to be kidding me. When had he had the time?

Alec clenched his fist at his sides and cast a gaze of fire at Lucas.

Lucas just shrugged his shoulders. "Don't look at me, man. I've got my own problems."

"OK, enough!" I grumbled, pushing in front of Alec and stepping before the hedonistic, shape-shifting force known as Kane, positive I heard mumbled curses behind me. "Hello, I'm Olivia. It's nice to meet you . . . I think. But if you ever shift back naked in front of me again, you'll find yourself crumbling from a hard knee to those very private parts."

His scorching gaze slid over me from head to toe. Under that gaze, my clothing seemed pointless. "I'll consider myself warned," he replied lazily, then added, "But what if I'm not shifting? What if I'm just walking around naked?"

Oh yeah . . . A very naughty boy.

Rolling my eyes heavenward, I started marching back towards the hotel.

"Where are you going?" Alec called after me.

"Gideon's trying to find me. Evidently, Dr. Li has my test results."

Lucas just snorted grudgingly. "Dhampir hearing. Shape-shifting bastards. How does a person stay sane in this place?"

✱✱✱

Dr. Arnold Li, MD, was the on-staff physician for The Oracle and one of the foremost authorities on the anatomy of the Dhampir. His extensive reputation was well deserved, thanks to over 43 years of researching and treating Dhampirs, and yet he looked as if he were only a few of years out of medical school.

Dr. Li was also a Dhampir.

A Chinese man of less than average height, his inky-black hair was stick-straight and thick, emphatically defining his face and calling attention to the thick lenses of his glasses, which looked much too heavy to be safe in the thin-wire frames he had chosen for them. Though I was nervous, not even needing one full hand to count the number of times I had ever seen a doctor, it eased me to know I was being examined by someone acutely aware of the differences between my body and that of a human . . . since I didn't even really understand them all yet myself.

But I still hated seeing this man—or any doctor at all.

Perched atop an exam room table, I tapped my fingers wildly against my pant leg and was wishing I could work out all my current anxiety on a keyboard while impatiently waiting. Gosh, I missed playing—especially when I was stressed. I never realized how much I used my time at the piano to just cope with life—until I no longer had one at my disposal. Actually, there seemed to be a lot of new things I was discovering about myself here. Finally, the door opened and Dr. Li appeared, smiling. "Olivia, welcome back." He opened my file, reviewing the pages as he spoke. "I've good news. Your test results all look normal, and the injuries you sustained from your battle on Vancouver Island are fully healed, so I'll approve you to begin training right away."

I inhaled a relieved breath, feeling a bit ridiculous about the tension I had been experiencing, because I hadn't really expected him to find anything wrong.

"There are a couple things I need to make you aware of . . ." He typed notes onto his tablet, barely looking up at me as he talked. "We ran test on the saliva sample we took—"

"Saliva?" I interrupted. "I thought you were taking a DNA sample."

"Well, yes, that, too. But we test all Dhampir saliva. It contains toxins, just as in a vampire bite, though not nearly as debilitating to the prey. We have to know how potent your bite is in combination with blood."

At his words, I felt as though someone had dropped a brick on my chest. "My saliva can hurt someone?"

Dr. Li glanced up from his notes. "Not to worry. Your toxin levels tested at only a fraction of a vampire's bite. It's what I would expect from a Dhampir who is three-quarters human. But you do need to be aware that your saliva can make a human very sick. That's why we give the humans here shots every six months . . . to protect them from illness if an accidental bite occurs while training. Kind of like a tetanus shot."

I let out an almost choked laugh. "Don't be ridiculous. I can't bite a human—not like a vampire, anyway."

Dr. Li glanced up at me in surprise. "You have fangs, Olivia," he said, calmly, while another brick landed on my chest.

"I don't *have* fangs," I cried, jumping off the table. "I don't *want* fangs."

Dr. Li calmly raised a hand to my shoulder. "It's all right," he said as he motioned for me to return to my seat. "It's perfectly natural. All Dhampirs have fangs."

"Then how's it possible that I've never seen them?"

"After reviewing all of your tests . . . and in my professional opinion . . . it's because your body has been denied blood."

I stared back at him dumbfounded. "Denied? B—But I don't thirst for blood."

"On the contrary. Your body does thirst for it . . . quite desperately, in fact. It would seem that the Greysons pulled off the impossible, limiting your exposure. Because your body should've responded to the scent if you were near it for any length of time."

A small gasp escaped me as I remembered the Greysons telling family friends and teachers that I suffered from Hemophobia, a fear of blood. They were warned to keep me as far away from any blood as possible.

"Your body has probably been giving you signals that you've missed," Dr Li continued. "Alec mentioned to me that you've been struggling with your strength. That would make sense if your body's been weakened. I'm going to recommend that you start drinking blood with at least one of your meals each day. That'll help significantly. You should notice a change within a couple of weeks. As you begin to drink, your fangs will emerge. Eventually you'll be able to control when they come out, just as a vampire does."

And there went another half dozen bricks, battering me almost insensible.

I hadn't had a problem being around vampires who drank blood on almost a daily basis—though never around me—but I couldn't imagine drinking it for myself. And there was no way I was drinking blood if it caused my fangs to come out. *I'd look ridiculous.* But really, I knew, I just wanted to hold onto the human woman inside of me, the part that Caleb loved. But it seemed as though the longer I was here at The Oracle, the less human I felt. "If I refuse to drink the blood, will these fangs still pop out?"

"I wouldn't advise that," came Dr. Li's quick reply. "You'll continue to weaken your body over time. That would prove most difficult, considering the challenges ahead of you."

Dr. Li then looked up at me, his expression far more concerned as he held my gaze directly.

This couldn't be good.

"There's one more thing," he began. "I believe this may be even more difficult for you to hear." The breath I was taking stopped halfway into my lungs for a moment as I waited for what seemed like minutes to hear what was wrong. "You mentioned when you were here last that you were taking shots for birth control."

"Yes," I replied carefully. "I have been for a couple years."

He once again tapped his pen against his chin. "Olivia, I know you said the Greysons almost never took you to see a physician, but can you tell me about when they did take you? What it was for?"

"They took me only once, really. I had a cyst removed from my ovaries when I was seventeen. I guess there was also a follow-up visits after the surgery."

The pen he had been holding in his hand stopped against his chin. "I don't believe that was the procedure you had done."

"I don't understand?"

"When I read your MRI scans, I noticed that you have tubal implants. They're a blocking device that is inserted into each fallopian tube through the vagina. It prevents the passage of eggs and is a permanent method of birth control. It's a simple procedure to insert them and would need only some minor follow up to insure they were placed properly. But I'm very concerned that you seem to be unaware of this and have continued with other forms of birth control."

I sat there in stunned silence. When I finally regained control of my voice, only muttered sounds came out for a full minute as I tried to calm my alarmed mind. "Are . . . are . . . are you saying . . . th . . . that I can never have a baby?"

"It's highly unlikely, yes."

Suddenly, I felt as if my heart was in my throat. "But . . . but how? How would I not know?"

"That's the disturbing part. The only way this procedure would ever have been done without your consent would have been with signed parental consent. And even then, I know of no ethical physician who would perform this procedure on such a young girl. You said your operation was done when you were seventeen?" I nodded, unable to voice any words. "You would've been a minor, so your parents may have signed for you."

"But that would mean they lied to me! Why would they do that?"

"I'm sorry, I can't answer that."

Shaking my head back and forth, I tried to take it all in, but it wouldn't fit. The size of this lie seemed too big to contain. "Can it be reversed?"

Dr. Li seemed to purse his lips at me in empathy. "It's possible . . . but usually unsuccessful. I can, of course discuss the procedure with you—give you all the—"

"Are we finished?" I interrupted him before he could finish.

Dr. Li hesitated for a moment. "We are. But is there anyone you can talk to about this?"

"I'll be fine." My tone failed to convince even myself. "But there's no reason The Brethren needs to know of this, is there?"

"None that I can see."

"Thank you, doctor." I fled Dr. Li's office so fast I was practically flying down the back staircase as tears began to blur my eyes. Once I secured the lock inside my room, I collapsed to the floor at the foot of the bed, my breathing feeling more like winded gasps as I tried to take it all in. I'd never be able to give Caleb a baby. My humanness was what Caleb found attractive about me, yet I was unable to do the one thing that was most human—create life.

I might as well be a full vampire.

I couldn't understand how the Greysons could do this to me. What possible reason could justify taking away my choice for a child—and their chance at having a grandchild? It didn't make any sense.

I wasn't sure how much time had passed when I heard the inevitable knock at my door. "Olivia, it's me," Alec announced. "Can I come in?"

"Not now," I replied weakly, my voice sounding foreign even to me.

My response was met with stone silence, which at first I believed meant that Alec had left as I asked, but no such luck. "Have you been crying?" he asked with surprise.

When I didn't answer, his gentle request became more of a demand. "Open this door right now, Olivia, or I'll break it in."

"Go away, Alec!"

"You have until the count of three . . . One . . ."

Frustrated and wanting just to be left alone, I grumbled as I rose to my feet.

"Two . . . I mean it!"

As soon as I slid the latch back on the chain, he came barreling in and saw my mess of a face. I wiped my hands over my cheeks and turned away from him, walking deeper into the room. "Everything's fine, now just go."

He was quick on my heels, spinning me around. "Don't give me that *fine* bullshit when your face looks as though you've been crying in here for hours. What the hell's wrong?"

"Nothing! You've been hanging out with Lucas too much, you foul-mouth jerk. Now leave me alone!"

"Uh—uh. Not good enough. I'm not going anywhere until you tell me."

Furious at the world, I took it out on him. "It's personal, OK! Now get out of here you asshole! How's *that* for a curse word?"

His responding expression was one of complete shock.

Unable to face him, I turned my back and walked a few steps toward the window, covering my tear-streaked cheeks with my hands. He remained silent, but when I realized he was refusing to leave, I slowly crumpled to my knees on the floor. He was there in front of me within seconds, curling his arms around my back and pulling me against his shoulder.

"Olivia, you're scaring me. Did Dr. Li say something was wrong?"

I couldn't answer him, but I felt so exhausted I allowed myself to fold against him. He said nothing and leaned back against the foot of the bed as he held me in his arms, patiently waiting for me to say something. "I can't have a baby."

"I'm sorry, Olivia," he said with gentle sincerity.

I shook my head against his shoulder. "You don't understand. The Greysons did this to me."

"What?" His surprise was evident in his voice as he drew me back from him.

"The Greysons consented to a procedure when I was seventeen. Why would they do this Alec? Why?" My voice sounded so lost that I knew I was worrying him.

He pulled my head back into his shoulder, kissing the top of it lightly. "Everything the Greysons did was out of fear," he began. "They stole you away . . . moved you clear across the country. They suppressed your abilities and never told you the truth about who you really were. They did this because they feared for you—feared losing you. Does it really surprise you that they also feared you'd be attacked and possibly impregnated against your will?"

"You mean by a vampire, 'against my will'?"

He stroked my hair. "If I had to guess, yes. They knew that your being a Charmer meant that vampires would be lured to you, want to posses you physically. They probably just didn't want to take a chance on the daughter they loved going through that."

"But even so . . . to take this choice away from me for something that *might* happen was wrong. Eve and James would've never done this to me."

"No, you're right about that. But *they* had the ability to protect you—the Greysons didn't. They were protecting you the only way they could."

I curled my hand into a fist against his chest, squeezing my fingers until they were bloodless. "This hurts so much, Alec. I'm supposed to be this Charmer. This woman that men desire . . . and I can't even—"

"Don't," he interjected sharply, holding my face in his hands, forcing me to look at him. "There are other options available to you if you want to be a mother. And any man who sees your value only in terms of giving him a child isn't worthy of you."

Staring at him in amazement, I realized at that moment how important this man of truth had become to me. I wrapped my arms around him, hugging him tight. "Thank you, Alec . . . for being here for me."

"I'll always be here for you, little Charmer."

Chapter Six

Over a month had passed as I watched summer in the lush valley of the Canadian Rockies transform into a crisp September fall. Every day I thought about stepping off sacred ground so Caleb could sense me again, but I couldn't. Alec had been right. Davin and his soldiers were spread out for miles, circling the perimeter in targeted spots, and staying close to The Oracle, just waiting for any small opportunity.

So Caleb was safe for now . . . but I was not, and the pain of missing him never dulled.

However, I had gotten used to my daily training routine at The Oracle. I was becoming faster, sharper, my senses more open and acute. There was something incredibly freeing in discovering my power to defend myself. My strength was still not where it should be because I was refusing to drink blood as Dr. Li had prescribed, but I was OK with that for now. Alec and Gideon were both concerned, but while Gideon offered patience, Alec, at times, was downright pushy. I knew, though, that even if he pushed me too far, I would forgive him. I could understand that he was pushing because he cared, because he wanted me to be stronger and safer.

Alec also had convinced his Uncle Reese to have The Brethren hold off on beginning my Advance Situations class until I was farther along, so that left me with more time in the afternoons to work on one of my favorite new activities. A few days into my kickboxing training I burst through the third floor training room doors to enjoy my new afternoon ritual when I was stopped dead in my tracks. Kane, the hedonistic wonder, had his arm wrapped around a pretty Dhampir while grinning from ear to ear and twirling what looked to be a lacy thong around his index finger. Completely unrepentant that he had been caught, he slid his gaze over to me before giving the buxom blond a scorching kiss, sending her off with a not-so-light spank over the swell of her jeans-clad bottom.

I rolled my eyes in disgust as she scurried out the door and he turned and began waltzing toward me, his long, lazy strides giving the appearance that he was stalking me with the same seductive ease of his jaguar form while he balled the thong in his hand and shoved it into his pocket. "So, Charmer," he drawled. "When are you going to take me up on my offer to ease the burning need you have for that vampire of yours?"

To say the least, Kane had a one-track mind and could be overwhelming to a woman's senses. As he neared, I was proud that I stood my ground unflinchingly . . . though admittedly there wasn't much ground to hold, since I was practically backed up against the wall, anyway. His arms braced the wall on each side of me as a devilish smile flickered within those sultry silver eyes of his and he leaned in close. "Now, this is better . . ."

I wasn't afraid of Kane. In fact, it was almost comical how *un-seriously* he took his own skirt chasing. It was as if he was oblivious to the possibility that anyone could see the subject of sex any differently than he did. He seemed a free man in that sense and quite harmless most of the time. But there were other times . . . Kane, like all my Guardians, had a hard time controlling the need to touch me when he was around me for any length of time—like right now. "As tempting as that kindhearted offer for your services is," I replied calmly. "I think I'll pass."

Not surprisingly, that just widened his pearly white predatory grin. "Are you sure? I can make quite a good substitute."

I blinked back at him. "You're unbelievable—"

"Thank you," he interjected.

"You just finished . . ."—having no more articulate way to describe the moment, I tossed my hands up wildly—"'*plowing the fields*' so to speak, and not five minutes later you're hitting on me?"

"For you, darlin', I'd give up all my other *plowing*."

I snorted in reply but found myself gasping in a quick breath as his hand slid down to caress my hip and his lips were suddenly brushing over my ear. "For one night you'd forget all about your vampire—and you'd enjoy it. I promise you that."

Caught off guard by Kane's stronger than usual pick up artistry, I tried to squirm away from the wall but there wasn't really a lot of room to move, so I had to be more direct with him. "Um . . . let me think about it . . . NO!"

I then shoved away from him, and found myself yelping as he smacked me full on my ass. "Same time tomorrow, darlin'?" he winked, disappearing from the room as I stood there with my mouth hanging open.

"Of all the . . . Ooohhh!"

Minutes later I was picturing Kane's face on the bag I was pounding on with even greater force than normal. I was heavy in concentration, but not so heavy that I would miss the fact that Alec had come into the room and was trying to sneak up behind me. He often liked to surprise me as a way of testing my new highly attuned senses; a tactic that never worked for him.

Pretending to be completely absorbed in the bag, I waited until he was just behind me and then let my sensitive Dhampir ears take over. I listened for the smallest rush of air as his arm swung from his side to come around my throat. Ducking just in time, I came back up as his body was following through with his swing and jammed my elbow into his side. He grunted out a hard breath, while I returned to my feet and smiled victoriously at him.

My celebration, however, was a little premature.

Alec swiped his leg beneath my knees, sweeping me off my feet and letting my own weight send me crashing back to the mat. His fit form then followed me down, looming over me and bracing his arms at each side of me. "Remember, always stay focused. Be strong and balanced. Don't let me swipe your legs out from under you like that."

I blew out a rough breath. "I know. Why haven't I gotten that yet?"

He released his arm and helped me back up from the mat.

"Give it time. You're doing well. I may be only human, but I've had a lot more training than you."

"Showoff," I grumbled as I shoved my gloved hands forward, silently asking for help in removing them. He obliged without hesitation, pulling loose the strings. "So, are you checking up on me?"

He grinned as he shook his head. "Gideon's meeting—," he started, just as the man walked through the door.

"What's this?" the Englishman asked. "More training?"

"Yes," I piped up before Alec could respond. "I almost had him today."

Predictably, Alec's features scrunched in a hard scowl. "I don't think so."

"Well, you two can finish this debate later," Gideon said. "Olivia, I asked Alec to join us today so we can work on your mirroring skills with a human."

I turned to Alec and then blinked back at Gideon. "Do you think that's a good idea? I don't want to hurt him."

"Do I look worried?" Alec replied without delay.

"You won't hurt him," Gideon assured me. "You can only cause him pain if his nature's bad. But I want you to describe to me what you feel when you connect with him."

"OK," I nodded, still a little unsure about whether this was a good idea. But Alec stood there with a confident smirk on his lips, not the least bit worried.

"Go ahead and place your fingers at his temples," Gideon instructed. "Try to relax."

I took a deep breath and closed my eyes, focusing the energy in my body toward my fingertips. Everything felt peaceful, calm. Then . . .

"*Oh, God!*" Alec suddenly cried out as if he were in tremendous pain.

I jerked my hands back instantly, just as he fell forward in laughter. He was playing! "Alec!" I cried, slapping him hard across his arm. "That's not funny."

"Alec," Gideon warned in a reprimanding tone. "Let's stay

focused."

"Sorry," he said with a shrug of his shoulders, while I disapprovingly pitched my hands on my hips. "What?" he added innocently. "I won't do it again."

We tried once more, and this time Alec was still as my hands locked on his temples and I focused on the energy I was able to feel inside him. He responded almost immediately, closing his eyes as the powerful muscles in his arms began to relax, and he raised his chin slightly to breathe a little deeper. I could feel that I wasn't hurting him; far from it, actually. He was enjoying the connection we had just then.

"OK, Olivia, that's good. He's nice and relaxed. Try focusing a little more—focus on what you want to see. Can you see that light you described to me?"

"Yes, I can see it," I replied. "It's the same light I saw inside Caleb, only much brighter." My fingertips pressed at his temples as I tried to reach even deeper.

"Do you see any of the darkness you described feeling with Davin or Isaac?"

"No. I don't see any."

"All right, very good. Now ease away from him very slowly. Remember, magnified like this you're increasing the illusion for him. You're drawing him to you, so you need to control how you pull away."

I did exactly as Gideon instructed and opened my eyes to see Alec stand there, smiling and relaxed. "Am I hurting you?" I asked him.

He shook his head and reached up to brush his hand over my cheek. "It feels nice, peaceful—like I don't want to let you go."

I turned to Gideon, who was watching Alec carefully. "It was amazing, Gideon. It felt as if I could connect to the light—connect to his soul. He's beautiful inside. I could see pleasant images—like good memories."

Curious, Alec stepped closer to me. "What did you see?"

"I saw your father. You were tossing a baseball back and forth here at The Oracle."

A small frown flickered over his features and I realized how careless I had been to blurt out such a personal memory like that of his now deceased father. "I'm sorry, Alec. I shouldn't have said anything."

"It's not that," he replied, shaking his head.

"Do you realize what you're saying?" Gideon asked in amazement. "Your mother was never able to connect with a human's soul . . . take in the images of their nature. Your gift appears to be stronger and more developed than hers—especially with humans."

I heard what Gideon was saying, but my attention remained with Alec, who was still frowning. "I'm concerned, Gideon," he finally said, his fingers tracing down my arms. "She has felt both the light and the darkness inside the vampires. What happens when she touches the deepest darkness? What images will she see then? Painful ones that could distract or hurt her at the most critical time for her to stay focused?"

"Yes, I see your point," Gideon replied, noticeably concerned by this new insight.

"But if that were true," I defended, "wouldn't I have seen those images when I mirrored Isaac or Davin?"

"Perhaps not," Gideon answered. "Now that you understand your gift of touch better, you're much more targeted and controlled with it. I think Alec's concern is valid, but we won't know for sure until we test it. But don't worry, I'll think of a way to do that that is safe for you."

Gideon then walked back across the room to the items he brought in with him and returned with a cup. I could already smell the blood inside—as if it were right beneath my nostrils—and it irritated me that my body was responding so strongly to the scent. "There's something else I'd like to discuss with you," he began. "You've been very resistant to Dr. Li's recommendation to regular blood drinking. I've tried to be patient and give you time, but I'm very concerned that this reluctance is preventing you from getting stronger. I sincerely would like to understand your fear of this."

As the scent from the cup continued to overwhelm me I

slammed my hands over my mouth. Gideon recognized immediately what was going on, but Alec stared at me as if I had just sprouted wings. "What're you doing?"

"Nothing," I mumbled behind my hands.

"What do you mean nothing? You're covering your mouth as if you just lost a tooth."

Gideon pulled the cup back. "You're afraid because you know your fangs will come out?"

I turned away from them both, needing to get some distance from the blood. Alec followed me, stroking his hands once again along my arms in a calming gesture as he reached me and asked quietly, "Olivia, what is it?"

"I don't want to lose my humanness," I whispered, my whole body becoming weak with the sadness of all this.

Alec turned me around to face him, his hands moving upward to steady me at my shoulders. "Your fangs are part of who you are. There's nothing wrong with them. All Dhampirs have fangs. In fact, many of the human men here have been bitten by Dhampirs, and they rather like it."

"Alec!" Gideon said with a start. "The human men's enjoyment of a Dhampir's bite isn't an appropriate discussion. And certainly not the intended purpose of the anti-toxin shots you and the other Guardians receive."

Alec shrugged his shoulders negligibly. "It's the truth."

I blinked up at him in surprise. "Have you been bitten by a Dhampir?"

An involuntary, clearly guilty grin twisted his lips. "Many times."

Gideon rolled his eyes, the older man obviously well aware of Alec's sexual prowess. But then again, Alec's overabundance of female Dhampir attention was not a well kept secret at The Oracle. Though not as obvious as with Kane, the women swooned over Alec's attention, and he knew it. "Alec, you could get sick. And isn't it painful for you to be bitten like that?"

Alec almost laughed. "As long as I get my shots I'll be fine. And pain is a relative term. I find a Dhampir's bite rather exciting actual—"

"OK, Alec, that's enough," Gideon objected, flustered that the original intent of the conversation had gotten so off track.

Alec frowned at the older man, disregarding his concern. "You should drink the blood. It'll be healthy for your body, and it'll make you stronger."

I was quiet for a long moment. "I'll think about it."

"Good," Alec replied as his hands seemed to slide lower to my waist, then still lower until he was caressing my hips and pulling me closer towards him. I was caught off guard for a moment but soon realized that he was having trouble controlling the illusion again. With so much focused contact with me today he wanted to touch me.

I said nothing, knowing he was not even aware of what he was doing it, but it didn't escape Gideon's notice. "That's enough, Alec," the Englishmen said, sharply, and Alec's head lifted, surprised by the sharp tone. "I'd like to speak with you outside. Now."

As I watched them leave, I sighed in frustration. My mother's gifts made things so difficult for Alec . . . for all of my Guardians.

Chapter Seven

Another two weeks had passed, and as I promised Alec, I was a good student. I worked hard and was improving my skills at a rapid pace, though still refusing to drink blood. Both Alec and Lucas pressured me about it almost every day, agreeing with Dr. Li that my body was thirsting for it. I couldn't very well argue the point, since it seemed I was the only Dhampir at The Oracle who wasn't drinking blood, but I still resisted. I just wanted desperately to hold on to the human woman inside of me.

Phin had become my only ally in this cause, helping me argue back against the other two by championing the idea that it had to be my choice and that they shouldn't push. I had come to rely on him for this, and also for his nightly updates reporting that Davin was still going nowhere near Seattle.

I would have appreciated Kane's support, but that walking excuse for a pick-up line seemed to be avoiding me of late. Evidently, my constant refusal to be led to bed by the Casanova was bruising his abnormally inflated ego. His assignment to the team by Reese did seem an odd choice. Putting him with a woman whose very nature attracted men seemed more like a punishment than an assignment. Yet, even Alec had to admit he was doing a good job. No matter what their personal differences, when it came to my safety, all of the men worked together, no questions asked.

My time with Gideon had proved most beneficial. I had really grown to like the awkward Englishman and could see why my mother had found his company so enjoyable. Aside from his sharp intellect, he possessed a gentle quality that was truly engaging. Unlike when I first met him—when he feared for me—he did not push, letting me learn, discover, and accept who I was in my own time. I now understood better how my luring attraction worked and how to go between connecting to calm a situation and channeling my energy to become the mirror that would undoubtedly be the key to saving my life many times in the future.

The hardest thing was continuing to be separated from Caleb.

Each day seemed more painful than the last, and I wondered if his heart was breaking anywhere near as much as my own. I hadn't been off sacred ground since I arrived, which meant that he had not been able to sense me for nearly seven weeks. The absence was either good for him—in that it allowed him the freedom to move on—or it was an agonizing one, like mine.

I was desperate to see him again, but at the same time I knew I was not ready to leave The Oracle. I would have to do something about my strength if I was going to be able to defend myself against a vampire, and that was something I wanted more than anything right now because it signaled that I could go home . . . back to him.

Knowing that this was what I wanted most, I was staring almost obsessively at the cup of blood Alec set in front of me that night at dinner. The salty fluid that I sensed my body craved would make me stronger, which meant my training would progress faster and allow me to defend myself against Davin and return to the man I loved.

I had to do this!

The group surrounding me had stopped eating and just watched. "You can do it, Olivia!" Maya cheered as the sole feminine voice of support.

The four men's gazes all slid in unison from me to her while I brought the cup to my lips, practically throwing its contents to the back of my throat. Once the cup was empty, I began to choke against the speed at which I inhaled it. "Are you OK?" Alec asked while rubbing his hand over my back. "You didn't have to shoot it."

"Yes, I did," I coughed, and then closed my eyes to focus on the energy sparking on my tongue. The blood was salty as it warmed—like brandy—all the way to my stomach. Nerve endings and muscles instantly came alive as the blood coursing through my veins seemed to race at hyper speed. I didn't just like it . . . I *loved* it.

My heart beat faster, my breaths becoming more shallow as heated warmth wrapped around me like a blanket, along with an intense desire to be touched—a desire that quickly bloomed out of control. Sliding my hands over my arms, at that moment I swore I could feel Caleb's cool caress on my skin. The memory of his touch, of his loving kisses, was so strong it was as if he were right there beside me.

When I remembered where I was, my eyes popped open to find everyone staring back at me. "Can I have some more?"

Unthinkingly, Alec reached over and kissed my cheek before running off toward the kitchen.

"Are you all right?" Lucas asked. "You look a little—"

"Bothered," Kane finished for him dully.

I stared back at them both, unable to sit still. When Alec returned with another cup I grabbed it from his hands, this time tasting the salty fluid as it poured over my tongue.

Alec once again rubbed his hand over my back. "No, don't touch me," I complained, not meaning to sound so abrupt but wanting nothing to interfere with feeling Caleb at that moment.

Alec blinked back at me with surprise. "Olivia, are you all right? Am I hurting you?" he asked worriedly, pulling the cup out of my hands, but it was too late. I had already finished every drop.

Closing my eyes, I licked the last of the red juice from my lips and that's when I saw him, clear as day. Caleb's soaring frame stood proud at the edge of his favorite rock perch, from which he scanned the moonlit valley below. A cool wind was swirling around him, blowing his hair against his bristled cheek, a wind that carried the scent of young fir trees and fresh rain. I could smell it just as surely as if I were standing there with him. Dressed in his favorite dark jeans and a gray, button-down shirt, he scanned the darkness of the forest below him, his arms relaxed at his sides. But his expression seemed lost, like a man searching for answers.

Concentrating harder, I tried to connect to even the smallest part of him, to feel the rhythm of his breathing in his chest, to touch the coolness of his skin or the flex of his hard muscles. His face appeared almost youthful in the soft light as he raised his chin and closed his eyes, ironically mimicking my own curious movements just then. In unison our hands lifted, fingertips reaching for one another, the need to make contact an absolute imperative. My breath caught at feeling the faintest pressure on the edges of my fingertips. At the same moment his eyes shot open, urgency now replacing the previous sadness. His gaze swept around him as if desperate to see something, and short, shallow breaths worked hard within his sizeable lungs.

"Caleb," I whispered, "please *feel* me. I'm with you."

He closed his eyes again, his body rigid, his mind focused as if devoting every ounce of energy he had into trying to *feel* something. His lips moved, forming a single, silent word that was as clear to me as the memory of the deep voice that spoke it. "Olivia?"

Caleb repeated it, over and over. Within seconds, I felt as if the temperature inside my body had increased ten degrees. I squeezed my hands over my crossed arms, pleading to the heavens to feel him holding me for just a moment, wanting desperately to maintain this connection to him, but just like that . . . he was gone. "No," I cried softly.

To feel him again at this deep level and then to have that wonderful sensation snatched away was excruciating.

Suddenly remembering where I was, I opened my eyes to all the worried faces around the table. Then reached my hand up to feel the length of my new fangs as they push against my lips. What was happening? I felt as if I had no control of my own body's responses. Embarrassed, I pushed from the table and raced from the dining hall. "Olivia!" I heard Alec call after me.

"I'm fine, Alec," I called back.

Once I reached the quiet darkness of my own room I inhaled deeply and released a huge sigh of relief. But the feeling didn't last long. I didn't understand what was wrong with me, but as I stood at the foot of my bed, staring blankly out into the night, I began to curse this place, to curse my gift. And most of all, to curse the circumstances that forced me to be separated from the one man I loved. "I just want to see you again," I whispered painfully to the empty room.

Sliding my hands over my arms, I felt a cool sweat beginning to form over my skin as my own touch seemed to be a thousand times more sensitive than normal. I closed my eyes and inhaled several deep breaths until I was relaxed once again, and that was when the image of Caleb returned to me. He was racing through the night faster than I had ever seen him moving before, so fast it appeared he was flying over the terrain. One moment the thick forest around him was just a blur, and the next it was halted in place as his hard gaze completed another sweep through the darkness around him. He was feeling something.

"Yes! Feel me, Caleb. I'm right here."

Then *I* could feel *him!* Just as if he were standing right there with me. His tall form pressed against my back as his fingers traced over the edges of my shoulders then stretched down my arms slowly before his hands caressed my stomach. To feel his strong hands touching me again so possessively sent a sharp, visceral response all throughout my body. My skin tingled and my stomach clenched as he brushed my hair back from my neck, replaced by his heavy breaths on my throat. "*God*, how I want you," his deep voice whispered against my skin. "Just let me touch you."

But he was already touching me—everywhere. His large hands massaged my hips and stomach then slid upward to cup my breasts as I leaned back against him. His touch felt so wonderful! I wanted more. Swinging around to grab him by the edges of his shirt, I dragged his body against mine, my lips taking him in a hard, open-mouth kiss that seemed to shoot sparks straight through both of us the moment we made contact. A deep groan sounded from within him as he angled my head back and pressed his tongue in a forceful sweep of mouth, his body now fully aroused as the hard length of him pushed against my stomach. "Olivia, are you sure?" he panted against my cheek.

Was he kidding? Of course I was sure. Why was he wasting time talking right now when we could be together again for the first time in weeks? I placed a hand over each of his cheeks and moved his lips back over mine, not wanting to be separated from him for even a second as the blood energy continued to pound its way through my veins. "Please," I murmured.

"Please what . . . ?" he asked as he walked me backward till I could feel the bed pressing behind my knees. He leaned in and eased our bodies down until I was flat against the mattress and he was directly on top of me. Then his strong arms pulled me to the center of the bed, never once releasing me from the fervor of his kiss. He parted my thighs with his knee and opened me wide to cradle his body. "Tell me that you want this—that you want me inside you. I need to hear you say it, Olivia."

This was happening. After all this time of being apart this was really happening. Every cell in my body was on fire and as I rolled my tongue over the artery in his neck I could feel my sharp, new fangs graze along his skin. He groaned hard in response, his hands now working fast at the clothing that was left between us. "I want you, Caleb," I answered him in a rush of breath. "Only you. Always you."

Everything stopped.

He froze above me, his body held fiercely rigid.

I tried to pull him closer. "No, Caleb. Don't pull away from me."

"Stop!" he ordered in a hoarse voice, almost as if he were in pain. "Don't move. Just stay still for a second."

Stop? Was he crazy? I could feel how much his body wanted me, even with all the clothing still between us. I squeezed my legs around his hips, trying to encourage him to continue. A low, guttural curse sounded beneath his breath. "Olivia, stop!" He then held my face in his hands. "Look at me!" he ordered.

My lashes fluttered up to see *Alec* staring down at me in the moonlight. My arms and legs were curled around him like a vine when reality hit me like a bucket of ice water.

"Alec? What . . . ?" Blood was running down his neck where I had scratched him with my fangs. "*Oh, God,* Alec, I'm so sorry."

I wanted to try and find some earthly explanation for what had just happened, but I was at a complete loss for words, and I couldn't even understand myself how I lost such control.

Muttered curses snarled under his breath and he pushed away from the bed. "No! Please Alec, let me explain." But he was gone from the room before I could stop him, the door slamming against the frame just before the room fell deathly silent.

I rolled over on the mattress and curled my knees up to my chest, the absolute burning need inside my body still pounding away at me. Seeing Caleb's face so clearly hurt like a thousand little pin pricks against my skin. I couldn't focus on anything else, including the inexcusable way I had just treated Alec, realizing he must have been concerned about me and followed me up from the dining hall.

I wrapped myself around one of the large pillows, trying to quell the pain.

It was the blood! The blood was somehow doing this to me!

Chapter Eight

Three long weeks had passed and Alec still wasn't speaking to me. Though I had tried to apologize numerous times for my outrageous behavior, he avoided me like the plague. My Guardian still did absolutely everything by the book, but he ordered the others to handle everything when it came to having any kind of contact with me. He had stopped eating with me, but thanks to the others, I never had to eat alone. And in defense class he wouldn't touch me, opting instead to assign Lucas to run through drills with me.

His cold distance and lack of affection hurt me, but I had no one to blame but myself. I had been so wrapped up in my own pain about Caleb that I hadn't realized how important Alec had become in my life. He was my Guardian and my friend, and now that he was avoiding me I felt as if I'd lost something vital.

Gideon recognized pretty quickly that something was terribly wrong between us and must have confronted Alec about it at some point. And, par for the course, Alec was completely honest about what had happened, because Gideon immediately started looking into why I had such a strong reaction to the blood. I hadn't touched another drop since that night, even though my body craved it and I ached to see Caleb again, but I didn't like how I felt so out of control.

Did my body need it that badly?

It didn't take Gideon long to discover that there had been some sort of mix-up and that I had not been given human blood, but vampire blood. Evidently, Dr. Li had supplies of vampire blood stored in his office for healing purposes, but how it got in my cup was a mystery. Gideon explained to me that in large quantities—like the two full glasses I chugged down—I would feel an enormous amount of excited energy. That was his polite, English way of saying that my body would go into an erotic state, which was exactly what happened.

I was so relieved to know that there was a reason for my behavior, and I hoped that once Alec knew the truth—that I never intentionally meant to hurt him—he would forgive me. But he didn't. He still kept his distance, and that hurt even more. I started to worry he would never forgive me.

With Alec no longer there to bend Reese's ear, The Elders saw no reason to hold off any longer on my Advanced Situations training with instructor Jude Gehring. They were anxious to see where my new-found abilities could take me, and so was I. Training with Jude would be a nice distraction from the awkward mess I had made with Alec, plus I would do anything to get stronger and be ready to defend myself in the outside world so I could return to Caleb and return to my music, which I missed dearly. I had never planned to be apart from Caleb this long without so much as a word between us. And now I regretted even more that I did not find a way to tell him where I was going that last night before I left.

I had only seen Jude a couple of times throughout my almost three months here at The Oracle, never actually met him, and today was my first class with him. I entered the special training room for this course, a gymnasium-style room somewhat hidden on the outer wing of the second floor. I immediately noted the unusual weaponry and absence of any windows, and the entire floor space was "upholstered" with thick mats, so I naturally assumed that we were going to be hitting the ground a lot. Finally, I noticed that all four walls were lined with full height mirrors. In the center of the room was a strange looking piece of equipment, reminding me of some sort of torture contraption from an old black-and-white horror film. The steel frame was about waist high and was bolted to the floor. Several curved pieces of metal hooked together with bolts, seemed to form a kind of vice grip to hold items or occupant in place when closed. I had never seen anything like it before.

Jude entered the enormous room with long, effortless strides. He was a Guardian—and human, like Alec and Lucas— but he glided across the floor so smoothly, so quietly, it reminded me of Caleb. His body was lean, not overly muscled—

and tall, about Alec's height, I guessed, which was still a couple of inches shorter than Caleb. As he made his way toward me I noticed his ebony hair was trimmed neatly, but his deeply tanned skin looked artificial, having an almost gray cast to it. His eyes were dark, a sort of muddled gray-brown color—nothing like Caleb's vibrant shades of gray. And his expression was tight, focused. "Olivia," he acknowledged, with scant warmth.

"Jude," I smiled, unsure why I felt the need to lighten the already crisp mood of the room.

"This is an Advance Situations class," he began as he stopped in front of me. "We'll be simulating real battle situations that are most common for injury, and we'll work on how you can maintain your focus while fighting your way through whatever challenges you may face. And, of course, in your case, how you can use your rare gifts to your advantage."

"Of course," I echoed with a proud smile.

Noticing the smile, he cautioned, "This class will not be easy and will require your complete focus. Do you feel you are up to the challenge?"

I nodded at him with confidence. "Yes, I'll be fine."

He motioned for me to follow him to the metal contraption bolted to the floor. Opening two of the vice grips, he positioned me so that my right leg was placed inside the larger of the openings he had just created. Clicking the metal shut, he locked my leg inside, I was left with virtually no room to move within the machine's grip and my other leg was still free. I was confused as to how this worked.

Jude then walked over to a weapons case that contained a number of swords, knives, lances and bows, most of which had some type of silver on them, since neither vampires or Lycans care for silver very much. He reached for one of the swords, then returned to me, placing the sharp blade at an angle inside the smaller vice and pointing the tip toward the fleshy part of my thigh. As I focused on the sharp blade only a few inches from my skin, I began to reconsidering whether or not I was really ready for this. When my uneasy gaze went to Jude I thought I saw a flicker of something in his eyes, as if he was actually enjoying my nervousness.

"One of the most common injuries within battle is to be impaled by an unseen weapon at your flank. To avoid this, you must always be aware of what is around you and learn to fight off an oncoming attack while maintaining your ground. If you lose ground, you inevitably have a greater chance for injury."

He took several long steps back. "I'm going to come at you like an attacker. We won't add handheld weapons to this drill, not yet. I want you to just focus on holding me off with your hands and standing your ground so you're not pushed into the blade. Understand?"

I nodded at him slowly.

"Good. I'll come easy at first, until you are more comfortable with the exercise."

Jude then wasted no time in charging me. My hands flew up to meet the force of his body, which slammed into me with what felt like the impact of a speeding car.

This was easy?

In no time, my arms began to shake as his strong frame continued to push forward, even after I held off his initial charge. He seemed even stronger than Alec or Lucas, but I held my ground. "Good," he praised coolly as he finally let up. "Now —again."

I wanted to ask for a moment so I could regain the strength in my already spaghetti-like arms, but I knew there were no breaks in battle. He backed off by a dozen feet or so, then exploded towards me once again. My hands caught him spot on, but this time I gave more ground, thanks to the shocking impact of his body. I felt the cold blade begin to pierce my skin, and the pain was instant.

I had to do something or he would continue to drive me into the blade. From the hard expression on his face, I judged that either he didn't seem to notice how the blade was to cutting me —or he didn't care. And that was starting to piss me off, so I decided I wouldn't play fair, either. Using all the strength I had, I pushed him back just a few vital inches. Then, when he came at me again, instead of grabbing his arms I threw my hands to his temples, focusing all of my energy. To my shock, I felt nothing except the cold steel of the blade cutting deeper into my leg. My touch had absolutely no effect on him! And now I had lost my leverage against his body, so he was sending me easily into the sword.

As the blade lodged deep in my thigh, I tried to hold back the piercing cry of pain, but it was no use. I didn't even recognize the shrill sounds in my own voice as the sword sliced like fire through the layers of skin and muscle.

At my loud cry of pain Jude finally released me, but to my amazement, he stepped back almost casually. My body was shaking with uncontrolled pain from head to toe, my breath shallow and panting as we both watched the blood pour from my wound onto the floor. I stared at Jude, bewildered because he wasn't even moving an inch to help me, his dark eyes taking in the whole scene with no apparent emotion.

At that moment both Jude and I were shocked as Lucas burst into the training room. Having heard my cry from far down the outer hall, he responded immediately but was momentarily stunned at seeing the long blade buried deep in my leg. His reaction was virtually instantaneous. His eyes flashed in rage as he hurled himself at Jude and shoved him back several feet from me. "Fucking bastard! What the hell's the matter with you?"

In that instant, I really didn't have a problem with Lucas's colorful vocabulary. He was saying the words I was in too much pain to say.

When Jude failed to answer him, Lucas dropped to his knees before me and quickly worked to unlock the grip holding the sword. Continuing to curse under his breath, he pulled the punishing blade back in increments of a half-inch as my hands gripped his shoulders so tightly my knuckles blanched white. I was just hoping I wasn't going to pass out from the pain at any moment.

With thready breaths, I watched the weapon gradually withdraw. I stared with fury at Jude, who just stood there, watching. After the blade was finally out, Lucas quickly released me from the vice grip of the machine, then tore off his cotton tee shirt and ripped it in half, wrapping it around my wildly shaking leg. When he cinched it tight, I screamed like an uncontrolled infant and collapsed toward the floor as both of my legs gave out. Lucas caught me at my waist, swinging me up into his arms, where I cried out for a third time as my injured leg settled into the crotch of his supporting arm. "I'm sorry, Olivia. I needed to slow the bleeding. Let's get you upstairs to Dr. Li."

As Lucas carried me out of the room and, thankfully, out of sight of Jude, I fought off waves of tears and tried to calm my out-of-control breathing, but I couldn't. I turned my head into his shoulder, my cheek resting over another scar on his chest as my limbs began to shake violently. "It's going to be OK," Lucas promised. The anger in his voice was barely contained. "We're almost there."

"I don't understand," I murmured weakly. "He was enjoying hurting me."

More curses rumbled under Lucas's breath. "I promise you, I'll get to the bottom of it. He won't hurt you like this again."

I released a hysterical laugh over his shoulder that I couldn't begin to explain just before he kicked the door in to Dr. Li's office. The doctor was already standing in the waiting area as if expecting us.

"What room?" Lucas growled.

Dr. Li stepped forward to see the damage, but Lucas had run out of patience.

"*What room!?*"

"First one on the right."

Seconds later, Lucas kicked open the door to the exam room open and gently lowered me onto the examination table. From the loss of so much blood, my body felt cold, really cold.

"Stay with me, Olivia," Lucas said—but the room was now spinning out of control.

Then there was nothing.

∗∗∗

I awoke sometime later to see Lucas still at my side, holding my hand as he sat in a chair beside the exam table. I glanced down at my leg, which had been cleaned, stitched and bandaged. Dr. Li must have given me something for the pain, because I couldn't feel a thing, only the dreamy sensation of floating. "How are you feeling?" Lucas asked me.

"Better." I croaked. "Thank you for helping me."

Shaking his head, he worked to push back the anger that was still bubbling just beneath the surface. It surprised me. This often gruff man, whom I had clashed with from the very beginning, was, after all, not the unfeeling jerk I had made him out to be. He was worried for me. "You shouldn't have needed my help. This never . . ." his voice trailed off. Then he took a calming breath. "Tell me how this happened."

"I . . . I'm not sure. I held my position the first time he came at me, but the second time I lost ground. I tried to use my gift to help me, but it had no effect on him. And when the sword started penetrating my leg, he didn't stop. He just kept pushing me into it."

Lucas closed his eyes in a long blink, then ground his teeth until the scar on his right cheek started turning white with the tension of his anger. "Your gift had no effect on him?"

I shook my head. "Unless I did something wrong."

"You did nothing wrong," he countered quickly. "But it doesn't make any sense. Alec and I have known Jude for almost ten years. This just isn't like him."

Just then, Dr. Li entered the room. "How are we feeling, Olivia?"

"Better."

"Good," he added, handing me a cup of blood. "I want you to drink this. This is a pretty deep wound and the blood will help it to repair itself more quickly."

Reluctantly, I took the cup, but didn't make a move to drink it. "This is human blood?"

An odd quirk came over Dr. Li's lips. "Of course."

Lucas squeezed my hand. "It's all right. You can drink this."

As I sipped carefully from the cup, I could indeed tell that the blood tasted different. It was thinner, more coppery. And my body, while liking the taste of it, didn't respond as it had to the vampire blood. Confident I had the right blood, I finished it quickly but once again began to feel the small protrusion against my lips—from my fangs.

Lucas was turned to Dr. Li just then so I was able to cover my mouth discreetly with my hand.

"Thanks, doc," Lucas said. "Can I take her back to her room now?"

"Yes, that'd be fine." Dr. Li then looked at me and added. "Don't be afraid to walk around on it. The leg will be a little stiff, but the blood repairs the tissue quickly, so it'll be good to get movement in the muscles."

"I will. Thank you," I mumbled through my fingers, still trying to be discreet.

Lucas cocked his head, his brows pulling straight over the light brown eyes that reminded me of Alec's. "Why are you covering—?" He stopped himself, a sly grin coming to his lips. "Let me see them."

I shook my head. "No."

"Olivia, let me see them."

Stubbornly, I sat there until I realized we weren't about to go anywhere unless I showed him. Removing my hand, I opened my mouth. He lifted my chin, responding to what he saw with a deep-throated chuckle, which I didn't find very reassuring. "This is what you're so worried about? These are like baby fangs. Actually, they're kind of cute."

"I don't look less human to you?"

"Nope," he smiled, leaning in close, positioning himself on his elbows, almost as if he intended to kiss me. *Lucas, kiss me?* That was crazy.

At my wide-eyed blink he drew back instantly, obviously coming to the same conclusion. He cleared his throat and rose to his feet, a little awkwardly, it seemed to me. "Would you like me to carry you back?"

It seemed even a man who I thought despised me was not immune to my gifts. Once again, there had been too much contact. "No. It'll be good for me to walk . . . if you don't mind plodding along beside me."

He smiled. "Not at all."

***

After Lucas had left my room, I relaxed for an hour or so, then decided to walk around a bit on my stiff leg. While everyone was at dinner I went outside and walked—a little more steady on my feet now—to my favorite rock to stare out at the lake, still feeling some of the floaty effects from the painkillers. I wasn't sure how long I had been there when I heard Maya's voice call out. "There you are. I've been looking for you. I was so worried." She sat down beside me on the rock.

"I feel much better."

"Here," she said, offering me another cup of blood she had brought with her. "Alec asked me to give this to you if I found you first. He wants you to drink it."

"What? Does this mean he's speaking to me again?" I asked as I took the cup.

Maya's happy face immediately furrowed with concern. "Olivia, I think he feels terrible for not being there for you today. You should've seen him tonight. After Lucas told him what happened he marched right into the dining room and punched Jude in the face—in front of everyone—shouting that it had better never happen again."

I blinked back at her in surprise. "Alec couldn't have stopped what happened, even if he hadn't been mad at me. He wasn't allowed in the class."

She shrugged her shoulders. "I don't think that matters much to him. He still feels responsible. He says he knew it was too soon for you to be doing this class."

I snorted in reply. "It wasn't the class . . . it was Jude." I paused, remembering how Jude had just stood there. He had acted as if he despised me, even though I had never done anything to him. "Maya, I'm afraid to go back. I really felt that Jude took pleasure in seeing me in pain. He frightens me."

"Maybe he's sick or something. I've known Jude for a while. This just isn't like him."

I sighed inwardly. "Lucas said the same thing. It's probably just me. My gifts tend to bring out the worst in people."

"Don't say that. This isn't your fault."

I drank some more blood from the cup. "Then who should I —"

I stopped myself just then because another image of Caleb appeared in my mind, this one even clearer than my earlier connection. He was on the roof of the tree house, setting a sheet of plate glass way too large for a normal man to be carrying on its surface, when suddenly he abandoned his task and rose to his feet, his gaze sweeping the landscape all around him. Closing his eyes, he took a deep breath, as if trying to focus his mind. After a few seconds his hand moved to his right thigh, his fingers rubbing over the exact spot where the sword had gone into my leg. He then curled both of his hands into tight fists and snarled through a tightly clenched jaw.

He could *feel* the pain in my leg!

Once again he called out my name—and how I wished I could hear his voice saying, "Olivia." If my vision was real, then his special gift seemed to be getting stronger, *feeling* me, even while I was here, on sacred ground, masked from the consciousness of all in the outside world. Then, just as quickly, I lost the image. I slammed back the rest of the contents of the cup, hoping to get it back again—but he was gone.

Maya clutched at my sleeve. "Olivia, what's happening? Your heart's breaking again."

"Oh, Maya, sometimes I can see him so clearly—like he's right here with me."

"Caleb?"

"Yes. I get these images of him that are so vivid! But I don't know if they're real. I thought it was the blood that was causing me to see him, but now I don't think so. I think his gift—his connection to me—might be getting stronger, even though we're apart. But maybe it's just wishful thinking."

"Try it again," she encouraged. "Try to see him. Maybe it's not just him. Perhaps it's both of you together."

I took in a deep breath, my mind focusing only on him, but I couldn't seem to relax now, and my heart felt like it was breaking in two.

"Olivia, this pain in your heart is overwhelming, it's hard for me to take in. How can I help you with this?"

"You already are, Maya. You let me talk about him without judging me on the fact he's a vampire. You're the only person here I have to talk to."

Even though Maya had been brought into this world of The Brethren where vampires were the enemy, she still had tremendous compassion. A reflection, I believed, of her special gift. Things were not just black and white with her. She was like me, seeing the world around her in much more subtle tones, a broader palette of significance and meaning.

"I didn't know I'd be here this long," I said sadly. "I'm just not sure . . . Maybe these visions are all in my own head. Maybe it's what *I* want to believe." "I don't know if he remembers me."

Maya placed her finger on her lips, held it there for a moment, and then a light bulb seemed to go off in her eyes. "I might be able to help," she said, her voice becoming excited. "I have personal leave next week to visit some friends in Vancouver. I could go to Seattle and check on him for you—find out if he remembers you."

With those words I felt my heart jolt back to life. "Oh, Maya, that'd be wonderful! But it'd be difficult for you to find him at the top of the mountain. And if he *has* forgotten me, I don't want to bring any pain back to his life."

"Then what do we do?"

I tapped my fingers against my own lips, knowing the solution was right there, on the tip of my tongue. "I know . . . Gemma!" I exclaimed. "You can go see Gemma at the blood clinic downtown. It's easy enough to find, and you should be able to tell pretty quickly if she remembers me. I know the perfect question for you to ask."

"That seems easy enough. I'll do it!" Maya replied cheerfully.

"Oh, thank you, thank you, thank you!"

Maya then glanced back over her shoulder toward the hotel. "I have to get back inside. I'm late for my meeting with Gideon. Do you want to come in with me?"

Wriggling around excitedly on the rock, I replied, "No, I think I'll stay a little longer—enjoy the night."

"OK. I'll catch up with you tomorrow, then. We'll make plans."

I nodded happily as she scurried off towards the hotel. With Maya's help I would find out, once and for all, if Caleb remembered—

"Hello, child."

I froze, recognizing instantly that dark voice. Glancing over my shoulder at the border of the sacred ground, my breath whooshed out of me as though I'd been punched in the stomach. The black-eyed demon from my nightmares was standing only a few feet away.

Davin was back.

Chapter Nine

Davin stood there, alone, his ghostly frame appearing to float above the ground in the moonlight. He was still wearing the almost symbolic long, ceremonial black coat he had on the last time I saw him, as if to underscore his importance. His ugly, blanched expression exuded true malice, and for the second time since I'd been here I felt completely at the mercy of the invisible line of sacred ground that separated us. "Maya," I spoke in a normal tone of voice, knowing that her Dhampir ears would hear me regardless. "Get, Alec, now."

"Well, that's awfully convenient of you to bring him straight here to me," Davin smiled. "That should expedite things quite nicely."

I made fists with my hands at my sides, realizing what a stupid thing I had just done. Davin had warned me he would hurt Alec, and I had just put his life in danger by calling him out here. "What do you want, Davin?"

"Oh, nothing much," he responded with a dull sigh. "I'm bored, really. Playing games with those bothersome Hunters you have following me around is getting old. Maybe I'll just have to go back to the mountain and see if killing your tortured vampire will entertain me."

My mind screamed that this was just part of his game, a very sick game. But after witnessing the horrific methods he used on his own kind I couldn't afford to be wrong. That meant keeping him close to me. "You could, but then you might miss your opportunity to nab me."

Stiffly, I made my way off the rock on my injured leg. Davin seemed to almost salivate with each step I took toward him, until I was right at the line of sacred ground. We were separated by mere inches, yet the vampire didn't even try to reach for me. He knew this time I had not stepped over the line. Instead, a smooth veil of calm came over him as he tapped his index finger playfully against the invisible wall that separated us. "Clever girl," he said in reply. "You think you have this all figured out, don't you? But I've already been to see your tortured vampire. He doesn't remember you. So there's really nothing for you to go back to."

I knew from Phin and Kane's reports that he hadn't been anywhere near Seattle. Now it was my turn to smile. "You're lying."

"Lying?" He feigned an incredulous expression in response. "What would I gain by lying to you about this? Think about it. Now that you know the truth that he's moved on, there's no reason for you to cross over this line. Really, I'm hurting my own cause here."

Davin was playing games and trying to confuse me, and *damn it all*, it was working. Doubt was circling through my head like a vulture. If only I had risked stepping over this line just once before now, Caleb would've been able to *feel* me.

"I can prove I'm not lying," he pressed. "There was another vampire with him—a beautiful female. Celeste, I believe her name was." He tapped his finger over his bottom lip, while my heart dropped in my chest with the gentleness of a cannonball. "At least, I think that was the name he was moaning. One can never be quite sure of these things in the throes of such passion."

Celeste was with him? Moaning?

"You see, his attentions were a bit distracted when I saw him. He was making love to the female on a rock perch. Rather fervidly, I might add. I'd say you were the last thing on his mind right about then."

I pressed my fingers to my temples in an effort to quiet the doubt that was ringing in my head. Davin was lying. *He had to be lying!* Caleb loved me . . . but had Alec been right when he said Caleb would forget me once my illusion wore off of him? I swung away from Davin, no longer concentrating on the line that I couldn't afford to cross.

"I told you. He doesn't remember you. And now he's free from your illusion, free to move on with her."

"No . . . it's not true. It can't be true."

"I'm afraid it is. His life is with her now. I sensed the love he had for her. She's his mate."

Oh, God, Davin was telling the truth! Celeste was Caleb's mate ten years ago. He had told me as much himself. But he said it was over, that he hadn't seen her in all that time. It didn't make any sense why he would go back to her now. Shaking my head wildly back and forth, I was trying to reinforce that what he was saying was not possible. "No! You're lying!"

"Oh, poor child. Are you trying to hold onto the idea that he could still love you? A Charmer? You're his enemy. The female vampire is his own kind. But I will love you. I'll show you every day how much I appreciate your gifts."

"Stop! This isn't true."

"I'll take you to him so you can see for yourself that I'm not lying. If he remembers you, I'll let you stay with him. If he doesn't, then you can stay with me. You have to admit, I must be pretty confident to risk such a wager."

"Stop. Please." My head was pounding, and I just needed him to stop so I could think for a moment.

"Just one step closer. Just one. Come to me."

"No," I said, shaking my head. "Soon I'll be strong enough to fight you. And then—"

His laughed deeply. "I saw your pathetic strength at the prison. You can't fight me. You can't fight anyone." He tapped at the invisible wall again. "You know this is what you want. This is all you want—to know the truth of how he feels. I'm offering that to you. Just step forward and I'll give you what you want."

"I . . . I don't know."

"I swear I'll take you to him," he pressed in a soft whisper. "Then you'll know once and for all how he feels about you."

He then stepped back a few paces, motioning with his hand

for me to follow. I took a single step forward just as Alec's voice boomed like a cannon behind me. "Olivia, stop!"

Davin flew back at me hoping I had crossed far enough over for him to grab any part of me. He crashed against the invisible wall so close to me I fell back, stunned, to the ground. Then the vampire seemed to dissolve into the moonlight right in front of me, his voice trailing off as he said, "I'll be waiting."

"Olivia!" Alec shouted again as I dropped my head into my hands. When Alec, Lucas and Maya reached me, Alec wasted no time in hauling me into his arms and carrying me back over to the rock. After setting me down gently, he drew my head up, his hands gently rubbing my temples as he exhaled several quick, anxious breaths. "Olivia, you almost walked right to him again! What were you thinking?"

"I don't know. I'm so confused. I want to believe what he was telling me was a lie . . . but I think it might be the truth."

Alec wrapped his arms around me, his warm body like a blanket trying to cover the sudden chill that had come over me. "Shhh, it's OK. He was using his gift to persuade you. Just give yourself a minute to get clear. Whatever he told you was a lie. He's trying to trick you."

"*Goddammit!*" Lucas cursed. "We need to find Gideon. The Elders need to know what's happening with Davin. He's too familiar with how we operate."

"I'm supposed to be meeting with him right now," Maya offered.

"Go," Alec said to Lucas and Maya. "I'll stay with her. And find Phin and Kane. We need to get a tracking group going right away."

The two headed off while Alec carefully appraised the injury to my leg. "Talk to me, Olivia," he said gently. "Did he threaten Caleb again?"

How could I tell him that I was this upset over the possibility that Caleb had been with another woman—*his mate*, for Christ's sake? He would think I was completely ridiculous. "I don't want to talk about it."

"Davin's a liar. Whatever he told you, he said it to cause just this kind of reaction in you. You have to see that."

I *really* needed to change the subject. "Does this mean you're not angry with me anymore? 'Cause I miss my Guardian, Alec. I honestly didn't mean to hurt you."

"I know," he said. "I should've recognized the effects of vampire blood. I'm sorry I haven't been here when you needed me."

"But if you knew that the problem was the blood, why've you still been so angry with me?"

"I haven't been angry with you," he said, stroking my hair. "I've been upset with myself—that I haven't had better control around your gift. I needed some distance so Gideon could teach me to handle it better."

I sighed. My mother's gifts—my gifts—kept hurting him, and I hated it, but I was helpless to change it. I tried to pull free from his arms, but he drew me right back to him. "You shouldn't be touching me. I understand my gifts are difficult."

"I promise you," he began in a sincere voice, "you won't have to worry about control from me, Lucas, Phin or Kane again. Gideon has been working with all of us."

Then a humorless snort escaped him. "Well, you may still have to deal with Kane. He doesn't know how to have a conversation with a woman without trying to hit on her."

I managed a small smile. "Thank you, Alec. But I'm just thankful you're not upset with me any longer. You're not just my Guardian, you're my friend. I don't know what I'd do if I ever lost you."

"You won't lose me."

✳✳✳

Over the next few days, Alec, Lucas, Phin and Kane went hunting for Davin with a whole team of Vampire Hunters. They targeted their search in the mountains above us, because Alec believed that's where Davin was hiding. I begged all of them not to go, insisting that I didn't want to face Jude again alone. It was the first reason I could come up with to guilt them into staying here, staying safe. But Alec assured me that he and Jude now had an "understanding"—which, if I read between the lines correctly, was sealed by the fist he had planted in Jude's face.

In the meantime, I had been taking it easy over the weekend, resting my leg, which was almost completely healed. It appeared that I wouldn't even have a scar to remind me of the horrid event. But as I brushed my fingers over the now healed skin I realized my memory of that day would not be so lucky.

Having an easy weekend, though, meant that Maya and I could put our plan in place for her visit to Gemma. I had to find out—one way or another—if Caleb had forgotten me and was now living with his mate, Celeste. By the time Maya would see Gemma, I would have been gone just over three months. And in that time, Caleb had no idea if I was safe, or even alive, and no notion of just how much I missed him.

"Thank you again for doing this," I said to Maya as she prepared to leave. "I don't know how I'll ever repay you."

Maya smiled brightly. "You'll repay me by healing that sadness in your heart."

***

I faced a gloomy, wet Monday morning with dread.

Although I had played up my fear of seeing Jude again to try and keep Alec and the others here, now that I actually had to face him, I wasn't so sure it was far from the truth. Alec had promised that everything would be fine, but I hadn't seen the cruel Guardian since the day I hurt my leg, and I had a whole lot of trouble believing he was going to suddenly morph into a nicer person.

Dressed in a pair of red shorts, a couple of colorful sleeveless tees and a light jacket cinched around my waist, I was prepared to go for a walk after class in the cooler weather if I felt like it. When I got to the second floor workout room, Jude was nowhere in sight. So I glanced around the room, jolting to a stop when I saw the chain that was bolted to the floor in the far corner—about five feet long, split into a "y" at that point and terminating in a wicked-looking shackle at the end of each extension. It was almost an exact replica of the chain I'd been unable to break during the battle with Davin on Vancouver Island!

You've got to be kidding, Alec! This is how it's supposed to be better?

At first, I had a hard time believing that Alec, Lucas or Phin knew anything about this. They had seen first-hand how awful that day was for me. But as I thought about it more, I wondered if that was my problem. Maybe that's why The Elders wanted me to take this class . . . because my fears of the past were holding me back. So I decided that despite my unease I would work hard and try my very best. I rationalized that the chain was probably just to be used as an example to show how I could escape such a restraint in the future.

The door flew open as Jude strode into the room. His flat, dark gaze was still emotionless as he approached me. "I'm glad to see your leg is healed," he said with *zero* emotion in his voice.

Chewing back a scowl, I decided to just ignore the jerk and focus on what I needed to do.

Straightaway he walked to the chain. "I understand that you were unable to escape the chain and shackles you were placed in during your battle with Davin. Today, we're going to mimic that situation. We'll see if your strength has improved any, and I'll show you how to escape such a rig in the future."

He motioned for me to step forward to the chain.

"You . . . you want to chain me?"

His face was expressionless. "Is there a problem?" he asked, his flat, emotionless voice not really sounding as if it were a question. "I've already made several adjustments to the training to work with your Guardian's request," he added, rubbing his hand over the jaw where Alec had hit him.

They knew about this? How could they do this? How could Alec let me walk in here and not be prepared? My blood came to an instant boil when this notion occurred to me, so I tried to get past that and calm myself down before I made things worse by exploding on Jude. There had to be a reason for Alec and the others to feel I needed to re-live this particular experience. They must believe I could have done more to escape my situation, that I had been too weak, and that it had therefore put them all at risk. Telling myself I needed to face this possibility, I tempered my anger and tried to look at it more rationally. Maybe I could escape the chains now that my strength had increased from the blood I was drinking regularly.

I stepped forward, and I couldn't help but flinch as the hard clank of the shackle being locked over my wrist sent an emotional jolt through me. *It's OK, Olivia. This is just a strength test.*

Jude handed me a cup of blood. "Here. This will help increase your strength before you start." Wanting any advantage I could get, I took the cup and slammed down its contents. The salty, red liquid sparked on my tongue, and my body responded to it almost instantly . . . but so did my fangs. Well, there was no time to worry about what I looked like at the moment.

"All ready now? Go ahead and try to pull yourself free."

Yanking on the right chain, I thought that I would be able to snap it at a weak link, but no such luck. Instead, I felt the skin on my wrist cut against the shackle. Then a sudden flash, a moment of déjà vu, swept me back to that night on Vancouver Island. I was trying desperately to escape the exact same bonds as Isaac barreled towards me.

"Again," Jude ordered.

I shook it off and this time pulled on the chain with both arms. Within a few seconds I went flying back across the room, the heavy steel chain coming with me and whacking me on the forehead. Stunned for a moment, I sat up and rubbed my head.

Well, that was going to leave a bruise.

Then I realized I had just successfully escaped the chain. I did it!

"Good," Jude praised dully. "There's still room for improvement in your strength, but that's a big step."

Standing back up, I felt great. Victorious, in fact! My fears of that night had been good for me to face, but I wasn't sure I wanted to admit that to Jude, who motioned for me to come back to the chain. Pulling another O-ring from the wall, he clicked the thick metal piece between the floor attachment and the next ring up on the chain.

Soon, one wrist was bound once again.

"The next exercise we're going to do will involve hand to hand combat with one of your hands restrained. This would simulate a situation where you've injured one arm but must keep battling."

Jude wasted no time lining up to charge me, but I wasn't nervous about it, since there were no sharp metal blades anywhere nearby. Crouching lower, I braced my stance and prepared myself for his charge. I was feeling pretty good about this because I could use several of the tricks I had learned in Alec and Lucas's defense class. "Focus, Olivia," he said. "Try to get a shot in at my torso."

Just then I remembered the move that had worked on Alec. I stepped towards Jude, and when he came for me I ducked under his arm, making sure I had a good deal of slack in my chain. When I shot back up, I swung my elbow hard into his ribs. He acted as if he'd not even felt the hit, but I stood up, smiling and feeling victorious for getting a shot in.

Then, without warning, he swiped my legs with one of his, sending them out from under me, and I landed, unceremoniously, flat on my back on the mat. I was shocked by the strength he used. I had worked with Alec on my stance—precisely to make sure my legs couldn't be swiped from under me, but obviously it wasn't enough. When Jude tried to come down on top of me, I rolled towards the chain I was still locked into, then rolled back and hit him square across his back with my elbow. *Take that, asshole!*

But Jude was not amused.

He roared like a lion as he snagged his arm around me like a hook and yanked me hard beneath him. The air was squeezed from my lungs, so I couldn't cry out against the searing pain I felt as my arm stretched straight on the chain 'til I thought it would rip off.

As the metal cut deep into my wrist I tried to understand what he thought he was doing. He pinned my legs down with his own before crawling over me, his heavy body nearly smothering me against the floor. Suddenly, this no longer felt like a training exercise

"Get off of me, Jude! You're hurting me!"

"What?" he bellowed. "You think an attacker's going to leave you alone because you ask him to? He'll keep coming. They all will! Stop being so weak-minded and fight through the pain!"

Soon I was struggling to breathe as my mind flashed me back to images I had wanted to forget of that night on Vancouver Island. Isaac was holding me down on the concrete block, the stench of his rotten breath choking me as I pulled helplessly against the chain. "Stop!" I said, not to Jude but to myself, as I tried to shake the images from my mind. Then, yanking one arm free from beneath him, I used every ounce of strength I had to push at him, but he wasn't moving. This lack of strength was getting ridiculous. I was a Dhampir and I couldn't even muster enough strength to push this human asshole off of me.

"*Fight me, dammit!*" he hissed, his dark eyes glassy, as if he were about to come unhinged. Now I feared that something was really wrong and I tried to scream, but he clapped his hand over my mouth with such force that I suddenly couldn't breathe.

He then pushed my legs apart and thrust his hips forward until I felt his hard erection pressing against my inner thigh. "*Oh, God, this can't be happening!*" I thought as his body became more and more aroused at my fighting him. Frightful memories assailed me of Isaac licking my cheek with his cold tongue as I had failed to push him off of me, as well. It was as though everything was getting mixed up—as though the present and the past were happening all at the same time.

Jude stretched my free arm above my head as I lay completely pinned beneath him, already feeling bruised in several places where he had grabbed at me. Finally, he removed his hand from my mouth and I started to shout, "Get off—" but he cut me off with punishing lips, violent in their assault on mine as he pushed his hands between our bodies to tear at the jacket around my waist. Then the sounds of my other clothing being ripped to shreds permeated my now stunned consciousness.

For a moment it was as if I were outside my own body, feeling this happening to someone else. But this wasn't someone else—it was me! And I had to find a way to stop him or it would be all over before my mind could fully process what was occurring.

The taste of blood on my tongue seemed to snap me out of my daze. I hadn't realized I was biting his lips. His body jerked up with a yell as a cool draft blew over my skin and I knew my clothing was now just in rags around me. I took that moment to scream at the top of my lungs, but a hard slap across my cheek stunned me back into silence and his hand clapped fiercely over my mouth.

Severely dazed by that point, I became a forced spectator as he tugged his pants down on his hips just enough to come back at me. I cursed Alec and the others for making me be here as Jude settled between my thighs, ready to steal what wasn't his to have.

I did the only thing I could and bit the hand over my mouth as hard as possible.

"Ahhh!" he groaned. "You bitch!"

"NOOO!" I screamed until my throat was hoarse and no more sound could come out. And this time, someone responded. Gideon burst into the room with three other men. Within seconds, they had hauled Jude off of me and were restraining him against the floor while I rolled onto my side and curled up in an effort to cover my near nakedness.

Shocked by what he was seeing, Gideon shrugged off his jacket and draped it over me, then moved quickly to unlock the shackle from my wrist. As soon as I was free, I wrapped myself into the heat of the worn jacket like it was the only heat I'd ever known.

Gideon reached for me, but I pushed away from him. "Don't

touch me," I said in a voice surprisingly lacking any real force or volume—almost a whisper.

"Olivia, it's going to be all right. I just want to help you." Gideon's voice was calm and gentle, but I didn't want to hear it, and I continued to crawl away from him until my cut, bruised and shaken body was nestled safely into a thickly padded corner of the room. In that moment, the chaotic sounds of the room faded to an undecipherable blend of muffled voices, while the banging of my own heart became thunderous inside my head. Tears blurred all the movements around me as I pulled my bleeding wrist protectively to my chest. I was so shocked by what had happened—how fast it had spun out of control—that none of it seemed real to me—at least nothing I could process rationally. "I can see you've hurt your wrist," Gideon said quietly. "Why don't we have Dr. Li take a look at it?"

"No," I said, still shaking my head at him.

Meanwhile, Jude still bellowed his rage behind me as he fought against the three men who could barely restrain him. Then more people suddenly burst into the room. "What the hell's going on here? We could hear her screaming on the next floor!"

"It's her fucking Charmer abilities!" Jude yelled. "They mess with your head. She's a devil!"

Gideon snapped his head around. "Get him out! Now!" That was the only time I ever heard Gideon yell in outright anger. He then turned back to me, softening his voice once again. "Olivia, listen to me. We need to take you to see Dr. Li."

I didn't respond, curling tighter into the perceived safety of the corner. When Gideon slowly tried to ease towards me I threw my hand out to block him. "Stay back!"

Just then, Dr. Li came rushing into the room, along with another man who must have alerted him as to what was going on. The doctor moved straight to me. "Olivia, I'm going to give you something to help you relax."

"No, I don't want it!" I cried, balling myself up tighter.

Suddenly, several arms were around me, holding me still as I screamed in suffocating panic. Then I felt a sharp pinch in my arm, followed a few seconds later by blackness.

Chapter Ten

The first thing I noticed when I opened my eyes again was the darkness outside the glass balcony doors to my room. It appeared so black and still, surely one would be chilled to the bone the moment they moved within it. *That* kind of steely cold could reach inside a person and penetrate every bone and sinew until one was forced to find a heat strong enough to defeat it. *That* kind of cold was warring within me now, and the only heat I had to fight it with was coming from the cast-iron stove warming my room . . . and it wasn't enough.

"Olivia?" Dr. Li spoke softly above me. "Do you know where you are?"

I nodded but offered him no words.

"We brought you back here because we thought it's where you'd be most comfortable. Do you remember what happened?"

I nodded again, finally noticing his concerned face.

"You have some cuts on your wrist that I've stitched up. And that arm was hyper-extended, so it'll be pretty sore for a few hours. You also have some deep bruising on your face and thighs. Your physical injuries should be healed in a day or so, but I'll want to check on you a few times over the next twenty-four hours just to make sure there are no other problems."

"Thank you, doctor," Gideon replied when I didn't. "I can see to her from here."

Dr. Li nodded. "Let me know if there are any changes."

After Dr. Li left, Gideon pulled a chair close to my bed but maintained a good distance. His expression was grim, quiet, like a father who was unsure what to say to his daughter after an incident like this. "Olivia, I—"

"Thank you," my raspy voice scratched against my throat.

His brow arched high in surprise at that.

"For getting there in time," I finished.

His eyes glistened with tears as he fought back some very real emotion. "I'm sorry I wasn't there sooner. I'd give anything to have protected you from this." He paused, his words coming out with great difficulty. "Can you tell me what happened?"

Quiet for a long while, I gazed absently into the cold night outside my window, not quite sure whether I wanted to talk about it, but somehow knowing that if I had any hope of taking away its power over me, I needed to get it out. "It all happened so fast," I finally said. "H—he restrained my wrist in the chain, just like . . . I kept flashing back to that night. I wanted to forget that night. He charged me, and once he had me pinned to the floor, he just wouldn't stop."

I realized my words were a jumbled mess, but I couldn't seem to get them to come out in any logical order. "Why would they tell Jude to shackle me?"

"What?" Gideon asked. "Who?"

My voice was nothing more than a whisper. "Alec, Lucas and Phin. They were there that night. They saw how awful it was. Why would they let him shackle me? Jude said he altered the training to meet my Guardian's request. Why would they—he —do that?"

Gideon seemed to be working hard to control himself and maintain an expressionless gaze, and he paused for quite a long time before he responded. "I don't believe they would. But I'll speak with them. What else—?"

Just then we heard hard, pounding footsteps racing down the corridor until they stopped right outside my door and were followed by several loud knocks. "Gideon, it's me. Let me in," Alec said, urgency permeating his voice. When Gideon didn't respond right away, Alec added harshly, "Is she all right?"

I glanced up at Gideon with sadness, shaking my head. He nodded in understanding, rising from his chair. The second the door opened, Alec tried to burst in, but Gideon wouldn't allow it.

"Gideon?" he questioned angrily.

"Step back, Alec. She doesn't want to see anyone right now."

"We just want to know that she's OK," Phin said.

The door shut and locked behind him. Gideon walked the men to the other end of the floor, but I could still hear them as Alec demanded, "What the hell happened?"

"All we heard was that there'd been another fucking incident with Jude," Lucas snarled.

"It can't be true," Phin added. "He'd be crazy to try something after what happened last week."

"*Gideon, what happened?*" Alec's patience was long gone at that point.

"Calm down," The Englishmen began. "Yes, there was another incident. He—"

"*Dammit!*" Lucas cut in.

"—set up an exercise where he chained and shackled her wrist. It brought her mind back to the night at the prison."

There was total silence for several long moments, and I feared that silence meant they felt guilty for saying something to Jude. "*He did **what**?*" Alec finally raged.

"Aahhh! What was he thinking?" Lucas fumed.

"I know," Gideon replied. "I need to ask. Did any of you tell Jude about that night on Vancouver Island? Anything that would give him the idea to do this to her?"

"No!" they all said, in almost perfect unison.

"But we reported to The Elders about it, of course," Phin pointed out. "Jude has been taking all of his orders from them."

"Yes, but why would The Elders encourage this?" Kane questioned. "It doesn't make any sense."

Hearing all of this, I at least felt better that they had not given Jude the idea to do this to me. I would've felt completely betrayed if they had.

"What're her injuries?" Phin asked. "Will she be all right?"

"Physically, she'll be fine—"

"*Physically?*" Alec echoed. "What the hell does that mean?"

Gideon paused for a long moment, probably trying to figure

out the best way to word things, but that added time only served to rile up the other men even more. "What the fuck did he do, Gideon?" Lucas snapped.

"He attacked her while she was chained. When we came in he had her pinned down and her clothing was ripped to shreds. If we'd gotten there any later . . ."

Again, shocked silence. The only sound I could hear was Alec's hard breathing. It seemed they were all momentarily speechless. "Gideon, are you saying he tried to . . . to rape—" Phin began, but Alec didn't give him a chance to finish.

"*I'll kill him!*" he said, flying into a rage. Multiple curses and several loud bangs and thumps occurred as the other men tried to stop Alec from taking off to hunt Jude down at that very moment.

"Alec!" Gideon barked. "Calm down. The Elders are on their way. They'll be here within the week to deal with the situation."

"They'd better deal with it!" Lucas shouted. "Or we will!"

Alec was still livid. "What the hell's the matter with him? He's a Guardian, for Christ's sake! He's supposed to be protecting her, not trying to rape her!"

"The Elder's will take care of Jude," Kane replied in a cool voice. "They'll know what to do?"

"She needs time and space, all right?" Gideon said. "You all need to respect that and give it to her. Are you listening, Alec?"

After that, I didn't hear anything for a long time, and I assumed the men had moved on. I tried to relax and get some sleep, but I couldn't, my mind still flashing back and forth between those two awful thoughts. Then I heard the lightest tap at my door. "Olivia?" Alec's voice was so soft it was almost a whisper through the door, but there was such misery in it that it broke my heart. "Olivia, it's me."

I didn't respond. I knew he was hurting, but I just couldn't give him the assurance he needed from me right then. "I want you to know that I'm sorry. You were right. I should've never left you alone with him today. *Never.* Forgive me."

Then after another quiet minute with still no response from me, he left.

Lying there in my room, staring at nothing in particular for most of the night, I knew I was not *all right*. I wouldn't even be able to utter the words. I had come here to learn how to defend myself against the supernatural world's most dangerous creatures, and instead I was being attacked by the very people who were supposed to be training me. Even my Guardians, whom I adored most of all, had trouble controlling their touches. I still cared about them deeply because I knew they were trying so hard and it was not their fault, but I didn't want to be here any longer. I wanted to go home. Home to the mountain. Home to *him*.

I was terrified that Maya would come back and tell me that Caleb had forgotten me, and that he was now with Celeste. I felt nauseous. If I didn't have a home there and I didn't want to be here, and I had no family, then where I would go.

Please! Please, let him remember me.

***

For the next several days, I didn't leave my room. Only Gideon and Dr. Li were allowed to see me. I trusted Gideon because he had been around my mother's gift, and it seemed he truly knew how to control his mind inside the illusion my gift created. Most of the time, he would just sit quietly, watching me as my thoughts drifted off into the distance. He was waiting for me to say something, which I didn't.

Each day he would tell me how Alec had requested to see me, sometimes two or three times in a matter of hours. Lucas, Phin, and even Kane wanted to make sure I was OK, but they didn't push like Alec. I felt bad because I knew all of them needed to see me to ease their worry, but I just didn't have it in me to speak with anyone. All I wanted was to be held securely in Caleb's arms, listening to his deep, husky voice telling me that everything would be fine, good—wonderful, even.

By the third day, I managed to dress myself in a pair of jeans and a comfortable red stretch shirt. Sitting with my legs pulled to the side of me on the sofa, I squeezed my fingers against the furniture's rounded, fabric-covered arms, wishing I could be pressing those fingers onto the eighty-eight keys that were so familiar to me. I didn't want to talk with anyone, didn't want fight anyone—I just wanted to play the music blaring in my head until it would become painful for my fingers and the muscles of my forearms.

When the eventual knock came, I crossed the room and let Gideon in before returning to the sofa without as much as a single word. He sat in the lounge chair beside me, placing a shoebox-sized wooden case on his lap. I was curious what was in it, but not enough to ask. "Alec asked to see you again this morning."

My gaze remained focused outside. "I know he's worried. Assure him that I'll be fine."

Gideon sighed roughly. "I don't think my assurances will help him much. He's been feeling pretty low the past few days. He believes he's failed you."

"He hasn't failed me. It's not his fault that Jude . . ."

I couldn't finish, and I hated how my lip quivered slightly before I could pull the emotion back in.

"The Elders will handle Jude. Alec has already given his Uncle Reese an earful . . . and then another earful. It's been all I could do to keep him from finding Jude and bashing his head in."

"I'll think about it," I replied, returning my gaze outside. "I know I can't hide in here forever." Then shaking my head in disgust, I added, "Wouldn't my mother be so proud . . . seeing me cower in my room like this? I bet she never did this. She was probably brave and faced her challenges."

"What happened to you was not a *challenge.*" Gideon's normally gentle English voice was sharp with anger. "It was assault and attempted rape. Eve never had anyone here attack her like that. I'm quite sure if someone had, James would've killed the man."

"But still—"

"No! Olivia, I'm convinced that with all of the problems the

human males are having keeping their touches to themselves—
even your own Guardians, whom I know would never want to
hurt you—that your gift to draw them is much more powerful
than your mother's. Eve never had these problems with the
human men. The Elders must be made aware of this."

"But that would mean that Jude was *right*. I caused him to
do this."

"No, he's *not* right," he responded sharply. "There's no
excuse for what I walked in on. You don't see Alec or the others
hurting you like this, do you? And they'd be just as affected as
Jude, if not more so, given their proximity to you."

I didn't respond, and after a while Gideon seemed concerned
with my wordless trance. He tapped his hand against the wood
case in his lap, the sound drawing my attention back to it. "I
know you don't feel much up for class today, but I thought I
could share this with you. This box belonged to your mother.
Just before she died, she asked me to give it to you when you
were older. I had forgotten about it until recently."

Unexpectedly, my heart jumped. Something of my mother's,
something that would tell me even the smallest bit about her
and how she dealt with her gift, seemed very important. I
straightened on the sofa, sliding my feet to the floor and
reaching my hands outward. "May I have it?"

Gideon nodded and handed it to me. "This box carries her
mementos and personal items. I thought it might help you to
know her a little better."

Without delay, I opened the lid and pulled out several
handwritten letters that were bundled together with a lilac-
colored ribbon. Upon closer inspection, I could see that they
were love letters between her and my father. I pressed the
precious pages to my heart, excited with the prospect of
reading some of them later and learning more about their love
for each other.

Below that was a picture of a man and a woman, but I didn't
need to ask Gideon who they were. I could tell from looking at
the woman's face that she was my mother. I looked just like her,
and the man beside her was handsome. Not in that 'stop you on

the street' kind of way, but that 'everything works well together' sort of way. His hair was light, with long bangs that swept to one side, and his eyes were green, framed with thin glasses. He looked so kind and gentle, it was hard for me to imagine the fierce fighter I had been hearing so much about. I smiled, holding the picture out for Gideon. "This is my father with her?"

Gideon nodded. "He was a good man—the very best. And though he was only with you for a short time, he adored you. You were his little princess. There was nothing he would deny you."

I felt my eyes begin to well with tears as I continued to stare at the picture.

"I didn't mean to upset you with this," Gideon said.

"No, it's not that. I'm just so happy to see their faces—to know something of who they were. It's so hard sometimes, not having any family." I touched my finger to the surface of the picture, outlining their faces. "How old were they when they died? It didn't say on the gravestones."

"That's because your mother was so much older than your father," he replied as I pulled out her journal, excited to read just a few pages. "He was thirty-two, but she was fifty-seven."

"Fifty-seven!" I said startled.

Gideon laughed. "Don't worry. She looked not much older than you. Your father actually appeared older. Look at the picture again." I did and was amazed to see he was right. "Dhampir's age much more slowly and have a much longer life span than a human—usually three to four times longer. You will, too."

As I thumbed through the pages of her journal, another photo fell out of the back of the book. I picked it up and read the inscription on the back: *Jackson and Isabeau Walker*

Walker?

Turning the photo over, I was stunned to see the handsome face of the man, vampire, and coven leader I had stayed with at the tree house. Jax!

Chapter Eleven

"Gideon! Who're these people?"

Taking the photo, Gideon looked at it, then glanced at the inscription on the back.

"Ah, yes. These were your grandparents. He's your vampire grandfather."

I gasped, barely able to believe it. "They're Eve's parents? He's her father?"

Gideon nodded, pleased that the box had lifted my spirits to resemble some sliver of the woman they knew and cared for. "Yes."

Jax is my grandfather! I have family! I'm a Walker! I'm a Walker! I'm a Walker!

I felt as if I was about to explode out of the confines of my own skin. I couldn't believe I was the same girl who only minutes ago felt utterly beaten and defeated. My recovered mood, however, was soon tempered with Gideon's next words. "Your grandfather was the reason Eve was with The Brethren. She hated that he brought your human grandmother into his vampire world. When he impregnated her, it was a virtual death sentence for your grandmother. Eve also carried the scars that her birth caused the death of her mother."

Isabeau Walker was the human woman Gemma had told me about, the one Jax had loved with all of his heart and soul—my grandmother. This was just all so unbelievable. She was also the woman that Jax had so many painful regrets about. Losing her had nearly destroyed him, but eventually Jax's love for her was the reason he became a better vampire, a better man, a Daywalker. "Sometimes love doesn't give us a choice, Gideon."

"True. I do know your mother wanted the resources to find Jackson. She wanted to destroy him."

My mother wanted to kill Jax? Her own father? Learning about my true family brought such a mixture of emotions: blessings and pain. There would never be a point in our lives where we would all be together. Circumstances had plotted paths for each of us that would separate us, even pit us one against another. If there was nothing else I accomplished in this life, I swore I would heal old wounds with Jax, my grandfather. I didn't care about the past, I just wanted a future. I wanted to belong to a family. He was all I had . . . and he was more than enough.

I realized I had to keep Jax's identity concealed from Gideon and The Brethren. I had no idea what they would do if they knew the truth. Gideon had not come with Alec and the others to get me off the mountain, so he had no idea I had been staying with my Grandfather that whole time, but I would have to keep this picture from Alec. He would put it all together in about two seconds. "Thank you for showing this to me," I smiled. "I can't tell you what this means."

"You're welcome. I'm glad it's cheered you up."

I pulled my arms around the prized possession. "It has. May I keep this?"

"It belonged to your mother. It's rightfully yours."

Gideon watched me carefully as I held the box close in my lap. "Olivia, when you're ready, I think it would be good for you to talk to someone about what happened. None of us want to see you go through this alone. If not me, then perhaps someone else?"

"I'll be all right, Gideon. I don't need to talk about it."

Discovering Jax was my grandfather was all the remedy I needed right now, but it was obvious from Gideon's strained expression that he didn't agree.

"Will you tell Alec he can come see me . . . if he still wants to?"

A soft laugh of release escaped him as he stood. "I'm sure he'll be here about two minutes after I tell him."

***

I had just enough time to find a good hiding place for my new gift when the light rap that brought back my smile sounded on my door. I had returned to the sofa but left the door cracked so Alec could let himself in, which is exactly what he did.

My recently tear-filled eyes met his as he crossed the room, and his widened with concern as he knelt before me, mistakenly believing I had been crying about Jude's attack. Touching his hand to my pulled knee, he cautiously, slowly lowered his head as he spoke. "I'm so sorry I wasn't here to help you," he began. "I'm a miserable excuse for a Guardian."

I rested my hand the crown of his downturned head. "Alec, don't. You couldn't have known what Jude was going to do."

His head snapped up and I removed my hand. "You did. You said you were afraid of him—and I didn't listen." His self-critical expression quickly turned into a grimace of pain as he observed, "It's just that I've known him for so long. I wouldn't have thought it was possible he could do something like this."

I lowered my upraised hand onto the sofa cushion, silently asking him to join me. He didn't hesitate, and once he was seated I wrapped my arms around his waist, lowering my head comfortably onto his shoulder. A relieved breath seemed to seep from him as he tilted his head against mine. And after a few quiet minutes, he lay back against the sofa arm, pulling me with him but keeping one of his feet resting on the floor. I relaxed against his chest as his hand gently stroked my hair. The moment felt peaceful—safe. "How badly did he hurt you?"

I squeezed my arms around him. "I was so scared, Alec. I kept flashing back to being in chains the night at the prison. It was as if what he was doing to me in the moment and that night blended together. I couldn't think clearly."

"He'll pay for what he's done," he whispered into my ear.

"When you said you'd talked with him, I thought you knew what he wanted me to do that day in class. I didn't understand, but I wondered if you were trying to tell me that I needed to be stronger about dealing with that night." The pitch of my voice was rising uncontrollably as I spoke. "So I let him put me in the chains."

"Shhh. You went through hell at that prison. I wouldn't have believed it if I hadn't been there myself. The fact that you survived tells me all I need to know about your inner strength." He paused and picked up the wrist that had been injured by the chain, smoothing his thumb over the skin that was now completely healed. "Was this the hand he chained?"

I nodded silently.

"Tell me exactly how he hurt you. I need to know what he did."

I didn't respond, just continued to breathe against his chest. "Olivia?"

"I'm all right now, Alec. I don't want to go back. Please say you understand."

He said nothing for a long while, then lifted my chin to meet his gaze. His eyes reflected his questioning expression and I worried that he would try to push the subject, but he didn't. "You look exhausted. Have you been able to sleep?"

I shook my head. "I've been having nightmares."

"Try to get some rest now. I'm not going anywhere, and I'll let nothing hurt to you."

I tried to sleep, but instead lay there for several minutes trying to figure out how to tell him the truth. "You're supposed to be trying to sleep," he murmured.

"I know . . . But I have to tell you something. I don't want to hurt you, Alec . . . but I can't stay here anymore. I want to go home."

His inward sigh was barely audible. "By home you mean to the mountain—to *him?*"

"Yes, if he remembers me . . . and if he'll still have me."

"He's not going to remember you. I'm sure of that. It's been three months now. He's been freed of the illusion you projected on him and has now moved on with his life. Do you want to bring him pain again by seeing you?"

"No. I'd never do that to him. But I need to know for sure

he's forgotten me before I make anymore commitments with my life."

"I understand. But you must also consider your own safety. Davin has been just waiting for you to leave sacred ground. I can't just let you to walk out of here so he can simply take you. Surely, you must know that."

I turned my head into his chest, inhaling his scent of sand, sea, and sun. "There has to be a way. Please help me."

"Get some rest," he whispered. "We'll talk about this more tomorrow."

***

The next morning I woke to knocking at my door. I was lying on top of my bedcovers with Alec behind me, waking up from his own hazy dreams. He stood up and stretched beside the bed, then walked to the door, still fully clothed except for his shoes.

A startled Gideon stood on the other side. "I'm not interrupting, am I?" he questioned, and I could tell he was worried his student had crossed another line.

"No," Alec said in a raspy, 'morning' voice as he scrubbed his hand through his hair.

"Oh. Well, good," he replied, unconvinced.

He found me as I sat up, fully clothed, on the bed. Then he seemed to relax. There was no need for him to worry, though. Alec had been a perfect gentleman the entire night, joining me on the bed only when my nightmares had returned early in the morning hours.

"Olivia, The Elders are here. They'd like you to meet with them tonight after dinner in council. With his Uncle Reese's permission, Alec can show you where that is."

"OK," I said nervously, my mind and voice still waking from sleep.

Alec glanced over his shoulder. "It's all right. I'll explain to you what to expect."

Gideon continued. "I've also been instructed to bring you up to meet with one of The Elders before tonight's gathering."

"Only one Elder? Not all twelve?"

"You'll meet all of them tonight," Gideon began. "But The Elders are never assembled together outside of chambers."

"Why is that?"

"It's too dangerous for them," Alec replied. "They're at their most vulnerable when assembled. Most of the people here haven't even seen all twelve, much less all of them together."

Alec turned back to Gideon. "Who wants to see her?"

"Joseph."

Alec's shoulders went stiff. "That's not a good idea. Not now, anyway."

Gideon frowned at the young man. "You know how this works, Alec. It isn't a request."

"Gideon," Alec pressed, but the Guide just stepped around him and proffered his arm.

I ran my hand through my hair. "Can't I at least freshen up a bit before we go?"

"You look fine. Come on, let's go."

"I'll be right here when you get back," Alec said tensely.

Gideon led us toward the designated elevator for the twelfth floor. No one was allowed to come onto this floor unless they were in the mood to challenge about a dozen guards. When we were greeted by four of them just off the elevator, I thought we were going to be turned right back around. The Elders Guards were hardly friendly, a couple of them showing scowls that could compete with Lucas on a bad day, but they motioned for us to follow them.

As we passed a couple of rooms that looked like high-end parlors, I noted that the décor on this floor was the same European styling as the floors below but in darker, richer tones, something resembling an affluent men's club. Then it hit me how deathly quiet it was up here. It was strange to think that this was where Reese Lambert stayed and that some day Alec would reside on this floor. It didn't seem to fit him.

Gideon knocked on a ceiling-high, ornately paneled wood

door and was received on the other side by a rather mild-mannered looking Englishmen. I could hardly understand Alec's concern over meeting such an unthreatening figure. Slightly less than average height and appearing to be in his mid- to late forties, Joseph was far from the big, bad Elder I had envisioned. He more resembled an average family man, with dark brown eyes that in some way seemed familiar, and wavy brown hair that fell a bit wild on his forehead. He had a peculiar bend in his nose, as if it had been broken and never fully healed, yet it brought character and distinction to his face.

"Gideon. Thank you for escorting her up so quickly." He then turned to me and offered his hand. "And you must be, Olivia. I'm Joseph."

Shaking his hand, I smiled. "Yes, hello."

"That'll be all," Joseph said, dismissing Gideon with a simple nod of his head, to which I blinked back with surprise. I had expected that Gideon would stay, but he left as if already knowing he would not be invited in.

Joseph then waved me inside. "Come in. Come in. Would you like anything to drink?" He pointing to the lavish bar set up just beyond him that offered just about anything anyone wanted to drink, but my attention was pulled several directions as I took in the grandness of his penthouse suite. The masculine room gave new meaning to the word "rich." With mahogany-paneled walls, traditional furniture upholstered in neutral tufted leathers with nail-head trim, and dark velvety accent throws and pillows, the room screamed wealth. Gazing deeper into the suite, I saw several sliding doors, also richly paneled, that were partially opened, showcasing a huge, four-poster bed beyond, each post distinguished by its ornately crafted carvings, obviously done by hand.

"No, thank you. I'm fine."

Joseph motioned towards a couple of leather wingback chairs. I took a seat across from him, resting my hands politely in my lap while trying to pull straight the wrinkled shirt I had slept in. Once the Elder seemed to relax into the full depth of his chair, he crossed his legs and draped his arms comfortably over the sides with the ease of a man who knew he was in charge but didn't have to prove it. "I thought it would be a good idea for us to meet before tonight's council session . . . though, I wish it was under better circumstances. I am truly bothered by what has happened."

"I appreciate that, but I don't understand. You speak as if I should know you?"

He hesitated, a quick half-hearted smile flashing over his lips before returning to a neutral expression. "I'm Joseph Davin. Luther was my father."

Chapter Twelve

I shot to my feet, feeling like an animal that had just been cornered. Joseph, meanwhile, remained perfectly calm in his chair. "I guess I shouldn't be surprised by your reaction," he offered. "Luther certainly has not made your life easy these past few months."

It was interesting how Joseph referred to his own father by his first name. Almost as if he already accepted that Luther "the vampire" was not his father.

"When we believed my father was killed, I assumed his seat in council. As Elder I may be my father's son, but I assure you my intent where you're concerned is quite different."

"Your father wanted to use me as a weapon to fight against the Lycans," I answered, in a somewhat stern and clipped voice. "Still does. You and your Brethren are training me in hopes I'll fight for your cause—again as a weapon. I see no difference."

Something resembling amusement crossed The Elder's features, as if he'd been caught off guard by my directness. "I believe, Olivia, it's more complicated than that. This war we are engaged in against the Immortals isn't easy—"

"War never is," I interjected.

"Yes, but *my* intent is different." He then raised his hand, gesturing for me to return to the chair I had vacated when I came to my feet. "Sit. I'll explain."

Stubbornly, I didn't budge.

"Please."

Finally, I slowly sat, just at the edge of the chair, my eyes never wavering from his.

"As a young adult I was living here at The Oracle for a while, being prepared for my future responsibilities as Elder—not unlike your Guardian, Alec. Your mother lived here, with you, at that time, though you were just an infant. And I'm sure like a lot of the young men here, I was completely smitten with your mother. She was beautiful, patient and kind, full of motherly affection."

Surprisingly, I could see the sincerity in the dark eyes that so resembled his father's. He gazed outward, his eyes becoming unfocused as though searching something very distant, perhaps sifting through cherished memories. For a moment, I nearly forgot he was a Davin. "My intent *is* different, Olivia," he continued, "because I want to do right by your mother. She loved you with all her heart. I saw it with my own eyes. She wouldn't want you to be forced to do anything against your will, even if it were for her own cause."

For a moment I was caught up in the emotion of seeing her face in my mind now that I had a picture of her. I was lifted by the smallest sense of hope that somehow, in some way, this man might give me what I wanted—freedom. "If that's true, then you'll agree to let me leave The Oracle?"

Another smile crossed his lips, this time completely without humor—more like with some sadness or regret in it. "Once again, it's not that simple. I share this responsibility with eleven other men, and I'm quite sure—even though my vote as a descendant of the founder is highest—the others won't put a single woman's wishes ahead of the overall mission."

"But I'm a free person," I cried. "You can't keep me here against my will."

His eyes narrowed. "I'm sorry you see it that way. I see that I'm honoring your mother by keeping you safe. That's what she would've wanted. I don't expect you to fight as she did—that was her choice. But I do expect you to stay here where my father and the rest of the Immortals bound to be drawn to you can't harm you."

I inhaled deeply, reaching deep inside for some powerful reason that would change his mind. Even though this man was denying me what I wanted, I sensed there could be room for compromise. "What if there was a way for me to live outside of

The Oracle safely. Would you consider it then?"

"That's not really possible, Olivia. My father captured you while we had four of our best trained men guarding you. Imagine what would happen if you were unguarded?"

"But what if . . . ?" I pressed, then hesitated in an effort to further develop my idea with some quick thinking.

He said nothing, but he, too, was thinking . . . and for now, that was something.

After a highly charged moment between us that seemed to speak volumes even though nothing further had been said, Joseph stood up, silently letting me know that our brief introduction was over. "Gideon will be waiting for you by the elevators to take you down. Again, it was nice meeting you, Miss Greyson."

When Gideon returned me to my room, Alec was wildly pacing back and forth, raking his hands through his wet hair. He had obviously taken a quick shower and changed while we were gone. Stopped by the sight of us, he threw his arms up expectantly when I didn't say anything, and said, "Well?"

I walked straight up to him. "I'm hungry. Can we go get some breakfast?"

Gideon tried bravely to conceal a laugh.

For his part, Alec stared back at me in complete bewilderment. "Olivia?"

I laughed. "Honestly, Alec, you're working yourself into white hair. Everything's fine. Now, will you please give me a few minutes to freshen up, then you can escort me to the dining room so I can see the others?"

He stood there, once again ruffling his hair with one hand as if debating with himself whether that was a good idea.

I squeezed the hand at his side. "Please?"

Finally, a crooked smile edged across his lips. "Sure. They'd very much like to see you."

"Well, if you'll both excuse me," Gideon said. Recognizing that everything was fine with Alec, he headed for the door.

"Thanks, Gideon," I said, then walked over to the basin to

clean myself up.

After what must have been several painfully long minutes for him, Alec finally blurted, "So, are you going to tell me what happened?"

"There's not a lot to tell. He wanted to introduce himself before tonight, knowing how his last name would upset me."

"And did it?"

"Yes . . . at first," I answered truthfully. He would expect no less from me. "But I think we've found some common ground."

Alec turned to face out the window while I changed my clothes behind him. "And that would be . . . ?"

Tucking the last of my shirt into my jeans, I walked up to him and twined my arm around his, letting him know I was ready to leave. "My mother," I answered simply.

***

Later that night, I showered and dressed in a gray cotton skirt and my favorite cypress green cardigan, the one Gemma had bought for me when I was staying at the tree house. It gave me some comfort to have Caleb, Jax and Gemma fresh on my mind in the midst of what I was about to do. I had no idea what to expect from the Elders, but I had faith that Jude would get what he deserved for hurting me like that. Slipping into some comfortable flats, I awaited the knock on my door I had been waiting for, and soon it came.

Gideon walked me back to the elevator that would take us to the twelfth floor. Only this time, he turned the key to unlock it and pushed the button to go down. As I stepped inside, I took a deep breath. "Relax," Gideon said. "You'll do fine."

Just before the door closed, Gideon stepped back and I saw that Alec, Lucas and Phin were quietly sitting on some benches in the hallway nearby. They were letting me know that they would be there when I returned. I smiled at them, though I could tell my nervousness prevented it from being very sincere.

When I reached the lower level I was surprised at how dark it was . . . and how cold. As soon as I felt the chill hit under my skirt I realized I should have worn pants to cover my legs. The floors and walls were all a rough, natural stone, with only a few candles lit inside decorative glass lanterns along the long hallway that led toward the chamber. As I approached the entry doors, four heavily armed guards in formal, velvet coats opened the huge, hand-carved doors and motioned for me to enter. Honestly, when it came to this secretive group, it felt often as though I was living in another century.

Once inside the chamber I was immediately struck by the enormous, custom-built table, shaped like a horseshoe, where all twelve Elders now sat. It was built on a platform raised at least a foot from the floor and boxed on the front and sides in what looked to be solid silver. The incredibly ornate trim and detail was broken up by twelve velvet panels in a rich eggplant color inserted just in front of each Elder's seat. Over the panels were the individual family crests and the last name of the family the crest represented. Each Elder was seated an equal distance from the next in chairs that looked more like silver thrones, and their full names, large enough for me to read, were inscribed on silver placards bolted into the stone floor inside the circle.

The Elders surely knew how insignificant someone would feel standing beneath them as they flanked all sides, never able to see all of their faces at once. Right away I spotted Joseph Davin at the top center of the horseshoe, marking his importance to the group. Alec had explained that The Elders were ranked based on the original family's entry into The Brethren more than two hundred years ago. And those positions had not changed. I found it ironic that I was comforted in some small way by seeing the face of the son of the man who was hunting me.

Directly to Joseph's right was Alec's uncle, Reese Lambert. Though Reese appeared to be in excellent physical condition, he couldn't be called handsome. His features were a bit sharp, especially his pointed nose, and his eyes were a bit dull, void of any of Alec's sunny warmth. I tried discreetly to search for a resemblance to his nephew, but there was none. Not even Alec's trademark chin dimple.

Reese looked to be Joseph's senior by about twenty years,

and by the rigid set of his features it seemed apparent he didn't like having to be seen as less important than the much younger Elder.

As I waited for them to speak amidst the eerie quiet, I nervously fussed with my skirt between my fingers. When I glanced down in an effort to silently will myself to stop, I noticed an etched design in the stone floor beneath my feet. It was an intertwined, braided knot. I assumed it was a trademark or symbol for the group.

Just then the heavy chamber doors opened again. I turned around and was struck with horror at seeing one of the guards bringing Jude inside the circle to stand only a few feet away from me. It was the first time I had seen the man since the day of the attack, and just seeing him brought back images I wanted to forget.

With a cast-iron expression, emotionless, he continued to hold himself as if he felt no remorse. I couldn't understand it. What had I ever done to this man to make him hate me so much?

"Olivia," Joseph began in a relaxed but confident tone. "First, let me say that we are all deeply disturbed to have to meet you, the Charmer—one whose gifts this group holds in high esteem —under these circumstances. We are aware of the attack the accused here"—he lifted his hand to Jude—"committed against you. The Elders have gathered tonight to decide Jude's punishment. But before we do, we'd like to hear your version of events."

My heartbeat was so strong now that it thumped against my throat. I hadn't prepared myself to retell that day's events with Jude standing right next to me. Not surprisingly, I struggled with my words. "I—I . . . I mean he . . . he recreated the situation where I was chained on Vancouver Island . . . so I could practice getting free from the chains. I was having trouble focusing. I kept seeing flashes of that night in my head."

"You see? She's a weak-minded girl," Jude scowled.

"Jude, I would advise against you speaking, if you know what's good for you." The angry man two spots to Joseph's left,

Callum Maberey, appeared to be about the same age as Reese, and his disposition was certainly surly. Even though he had just defended me in some way, I sensed no kindness from him. It was almost as if he was more upset that Jude wasn't keeping his mouth shut than concern for how he treated me.

That was when I realized how The Elders saw me. Jude was one of them. He had been with them for nearly ten years. Even Alec and Lucas said he had always been a '*nice enough*' guy. I was the newcomer, the outsider, and it would be my word against his as to what happened that day in the training room.

"H—he charged me," I continued, "while I had one hand chained. The next thing I knew, he swiped my legs out from under me and had me pinned to the mat." My voice began to shake and I cursed my own nervousness. "I screamed for him to stop. He was hurting me . . . but he continued to hold me down —began tearing at my clothes and forcing himself between my legs. I . . ." I stopped, unable to continue.

The voice of an Elder behind me snapped out. "Jude, what possible explanation could you have for this outrageous behavior? And only four days after the girl was rushed to the doctor for being impaled by a sword in your class."

Jude visibly stiffened, appearing angry at having to defend himself, but he kept his voice calm. "You all know what this girl is. You can't even be near her without feeling as if the entire world around you is a lie."

Another Elder to the left of me replied, "The Guardians and Hunters assigned to protect her haven't tried to rape her. And they are around her more than you."

"They've touched her inappropriately, though," Jude defended and then pressed, "just ask her."

"Is this true, Olivia?" an Elder named Nathaniel Hawkings asked. He sat to the left of Joseph and looked closer to Joseph's age. His tone was respectful and held sincere concern, but I didn't want to answer the question. There was no way I wanted Alec, Lucas, Phin—or even one-track-minded Kane—to be lumped in the same category as Jude. There was no comparison.

"Answer the question," Callum ordered.

My gaze wandered up to Reese Lambert. This was the most wretched moment for me. How could I do this to Alec? After everything he had done for me. I tried to reassure myself that he would always want me to tell the truth. "At first, yes, but Gideon—"

"You see!" Jude snapped.

"Jude, I hardly think inappropriate touches are in the same league as ripping the woman's clothes off while she's chained," Joseph finally spoke up.

"Yes, but we must make allowances considering who she is —what her gifts are." It took a moment for my mind to register that statement. And then another to register that it was *Alec's uncle* who was saying it. I stood there dumbfounded as Reese continued. "All of the human males have been drawn to her, much more so than to her mother. Gideon has spoken to me of this."

"So you're saying we don't hold the men accountable for their actions simply because of who she is?" Nathaniel questioned, his tone hard and clearly objective.

"No. But we're still learning what her capabilities are. Jude, as with my nephew and the others, was not properly prepared for how strong her gifts are. Everything we know we learned from Eve. But Olivia is showing us that we still have much to learn, and we have to better prepare the men."

"I agree," Callum said. "If they are better trained to handle her gifts, and Jude or any of the others have even the slightest incident with the girl, then I think he should face severe punishment. But how can we do that now, when we're the ones who put him in this situation—inadequately prepared?"

I couldn't believe what I was hearing. They were practically saying the whole thing was my fault. I wanted to scream, but I stood there silently, anger welling inside me at being betrayed by these men who said they wanted to protect me.

"I'd agree to this only on one condition," Nathaniel began. "That Jude is to be kept confined to his room and allowed nowhere near the girl until Gideon is absolutely sure he can handle it." Three other Elders around the table quickly agreed.

Joseph, who had been quiet for a while, finally spoke. "I must say I'm disappointed, gentlemen. If this were one of our wives or daughters we were talking about here tonight, I don't believe you'd all feel so lenient."

Voices rang from around the table.

"I agree."

"So do I."

"Yes."

"Our wives and daughters are not Charmers," Reese responded, his high chin and narrowed gaze challenging Joseph at every turn. "This is appropriate for this circumstance."

Joseph then called for a vote, and I stood there feeling as though I were about to crumble to my knees as he called them off. There were seven in agreement to release Jude and five against.

"Very well," Joseph said, and I was hurt even further that he didn't try to use his weighted vote over the group to defend me. "Jude, you're to remain in your quarters until further notice and you're to have no contact with Olivia. You will receive meals there and undergo daily meetings with Gideon while guards are placed outside your door. Do you understand?"

"Yes."

I risked glancing up at Jude just then. His expression was victorious.

"Take him away," Joseph ordered.

As the chamber doors shut behind Jude, I could feel Joseph's eyes on me. "Olivia, is there anything else you would like to say?"

You're darn right there was! I wanted these men to understand what they just did to me. For whatever reason, I wasn't afraid of these men of great power. I was a free person. As Caleb once said to me—'*Your life is your own. It does not belong to this Brethren.*'

"Yes," I replied, finding strength in my voice. "If this is your decision . . . if you believe that my gift was responsible for this act against me—then I want to leave The Oracle. I can't stay here any longer."

I could literally feel the weight of all the stunned gazes around me at that statement.

"Remember who you're talking to, child," Reese snapped, and I cringed at hearing the way he addressed me, sounding so similar to Luther Davin.

But it didn't stop me.

"The inappropriate touches that my Guardians and Hunters had trouble with in the beginning can't be compared to what Jude did to me. Jude assaulted me. He nearly raped me while I was chained and couldn't defend myself."

"What Jude did was absolutely wrong," Nathaniel began. "There's no denying that. And if there's another incident—"

"There won't be another incident—because I *will not* stay here!"

Callum's eyes bore into me like fire, outraged at the lack of respect I was showing the group. "You'd be dead inside a month if you left sacred ground. Are you saying you'd prefer to be killed by vampires than remain protected here? That's ridiculous!"

"I don't agree with you that I'd be dead in a month. This group looks at the vampire world only in black and white. You accept what you've been told by men who lived two hundred years ago, and you've never questioned it."

Though my hands were now shaking, I kept going. I couldn't seem to stop the words from spilling out, and it shocked me. "If you truly are men of great power, then you should question it until you know with absolute certainty that you're right. And I'm telling you, in this matter, you're not right. I've seen it with my own eyes. There are vampires out there who do not take human lives, vampires who want to live in peace with humans."

"This is blasphemy!" Reese raged, and I knew Alec would get an earful from his uncle about my uncontrolled words after this was all over.

"Not so fast," Nathaniel replied. "While I don't appreciate the girl's tone, I want to know if she speaks the truth. If there *are* vampires who want to live in peace with humans, I know that we all want to see evidence before making further judgments and policies."

An easy smile crossed Joseph's lips as he watched me, almost as if he were impressed. "Yes. Olivia does speak the truth. Gideon told me she lived, unharmed, with a coven, even when they couldn't sense she was a Dhampir. They were the vampires who challenged Alec's team during daylight hours. 'Daywalkers,' I believe you called them."

I nodded.

"This is insane," Callum snarled. "We have been at war with these creatures for two centuries, and until the incident in Seattle not one of us has ever heard of these *Daywalkers*. It's much more likely that they're another hybrid species. And this isn't even why we're here!"

Another Elder spoke behind me. "Perhaps it should be. I don't see the harm in further discussion."

"That's it! Get the girl out of here," Reese bellowed.

I was startled. Until this moment, I hadn't stopped to consider how Reese's rage would affect Alec. He didn't deserve the anger Reese would dish out because of me.

"Calm down, Reese," Joseph ordered, then looked at me. "You can go, Olivia."

I nodded, walking quickly out of the room and not once looking back. When I reached the stone hall I started to run, but my arm was caught by one of the guards. "We'll escort you up," he warned, his tone clearly indicating that there would be no further discussion about it.

"Fine," I murmured, just wanting to escape from here, but that soon changed when I saw in front of me the man also waiting to go up.

"Hello, Olivia," Jude smiled.

Chapter Thirteen

When I squished into the corner of the small elevator, I felt sure I was about to shatter like glass. He had won. And now Jude stood less than three feet from me, savoring the taste of victory. He nudged the guard beside him, who seemed to not care about anything except following the strict protocol of escorting people to and from the chamber. "Careful. Don't touch her skin. She's a devil."

As the elevator door opened, I tried to hold back the tears long enough to make it back to the quiet of my room, but my hands couldn't stop shaking and my bottom lip started to quiver. Alec, Lucas and Phin instantly knew something was very wrong. They all seemed to freeze for a second, studying my broken expression. I stopped in my tracks, believing I was about to be bombarded by questions, but I was surprised when all three men's attention instead shifted to the still smirking Jude as he strolled off the elevator behind me.

Fury suddenly filled their eyes.

Without warning, they bolted towards Jude. I jumped to the side to avoid the fist-throwing anger that had now broken out between them and Jude. The two guards stepped in to try and break up the fight but only ended up getting punched themselves.

My confused gaze found Gideon. His expression was bleak as he saw my tears fall. I could tell he wanted to comfort me, but the fight was already out of control. Gideon ran forward just as Kane came around the corner to respond to the loud commotion, helping the older man to try and pull Alec and Lucas back. Alec was spouting as many curse words as Lucas, while Jude just kept repeating that I was a devil.

I couldn't take any more.

Stumbling away from the fight on my unsteady feet, I turned and raced for the main elevator, hitting the button for the first floor, pretty sure that everyone was too distracted by the fight to notice my absence. I just wanted to be alone. I couldn't go to my room, or to any of the usual places. Alec would find me in a heartbeat. I didn't want to see him. How could I face him after enraging his uncle like that? Once Reese finished tearing into him, he probably would never speak to me again.

Darting out of the hotel lobby, I knew exactly where I wanted to go. Within minutes, I was in front of my mother's gravestone, collapsing to my knees in the darkness and the cold. "*Why?* Why did you have to give me these gifts? They're hurting me. They're hurting everyone around me," I cried out. "I just want to go back—back to being a normal human girl."

But suddenly I realized that what I was saying wasn't true— not at all! If I had gone back, I wouldn't know true love with Caleb, love that had sustained me through every hard moment here. I wouldn't know the truth about my real family, Eve and James. I wouldn't know that I had a new family, Jax. And even here, in this sometimes miserable place, I wouldn't know the protective kindness of the man who was my Guardian, Alec.

Now bitterly cold in my short skirt, my knees and lower legs covered in wet grass stains and dirt, I moved inside to the one place I hoped I could find comfort—the chapel. The dim, candle-lit space was quiet and peaceful as I walked toward the front wood pews and stretched out my tired body on one of the benches. My thoughts went to the one man I wanted to be with right now more than any other, Caleb. "Please, please, let him remember me. I want to go home. I want to go back to him."

Eventually, my unsteady heartbeat began to fall back into rhythm as I relaxed and thought about the past. I remembered how it felt waking in Caleb's arms. I cherished the warm rumble of his voice when he was laughing, the quickened pace of his breath when he was angry, and the depth of those breaths when he felt desire. I recalled what it felt like to trace my palms across his broad shoulders, the superhuman strength in his rock-hard chest and corded arms. I remembered the gentleness of those powerful arms, too, as he'd wrap them around me like a blanket of protection.

Oh, God, I wanted to see him—to feel him—more than anything, more than the oxygen I required at this very moment. *Please, Caleb . . . please don't forget . . .*

As my mind silently willed the words, an image appeared—so clear to me that it was as if I was truly in two places at once. Caleb's face, his beautiful yet uneasy face, reflected from the moonlight of the cloudless night as he raced through a dense forest setting that was completely unfamiliar to me. The trees weren't as perfect as the ones in the Cascades, not quite as green, their spacing uneven, and they didn't stretch quite as high. The speed at which he traveled pushed his now longer hair away from his face and over the edges of his shoulders. And the normally shadowed stubble over his jaw and cheeks was thicker, trimmed and shaped, but definitely more of a short beard. I wanted to touch it, to touch the hard, angled lines of his face and will him to relax, to take away the pain currently distorting his determined features.

Then, suddenly, he halted with such quickness it was like being fixed in place after flying on a roller coaster. He swallowed hard as his lively eyes swept around him, and his chest swelled with his breath. He could *feel* me! I was sure of it. The recognition was there—in those incredibly expressive eyes.

Inhaling a second deep breath, his hands curled into tight, white-knuckled fists at his sides. His jaws ground together, causing his facial muscles to flex just before he released an angry roar that seemed fierce enough to expel all of the energy inside him. *God,* how I wished I could hear him, even the deep rage of his voice seemed important at that moment.

At first, his anger confused me, and then, as I watched him try to contain it and regain his focus, I understood. He could *feel* the pain and betrayal inside me at that moment.

"Caleb!" I called out to him, hoping somehow he would hear me. He froze as if had, indeed, heard my cry. His shoulders held stiff, he sniffed into the night air, his nostrils flaring wide before he shook his head as if he had lost it again. Now frustrated, the vampire pounded an iron fist against the base of a tree, creating a deep crater in the bark.

He was hurting, and there was nothing I could do to help him. I wanted to reach out to him, comfort him . . . but just like that, the image was gone. Emptiness and fatigue seemed to swallow me at that moment, until—as a blessing of sorts—my exhausted mind refused to stay awake any longer and I finally cried myself to sleep.

Throughout the night, the hard seat beneath me prevented any meaningful sleep. My bare legs were freezing under my skirt, and my back found little comfort in being plastered against the rigid wood surface of the chapel pew. At some point, though, I felt the warmth of a blanket being placed over me and the softness of a pillow being slid beneath my head. Assuming I was dreaming, I continued to rest my tired body through the remaining hours of night until the bright rays of the morning sun began to filter through the chapel windows.

When I woke, I discovered the blanket and pillow were real. My first thought was that Alec had found me, and I dreaded having to face him. But as I carefully glanced around I didn't see him. Then I peeked over the wood pew in front of me and saw the sleeping form of a woman I had missed for a week. "Maya!" I cheered as my blue-eyed friend fluttered her lashes open from a deep slumber.

I jumped over the pew and threw my arms around her as she sat up, hugging her so tight I wasn't sure I would never let go.

"Good morning to you, too," came her startled reply. When I finally did pull back, a worried expression transformed her face. "Are you all right?"

"No."

"Phinneas told me last night what happened with Jude. I can't believe it. I hate him for what he's done to you."

"I appreciate that. Maybe you could talk to The Elders. They might listen to you," I remarked with no humor. "How did you find me?"

"I saw you run out here while unpacking in my room, and I came over as soon as I could. You were already asleep, so I got you some covers and a pillow, and I wanted to stay with you until you woke up."

My heart jumped. "Did you tell Phin or the others where I was?"

Maya shook her head.

"Thank you for that. I just can't handle seeing them right now. And I can't face Alec."

"Why do you say that, Olivia? He's so worried about you. He was running around like a madman trying to find you last night. All of them were. I think Alec's terrified that you've gone off sacred ground. And Phinneas will probably be furious with me when he finds out that I knew where you were and didn't tell him."

"I'm sorry, Maya. I don't want you to have to lie to Phin for me. I know how much you care for each other."

The pretty woman's alabaster skin flushed in seconds. "Oh, don't be silly. We're just friends."

I smiled at her. "If you tell him that, you'll break his Vampire Hunting heart. It's obvious he adores you, which I know you can *feel* . . . and I can tell you care a great deal about him, too."

"I *feel* how much he cares for you," her quiet voice replied.

I took both her hands in mine. "Maya, you know that's my gift. It's not real for him. You have to trust what you feel inside him when it's just the two of you. And I know the truth. I saw it the day you touched his arm."

Her blush deepened before shaking her head. "Don't try to change the subject. Why are you hiding in here from Alec?"

I sighed roughly. "Oh, Maya . . . I was just so hurt and angry when The Elders sided with Jude that I spoke without thinking. By the time I was done Reese was so furious he was practically throwing me out of the chamber himself. I've just made Alec's life ten times more difficult with his uncle."

"That's not true. Alec's furious with The Elders for letting Jude off so easily, and he's angry that Reese didn't do more to convince them."

"*More?* He did nothing!" I snapped bitterly. "Reese was the one who defended Jude."

Maya's eyes widened in surprise as she replied, "Alec doesn't know that."

"I know, and I'm not going to be the one to tell him. I won't hurt him like that. Reese is his family."

Maya's disapproving frown caught me off guard. "He needs to hear the truth from you. You know how much that means to him."

"Yes, but I can't come between him and his uncle. I won't. It's not right."

"Olivia, Alec needs to know this about his uncle, about The Elders? I can tell there are cracks forming in his once impenetrable resolve regarding this place, this mission. He's having doubts. You already know I am."

"I can't, Maya. The Oracle is his whole world—his future."

Maya sighed audibly as she shrugged her shoulders. "We'll have to agree to disagree on this point, but I want you to really think about it." Then a small smile spread over her lips. "Let's talk about something else . . . like my trip to Seattle."

I sat up straight, unable to believe I had forgotten about the one thing that mattered most to me right now. *Caleb!* "Oh Maya! Did you see Gemma at the clinic?"

"Yes, and she's as spirited and feisty as you said she'd be."

I squeezed her hands, wriggling back and forth excitedly over the bench seat. "Did she remember me? Tell me everything."

A frown crossed her face. "At first, I didn't think so. Actually, she gave me a pretty good scare there with a needle for a minute."

"So you asked about the over-protective sods?"

She nodded quickly. "Yes, but she showed no reaction. So I did what we talked about—I got up and left."

"Oh, no!"

"Don't worry. I didn't even make it to the door before she stopped me. She asked if my *friend* was all right." Maya's whole expression seemed to brighten. "Don't you see? She knew I was talking about you. She remembers you, I'm sure of it."

"And Caleb?"

Maya squeezed my hand in hers as if to offer reassuring comfort. "That I don't know. We didn't have long to talk because Caleb and Jax showed up at the clinic."

"You saw Caleb?" I gasped. "Did he look well? Did Jax look well?"

Maya blew out a startled laugh. "Believe me, they looked more than well. I thought I'd never get away from those two giants. *Good Lord,* you said Caleb was tall, but mercy . . ."

I had a hard time sitting still I was so excited. "Thank Heavens for the necklace and some help from Mother Nature. The sun cracked through the clouds, forcing them inside the shadows. That was the only way I got out of there."

Caught off guard by my own emotions at that moment, my hands began to shake.

"Hey, no more worries," Maya said, squeezing my hands. "Caleb's safe and you'll be with him again soon. We'll find a way."

"Are you sure Gemma didn't follow you? I can't risk any of them coming back here with Davin just waiting. He'll hurt them."

"I'm sure."

"But we still don't know if he remembers me, or if he's now with Celeste."

"I'll go back."

"No. It's much too dangerous—"

I was interrupted just then by the sound of a familiar voice outside the chapel.

" . . . My nephew won't be a problem. I've made arrangements for him and the others to be reassigned."

"Will I still have access to her?" Jude asked.

"Yes, but maybe this time you won't be such a sodding idiot!" Reese Lambert snapped as he waltzed right into the chapel with Jude beside him. Jude was already looking straight at me, as if he knew I was there, but he did nothing to alert Reese to our presence.

Unfortunately, my startled gasp did.

"Olivia! What're you doing here?" Reese demanded.

I stood there, dumbfounded and speechless. What did he mean 'Alec and the others were being reassigned?' That Jude would 'still have access to me.' Maya must have been thinking the same thing because she grabbed one of my hands and squeezed it reassuringly.

"Come here!" Reese ordered, while Jude stood back and crossed his arms over his chest.

I didn't budge.

"I'm an Elder and head of this station. You *will* respect me, something you managed very little of last night. Jude, bring her here."

Jude stepped towards us. Maya and I turned to take off just as Phin blasted through the door, anchoring himself between us and Jude. Reese stepped forward, but Phin gave The Elder a deep-throated warning growl. "You dare threaten me?" Reese hissed. "I'll have you thrown out of here on your ass!"

Phin just smiled, his bright blue-gray eyes almost twinkling at the challenge. "I'd like to see you try."

He then turned back to us. "Everyone all right?"

We both nodded in wordless response.

Alec and Lucas barreled in just then, both breathing hard from their effort to keep up with a Dhampir. Alec's shocked gaze went from me to Jude as if he couldn't quite comprehend what he was seeing. "What the hell's he doing here?" he snapped. "He's supposed to be confined to his damn room!"

"Careful nephew, I'm still an Elder. And you'll watch your tone."

This was not good.

Lucas then mumbled several expletives that would have shocked a truck driver, while Alec took a warning step towards his uncle. "Then start acting like an Elder." He whipped a pointed finger towards Jude. "This animal isn't to be anywhere near her, yet you have him standing not ten feet from her. Can't you see she's terrified?"

Reese moved to stand before his nephew, displaying no fear that Alec would strike out at him in any way. "You raise your voice to me again and you'll be joining him in confinement. Not that I have to explain myself to you, but Jude's in my custody. We didn't know the girl would be here. She's supposed to be in classes."

Alec's expression was stunned, as if his uncle had just spoken to him in a foreign language. "Does it really surprise you that after what The Elders did to her last night that she wouldn't be in classes today? What the hell's wrong with you?"

"Enough, Alec! I'll see you in my office in one hour. That'll give you some time to cool down and reflect on the mistake you just made here." Reese then swung around on Phin. "And *you* had better start packing, because you're going on a very long trip."

"Excellent. First class or coach?" Phin mocked in reply.

Reese's eyes widened in a mix of shock and rage as Jude stood back and seemed to enjoy the entertainment.

"Phin, don't," Alec said calmly. "It's not worth it."

Maya released my hand and stepped forward to reach for Phin's. He gripped it tightly, a movement Reese followed with a narrowed gaze as he walked towards the door. A low growl, as fierce as any I had heard even from Caleb, rumbled from Phin's throat as he stepped protectively in front of Maya.

When they were gone I felt as if I could finally breathe again. I steadied myself with a stiff arm holding onto the back of the wood pew, watching Alec's disillusioned gaze drop to the floor. His expression spoke of trying to understand the actions of the man he believed was as close to him as a father. He then seemed to catch up to the moment, his head lifting to find me. "Are you all right?"

I nodded silently.

"How did you find us?" Maya asked Phin.

"Someone mentioned that they saw you come out here last night. We were on our way to check it out when I heard your voices," he replied, then he frowned when he saw the blankets and pillows on the pew benches. Addressing himself to Maya, he asked, "When did you find her?"

Maya stared up at him with a guilt-ridden smile. "I found her last night and stayed with her. We were talking this morning when they came in."

Phin's dark brows furrowed deeply, looking almost like a single slash across his forehead. "Maya, you knew we'd been searching for her. Why didn't you tell us she was here? You know I can't sense her well on sacred ground."

"I'm sorry, Phinneas, but she needed time. She's frightened, and she should be. Something's very wrong here." She turned to a very quiet Alec. "I know he's your uncle . . . and Olivia doesn't want to tell you this—"

"No, Maya!" I cried as Alec swung to face me, his body stiff and his face filled with a confused expression.

"What don't you want her to tell me?"

I stood there, unable to answer him, the words seeming frozen in my head.

"I'm sorry, Olivia, but he needs to know the truth."

Normally more reserved and shy, Maya now commanded the attention of an entire room. All of the men understood that if she was this upset, something was definitely wrong.

"What truth?" Alec demanded.

"That Reese is the one who pushed to have Jude released. He used the troubles all of you were having touching her to insinuate that she was the problem, not Jude."

"What?" Alec answered in slow shock.

I moved to his side, my hand hesitant as it touched his arm between elbow and shoulder. "I'm so sorry," I whispered, but he didn't respond. I kept direct contact with his arm, tightening my grip just a little, trying to give him some added reassurance.

Maya pressed on. "And now we just overheard him say he's having all of you removed as her Guardians."

"Alec, what the fuck's going on here?" Lucas growled. "What's Reese up to?"

"I . . . I don't know," Alec replied, still appearing stunned.

"Alec!" Maya shouted, and Alec whipped his head up. "Reese told Jude that once you and the others were removed that he'd still have access to Olivia."

"*What?!*" Alec and Lucas both snapped the same word at the same moment.

Phin pulled Maya into his arms, kissing her on her head. "Easy," he whispered.

Alec snatched my hand from his sleeve and almost pulled me out of the chapel and into the morning light. Everyone followed, including my hero, Maya. "We'll get to the truth," Alec snarled, the determined set of his face almost frightening. "Where the hell's Kane?"

"Reese sent him out tracking last night after the fight," Lucas replied.

"I'll just bet he did," Alec snorted. "Phin, find him. Reese knows that Kane's feline senses can still track on sacred ground. I want to know everywhere Jude's been in the last twenty-four hours *and* where he's going."

He then turned to Lucas. "You're with me." Lucas gave one quick nod in reply as Alec squeezed my hand. "I'm taking you back to my room. I want you to stay out of sight. People won't be looking for you there. Is that all right?"

I nodded quickly.

"Maya, will you stay with her? I have a meeting with my Uncle—I'm not going to miss it!"

***

During the next several days I did as Alec asked and stayed hidden in his much larger room. As a future Elder, Alec was staying on the eleventh floor in a mini-suite which was decorated in the same rich finishes as Joseph's room. I slept with Maya on the queen-size bed in the separate bedroom, while Alec and Phin shared the sofas out in the main area.

Alec already kept his room fairly tidy, but Maya and I made sure it stayed that way despite finding the occasional woman's jewelry piece or hair accessory in the most unexpected places. I frowned as I held up the latest addition, a light pink lace push-up bra that matched the thongs we found a couple days earlier . . . in a completely different room.

"Seriously, Alec? What are you grumbling at Kane about?" I mumbled, ostensibly to myself, but I could hear Maya's giggles at my comment coming from the next room. Her Dhampir hearing obviously picked up every word. To no one's surprise, my handsome Guardian enjoyed an active sex life, but he did differ from Kane in that he knew how be discreet. Yet, I sensed no real fulfillment from these little trysts. When I tried to tease him about it, he would just shrug it off and order me to stop cleaning so much.

Alec's meeting with his uncle had been basically a chess match, with neither side divulging what the other knew. Reese did admit, however, that he was having Alec removed from being my primary Guardian. Alec responded by saying only that he would challenge the decision with the other Elders. That, of course, did not make his uncle happy, but until a final decision could be made, Alec and the others were allowed to remain my Guardians.

Dressed in jeans, a bright tee shirt, and a thin sweater—a 'happy' outfit—I stared outside into the unusually warm fall day, trying unsuccessfully not to think about how yet another week had passed without my seeing a vision of Caleb. The sense of emptiness in my heart now seemed almost unbearable. I feared my connection with him was fading, and those connections had been the only thing keeping me moving forward on some days, it seemed. Pulling my hair back in a clip, I let a few long wavy strands dangle along my face and was inspecting my handiwork when Alec, Phin and Kane showed up with trays of breakfast food from the dining hall. Maya and I already had the round table set up with plates and silverware as they piled the trays onto the table. "You look pretty today," Alec smiled as I came to greet him, kissing me lightly on my temple.

"Thank you," I replied cheerfully. "Where's Lucas this morning?"

"He's with Gideon." Alec sat down beside me at the table. "We've some good news. Gideon was able to get a hold of

Joseph. He's returning to The Oracle today. He should be here by late this afternoon."

I placed some eggs and fruit on my plate. Alec frowned, adding two more slices of bacon and a roll before sliding a glass of orange juice forward. "That *is* good news. But does Joseph have the power to really do anything?"

"Oh, yeah," Phin snorted, handing Maya a small plate of jams as he continued. "And sorry to say, Alec, Reese hates having to take orders from Joseph."

I glanced at Alec, who seemed to have very little appetite. Reaching my hand under the table, I found his and squeezed it gently. He gave me a slight smile then acknowledged Phin. "Don't apologize. There's no excuse for my uncle's behavior."

"Does Reese know Joseph's coming?" I asked.

Alec shook his head. "My guess would be that he doesn't. Gideon has been pretty quiet about this whole thing. But once he's here, it should be safe for you and Maya to leave the room."

I clapped my hands together. "Really, Alec? Not that I haven't been comfortable here—it just would be good to walk around in the fresh air again."

"Well as soon as Joseph arrives, you can take in the fresh air to your heart's content."

***

Later that night, after it was confirmed that Joseph had arrived at The Oracle, I wandered out to the rock perch that I had so missed while confined inside. Staring out onto the scenic beauty of the lake, I appreciated that the night was peaceful and the dark skies were holding back the evening chill. "You really like this spot don't you?" Alec laughed as he walked up.

"Yeah. It's beautiful here," I murmured, then added. "Any word yet from Gideon?"

"Not yet."

Alec stared off into the distance, his mind deep in thought. "I was actually hoping to find you out here. I wanted to talk with you privately about something."

His features began to distort, then, into an awkward

grimace, as if he couldn't decide whether he was hurt or angered by his thoughts at that moment. "What Jude did to you was unforgivable. But the fact that my Uncle and The Elders let him walk away from it, placing the blame on your gifts, has rattled me in a way I've never known." I curled my arm around his, resting my hand over his shirt. This situation with his uncle was tearing him up inside, just as I feared it would. And I felt responsible. "It's shaken my faith in this place—in our mission. For the first time, I'm questioning the path that's been laid out for me my entire life."

"How can I help you with this?" I asked, resting my head on his shoulder.

"I don't think you can. I'm going to have to figure it out on my own. But I know I can't do that here. I need to leave—get my head clear."

I pulled back with a start. "You're leaving me?" I didn't know how he possibly could think I would stay in this place one more minute if he were gone. But I hadn't expected what came next.

"I want to take you with me . . . find somewhere that you'll be safe. I'm not exactly sure how that's possible, but I'll find a way."

"Alec . . . ," I whispered, overcome with a deep feeling of loyalty and friendship to this man.

Shaking his head, he added. "I need to say this. I've sat here and watched how all this has changed you. That positive woman who used to say she would be *all right* to just about anything has disappeared. And I've let it happen."

"Are you saying what I think you're saying? That you'll take me back—back to *him?*"

Alec's hard sigh was a definite 'no'. "That'll be the first place The Brethren will search for you. I need to take you somewhere they can't find you. Lucas and the others have already agreed to —"

"No," I replied firmly. "I appreciate what you're trying to do, but I can't leave him again. Why can't you understand that I love him with all my heart? The woman you see is disappearing because her heart is breaking. I've tried to be strong every day while I've been here, but it's no use. I *need* him."

Alec let go of my hand, frustration building in his grumbling tone. "How many times do I have to tell you? He doesn't remember you. He's moved on with his life by now. You'll only bring him pain if you go back."

"I believe he does remember—"

Alec jumped to his feet from the rock. "No, he doesn't, Olivia! You had him trapped in an illusion. It wasn't real for him. And his memories will have faded along with that illusion"

I turned away from him, not wanting him to see the emotion that was coming forward in me.

"I'm sorry," he said more gently. "I'm not trying to hurt you —but to make you see the truth. Just think about what I said. We can talk more tomorrow."

Then, without another word exchanged between us, he walked back towards the hotel.

Bending my legs up, I curled my arms over my knees and dropped my head into them. I wanted to leave this place, and I wanted to help Alec in any way I could—but I couldn't go farther away from Caleb. I still believed he was my future. I needed to move towards that future, not away from it. In fact, I wanted it so badly at that moment, it was almost as if I could hear him again, hear the deep rumble of his voice. "He's wrong, Olivia. I've not forgotten you."

I sighed. "You've no idea how much I need that to be true."

"*It is true!*" his voice pressed. "I could never forget my sweet girl."

Suddenly, I realized the voice didn't sound like it was coming from my mind. Lifting my head from my arms, my eyes swept over to see him standing there at the edge of sacred ground.

"*Caleb!*"

Chapter Fourteen

Standing not ten yards in front of me with a determined Jax at his side, was the man, the lover, the soulmate I had not seen in over three months. I leapt from the rock; nothing could stop me from crossing the boundary of the sacred ground for the first time since coming to The Oracle. I bounded high into Caleb's arms, curling my legs around his waist and practically strangling him at his throat with my embrace. His deep chuckle at my ear was the most beautiful sound in the world to me at that moment. "You're here! You really *are . . . here.*"

My joyous tears fell onto his skin as I kissed along his neck, his chin, and then the sensitive hollow behind his ear. He responded by pulling me tighter in his arms, enveloping me in his incredible strength. "Vanilla and oranges," he murmured. "How I've missed that scent."

"You missed it? You remember me, then?" I questioned. "I prayed so hard for you to remember. Do you still love me?"

"Every single day, my sweet."

Caleb then threaded his fingers through my hair as he cupped my cheek and pushed me back to stare into my eyes, but his expression twisted into one of pain as he whispered with feeling, "But damn you for running away like that!"

"I didn't want to leave—"

Caleb silenced me by fisting his hand into my hair and dragging my lips over his. He kissed me hard, literally taking full possession of my mouth as if he dared anyone or anything to come between us at that moment. And, like a private dance between two people, he coaxed, caressed and eased me until I fell under his lead, taking his pleasure like a man who had been starved of warmth for three long months. *And, oh,* did it feel good. He tasted cool and crisp. He was a fresh breeze on a warm day. His kisses were so powerful, so consuming, I felt as if gravity had lost its hold on me for good. When I finally got a chance for air, I breathed against his cheek, "I feel like I'm floating. You have that power over me, you know . . . the power to make me fly."

Just then, the deep clearing of a throat reminded me that we were not alone. "Uh-um," Jax sounded. My head jerked up, remembering who this dear man was to me.

My grandpa was here!

"Jax!" I cheered, surprising Caleb at how suddenly I left his arms and went to Jax.

Jax was exactly how I remembered him. Though still as young and handsome as the day he was turned—more a mid-thirties looking twenty-nine—he was a wise, confident giant of a man who stood there dressed from head to toe in his favorite color, black. Yet, if one looked closer, beyond the fearsome set of his square jaw or the intimidating mass of muscle, they would see a warmth to his amber eyes that was as rich as the finest gemstone. I threw my arms around the man who was my family with such fierceness it astonished him.

"Are you all right?" he asked, pulling me back to face him, and I searched his eyes for any hint of recognition that he knew I was his granddaughter, but I didn't see any.

Shaking my head, I replied, "No. I want to go home . . . home with you."

He stroked the sides of my face, worry showing plainly on his brow. The woman they knew, the one who would constantly affirm that she was 'all right', couldn't even come close to uttering the words. The determined set of Jax's jaw showed no doubt, no hesitation. He would not leave this place without taking me with him. "You belong with us—with me. I know that now."

I smiled at him so brightly I had to be showing all teeth. He knew the truth—that I was his granddaughter—and I couldn't stop myself from hugging him again. "Thank you, Jax. I've missed all of you so much." It was then I realized someone was missing. I stepped back from him, I asked, "Where's Gemma?"

Jax cleared his throat again, but this time there was an amused uneasiness in his expression. "Uh . . ."

That certainly wasn't good. As a cultured man born more than two centuries ago, Jax never contracted his words or spoke in muttered sounds. "She is staying at the condo downtown. Our angelic girl is not very happy with me at the moment."

Reading between the lines, I pictured the little powerhouse redhead ranting over being left behind. But the over-protective sods were right this time. She needed to stay as far away from The Brethren as possible, which Jax already knew. "I did not want her anywhere near this place. It is too dangerous. She did not agree, and . . ."

I laughed. The first laugh I could remember in a long while. "Say no more, Jax. You did the right thing." I then turned to see Caleb's troubled frown. It was clear that my exchange with Jax confused him. Jax must not have told him that I was his granddaughter. I would ask Jax to remedy that right away because I wanted no secrets from Caleb. But now was not the time to get into it. I just wanted to get out of here.

With a happy squeal, I jumped back into Caleb's arms, smothering his face with kisses. His perfectly trimmed beard was slightly fuller, tickling me as I moved over it. "Thicker peach fuzz. I like it," I smiled, tugging at his cheek, "very masculine."

But Caleb was no longer in the mood to joke. "Tell me what's been happening. Davin found you here?"

I nodded. "I was so scared. He threatened to kill you—to hurt anyone important to me—unless I went with him. Alec said that you'd be OK, but that's why I had to send Maya. I had to know for sure."

"Yes, I got your message."

I tilted my head at him in question. "My message?"

"Maya's contact with Gem made me realize I needed to stop trying to *feel* you and start tracking Davin. It took us a week, but his trail eventually led us here."

He leaned his forehead against mine, his breathing heavy as

he spoke. "How dare you use yourself as bait to keep him here. You should've sent Maya to me sooner. I could've helped you. Just tell me he hasn't hurt you."

"He hasn't." Softly, I pressed my lips against his, feeling so secure in his arms, I just wanted to stay with him in this moment and until all the recent bad memories went away, to touch him.

But my amorous state was swiftly interrupted by the familiar, gruff tone of the man who had been protecting me in Caleb's absence. "Olivia!" Alec exclaimed from behind me.

Startled, I released my hold on Caleb and dropped back to my feet, turning to face my more than a little upset Guardian. Caleb curled his arm possessively around my waist, keeping me firmly planted against his body as he stared back at Alec with a hostile, warning glare.

"What're you doing?" Alec snapped.

My gaze fell to the jacket he had brought out with him, and I realized he had returned because he had been worried that I would get cold. "I . . . I'm sorry, Alec."

That apology didn't calm him much, as his angry gaze fixed on Caleb. "Davin's been just waiting for her to cross over that line. Are you so selfish that you'll put her life in danger like that?"

Caleb's low, warning response was hard and direct. "Don't talk to me about selfish. I've remembered her every day that you've kept her locked away from me here." Alec seemed to blink back with genuine surprise for a split second as Caleb moved me behind his tall frame and took a step closer to the invisible wall separating them. "And you *won't* take off with her again. She's leaving here, and she'll be free to make her own choices from now on."

Uh-oh. Caleb and Jax had overheard my conversation with Alec about leaving The Oracle. That made me worried about what else he may have heard.

"Davin is not here," Jax stated plainly. "We would sense him."

I could see right away that anger was boiling inside Alec. It was clear he didn't want me going anywhere. "Olivia, get over here," he snapped. "This is too dangerous." By sheer reflex I started to move at his command, but Caleb held me back.

"She's not going anywhere with you!"

Alec hissed. "And that's why you're not capable of loving her. You'll always put your own lustful needs ahead of her safety. You're going to get her killed—that is, if you don't kill her yourself!"

Caleb's warning growl had now turned into a full blown roar as his hands clenched into tight fists. Alec had pushed him too far. Of course, when Caleb and Alec were involved, it didn't take much for either of them. "Please, both of you . . . stop this!"

I tried to turn Caleb to face me, which was rather like trying to turn a brick wall, so I had to use a gentler approach. "Caleb," I whispered softly so Alec wouldn't hear. He finally turned to look at me. "The Brethren won't let me just leave here with you."

"I don't care, Olivia!" he snapped, unconcerned about what my Guardian heard. "You're a free person. You may leave here if you wish to. *This Brethren*," he seethed the words, turning his hard glare back to Alec, "won't keep you here against your will."

"Yes, but we have to find a way to do this so they'll leave us in peace. I don't want The Brethren chasing us, and I think I might know a way. But you have to trust me."

His expression twisted, as if he were pleading with me not to ask this of him. "You know I trust you. It's them—*him*—I don't trust.

Jax spoke up just then. "You may try your idea, Gran . . . ," clearing his throat, he resumed, "*Olivia*. But ultimately you are coming with us, whether they agree to it or not." All those times when I admired Jax for putting his coven family first, I now realized applied also to me. I was his family. He would put me first, along with Caleb and Gemma, and that seemed rather remarkable to me for a woman who believed she had no family left.

"You're going to need to let me cross that line, then," I said to Caleb.

With an exasperated scowl, he sighed. "Olivia . . ."

After a few tense heartbeats, he released his arm. I crossed back onto sacred ground to face a quiet but equally grumpy Alec. "Thank you for bringing me the jacket. It is a bit cold out here. May I have it?"

"Don't try to sweet talk me," he snapped. "I know exactly what you're doing."

And at his sharp words, Caleb growled again behind me. Swinging around on my heels, I shot him a glare, "Not helping." Caleb's lip snarled as his gaze slid away from me and he muttered curse words under his breath. At the moment, he sounded almost no better than Lucas.

What was it with men and their curse words?

Returning my attention to Alec, I reached for his free hand and squeezed. "Will you find Gideon for me? Ask him to tell Joseph that I've found a way. See if he'll come here to meet with me."

Alec appeared astonished. "Are you crazy? He's not going to expose himself out here in the open with two vampires standing across from him. It's too dangerous!"

"They can't do anything to him from there, and I can't bring them to him. So this is what I need."

Alec still didn't budge. The man was as stubborn as Caleb sometimes.

"Please. I know, deep down, you want me to be happy, so I'm asking for your help." Without saying another word, he shook off my grip, shoved the jacket into my hand, and headed for the hotel, mumbling fragmented sentences, wondering aloud how the hell had I talked him into this.

Sliding into the coat, I returned to Caleb and heard his relieved breath as I wrapped my arms around him and rested my head on his chest. There, my ear against his breast, I felt once more the steady rise and fall of his lungs that had been so clear in my memory, and I couldn't help but smile. "I want you to tell me what's been happening," Caleb began quietly. "The few times I could *feel* you, you were in such pain—both physical and emotional. I can feel some of it now."

"It's been difficult here," I replied, squeezing my arms around him. "I want to go home with you."

My head moved with his chest on his heavy sigh. "Olivia, that's not really the detail I was asking for."

"I know," I murmured. "I promise I'll tell you everything when I'm home and we have more time." I gazed up at him sincerely. "No secrets."

He smiled softly, brushing the back of his hand over my cheek. "Are you not telling me because you're afraid I might do something about it?"

The thought had definitely crossed my mind, and my silence basically answered his question. Caleb didn't like it but continued to stroke his hand through my hair as I stared at Jax around Caleb's broad shoulder. "Jax, you can't be here when they return. Gideon will recognize you. He's seen old photos."

Jax scoffed at that. "I will not hide from these people."

"What are you two talking about?" Caleb grumbled.

But Jax's attention was already diverted. "Caleb," he warned quietly. We both swung around to see Alec walking toward us, along with Gideon and—to my relief—Joseph. But there was a fourth person in the group, and I soon recognized Reese Lambert. *Oh, just great.*

As Alec neared, he gave me a sour look that told me he didn't have a choice.

"Who're you afraid of?" Caleb asked in a whisper that the approaching men couldn't hear. As usual, I couldn't hide anything from Caleb. He could feel me too easily.

"Later," I answered.

Gideon's gaze went straight to Jax, his eyes flickering with instant recognition. I was a ball of nerves just then, fearing that he would say something in the middle of this very tense stand-off between the two sides, but he didn't. "Thank you for coming, Joseph," I said.

He nodded once in reply, but the angry Elder behind him was not so cordial. "This is outrageous!" Reese fumed. "We don't take conferences with bloody vampires! Do you think we're at your beckon call?"

The so called '*bloody vampires*' behind me responded with a fierce warning.

"Reese," Joseph began calmly. "We're here to listen. If you don't want to do that, then perhaps it would be best for you to go inside. But, of course, it's your choice." Joseph was walking a very fine line. Before now I hadn't appreciated the position he was in, coming on as leader of a group in which the other men were significantly his seniors. He wanted to lead with strength and purpose, to make sound judgments, and to use his weighted power with discretion.

"Joseph, I asked you once if you would consider letting me leave The Oracle if I could prove to you I'd be safe in the outside world. These men took me in when I was in transition. They never harmed me, and their coven doesn't feed on humans. I believe I can live safely with them—with the aid of one of the necklaces, of course."

"This is insane!" Reese snapped. "They're vampires. They'll be drawn to her more than the human males are. They'll kill her!"

"We'd never hurt her," Caleb calmly replied.

Joseph stepped towards us slowly as if his interest had been piqued. "Alec? Are these the vampires who helped get Olivia back from the man who was my father?" Suddenly Caleb pulled me tighter against him at hearing I was putting my trust—our future—in the hands of Luther Davin's son. "They are these Daywalkers?"

"Yes," Alec answered, then nodded towards Caleb. "He believes himself in love with her." Caleb merely gave a wicked smile in reply that said Alec could believe whatever the hell he wanted but it wouldn't change a damn thing.

"Vampires who walk during the day," Joseph replied as he directed his attention to Caleb. "Fascinating. And you claim to love her. I wouldn't have thought it possible—considering how much pain she can inflict upon your kind. Alec, are you sure?"

"He remembers her after three months. He's under no illusion."

Surprised, I stared back at Alec. Though his argument with Caleb indicated otherwise, he did, in fact, understand that the vampire loved me.

"Yes. True love would be the only thing strong enough to break through her gifts. It was like that for your father, James," Joseph said to me as he moved to Jax. "But what of this one? You can have only one true love, Olivia, and your gift is stronger since you left their coven. Eventually, this one will be drawn to you—hurt you like Jude."

Caleb went rigid behind me at Joseph's mention of Jude, his hand squeezing my arm rather painfully to let me know that he wanted answers later. I was confused about why Joseph would so clearly bring up the incident with Jude in front of Caleb and Jax. He had to know it would anger them, and that certainly didn't seem very smart if he was trying to keep a fragile peace.

Then it hit me.

It was exactly that. Joseph was testing them, testing the vampires' ability to control their anger. So far, even though he appeared frozen in place, Caleb was passing the test. He must have realized what Joseph was doing. It was the only thing that could explain why he wasn't furiously demanding that Jude be delivered to him on a rope.

Beside him, Jax's sly smile gave little away, except the fact that he also was very aware of what Joseph was doing. "Uh-hum," Gideon sounded, clearing his throat. "I don't believe he'll harm her, either."

Joseph turned to Gideon. "Really? Why is that?"

"Because she is my granddaughter," Jax announced proudly.

Joseph whirled on his feet, stunned speechless at meeting Eve's father, my grandfather. Alec didn't handle the information much better. When his expression slacked into involuntary disbelief, I smiled at him, nodding to confirm it was true.

Caleb wasn't move a muscle behind me, acting as if he knew the truth, but inside I was sure that he was just as shocked as the rest of them. He just understood that the first priority was to get me out of here. However, later, he would probably have a few choice words for Jax about why he was left in the dark. "Is this true?" Joseph finally asked Gideon. "Is this man Eve's father?"

"It's true. I've seen photos. Since he's related to Olivia by blood, I don't believe he'll be affected by her gifts either. It would explain why she was able to live with them before without coming to harm."

"I can't believe you're even considering this, Joseph," Reese continued to fume. "This isn't solely your decision. The Elders will never allow it."

Joseph showed no reaction. In my opinion, he was a true leader, remaining calm, assessing the situation, reserving judgment until he had all the facts. "I disagree with you, Reese. You made this decision mine when you chose sides in that chamber."

Anger and betrayal filled Alec's steely expression at Joseph's words, and it pulled at my heart. This man of truth had been lied to by his own family, and it was breaking him, little by little.

Joseph's discreet gaze watched Alec with interest as he continued. "As for our Brethren brothers, you may challenge me on this if you'd like, but after speaking with many of them I believe you'll find a consensus among the majority that if there's a better way, then the woman shouldn't have to live side by side with the man who attacked her."

Joseph's eyes swept back to Caleb. He was indeed testing him. Stiffly, Caleb shifted his stance, using every ounce of restraint he had so as not to give in to the warrior's temper. "Alec, are there any other members of this coven we should be concerned with?"

"There's just a female Dhampir. She's kind and seems happy."

Jax inhaled slowly, not happy at all that Gemma had entered this discussion. "Another Dhampir . . . ?" Reese questioned hard. Instantly, Jax's hands clenched at his side. "A female?"

"She's not enslaved, as we've seen in other covens?" Joseph pressed Alec.

"No, she's not."

"We would never enslave a Dhampir," Jax growled, losing some of his cool composure. Then he moved quickly to get his feelings back under control.

"Alec, how old is the Dhampir?" Reese asked from behind him. That seemed to me a strange question.

Alec's jaw was grinding. I could see the doubt in him, doubt about this cause he had given his entire life to. "As you know, it's hard to tell with Dhampirs."

"Her name?" Reese snarled, recognizing that Alec was being evasive.

Before Jax had a chance to explode, Alec, the man of truth, did something I had never heard from him before. He lied. "I don't know her name."

Alec was protecting Gemma from his uncle, from The Brethren!

Joseph turned to address me. "Olivia, you've shown me that you can live with these men, but there are a couple of things you haven't shown me." He moved toward Jax, having complete faith in the invisible line that divided them. "First, I need your assurance that you fully understand the responsibility you are saying you'll assume. We can give her items to help her hide herself, but she'll eventually draw in vampires that you'll have to protect her from. It's unavoidable. Are you willing to fight your own kind to defend her?"

Jax stood tall, strong, his stance nothing but confident as his gaze narrowed on Reese Lambert. "I will protect my granddaughter with my life, whether her enemy is vampire or human."

Joseph massaged his hand over his chin as he walked to stand in front of Alec, looking straight at him as he said, "There's just one very big problem then, Olivia. Luther." At that Alec's eyes slid to meet Joseph's in a momentary flash of understanding. He nodded, wordlessly agreeing to something with a determined set of his jaw. "If I let you leave with them tonight, he'd be on you in a heartbeat. My former father may already be listening to us as we speak."

"He is not," Jax replied simply. "We would sense him."

Joseph's exaggerated pause had me holding my breath. "Then I've made a decision."

Chapter Fifteen

"If you choose to not accept my terms and decide to take off with her—which you could easily do, since she's still on that side—I'll send Alec, here, and his team to retrieve the girl relentlessly."

Joseph was not at all surprised by my responding gasp. "I don't think Olivia likes that prospect much. She doesn't want to see all of the men she cares for battling against each other. Am I correct, Olivia?"

I nodded quickly, my eyes pleading with Alec. Joseph was using my friendship with him to control the situation, knowing if Caleb really did love me, he wouldn't hurt me by attacking Alec.

"In two day's time, Alec will bring Olivia to Seattle. We'll get her out of here safely without Luther sensing." The Elder then turned to my Guardian. "Alec, you're to remain there to observe how she's doing . . . be there in case she needs you . . . and report back to me directly. Do you understand?"

Alec nodded. Was this what he had wordlessly agreed to?

"That's ridiculous!" Reese snarled. "I need him here."

Joseph smiled. "You've got your prize bull, Jude. Let him take on Alec's duties," Joseph responded dryly, letting his tone communicate his dislike for the fellow Elder. Meanwhile, Alec seemed to revel in the fact that his uncle was being put in his place. "Of course, it's your decision, Alec. Would you prefer to stay?"

Alec didn't hesitate. "No. I'll go to Seattle. I'll make sure she's safe."

"Good. Olivia, I'll give you three months to prove to me that you can live safely with this coven. At that time, Alec, here, will update me. If things seemed to be fine, you may stay. If not, you must return with Alec to The Oracle immediately. Is that understood?"

"Yes," I answered without delay, just so happy that Joseph was giving me a chance to have the life I wanted. With his back turned to everyone else, Joseph shot me a quick wink. He had been telling me the truth the day I met him. He really did want to do right by my mother.

Joseph then focused his attention on Jax. "Do you accept the terms I'm offering?"

Jax didn't believe in living under any man's terms. I was sure that in his mind I was his granddaughter, and no Elder would keep me separated from him. But he would always put the safety of his family first. If this was a way to get me back and not have The Brethren at war with us, then he would agree to it. "Yes, I accept."

"Very well, then. Olivia, come." Joseph waved for me to cross back over.

Turning to Caleb one last time, I could see he did not agree with any of it. "If this is a trick, I'll be back . . . war with Alec or not," he warned me before brushing his fingertips over my temples and kissing me softly. My chin quivered as a soft sound too close to a cry escaped me. "Shhh," he breathed in my ear. "No tears. I'll see you in two days, my sweet."

I felt as if a cold wind had blown over me at having to step away from him once again. All I wanted was to leave with this man, whom I loved more than my own life, but instead I was remaining with The Brethren, trusting that Joseph would keep his word. Crossing back over to sacred ground, I went to stand beside an emotionally blank Alec. Taking my Guardian's hand, I glanced over my shoulder at Reese. He looked as if he wanted to punch me.

Caleb glared at Reese in warning, his tense expression already displaying regret at letting me step back over that line. "What assurances do we have that she'll not be harmed again by this Jude?"

"You've my word," Joseph replied. "I'll take care of it

personally."

Jax took a measured step forward, his amber eyes swirling dark with challenge. "If any harm comes to my granddaughter while you are *'taking care of it personally'*, you *will* have a war on your hands. And no amount of sacred ground will protect you."

Then Jax and Caleb turned to leave me again, but this time I knew it would be for only two days.

. . . two very long days.

As we all walked back towards the hotel, an uneasy quiet hovered over our group. I lagged behind Alec, maintaining distance from his uncle, who looked as if he was about to erupt more violently than Mount Saint Helens. Alec reached his hand out behind him, asking for me to take it. When I did, he gave a reassuring squeeze and pulled me up closer behind him. Then Reese, who was clearly containing the fury that had been building under his collar, suddenly swung around on his heels. "You may think you've won here, Joseph, but I'll challenge you with The Elders on this. That girl isn't setting foot off The Oracle."

My heart dropped.

"That's your choice, brother," Joseph replied, though the subtly mocking edge behind his tone could not be missed. Caleb was right not to trust that these men would actually let me go.

At my stillness, Alec squeezed my hand once more and then released it, marching right up to his uncle. "Just why is it, *Uncle*, that you're so vested in her remaining here?" Alec asked sharply. "Why does an Elder want a Guardian—who's done nothing but hurt her—to have access to her? It certainly isn't anything in her best interest. I think the other Elders would also be interested in that."

My jaw dropped. I couldn't believe that Alec was challenging his uncle—an Elder—like this, and it was because of me. His entire relationship with Reese seemed to have been ripped apart in the span of just a few days. I couldn't imagine the pain he must be going through trying to reconcile in his own mind what he believed to be true about this man and what actually was.

"Hold your tongue! I'm an Elder, and I've earned the right to question what is best for this group. I won't stand for you disrespecting me like this—nephew or not."

Suddenly, it was clear to me. The shift that had happened in Luther Davin when he was an Elder was also happening to Reese. These men were given so much power; they felt untouchable. Their decisions mattered—not for their content, but rather for their enjoyment of seeing someone else bend to their will.

"Easy, Reese," Joseph replied coolly. "Alec is also a future Elder and worthy of our respect. But even if he weren't, he raises some very good questions." Joseph then turned to a stunned Gideon. "Gideon, take Olivia upstairs to her room. Stay with her until I send for her." Turning back to Reese and Alec, he added, "We'll finish this discussion in private."

***

Back in my room, Gideon locked the door behind us and wasted no time before pulling a small overnight bag from my closet. "Gather a few items in here—just enough for a couple of days. Take only personal effects that are most important to you. The rest will have to stay."

"Gideon?" I questioned, not sure what was happening.

"Quickly, Olivia. You must be ready when Joseph sends for you." He then motioned once again for me to start packing. "Joseph's the only one with enough power to protect you from Reese until you leave The Oracle. I don't know where he'll keep you, but it won't be here in your room."

"You believe Reese will try to prevent me from leaving against Joseph's orders?"

Shaking his head, Gideon held me firmly at my shoulders. "I don't mean to frighten you. I just think that until we understand what's really going on here, we can't take any chances."

"Gideon, I'm sorry that I've caused all of this . . . that I've ruined Alec's relationship with his uncle."

"That isn't your fault. The path that Alec's now on with his uncle would've happened, regardless. Alec is a man of truth. Reese has become a man of secrets. The two were destined to collide at some point."

Feeling too unsteady to trust my own legs, I plopped down on the bed. Gideon kneeled in front of me, taking my hands in his. "The most important thing is that you're safe."

I stared at the Englishman, realizing how important he'd become to me over these last three months. "Thank you for telling me about my family—for helping me find my grandfather. I know what my mother believed, but she was wrong. Jax is a good man."

"I don't know this because I have not read it, but I believe you'll find in her journal that near the end, Eve started to question her beliefs about her father—about the kind of man he was. Seeing you with him tonight—seeing how much he wants to protect you, I know it's what she would have wanted. She would want you to be with family."

I wrapped my arms around him, hugging him tight. This once awkward and fidgety man with the outdated suits had become as dear to me as any uncle.

Just then there was a knock at the door. Gideon whispered to a guard on the other side, while I threw the first things I could find into the overnight bag. "Olivia, its time," Gideon said. I was almost out of the room before I turned back to the closet; I'd nearly forgotten the wood box filled with my mother's memories. Holding it up to Gideon, I said, "Now I'm ready."

A few minutes later, we were standing outside Joseph's room. Gideon knocked on the door and then gave me a fatherly kiss on my forehead. "Stay safe, Olivia," he said as he blinked back tears in his own shimmering eyes. I didn't even get a chance to respond before he was gone and a guard received me at the door.

Stepping inside, my bag and box were immediately taken into another room. Alec and Joseph were in a tense conversation when my Guardian looked over to me. My mind seemed as frozen as my feet, which refused to move from the spot where I was standing. Everything was happening so fast! Alec marched over, full stride, and pulled me into a secure embrace. "It's going to be all right. I promise you."

"How can you say that?" I murmured. "Look at the mess I've created."

Alec pulled back from me. "This isn't your fault."

"Alec's right, Olivia," Joseph added. "You've merely brought to the surface a problem that seems to have been brewing here for some time." He waved us over. "Bring her over to the sofa." Joseph then grabbed a couple of bottles of water, some ice, and glasses from the bar before returning, while Alec sat down beside me. "I hadn't expected Reese's severe reaction tonight," Joseph sighed. "He's acting like a man who's trying desperately to control something."

My heart sank. Was he saying what I thought he was saying? "What does that mean? Can I not leave The Oracle as you promised?"

Shaking his head, he replied, "I'll keep my promise and let you leave with Alec. But I think it needs to be sooner rather than later. Reese will try in any way he can to keep you here." I was fine with leaving The Oracle sooner, as long as Alec came with me. "The jet will be taking me back to London tomorrow. You two will be on it with me. I'll drop you off in Seattle."

There was a loud knock at the door that made me jump in my seat. "Relax," Alec whispered. "We'll get you out of here safely. I promise."

The guard on the other side handed Joseph a black satchel. "Is everything here?" he asked. After one sharp nod, Joseph dismissed him. He spilled the contents of the satchel onto the coffee table. There was a passport, a couple of sets of keys, and a thick bundle of hundred-dollar bills. "These are for you, Alec. There's about ten thousand in cash and keys to the downtown condo. Olivia, I want you to know where Alec will be, as well, in case you need him."

I nodded in agreement.

"The other set of keys is for the SUV parked in the garage under the condo. By the time you arrive, it'll already be outfitted with all the weapons you'll need to protect her."

"Good," Alec replied, reviewing the passport to see that everything was in order.

Joseph then handed each of us a cell phone. "These are set up and ready to go. I want you to use them to communicate with each other. There's also a contact number on the speed dial for someone who can get through to me if you need to. Oh, and I almost forgot." He reached for a blue, velvet-covered box on the end table beside us, while Alec noticed I was staring, transfixed, at my water glass. He touched my arm to bring my attention back from the glass with a curious look that clearly indicated he was wondering what I was thinking. "Here," Joseph said, handing the box to me. Inside was a beautiful sapphire necklace in a large, teardrop shaped design. The color of it was so dark and rich, one had to look closely to see the earth moving inside—sacred ground.

"You'll need to be wearing this when we leave here tomorrow so Luther can't sense you. And you'll need to get used to wearing it if you want to remain blurred to him and the Supernatural World."

My attention then returned to the water glass on the table. I picked it up, and then glanced at the black satchel. Alec put his hand over mine as I held the glass. "What has got you so fascinated?"

"It's the emblem. This is the same design I saw on the floor in chambers. What's does it mean?"

Joseph brushed over the design on the velvet pouch with his fingertips. "It's our symbol for The Brethren. My great, great, grandfather, Seamus, chose it. It's Celtic in origin—for Mary, his wife, who died giving birth to the child of the vampire who attacked her. She was Irish. The interwoven braid has no opening, which symbolizes no beginning and no end."

I glanced worriedly at Alec. "What is it?" he asked.

"Can you do me a favor?" He nodded. "Will you lift my hair and look at the back of my neck?"

Alec's brows pulled together with concern at the strange request, but he did what I asked. After a few moments, I could feel the slightly callused pad of his fingers brushing over the tattoo hidden beneath my hairline. "Joseph," he said, quietly. The Elder moved around the table to sit on the other side of me and looked at the mark. Then Alec dropped my hair back over my shoulders.

"Is it the same symbol?"

Alec nodded. "How long have you known about this?"

"Caleb and Jax found it the morning you came for me on the mountain. When Isaac was tracking me for Luther the night of the train crash, he knew how to identify me by this symbol."

Joseph sighed with clear concern. " . . . meaning that my father knew the symbol was there."

The tension in Alec's body was growing by the second. "Yes, but it also means he had to have known about the mark when the Greysons stole her away as a child."

I blinked at both of them. "Did The Brethren brand me? Do you mark Dhampirs this way?"

Joseph rose to his feet. Though he was a man of less than average height and plainer features, his presence was always commanding. He massaged his smooth chin with his thumb and index finger as if trying to work out a problem in his own mind. "No. I know of no other Dhampir who has this mark."

I came to my feet beside him. "Then why?" I demanded. "Why was I marked like this?"

Alec stood and pulled me back against his chest, speaking over the top of my head to Joseph. "We need to get her out of here!" he snapped in a hushed voice.

"We will," Joseph assured him. "Why don't you take her into the room and let her get some rest. Tomorrow will be a long day for both of you."

Alec led me to the room where my bag and my mother's box had been taken when I arrived. He sat me down on the edge of the king-sized bed and removed my shoes, then told me to lie back while he grabbed a blanket from the sofa. After wrapping the warm, woolen plaid around me, he sat beside me on the bed. "Will you stay with me?" I asked.

"I'm not going anywhere. I'll be sleeping right there on the sofa."

"I'm sorry I've caused you so much pain with your uncle, Alec."

"Shhh—just rest, Olivia. My problems with my uncle are not your fault."

"It's just that . . . I don't want you to end up resenting me because you had to give up the next three months of your life babysitting me."

He laughed. "*Babysitting?* You are a handful. I've said it since the day I met you . . . but you don't need a babysitter."

"I'm not joking, Alec. I don't want you to keep making so many sacrifices for me."

He seemed to reflect on something before he continued. "I told you, I need time away from here—time to get my head clear. Seattle is just as good a place as any to do that. Joseph knows this. Why do you think he's sending me there?"

"I just want you to be happy."

"I know," he smiled. "Now get some sleep."

***

The trip from Alberta to Seattle was a quick one by jet. Thanks to all of Joseph's preparations and the sapphire necklace, we had no trouble going unnoticed from The Oracle. Every mile closer to Seattle we flew, the deeper I could feel happiness sinking in. I hadn't realized how much I wanted to be free of that place. In all the secrecy and rush, though, I hadn't been able to say goodbye to Maya, Lucas, Phin, or boy wonder Kane.

As Alec unloaded my bag on the kitchen countertop at my condo, I stared at my familiar open surroundings and exhaled a huge breath. I was home, and it felt like it. I couldn't believe how much I had missed this place, a place that at one time I dreaded coming to because it only reminded me of the parents I had lost—the Greysons. But now it was home.

Most of all, I missed the precious gift waiting for me on the terrace, and I was more than a little anxious to get to it, which Alec seemed to notice.

"That's everything," he announced as if reading into my thoughts that I wanted to be alone. He stood before me, taking my hands. "I don't want you to feel like you're being babysat. You know how to protect yourself now. Take some time to get settled. Be smart, vigilant. I'll be back to check on you in a couple of days . . . make sure Caleb has returned for you."

"He'll be here."

"I know. But he isn't expecting you until tomorrow, and the necklace is blurring you to him right now. *And I do want you to keep the necklace on!*" He emphasized each word as if to make sure it sunk in.

"Don't worry—I understand," I smirked. "And don't worry about Caleb coming for me. I have a way to call for him. He'll know I'm here."

Alec raised a questioning brow at that, then handed me a piece of paper with a downtown address on it. "This is where I'm staying. Memorize it. I'm only about a mile from here if you need me."

Reading the address, I unthinkingly replied, "Oh, this is right by the blood clinic where Gemma—"

Oops.

His trademark crooked smile, which I hadn't seen in a while, quirked the corner of his lips with such ease. "The fiery redhead? Interesting. I may just have to go donate some blood, see if she still detests my existence." His crooked smile then got bigger. "You know, such a strong reaction from a woman is either an invitation to a lot of trouble . . ."—he wagged his brows—"or even more fun."

"Alec . . . ," I warned him. "Be careful. Jax hovers over her like —"

"I will, I will," he replied dismissively, then kissed me on my forehead and headed towards the door before quickly swinging on his heels.

"Don't let—"

"—Anyone in 'til Caleb gets here," I finished for him. "I know. Now, get out of here."

He smiled, winked, and closed the door behind him.

A few minutes later I was standing in front of my closet, all warm and freshly pink from my shower. I scanned the rack for something pretty to wear, wanting to look my absolute best for Caleb, but instead I found myself sighing deeply, dismally disappointed with the few lone selections. Before I met Gemma, the shopping guru of current fashion trends, my simple college wardrobe of blue jeans and white tee shirts seemed perfectly fine. But once she spoiled me with several wonderfully colorful and tailored pieces that hugged my curvier shape in all the right places, the comfortable basics no longer cut it.

Searching through the hurriedly-thrown-together bag I'd brought with me from The Oracle wasn't much better. I had been in such a state that last day I wasn't even paying attention to what I was tossing in there. There was one item, though, that would work—the cypress green cardigan Gemma had given me as a gift when I left the tree house. Paired with a simple white circle-neck tee and an a-line skirt from my drawer, it at least looked nice, if a little businesslike. But Caleb loved me in skirts, and this was the only one I had left after leaving most of my things in Canada.

Outside it was definitely stormy and consistently rainy, but it wasn't cold. I ran straight out onto the terrace in my bare feet, swishing through the large puddles of rain as I made my way toward the magnificent glass atrium Caleb had surprised me with the night I had left for The Oracle. When I turned on the sparkling interior lights that lit up the glass ceiling like a sapphire-cast night sky, the real gift was waiting there for me front and center—my grand piano. Only, it was not just any piano. It was a Fazioli, and I had never seen anything more beautiful. Just seeing it again, gleaming under the lights, made me realize how desperately I had missed playing while I was gone. My heart leapt, and I could feel my fingers just itching to race across the keys. I longed to hear a lively, brisk andante, and then a slow, leisurely allegretto, the familiar melodies that we a part of my soul. Music had been my life, the direction I was going before that fateful train crash. It was still strange to think back on how that one night had changed the course of my life. And yet, there was still a large part of my heart that pulled me towards the familiar—a previous life that was outside of Caleb. Was it possible for me to have all of them? To be a lover, a pianist and a supernatural fighting force?

I didn't think so. At some point I would have to choose.

Taking my natural seat on the bench, I inhaled in a slow, deep breath as I began to run my fingers across the keys in a relatively soft molto allegro piece, then increased its strength. My timing of the notes was a bit rusty and my fingertips were bit soft, but after a few minutes I relaxed and just let the music come to me. The rain outside pelted softly against the glass in perfect harmony with the tinkling highs and resonating lows of the grand's strings, radiating into the Seattle skyline. The more I played, the more I allowed myself to get lost inside the music, finding freedom and peace again across the eighty-eight keys. It was as if I were uncovering a hidden part of my soul that had been locked away for the past three months.

In the past, Caleb had always found his way to me by the music. He could feel my enjoyment of the music through me. But after nearly two hours, as I depressed the last note, he was not here. Perhaps he was still making his way back from Canada with Jax. I *had* taken a jet to get here.

It was OK, though. *He would come.*

Stepping back outside the protection of the glass, I realized that harder streams of rain had begun to fall. I should've wanted to use my Dhampir speed to seek fast shelter inside the condo, but in a way, the cascading showers felt like a balm to a spirit that had been slowly battered over the last few weeks. Removing my favorite cardigan, I tossed it inside the sliding doors. Then, closing my eyes I raised my face to the heavens and throwing my arms out high to my sides. I could feel the wide smile pulling across my lips as I just let the rain soak me in its freshness. Soon I was a sopping mess, which meant I would have to shower and start all over again to look my best, but I didn't care. I was free.

I was free!

I tiptoed back inside and across the wood floors, dripping onto everything in my path, and that was when I felt it—felt him. Tightness, mixed with excitement, pulled inside my chest. Wonderful tightness! An energy I knew better than my very own heartbeat.

Caleb was here.

Chapter Sixteen

When the wave of cool air crashed against my back, I swung around to face the man who still had the power to steel my very next breath just by the sight of him. He stood back from me—several feet back—his expression troubled and his breathing heavy, the air practically sawing in and out of his chest. Caleb Wolfe didn't appear winded; it was more like he was holding on, or holding back. "You're here," he whispered, his rain soaked clothes clinging to his wide shoulders and barrel chest like second skin.

"I'm here," I echoed softly. "Joseph arranged for us to leave The Oracle sooner."

His brows furrowed sharply. "Why? Did something happen?" I shook my head to quickly assure him, but it was still there in his eyes—uncertainty. I hated seeing it because more than anything I just wanted to be in his arms already, to be touched by him after being denied that for so long. But he kept his distance from me when I most wanted to be close to him. "I've thought of this moment every day since you've been gone," he said, the words seeming to come out with great difficulty, " . . . of seeing you again. But now that you're here, I'm afraid you'll disappear if I try to touch you."

His words pulled at my heart and he was still breathing deep as my gaze followed the wonderfully long, angled lines of his body to the single white rose he held delicately in his hand. "Is that for me?" He blinked slowly then looked down as if suddenly remembering that he had a flower. I couldn't help but smile as he silently lifted it towards in me. His eyes were so soft, filled with readable emotion, as I reached for it. "Then let's start here, OK?"

But Caleb had never been a patient man when it came to

waiting for what he wanted. Without warning, he closed the distance between us, placing the stem in my hand and raising them both until the sweet scent of the flower was just under my nose. He watched me as my free hand touched his wrist, sliding delicately but purposefully upward along his arm and tracing the line of his broad shoulder. "I'm still here," I smiled at him. "Please touch me. I've missed you so much."

Caleb's hand slid to my throat then wove into my hair, fisting through the long, wet strands as he angled my head back and sheer need seemed to take him over. He slanted his lips over mine and took me against his mouth in a sweet kiss that had me dizzy in seconds. Kissing him was just so easy. He moved his lips over mine with the absolute confidence of a man who knew exactly how I would respond to each gentle little tug, each tempting little lick. His kiss permeated my senses and coaxed with tender demand until I opened to him more, taking him deeper, brushing his tongue against my own till the familiar sensation of it left me trembling in his arms. "Are you cold?" he breathed, interrupting the kiss without ever separating his lips from mine.

My reply was to pull his lips back down firmly against mine. He didn't ask again.

Oh, the sensations were already too much. My entire body felt weak, as if my knees would buckle at any moment, but he held me upright, his hands exploring, circling over me greedily. I wanted it to go on and on, but without warning he pulled back from me, his excited breaths puffing against my cheek as a low rumble stirred inside his chest.

I knew that primal sound.

The blue-eyed warrior—the vampire within him—had come to the surface, and it meant his dangerous knife-like fangs were preventing our kisses from going any further. "I need you," his breathy voice spoke, his large hands now caressing my hips possessively. "I need to be inside you."

I nodded and answered with the only word that came to my head, "Yes."

Suddenly, he gathered the hem of my skirt in his fingers and began tugging the wet fabric up on my thighs, then became frustrated that it was taking more than two seconds to free me from the clinging material, so he abandoned that plan completely and ripped the skirt in half, tossing the remnants to the floor. "Caleb!" I gasped at the same moment his hands gripped the backs of my thighs and hoisted me up off my feet, drawing my legs instinctively around his waist. "I barely have any clothing left. I had to leave everything . . ."

I lost the thought in my head once I could feel the hard proof of how much he wanted me pressing low at my belly. I didn't even feel the motion of being moved across the room until I heard his foot kick at a couple of pesky barstools in his way, crashing them against a nearby wall before he roughly planted my bottom on the kitchen island granite. "I'll have Gem take you shopping," he responded with a bit of a growl. "You can have whatever you want." Then, in one sweep, his arm cleared the bags behind my back from the granite top. "*Damn it all!* This will have to do."

With an effortless pull, the delicate lace bikini on my hips was gone, followed quickly by his hands tearing at his own button-fly's. I slid my small hand to his now open jeans and began to stroke over his long length from base to tip. Up and down, up and down, his eyes seemed to catch on fire and he fell forward with a groan and braced his hands on the granite at each side of my hip, his breath hitching as he watched me. "*Damn*, your hand is perfection . . ."

Gently I squeezed around him. Long, thick, hard as steel but wrapped in sinfully soft skin, I was sure I could stroke him like this all afternoon. But as his piercing blue eyes began to dilate and it became increasingly difficult for him to maintain control of a steady breath, he wrapped his hand around my wrist and pulled it away, then spread my thighs wide as he dragged my hips right to the edge of the countertop. Shoving what was left of his clothing down his hips he lined up his body with mine. When his first, deep thrust impaled me fully, I gasped, struggling for any kind of solid breath as he held himself inside me for a long moment, pressing until every quarter inch my body had to give him surrendered. "Olivia . . ." he said with a crinkle to his brows. "*God,* am I hurting you?"

He was worried he'd entered me too hard. Caleb was a vampire. His strength was far superior to my own, and it was a constant struggle for him to contain that strength when he was with me like this, but I trusted he would never hurt me. In fact, I lived and breathed to feel his powerful body driving inside mine, as if I could somehow harness that part he worked so hard to control and take it inside me. "Again Caleb," I whispered, trying to reassure him. "Again."

He didn't hesitate. Rearing back, he plunged forward with another hard thrust that had my breath hitching at his shoulder. Then one more that forced me to grab onto his arms for support as he stilled himself deep inside me. "Look at me," he breathed. When I did, the amazing blue of his warrior eyes held my gaze, darkening, heating, and glazing over in passion every bit even more than a human man could. He was beautiful. "I've missed you," he said. "I've missed being inside you like this."

Caleb then flexed his hips, and my nails dug into his shoulders as he began to thrust into my body with steady, even strokes. Clinging to his arms, my heartbeats fell into perfect rhythm with his thrust. The rest of the world, the nightmare I had been living for the past few weeks, had now been shut away. Never in my life had I felt so safe in a man's embrace. It was like he sealed me in a protective bubble, the evil in this world no longer able to touch me.

Slowly, Caleb guided me back on the granite top until I was lying flat. Then he dragged his hand along my chest, making sure I felt the friction between his cool hand and the fabric currently caressing my skin. I arched to his hand as he drew it lower and lower along my stomach. Taking a firm grip of my hips, he continued to thrust, driving my body higher and higher. "Yes," he breathed, "open for me. Let me *feel* what your body wants."

He wasn't talking about my body. He was talking about my mind. He wanted to *feel* my pleasure, *feel* my response to him— share them with me. It was his gift, and it made his enjoyment of the act that much more powerful for him.

Caleb's hand once again followed the arch of my back until he found the exact spot he wanted and lifted my arch deeper. *Oh God,* it was the perfect spot! I inhaled sharply, my thighs now shaking around him. "Mmm, you like that, don't you?"

"Yes," I managed in panting reply.

"Would you like a little more?"

Without waiting for my answer—which there was no way I could've found voice to give to at that moment—he pulled my arch slightly higher and then began to thrust again. I felt as if I were hanging off the edge of a steep cliff. Each new plunge driving me closer and closer to something I desperately wanted to float from. "*Damn,* you're close," he groaned. "I can *feel* it. You're gonna come for me right here . . . right like this."

And he was right. My palms stuck to the granite as my mind tried to absorb every sharp, visceral sensation, every movement. "Caleb!"

"Yes, that's it! Scream for me," he said in a strained rasp.

And I did scream.

My hips rose and my heels dug into his low back just before my entire body locked, trying to just contain the waves of release rolling through me at that moment. Tiny lights sparkled in front of my eyes while he continued to power through my orgasm until every last flicker had been extinguished. Only then did his body let go. He drove deep, growling out in a powerful explosion as I felt him come deep inside me and then left me shaking beneath him.

I closed my eyes, panting for a long while as I tried to regain my wits. Caleb pulled my shaking and exhausted frame back up against his chest, his arms curled around me so I was surrounded by his scent, his strength. My head collapsed against his shoulder and I felt his tender kiss on my head. All the emotion of being separated from this man I loved for so long came crashing over me without warning. "I missed you. I didn't think . . ."

"Shhh," he whispered, straightening his clothes enough to carry me to the bedroom. He set me down gently on the bed, his long body staying close as I clung to his shoulder, unable to stop the emotion coming forward in the form of tears and tiny, little sniffs. "Shhh, my sweet girl. It's OK. I'm right here. You'll never have to be apart from me again."

Despite his reassuring words, the emotion continued to come. I feared this would all be just some heavenly dream that I would wake from and find myself back in my room at The Oracle. But for the first time in over three months, the frosty tingles I loved so much returned over the shell of my ear as he whispered, "I love you, Olivia. I've loved you every single day you've been away from me. And I *will never* forget you—not as long as I live. And that's going to be a very long time."

I suddenly found myself laughing through my tears. Lying back against the mattress, my face still wet from the earlier rain, I stared into his amazing eyes, which had returned to their normal, spectacular gray color—but now they were filled with worry. His thumbs brushed across my cheeks. "I've felt such pain in you these last weeks. I need to know that you're all right. I need you to tell me what has been happening." I continued to stare straight into his intense gaze, not wanting this perfect moment to be ruined by memories of the past that couldn't be changed. "Olivia," he pressed. "Talk to me."

I nodded at him slowly. "I know I need to tell you these things. And I promise I will." Caleb started to object but I touched my finger over his lips to stop him. "But for this one night, can we forget about The Brethren and Davin? Can it just be about us? Just you and me? Please. For just one night."

After a long silence, a playful glint entered Caleb's eyes. His smile tipped up just enough to remind me of a guilty boy trying to hide the chocolate bar with the evidence still smeared on his face. He feathered his lips against mine, teasing me at the edges of my mouth just before raking me once again with the velvet brush of his kiss. Slowly and deliberately, his hands caressed the entire length of my body while removing my clothes, and he never once broke contact with my lips. He was truly gifted in some areas. Soon I was curled up, naked against him, our bodies fitting together like puzzle pieces. "I promise you," he began as he licked at the sensitive hollow behind my ear, "tonight you'll be asking yourself only one thing: 'How did I not know that a man could please my body in so many intriguing ways?'"

I laughed again as he continued to trace a silky trail of kisses down my throat. He paused for a moment, his head lifting and his hand reaching for the sapphire necklace resting at my collarbone. He seemed curious and I wondered if he recognized the piece from when Maya came to the clinic. "I have to wear this," I said, my hand covering his, "to keep myself blurred to the supernatural world."

He closed his iron fist over the gemstone and I feared he would crush it right there in his palm. "This is why I'm having trouble sensing you? I don't like this," he complained. "I don't like not being able to sense you."

"Yes, but you can still *feel* me," I replied softly, trying to keep him relaxed so he wouldn't destroy the one item I had to help keep me safe in this world. " . . . when I'm close to you like this, can't you? Your special gift breaks through."

"I *feel* you," he sighed, his expression a hard grimace of frustration. I understood the idea of me being blurred to him was difficult, especially for a man who relied almost solely on his gifted senses. "When you're close," he continued. "But I need to be able to feel and sense when you're in danger all the time." His hands slid behind my back and cupped the swells of my bottom. Lifting my hips, he cradled me tighter against him. "I need to *feel* you," he breathed.

I wasn't sure what he wanted me to say when he had me so tingly at the moment. Luckily, I was able to put something together. "What if I promise that if I need you I'll take the necklace off?"

He said nothing in reply.

"Please, Caleb. I want this to work for us. I want The Brethren to leave us in peace. This is how we're going to make that happen."

"You know I can't refuse you," he said quietly, then surprised me by leaving the room in a cool rush of air, only to return a second later with the white rose he brought for me, its rained-on petals now dry. I reached for it, but he shook his head with a smile and pulled it back. His long dimples were deep around his smile as he began brushing the flower over my skin. The sensation tickled me and I squirmed beneath him. "We're going to stay here—all night," he said. "And I will take you again and again until you are breathless and begging beneath me." He warned me of his intent with his eyes, the soft glimmering in the evening light reflecting in his eyes as if silently verbalizing a promise. "*You will know* how much I love you by the time the sun rises again."

"Then I guess we better get started," came my breathy reply. "Sounds like I might have a lot of begging to do."

Chapter Seventeen

The next morning I awoke knowing that every single thing in my world was right. Outside, large raindrops fell, their impact resounding on my patio as though they were hail, while the urban rush of traffic and the wail of police sirens whistled in the distance, adding to the metropolitan symphony of sound. And inside, my skin tingled from the petals of the wilting white rose that was being brushed across my cheek. I rolled over to gaze into the relaxed features of the man who tortured me with such sweet bliss throughout the night. His face was even more handsome than I remembered, if that was possible—rugged and masculine with that neatly trimmed beard. And his body! Even in the dull, rainy daylight, his lean muscles and firm lines, mixed with an enticing balance of dark, manly hair, glistened to perfection, all the way to his feet.

I was one lucky woman.

"Good afternoon, my sweet," he rumbled as he nuzzled along my throat, and then lower until he was lightly licking my nipples, which were standing at attention for him.

"Afternoon . . . ?" I questioned with a sharp inhale as he bit lightly over the tip of one rosy peak.

"I'm afraid so. You slept quite soundly . . . like a lazy cat." I swatted him on the arm for the reference but he didn't move, just laughed against my skin before drawing that same nipple deeper into his mouth. *Oh*, it was sweet torture, and I hissed in reply, arching to him. "So tell me, my beauty . . . Is your body satisfied?" When I didn't respond right away, he lifted his head in question.

"No," I smiled at him. "I want more." He lowered his head again and continued with his task, not even bothered by my implied dissatisfaction. He knew better. I had panted and moaned and screamed for him repeatedly throughout the night. "Really?" he questioned playfully. "I seem to remember a lot of begging and pleading."

"Maybe a little, I suppose." I figured I could give him at least that much.

"Aren't you going to ask if you pleased me?"

"No—*oooh!*" My voice went up an octave after he bit my nipple again. I sucked in a quick breath before adding, "I *know* I did. I could see, hear and feel it."

He chuckled at that. "Yes you didn't really have to *feel* me to know how much I enjoyed you, did you? I guess I'm going to have to put in more effort today."

As he smiled at me I pulled him back up to my lips and kissed him softly. "Caleb, can we stay here like this forever? You're the only thing I need in this life."

"We could . . . but I think Gem and Grandpa Jax would miss you."

My eyes blinked wider and I clapped my hands together and involuntarily released a small squeal. "I've a grandpa, Caleb! I have family!"

"Yes, you do. And I think he's as excited about it as you are. So the question is, how long have you known?"

"Not long . . . a couple of weeks, I guess. Gideon was trying to cheer me up and gave me a box that belonged to my mother, Eve—Jax's daughter. There was a photo of him and Isabeau inside." I pulled my head back and glared at him—just a bit. "I hope you weren't too hard on him for not telling you."

A smirk was his response. "Oh, he got an earful for catching me off guard like that. But you know Jax. He never lets me push him too far." Caleb then rolled to his back, bringing me with him atop his body. We gazed at each other for several perfect moments as he stroked his fingers through my hair. "Why did you leave with Alec?"

I traced the slope of his jaw with my finger, trying to offer a tiny gesture to soothe away the hurt I knew I had caused by leaving without telling him. "I wanted to give you the time and space you needed to figure out how you felt about me."

"OK," he replied carefully, " . . . but why did you leave with *him?*"

I blinked back at him in surprise. "It wasn't about Alec. It was about keeping my promise to you—that I would keep myself safe. I needed to learn how to defend myself. When I realized that you truly did love me, I knew I wanted to be with you, but I didn't want my gifts to be a burden to you or Gemma or Jax."

"What do you mean '*when you realized I loved you*'?" he frowned. "When did you know?"

"That last night I played for you—before I left." His frown deepened, while I just kept talking, as if somehow it would help ease his response. "That night Alec told me that my illusion would wear off in two weeks, but I'd already been separated from you once before for an entire month. I knew then it had to be real."

"Then why the hell did you leave?" he asked sharply. "Why didn't you just tell me?"

"Because, Caleb . . . loving me had to be something you knew was true inside you—not just taking my word for it. And I didn't know how long it'd be before you trusted your own feeling that it was true."

"I knew after a week! The pain never lessened, it only got worse. And you had left, and I couldn't *feel* you. I didn't know if you were ever coming back."

Wrapping my arms around him, I held him tight. "I'm sorry. I didn't understand that they were taking me to sacred ground. I would've stepped off so that you could *feel* me sooner, but Davin found me the day after I arrived. He threatened to wait for me to cross over."

Caleb's expression just then was determined. "Tell me everything he said to you."

I lay my head on his chest and sighed as he lightly massaged my back with long strokes. "He said you'd forgotten me; that you'd moved on with Celeste; that you'd been . . . *with her.*"

Caleb was quiet for a long while, as if expecting me to continue. When I didn't, he tilted my chin up. "Hey, look at me. You know none of that's true, don't you? I've not seen Celeste. I've not even thought about her."

"I do. I just don't understand how Davin knows so much about you. How did he know about Celeste? The fact that he knew about her—that she was your mate—made me believe he was telling the truth."

"She's not my mate!" he snapped, then quickly dragged his hand through his hair as he attempted to regain control over his emotions. "But regardless, she needs to be warned. I don't want Davin to surprise her."

"*Oh,*" I replied as my heart seemed to skip a beat or two. "Of course, that's the right thing to do." And it was right for him to warn her. So, then what was wrong with me? Why was I insecure when it came to Celeste—a mate from ten years ago? . . . Because Caleb himself had told me that a mate in the supernatural world was meant to be for life. Did it matter then that it had been ten years since he'd seen her? They were still mated. Caleb must have been able to read my thoughts at that moment because his gaze narrowed on me. "*What?* You think I'm going to see her after ten years and want to fall back into bed with her?"

"I didn't say that."

"You didn't have to," he scowled.

He had felt my jealousy. *Damn,* but his gift was sometimes inconvenient.

Watching him as he let out a frustrated sigh, it surprised me when he pulled me closer to him and kissed me tenderly on my forehead. "Look where I am, Olivia," he quietly breathed against my skin. "Look whose bed I'm sharing. I'm just going to *warn* her." He then pulled back 'til his gaze met mine. "Now, get the rest of that stuff out of your head. You know it's *you* that I love."

I returned a smile as Caleb carefully covered my nude form with a blanket after feeling me shiver against him. "What else did Davin say to you?"

"Nothing, really. I stood up to him—warned him that I was getting stronger and that someday I'd be strong enough to fight —"

"*You what?*" Caleb threw himself up to a seated position, plopping me back onto the mattress and clean out of the blanket he had just covered me with "You're not going to fight him. I won't allow it!"

"*Whoa,*" I replied, heating up emotionally. "What do you mean, "*won't allow*"? It's not like I'm looking to fight him, but if he or his soldiers surprise me or something, then I need to be able to defend myself."

"No, you don't, because he's not going to get that close to you. Ever! Jax and I will protect you."

"Caleb, you can't possibly protect me every minute of the day. If there's one thing I've learned over the past three months, it's that this gift comes with burdens. I have to find strength in myself. I have to be able to defend myself."

Caleb was silent for a long while, and I thought he was reconsidering his position, but I soon realized that wasn't the direction of his thoughts at all. "I need to know what happened to you while you were at that place. I need you to tell me."

I was caught off guard just then at how I suddenly felt panicked. My pulse felt like it was resounding in my throat, and I was sure he would be able to hear it. How was I going to explain everything that had happened at The Oracle? I wanted no secrets between us, but I also didn't want him charging back there to impose revenge on Jude. It would serve no purpose. It wouldn't erase what had happened and would just serve to delay my attempt to move on past the whole horrid event.

Caleb nestled in closer to me until our noses were practically touching, his voice was rough but very sincere as he whispered, "Olivia, talk to me."

I licked my lips nervously and inhaled a deep breath as I stared back at him, knowing I just needed to find a way to tell him. "The human men were having trouble training me because they were drawn to me—even more so than my mother."

"Did they hurt you?"

"The Guardians and Hunters assigned to me didn't hurt me. In the beginning, they just touched me a bit more than they should have. But they worked very hard with Gideon to understand my illusion better—how to see through it, so to speak. And it worked."

"Did Alec touch you?"

Caleb asked the question with an even voice, but I saw something in his eyes that sparked of jealousy, and it surprised me. "Yes," I answered carefully, "but he learned to control it, like the others. You have to understand, it was hardest on him because he was my primary Guardian. He was around me the most."

Caleb's responding scowl said there was no chance of that happening. "He's been with you this whole time?"

"Yes," I answered, not sure where he was going with this.

"Have you been with him, Olivia?"

Shaking my head in confusion, I replied, "I just told you I've been with him this whole—"

"—That's not what I'm asking. Have you been *with him*—been *intimate* with him?"

"What?" I blinked back. "No! What is wrong with you! You're acting jealous." "I've reason to be. I've felt the love in your heart for him. I feel it now at mention of his name. And he's in love with you."

"He's not in love with me. He's just under my illusion. It isn't real for him. Now that he has some distance from me, his feelings will change."

My answer, to my surprise, didn't seem to satisfy him. "Olivia, are *you* in love with *him?*"

My eyes were suddenly watery—as if he had just slapped me across my cheek. "How can you ask me that after last night? After what we shared?"

He closed his eyes and shook his head. "Please, just answer the question."

I reached my hands to his face and stroked over his beard, pleading for him to see the sincerity in my eyes. "Yes, I love him . . . like a *brother*, and *only* like a brother. Caleb, my body, heart and mind desire *one* man. And he's the one I fought so hard to come back to—you! *You!* Don't cheapen what we have by suggesting I would share myself with someone else because I was away from you for a few months. I would never!"

He stared at me, expressionless, until finally a small smile crept across his lips. "You're right. I'm sorry."

"Good," I smiled, snuggling in impossibly close to him as I seductively suggested, "Now, why don't you get on with the business of showing this body how much you love it?" But I was surprised when he didn't jump on my suggestion. Something was still on his mind, and by the seriousness of his expression, I guessed immediately what it was. "Tell me what this Jude did to you?"

I knew this was coming, but somehow I was still not ready to explain it. Why was I unprepared? Or was it that I just didn't want to face it?

"He hurt you, didn't he?" Caleb pressed, the sudden stiffness in his shoulders visible.

Nodding my head against his chest, my voice was still escaping me as I tried to think of how best to explain everything. Caleb tried to help me along by sliding his hand down to my right thigh, rubbing his fingertip over the exact spot where the sword had gone into my leg. "The second time I felt you, I got an overwhelming sense of pain . . . here in your leg. Is this where he hurt you?"

I nodded. "He was the instructor for my Advanced Situations training. They reenact battle situations so that you can be better prepared to handle them."

Caleb snarled at that, displaying once again how he hated the idea of me battling anything or anyone. It was unacceptable to him. In his mind, it was never going to happen. "In the very first test, he charged me. I couldn't hold my stance against his strength, so the sword went in—"

"*What?*" Caleb snapped, pushing me back from him so he could look into my eyes, as if that could help him process it better. "*He did what?*"

"Calm down, Caleb. Lucas got me to the doctor quickly, and the wound is healed."

"I don't give a damn! That asshole will pay for what he's done."

I blew out a frustrated breath and pushed away from him, turning my back to him as I rolled over on the mattress. "Caleb, you're not making this easy."

I was clueless on how to tell him about the attack without sending him into the stratosphere. But he wouldn't let me go and followed me, nestling in behind me and folding his head into the crook of my neck, his voice much calmer. "I promise I'll try to remain calm. I'm listening. But I need you to tell me everything."

Quiet for several moments, I used the time to search for the right words. I knew he needed to hear the truth from me, but the added time to let his own mind run wild was not helping. So I plunged in, hoping for the best. "He had me do some exercises where I was chained . . . like at the prison." Caleb's body stiffened behind me, but, to his credit, he seemed to hold his anger in check, so I decided to keep going. There just wouldn't be any easy way for him to hear this. "He was charging me while I had one hand chained. I did OK at first, but I was having trouble concentrating. I kept flashing back to being chained with Isaac charging me, and I felt suffocated. That's when he was able to pin me down—"

I suddenly stopped. Caleb's body had begun literally to shake, to vibrate with anger behind me, and he finally rolled away to the edge of the bed. He sat up with his back to me, his head dropped into his hands, his elbows resting on his knees. "Go on," he growled, with a barely contained anger that seemed ready to unhinge.

"Caleb, I don't think—"

"Go on," he repeated, his voice completely steely now with a forced calmness, but I could hear his breathing getting harder by the second.

"Because I couldn't focus, he was able to pin me down on the floor beneath him, and . . . and . . . my struggling excited him."

I glanced over to see Caleb's chest swell and deflate like a balloon. He was trying hard to stay calm, but his body just couldn't contain it. "Did he rape you, Olivia?" he asked in a voice so lethal, so deep, I knew, even though I couldn't see his face, that the man was now gone—the blue-eyed warrior had taken his place.

"No," I answered quickly. "Gideon and some others were able to pull him off me before—"

Caleb suddenly exploded in an ear-shattering growl. Every muscle flexed and bulged as he rose to his feet, trying to regain control of his anger, but it was too much.

Before I could say another word to try and reassure him, he was gone.

Chapter Eighteen

After waiting several anxious hours for Caleb to return, and regretting my choice 'to tell him everything', I eventually lay back down and had to wrestle with my conscious in sleep. I had known that telling Caleb about Jude would be difficult for him to hear—that he might not be able to control the anger that was tied to his vampire thirst—but I still hadn't been prepared with the right words. Why couldn't I tell him in a way that would ease his mind? Telling Caleb the truth about what had happened was the last hurdle I had to face before I could put the whole painful event behind me for good.

I knew that . . . so why couldn't I convince him?

It was some time later when my lashes fluttered open and I immediately inhaled the scents of fir and sage—Caleb's scent. He was snuggled behind me, his arms enveloping me as if he had been trying to reassure me inside my own restless dreams. "I'm sorry, my sweet," he whispered against my skin. "My anger was too much for me to handle. I had to feed my thirst. But I'm in control again. I didn't mean to hurt you by leaving like that."

I turned in his embrace and reached for him, burying my head in his neck. "No, I'm sorry. I could've explained things better—found the right words—"

"Don't," he cut in. "You've nothing to be sorry for. I'm a grown man. I should've been better able to handle the truth." I tried to finish my sentence, but he placed his finger over my mouth to silence me. "There's nothing wrong with your words. I want you to feel you can always tell me the truth. And though I didn't do a very good job of showing you today, I don't want you to be afraid of telling me because of my vampire thirst."

"I understand your thirst, Caleb. And I know how hard you work to keep control of it. I'm not afraid of you. You would never hurt me."

He smiled tenderly at that, tracing that finger under my chin as he held me there in his gaze for a long moment. "Did he . . . physically hurt you?"

I stared back at him for a long while, debating in my own head whether it was a good idea to give Caleb any more detail, but considering what we just said to each other I didn't want him to think I was giving him anything less than the truth. "Some bruising, some stitches on my wrist where I was shackled," I finally answered.

He shut his eyes in a long blink. When he opened them again there was a new challenge sparkling within them. "Where was Alec when all of this was happening to you?"

I drew in my breath sharply. "It's not Alec's fault," I defended quickly. "He was out hunting for Davin after he had threatened me. Please," I whispered, "he's already struggling with this so much and—"

"He *should* be struggling with it," Caleb replied. "It was his job to protect you, and he let this animal almost—"

I pushed away from him just then, but he snatched me back firmly, crushing me against his body. It was clear I wasn't going anywhere.

"All right," he conceded calmly. "I'm sorry."

"You don't understand," I pressed. "Alec already blames himself for this. But it isn't his fault. Jude's the only one who deserves blame here."

"And he *will* pay."

"Caleb! You can't kill him for this. It would destroy everything you've worked for to become a Daywalker. No matter what he's done, it's not worth it to destroy that."

"I don't have to kill him to hold him accountable for what he's done," he scoffed. "But you're wrong. If I did kill him, it *absolutely* would be worth it."

"Please . . . leave it alone. I just want to live in peace with you and Jax and Gemma. I want to put it in the past where it belongs and focus on you and me."

He pushed the hair back from my cheek, a worried expression washing over his entire face. "Olivia, can't you see that this is hurting you?"

Shaking my head with a resolve that was born by pure determination not to revisit that day in my head, I replied, "It's not. Please let this go. I want Jude and The Brethren out of my life. I don't want you to go back there." My voice then rose in pitch. "*I* don't want to go back."

Caleb pulled my head into his shoulder, stroking his hand in my hair. "Shhh. Easy."

In the following silence I could tell he was *feeling* me—feeling the fear and pain—the scarring Jude had left behind that I didn't want to examine too closely. "I can't let this go," he spoke honestly, and I raised my head to object. But he cut me off, saying, "I won't do anything for now. And I won't go back there without talking to you about it first."

"But Caleb—"

"No buts. That's the best I can offer you right now. And it's a lot, considering I'd like to rip his heart out through his spine."

I decided that now was not the time to push. I would convince him later not to go back, when his anger of the event was not so fresh.

We lay there quietly, listening to the rain pat against the glass, a sound that seemed only to add to the somber mood that had settled over us. "I'm sorry if I was too rough with you yesterday," he finally said into the silence, " . . . when we made love."

Stunned, I blinked back at him. "You weren't too rough with me." He turned his head away, indicating he obviously didn't agree. "Caleb, look at me." He was slow to respond but eventually turned back to face me and I held him at his cheeks to keep him there. "When you're inside me, I feel nothing but safe. The incredible power of your body fills me with strength, just as my warm body calms you. We are right for each other. I'll not let what Jude did take that away from us."

Caleb leaned down and placed a tender kiss on the very tip of my nose. "I love you," he whispered. "I can't stand the thought of another man touching you—hurting you."

"I'm all right—better than all right—after being with you again." I stared up at him with a sincere and easy smile. "Will you make love to me?"

His eyes simply sparkled at that moment, their many hues of gray melting into one giant burst of color under the light. "Yes . . . If you promise to play for me later. I've missed your music."

And Caleb meant that. He and Jax both adored hearing live music played because of how the sound transferred through their bodies. Their senses were so highly attuned, so clear, the sound vibrated through them. "I love that you receive such joy from my playing. How you *feel* the music. I wish I could feel it that way."

Caleb's expression was absolutely sincere as he stared back at me. "I feel the music—but I can *see* the music in you. When you play it lights up your whole face. I'm not sure you're even aware of how much you see the world in music. It's beautiful. You're beautiful."

I couldn't help but smile. "Well, with a compliment like that I'll play for you all night, if you want."

A silky laugh escaped him as he yanked my tee shirt over my head. "Not all night," he replied as his skilled fingers deftly unclasped my bra. "There are other things to be accomplished." He kissed his way lower, his cool breaths rough against my stomach as he licked over my navel and tugged my leggings down.

"Caleb, I'm being serious," I gasped under the soft, wet strokes of his tongue. "Tell me what it's like to *feel* music. It must be wonderful."

Caleb's head popped up, a mischievous glint in his eyes. "Would that please you, my sweet? To feel music . . . ?"

"Yes, but I can't."

He pushed himself to his feet and shrugged out of his shirt—the last of his clothing—appearing like a statue of perfection standing there in the soft, cloudy daylight. I smiled and reached my hand for him. "Come back . . ."

But instead, Caleb reached for a blanket and wrapped it around me, lifting me into his arms in one easy motion. "What do you think you're doing?" I laughed as he led us out toward the rain-soaked terrace. He answered with a twisted smile, and before I knew it we were shielded from the rain again inside the glass atrium on the terrace. Caleb kicked out the piano bench then sat in the center of it, facing the keys, lowering me directly on top of his legs and removing the blanket from around me. We were both now completely exposed to the inner city lake and the fading light around us. "I don't understand," I questioned. "Do you want me to play something for you?"

He nuzzled his cheek at my neck, his short beard tickling me as it scraped over my skin. "We're going to let your body feel the music."

"Caleb, I—"

"Shhh," he sounded gently across my lips, drawing his fingers down my arms, leaving behind tingly trails of pure sensation. It was so nice I sank back against his chest, hearing only the sound of the rain tapping against the glass above us as he worked his palms with knowledgeable precision over my breasts, his thumbs and forefingers pinching the hard tips until he drew an aching gasp from deep within me. "First, we need to make sure your body's nice and sensitive," he whispered while smoothing his hands down over my stomach, then lower to wickedly explore through the soft curls between my thighs. I grabbed his forearm to brace myself against the incredible sensations hitting me as his fingers began to circle around the little knot he was teasing so patiently. "Just like this."

Mercy, any more sensitive and I would be rocketing from the bench. I desperately wanted him inside me. "Music is very powerful, my sweet," his deep, sexy voice murmured as my hips arched over his hand and he slid two long fingers inside the warm flesh that greeted him. My aching inner muscles reached to pull his fingers deeper as he stroked again and again. "I want you to *feel* the pleasure you give me when you play."

"But how?" I half sighed, half moaned, wriggling impatiently over his lap.

Caleb hissed in a sharp breath just then. "*Damn,* you're not going to make this easy for me, are you? Just hold still. Allow yourself to just *feel* the sensations." He patiently continued to stroke in and out with two long fingers, sometimes slowly, sometimes fast, depending on what he heard in the pace of my breath. There was an edge he wanted me on, but not to cross . . . and it was killing me!

"Caleb, please . . . ," I begged, reaching my hands back to run them through his hair, which arched me further over his hand. Everything around me now felt heightened. The overcast light of the city on stormy day seemed almost to glow as it reflected from the low clouds above us, and the raindrops sounded like sleet as they exploded onto the glass. And still he stroked. My flesh almost hurt from the increasing sensitivity generated by his deft fingers and circling thumb. I was so close to my entire world exploding like the raindrops, and he had to feel it.

Then, without warning, he drew his fingers away. My breath caught as if frozen in a state just short of bliss. "No! Don't stop—please."

"Shhh," he whispered at my ear. "Your body's near that peak where you can experience the most from the music. Trust me, sweet girl." One strong arm circled my waist as he raised me up off his legs and then carefully positioned himself beneath me. When I felt his wide flesh impale my own, I wanted to cry out at the perfect bliss of it—the perfect sensation of his hand curling at my hip and guiding me down on him in a long, slow slide. "*Damn . . . ,*" he gasped. "Feel how warm and ready for me you are? You feel amazing."

As I continued to stretch around him in almost intolerably slow fractions of inches, my breathing was—at best—erratic. For a moment I wondered if I could even fit all of him inside me in this position. But once he was finally buried to the hilt, I suddenly needed more and began to move on him. Caleb's body tightened as he released an almost pained growl, moving his hands and tightening them over my hips to stop my movement. "Easy, my sweet. We will get there. But first . . ." He pulled my knees out wide and then pressed them down, causing my hips to swing forward. My breath hitched as he positioned me over the piano keys in front of us, his strong, straight length stretching the insides of me until I thought I would scream. Every movement now caused a thousand sensations, and it was a sweeter rapture than I had ever known. "I want you to play for me," he breathed roughly. "Play for me, my beautiful girl."

I wasn't sure how I could focus on much of anything, let alone an entire piece, but as I depressed my fingers over the keys in an andante Schubert rhapsody, Caleb wrapped both his arms around my waist, blanketing me with his body as his chin rested on my shoulder. After a few seconds, I could feel vibrations from my music moving through his body. They were small at first, a little like being in one of those deep massage chairs, only the vibrations worked from the inside out. And the music was amazing, ultra-clear and sharp, like being in the middle of a live orchestra under a cloudless night sky. The notes became alive, three-dimensional, and part of the energy around me in a way I had never experienced before—from the inside out. I wanted to hold on to the feeling, commit it to memory so it would be there for me in the future.

But then the sensations got even stronger . . .

As the music echoed through my head, I felt searing little tremors—a lot like sparks—vibrating from him into my straining inner muscles, prompting them to clamp around him in a fierce grip. He groaned as more notes followed, the sensations became stronger, tighter, snaking deeper, like heated little spasms that excited and sparked my flesh to an almost unbearable level. I didn't know how much longer I could hold back the huge wave of sensation that was about to break over me.

"Not yet," Caleb growled as he released my waist and squeezed his hands around my hips.

Not yet? I was sensitive, swollen, and riding a very fine edge. My body was practically screaming for that final push into release and he was telling me *not yet?*

"Caleb, please . . ." My hands flattened against the keys to create one giant, blaring sound. All I could focus on was how much I needed him to move inside me—to release me from this sensual overload.

Caleb used his hands to rock my hips over him in several small, controlled movements. "Keep playing, my sweet. Let the music please you." Despite his calm, I could hear the breathless restraint in his voice, the excited man trying to hold off and give me this gift of feeling music.

My fingers somehow remembered how to move again and began to race over the keys, eliciting loud cries from me as the music seemed to rip through me from the inside. I had never felt it so clearly before.

Caleb's chin lifted from my shoulder and he raised his face to the darkening skies, his fierce pants heavy at my ear. He was receiving pleasure from both the music vibrating through him and the heat from the friction of my muscles working over him. A low, rolling groan escaped him, sounding as if he were drowning in a state of complete rapture. It was beautiful, so beautiful I wanted to give him more, so I played even harder.

Soon, the sensations were overwhelming. I dropped my head back against his shoulder. "Please help me."

"Olivia," he whispered, gripping his hands around my hips, shocking me when he lifted me up until he was almost withdrawn from my body, then pulled me back down over his full length. I cried out, the feeling of being filled so quickly, so fully, was better than perfect. He then repeated the movement, again and again, his thrusts becoming stronger. Up, down, up, down. I lost all dexterity in my fingers, and my palms went flat against the keys for support. The loud, unstructured cacophony that resulted from my pressing all those keys at once sent hard, thick pulses into my womb. It was the perfect sound for my climax! I knew the crest I'd been riding for a while was about to crash in one giant wave, a coda to end all codas. "That's it, my sweet! Let your body tighten. I will release you."

Shocked by the powerful and irrepressible forces suddenly gripping me, my fingers tried to dig into the ivory-clad piano keys as my body shuddered and I screamed out uncontrollably. Caleb wrapped his arms around me, pulling me back against his rigid body as my orgasm took over every part of my being and emerged as my very existence.

"*Christ!*" he choked just before I felt him explode within me, his body climaxing again and again in repeated, rhythmic spurts so violent that they seemed to startle even him.

For several long minutes after that, our breathing rose and fell, synchronizing exactly, allowing me to finally resolve the music of our coupling clearly in my mind. The incredible experience was wrapped around me, a sweet memory I would never, ever forget. Eventually, the blue-eyed warrior retreated and the cherished man returned to me, smothering my neck with kisses as his hands continued to massage my sweat-misted abdomen, my swollen breasts, my totally relaxed shoulders, seemingly every inch of me he could reach. "That was amazing," I breathed, my body still trembling. "To feel music that way is a gift. To feel *you* that way is a gift."

He nuzzled his face against mine, his breathing still rough. "I love you, Olivia," he said. "Tell me that I please you. Tell me that I please your body."

A rather unladylike snort sounded from my lips. "*Please* is an understatement. No one in my lifetime will ever please me as much as you do."

His deep chuckle seemed to permeate every other sound in the city at that moment. "I don't plan on you ever finding that out. I've something to ask you."

"What?" I asked, turning to blink up at him.

He lavished my lips with more kisses, pulling me to him as if he were afraid I might try to let go. "I want to be the man who pleases you," he breathed over my lips, "who pleases this body every day for the rest of your life. I want to be the one to give you shelter—keep you safe. Make me the happiest man and say you'll agree to be mated with me."

My eyes opened wide and I suddenly became completely lost for words. I couldn't get even the simplest muddled sounds to come out as I stared up at him.

I loved this man more than I ever believed it possible to love another. But I still had insecurities, doubts and fears—emotions that must have been plain to him in my expression, because his gaze focused, laser-like, on me with a mix of surprise and raw, wounded emotion. Every second of silence that went by now accumulated to form a huge and growing gap between us.

"*Olivia?*"

Chapter Nineteen

The stony appearance of Caleb's face did little to mask his disappointment. My silence had hurt him beyond words, but instead of pressing me further he reached for the blanket, wrapping it with care around my shoulders before moving me from his legs to sit on the bench beside him. Then he stood, squaring his shoulders to signify a visible distance he was placing between us. "You don't want to be mated to me," he said—more a statement than a question.

In that horrid moment, the rain drops that continued to fall outside sounded like ice breaking against the glass. "Please, Caleb, let me explain."

But he turned away from me, walking several steps forward toward the city lights, his hard, naked form etched perfectly into the fading light of darkening skies. "There's nothing to explain. You either want to be mated to me or you don't. I guess I have my answer."

I jumped from the bench, not caring that the blanket fell to the floor behind me. "No! That's not it! I do *want* to be mated to you . . . but . . . but you're already mated. And in your world she will always be seen as your—"

He swung around on me so fast it stole my breath. "No!" he snapped. "I'm not mated to her! I don't love her. I love you. I've told you this. Why can't you trust me?"

"*Trust you?* Caleb, you're saying you want to be mated to me. That you want to spend the rest of your life with me—an immortal life at that . . . but you won't even talk to me about *her!*" I dropped my head into my hands, swiping at the tears that had unexpectedly caught me off guard. "Don't you understand?" I whispered. "I love you enough to refuse to be second."

"You're not second!" he growled, gripping my shoulders as if he wanted to shake some sense into me. "You never have been!"

"Then why? If you don't love her, as you claim, why did you agree to be mated—?"

"I didn't agree!" The bellowed announcement caused my breath to start with surprise. I was confused. When I had stayed with Caleb the first time, recovering from my wounds after the train crash, he took me to one of his favorite rock perches in the woods and told me of how Celeste had 'turned' him—how they were mated. I remembered the words quite clearly because they had struck my heart with such force. So this new revelation that he didn't agree to the mating truly had me at a loss for words.

He raked his fingers through his hair as a pained expression pulled over his features. "I told you, when Celeste turned me from human into a vampire she let me know that she wanted a mate," he began in a much calmer voice. "When I awoke that next night, after the virus had finished with me, I didn't fully understand what had happened to me. And I didn't know how to satisfy my powerful thirst. She offered to let me drink from her." His hands fisted in front of him as he continued. "And I wanted it. *God,* I wanted it. The scent of her blood had me rabid. But in exchange, she said, I had to show her my loyalty in return—by letting her drink from me."

I swallowed hard, watching the shame cross over his face.

"In that moment, I would've given anything to drink from her . . . and I did. I didn't know what she was doing—what I was doing. The mixing and exchanging of our blood would keep me bound to her for life. When I felt the connection with her afterwards, she told me that we were mated."

I couldn't move a muscle; the impact of this virtually paralyzed me. I wondered if he had any idea how much he was breaking my heart. I hated what Celeste had done to him, how she had tricked him. Yet every cell in my body wanted to lash out in revulsion at the thought of him touching her. "From then on, she was like a drug that I couldn't get out of my system. For the month I was with her, I was also with her physically. I gave her my body, gave her pleasure, but I never loved her. She was never my choice." He brushed the backs of his fingers over my cheek as if trying to ease the pain that was choking my heart, pain that he could literally see on my face as I imagined him with Celeste.

"How were you able to escape from her?" I asked quietly.

"Jax," he replied. "He recognized that though we were connected by blood, a full mating never happened. He explained that vampires exchanging blood and making connections with sexual partners was quite common, and those connections often come and go. But when a pair is destined . . . when it is right . . . a connection will be made that cannot be broken. It's evident in a change of scent between the mated pair. Their scents will match. My scent was still different from Celeste's."

"So that's why you believe you can mate again?" I asked in a fading voice, then I stared back up at him. "But what if we try and our mating doesn't take, either? How can you be so sure?"

Caleb pulled me into his arms without warning. The moment his lips swept over mine I was lost. He caressed with the softest touch and even gentler hands as he stroked through my hair, his lips moving over mine with raw, open emotion that was right there at the surface and had me shivering against him. When he finally drew back, he was smiling. "That's how. Every time I touch you I feel it. I've felt it since the day I touched your hand after that train crash. *Damn!* Luckiest day of my life, actually." He then took both my hands in his and brought them up to his lips. "I know that when we are mated it will be right. You are *my* choice. I just need you to have faith in that—*in us.*"

Slowly, I pulled my hands from his and walked back to the bench, inhaling a deep breath of relief as I sat down, but it was a relief that didn't last for long. "Thank you for being so honest with me. I do want to take a chance on us. But . . ."

He picked the blanket up off the floor. Coming to me, he wrapped it around my shoulders and knelt before me, rubbing his hands over my arms. "Why are you hesitating? I know you feel what's between us every bit as much as I do. So, why?"

"Because I love you so much," I said, with no hesitation. "Because I want you to have everything in this life."

A questioning frown crossed his brow. "I don't understand. You *are* everything to me in this life."

Shaking my head, I said, "No. I alone am not everything. I . . . I'm not a family."

Caleb's confusion seemed only to get worse. "What does that mean? You're not making sense. *You'd* be my family, with Jax and Gem." When I still didn't respond, he touched my leg. "Olivia?"

"I can't have a baby, Caleb." The words were barely audible. "I can't give you a child—a family." I lowered my head, trying to hide the quiver in my chin. I wanted so badly to say 'yes' to this man and spend the rest of my life with him, but it wouldn't be fair to him.

In the silence that followed, I glanced up to see his stunned expression, and I felt sure it was a confirmation that my instincts had been right. "When I was at The Oracle, they ran tests. The results showed that the Greysons had a doctor do a procedure that would prevent me from getting pregnant. I can't give you a child," I repeated, as if I were trying to let the words sink into my own head. "It wouldn't be fair to you—to be mated to me when I can't give you this. You deserve the chance to be a father. I *want* that for you."

Words finally broke his stunned expression. "You want to give me a baby, Olivia?"

I nodded sadly. "I'm mostly human. As a woman, that's what I'm supposed to do, to create life. And I can't. It was the one thing I could've given you that she couldn't."

"*She?*" Caleb questioned. "You mean Celeste?" He grabbed both my hands, squeezing them tighter and tighter until I couldn't ignore it and raised my eyes once again to gaze directly at him. "Hear me," he almost pleaded. "Celeste could promise me a dozen children and it wouldn't matter. I love that you want us to have a baby, and if by some miracle that happens, I'll be twice as blessed. But I want you! You're my family. And I'll be happy if it's *just* you. Do you hear me, Olivia? *You're my family.*"

I was flabbergasted how I deserved this man who loved me so completely regardless of my faults. A smile pulled at my lips as he watched my acceptance of his words and the joy return to those beautiful gray eyes of his. "Now, I'll ask you one more time. Will you agree to be mated to me?"

Without hesitation, I threw my arms over his shoulders and around his neck. "Yes! Yes! I want to be mated to you."

Caleb pulled me tight against him. What he was offering me was not marriage, but it was the equivalent in his world, and I wanted it. "Hmm," he murmured into my ear. "There's my sweet girl's fluttering heart. I've missed that."

***

Early the next morning, Caleb and I were standing just outside the downtown Walker condo. It was located in Belltown, a trendy neighborhood full of restaurants, bars and boutiques nestled between historic Seattle Center and Pike Street Market. I had to admit, it surprised me that the coven's second home was so central to the noise and chaos of downtown, especially considering how little Jax cared for the hustle and bustle of the big city. However, if you're a coven of vampires, a well stocked blood supply would be the first priority, and the blood donation clinic Gemma managed for the Walker Foundation was on the first floor of the thirty-story residential and mixed-use building.

From the front entry I glanced southward a couple of blocks, half expecting to see Alec walk up at any moment. My Guardian probably didn't realize just how close he was staying to a coven of vampires. A city the size of Seattle, and yet they ended up blocks from each other. "Figures," I mumbled to myself.

"Figures?" Caleb asked.

"Nothing," I replied, then smiled up at him. "I'm excited to see Gemma again. It feels like so long since I have seen her."

"I think she's just as excited to see you. I told her this morning about your clothing situation, and she's more than ready to restock your closet with some new things while I'm gone for the next couple of days."

"Gone? But how can you leave me after we just found each other again?" My heart had jumped when he said he was leaving. I wanted to make certain that nothing prevented us from being together this time. But Caleb smiled at me reassuringly. "Hey," he said gently, cupping my cheek in his large, strong hand. "I'm afraid you're stuck with me, *soon to be* mate. I just need to get some things done before I bring you up to the house. It's winter up there now. The pass is already closed for the year."

"Well, I guess that's all right," I sighed, actually feeling a bit relieved, "as long as you make it up to me." Now I was smiling, too.

One corner of his lip turned up in a wicked smile just before he kissed me. "Oh, I'll make it up to you."

Caleb then guided me with his hand at the small of my back as he led me inside the formal lobby. The space was open, modern and shiny, with furnishings finished in luxurious mohairs and cotton velvets and tastefully nestled around a giant, limestone fireplace. Taking it all in, I could only imagine how spectacular the condo itself would be. "Is Jax here with Gemma?"

A small frown crept over his brows as he led me past the main elevator bank to a single elevator, its door open and awaiting our arrival. Caleb pulled a key from his jeans pocket, inserted it into the elevator's control panel, and hit the only button on the panel—the penthouse. *Of course.* "No," he finally responded to my question. There's been some tension between them lately. I'm not sure what it's all about, but Jax wants to give her some space."

I rolled my eyes, wanting to slap both Jax and Caleb upside the head. *The tension* was because Jax and Gemma were in love with each other, but for some reason or other, they were unwilling to acknowledge it. My guess was that most of the fault lay with Jax. He could be a stubborn two-hundred-year-old vampire. His dark, good looks, deep voice, and well sculpted body exuded power and authority, yet he was secretly collecting the woman's poems. It practically screamed '*fallen— hook, line, and sinker.*' Why Caleb couldn't see this, I would never understand. "How long has this been going on?"

"A couple of months."

"A couple of months?" I echoed, very surprised. "Aren't you concerned?"

He shrugged almost imperceptibly. "It's happened before. Gem just kind of gets in these moods. She'll work through it."

"Unbelievable!" I cried. "Men can be so clueless."

"And women can be moody," he countered with a laugh. "What? Are you implying you know what's wrong with her? You just got back."

"*Yes*, I know what's wrong with her." I exhaled a flustered breath to emphasize my frustration and turned to lean back against his chest, holding on to his arms, which he had wrapped around me.

Slouching just a little to bring his taller frame down to my level, he hooked his chin into the crook of my neck, the scent of fir and sage making my stomach all mushy. "Well, then, do you want to let me in on the secret?"

I was baffled. How could he not see it? "No. I'll talk to her."

"Here," he said, placing a small key in my palm. "You'll need this to unlock the elevator in the future." Perfect timing—the elevator doors opened to a sweeping penthouse view.

The twenty-foot-high ceiling of the penthouse capped what seemed to be more than three thousand square feet of windows. There was floor-to-ceiling glass around the entire perimeter, and the glass was tinted, just as it was at the tree house. Dramatic views of the Seattle city skyline, Puget Sound, and the Olympic Mountains surrounded the residence. The elevator had opened onto a modern living space, the focal point of which was a massive, glass faced fireplace that looked as if it had never been used to house a fire. To the right was a generous dining area and bar, with a huge, open kitchen just beyond. The modern finishes were similar to those at the tree house but a little darker, ebony walnut and granite, with stainless steel and textured glass details. But unlike the tree house, there was no concern for saving space.

"Why am I not surprised that this place is incredible," I said, just as a cheerful voice called my name.

"Olivia!" I swung around to see the beautiful face of the woman I had missed so much. Gemma's brilliant, ginger hair was pulled back neatly in a clip, with small strands dangling loose over her sparsely freckled cheeks. She smiled with full, broad lips, the kind of wonderfully pouty lips that would compel men to think of kissing her. Dressed in stylish boots, black leggings and a faux wrap skirt that looked to be keeping her warm from the wet chill outside, it was clear why she was in charge of the shopping bonanza that was about to occur. Everything fit her small curves perfectly, including the exaggerated v-cut sweater and simple white camisole underneath. "How dare you disappear on us like that," she teasingly scolded. "This tower of brawn beside you has been practically insufferable to live with every minute since."

I threw my arms around her. "Oh, Gemma, I missed you."

"Whoa," she replied at my enthusiastic hug. I missed you, too."

I was so happy to see her, I didn't think I would ever let go, until I remembered what I was doing—I was touching her. Without warning, I pulled back from her, leaving Gemma standing there with her arms dangling in an empty embrace.

Caleb was right behind me, rubbing my back with concern. "I—I'm sorry. I almost forgot. I can't touch your skin. If I do, my gift will affect you."

Gemma returned a sad frown. "I know I'll need to learn some things with regards to your gifts, but don't worry. It'll be fine. Caleb and Jax will help us." She then stepped back to fully assess my bland wardrobe choice for this morning—jeans— baggy, unbelted jeans at that—and a tee shirt. "My, we do have some work to do."

"I know," I sighed. "I had to leave The Oracle so fast . . ."

Gemma waved a dismissive hand through the air. "No worries. I've got everything figured out. I only hope we can get it all done in two days."

I swallowed hard. Shopping with Gemma wasn't going to be casual and fun—it was most definitely a 'mission.'

"I also understand we're buying you a gown," she squealed, clapping her hands several times in quick succession.

Caleb proudly wrapped his arms around me from behind, placing a chaste kiss on my cheek. "Gem, I want her to have the prettiest mating gown you can find. And two, if you don't mind."

Gemma smirked back at him under a narrowed gaze. "Yes, I understand." Then she looked at me. "Really, you're too good for him. The animal."

Caleb tightened his hold around me. "I need to get going while this rain holds up. I want you to stay here at the condo with Gem until I return."

I turned in his arms to welcome his goodbye kiss, intent on his gray eyes, which were gleaming with so much love it tugged at my heart. "Don't worry. I'll be no trouble at all."

He harrumphed at that. "Don't jinx things. And *take* the necklace off if you need me. Understood?"

I nodded. "Don't worry, Alec's nearby, too." Caleb replied to that with a rather ugly expression, muttering what might have been curses. "Caleb! He's my friend, and he's still my Guardian. You'd better start accepting that."

"We'll discuss it later," he managed. "But for now, I don't want you staying with him. Agreed?"

"Yes," I replied with an exasperated sigh.

"Geez, Caleb. What do you thinks' going to happen to her? We're not exactly in the middle of a vampire war zone."

He scowled at the much smaller woman. "Don't start with me, Gem. You know how Jax and I feel about your being careful while we're not here. In fact, he's going to insist that you return home soon."

Gemma snorted in response. "Over-protective—"

"Gem, just promise me you'll be careful," Caleb cut in, and I couldn't help but smile. I had missed this family.

"It'll be fine, Caleb. Chill."

His eyes narrowed in one final warning, though it was undermined by the amused half-smile that lifted the corners of his lips as Gemma innocently looked away from us and rolled her gaze around the room. Caleb then kissed me one last time. "I'll be back to take you home day after tomorrow." He dropped his lips over my ear and whispered. "I love you, my sweet." And then, just that fast, he was gone.

The whirl of air Caleb left behind hadn't even stilled when Gemma squealed in joy. "Are you ready to get started?"

Lord, help me. I liked to shop, but I was a rank amateur compared to this stylish diva. She began the undertaking by explaining that clothes were not just clothes, they were a statement—an extension of the person wearing them. She wanted mine to announce that I was a confident, beautiful young woman who was madly in love with one very strappingly hot vampire. "I'm not really sure I want to announce I'm in love with a vampire."

"Semantics," she replied, "but you get the idea. Now let's go."

Hours later, Gemma and I were lugging nine shopping bags full of shoes, clothes and accessories, and it was only noon. "Gemma, are you sure I need all of this?"

"You do remember how many pieces of clothing that sex-crazed beast of yours destroyed the last time you stayed with us, right? Now magnify that times ten when you're mated to him for life."

I chewed my lip between my teeth. She had a point.

Noticing my reflexive action, she chuckled, "That's what I thought."

Just then she stopped in front of an Italian restaurant in the mall. "Are you hungry?"

"Starved." And I wasn't exaggerating. I ordered a dinner-size plate of angel hair pasta to go with vast amounts of salad and breadsticks I began wolfing down as soon as they arrived at our table. Gemma teased me mercilessly about my uncontrolled appetite. "It's Alec's fault," I defended. "He had me practically doubling my portion sizes while I was training."

Gemma set down her fork and sat back in her chair with an amused glint in her eyes. "Speaking of your troublesome Guardian, he came into the clinic the other day to *give blood*," she said, making quote marks in the air with upraised hands. "He insisted that I be the one to draw his blood, and then complained the whole time that I wasn't *gentle* enough with him. The boy's sick in the head."

I gathered that Alec had some interest in Gemma, but that meant he went to see her the day we arrived here, even though I warned him about Jax. He was sick in the head—and asking for trouble.

"Honestly, I don't know what you see in him," she continued. "He's over-confident—arrogant, really . . . and stubborn. He won't take no for an answer. He just thinks all women will swoon over him because he's sort of good looking and has a few muscles." She then paused as if reconsidering something. "Well . . . maybe more than a few. Not that I noticed," she added quickly, splaying her fingers over her collarbone with utter sincerity. "Christian did." Her nose twitched as she giggled, staring off into the distance as if pondering a happy thought. Then her expression quickly shifted. "Oh, but he's just a rude cad!"

Gemma definitely seemed to protest a bit too much. "Yes, I see your point. Having a confident, handsome, six-foot-plus and deliciously muscled Guardian showering you with attention would be pretty tough to take."

Her gaze narrowed almost to a scowl. "You know what I mean. It's those naughty eyes of his. He's all Mr. Cool on the outside, but those eyes look at you as if he's imagining bedding you at that very moment."

"I would say that's more than likely, yes."

"Then he shows up unannounced with daisies, wanting to take me to dinner. When I said no, he returned yesterday with fresh cut orchids—asking again."

"What did you say?"

"I said no! Then he came back later with a calla lilies."

Now I had to work to hold back a rather unsupportive

laugh. Alec could be devilishly charming when he wanted to be. "And you said?"

"I said, if he didn't come back I'd think about it." She giggled at her own joke. "He didn't find that as funny as I did."

"And where're the flowers now?"

Her wide-eyed expression quickly became flustered. "That's hardly the point."

"So they're not in the trash I take it?"

Gemma scanned the restaurant as if searching for an eavesdropper in our midst, and then returned her gaze to me. "Do you even know how upset Jax and Caleb would be if they had any idea Alec—a Brethren Guardian—had come to see me? I'd have to pull them off the ceiling."

"Mmm," I sounded, "true." Gemma was probably wise to stay clear. Alec would eventually grow tired of chasing and move on. He never had any trouble finding or receiving female attention. But Gemma's next words surprised me. "Tell me about him. You know him as well as anyone."

I reflected for a moment on how far Alec and I had come since that first day I met him as the arrogant young man leaning against the base of a cherry tree. "He's a dear friend. I don't think I would've made it through my time at The Oracle without him. As you say, he's arrogant and stubborn, but he's also amazingly strong, caring and protective. And most of all, he's a man of truth. He wants his life to stand for something good. I think I admire that *most* about him."

A tight smile pressed Gemma's lips as her gaze slid away from mine, a bit evasively. "But what about the fact he's with The Brethren? Doesn't that concern you?" And her focus returned immediately to me.

I shook my head. "Alec's a good man. I met some really nice people while I was at The Oracle. Good people who are trying to do the right thing. I don't think The Brethren as a whole is bad, but there are some parts of it and some people associated with it that aren't all I'd hope them to be. Alec's struggling with that right now. I wish I could help him with it."

"Hmm," she responded, looking thoughtful.

"Gemma, can I ask what's going on with you and Jax? Caleb mentioned there's been some tension."

Her head lowered as she teased her salad with her fork. "I know. I heard you and Caleb talking as you came up the elevator." She then paused as if considering something, then sighed. "I'm not sure I should discuss this with you. Caleb doesn't know . . ."

I reached across the table to take her hand, squeezing gently. "I promise, whatever you say to me will remain between us. You just seem like you could use someone to talk to."

There was a long pause before she spoke, and her voice dropped nearly to a whisper. "Jax changed after you disappeared. He kept me at such a distance. I didn't understand at first. I thought he might be struggling with some sort of feelings he had for you."

My brows shot up. I wasn't expecting that at all.

"Of course, now I know that he was tormented over realizing that you were his granddaughter and that on that last day he had let The Brethren leave with you. I think in his mind as soon as he finished helping Caleb he was going to come get you. But then he couldn't sense you. He struggled terribly with regret over the decision he made that day."

So Jax realized I was his granddaughter during the confrontation in the meadow with Alec, yet didn't say anything. I wasn't quite sure how I felt about that.

"But if you know that's what was bothering him, why's there still so much distance between you?"

Shaking her head, her face began to crumble and she looked as though she might cry. "Before this happened I foolishly thought I might be in love with him. But when he pushed me away like that . . . when he wouldn't trust me to confide in—to help him with his pain—I realized that he didn't feel the same. What I felt wasn't love; it was dependence. He's been the man in my life for the last twenty years, minus a few dalliances with boyfriends. I saw that I needed to get away from him, get some perspective. That's why I moved here. I think it's been good for me."

"You *moved* here? Do Jax and Caleb know that?"

She uttered a startled snort, clearly spontaneous, and it seemed to catch her off guard. "No way. Have you tried to tell those two testosterone-loaded alphas something they don't want to hear? I figure they'll catch on in another month."

My heart ached for both Gemma and Jax. I had little doubt that Jax Walker, in fact, loved Gemma May. He was just afraid of losing her—and probably afraid of crossing a line after taking care of her for so many years. "I think he misses you, Gemma—very much."

Gemma shook her head as if trying to deny that possibility, and then she swiped at some tears that had surprised her by rolling down her cheeks, unwilled and unexpectedly uncontrollable. "The distance has been good for me. I needed to move on."

"Gemma . . . ," I said worriedly, reaching for her hand across the table.

She closed her eyes, and when she opened them again her expression had completely changed. "Enough of this sad stuff," she sniffed. "Let's talk about something happy. Like the fact that you're going to be mated to certain devilishly handsome vampire."

Just thinking about Caleb made me feel as if the whole room was lighting up around me. It hadn't even been half a day, and I already missed him. "I have to admit, I'm nervous. I know only a little of the ceremony. Is it like a marriage ceremony?"

She shook her head. "It's much more intimate. Just between you and Caleb. It's a sharing of each other's blood. Are you uncomfortable with that idea?"

"No. I was drinking blood at The Oracle to increase my strength. By the end, I was drinking it every day."

"Every day? That's quite a bit for a mostly human Dhampir. They weren't forcing you to drink it, were they?"

I shook my head. "But please don't say anything to Caleb. I seem to be having trouble getting off the blood now that I've gotten used to it."

"Why do you think that would bother Caleb?"

"Because it makes me less human. He likes the human woman in me."

"He *loves* all of you—not just the human part. If you're struggling with this, he'd want to know. He'd want to help you."

"I can't, Gemma. It's just . . . Can I ask you something?"

"Of course."

"Do you have fangs that come out when you drink?"

A half-hearted smile set on her lips as realization dawned on her. "Yes, Olivia. Every Dhampir has fangs. Are you worried about whether Caleb would find you less human if he saw them?"

I didn't respond, keeping my gaze averted.

"Olivia, you need to talk with him about this. I know he loves you and could care less about any of this stuff. But you need to know it for yourself, especially since you're going to be mated to him. Just promise me that if after a week or two you're still struggling with this, you'll talk to him."

I nodded. "I will."

***

Back at the condo, finally, I deposited a ton of shopping bags at my feet and collapsed into one of the lounge chairs with a heavy sigh of weariness. "I can't believe we've scheduled another day of this tomorrow. I feel like I bought an entire store's worth of clothing today."

Gemma just continued to move around the condo, depositing items with quick efficiency—including a few new ones she'd bought for herself—in their appropriate places, prancing from closet to closet as if she hadn't exerted herself at all during our marathon shopping session. "Don't be silly," she smiled. "We haven't even got you any warm, winter items yet."

Lord, help me. "Gemma? Do you mind if we run over to my place? It's not far from here. I didn't think about packing a night bag. My toothbrush and everything are still there."

"Sure, no problem."

I pushed slowly to my feet. "Do you mind if we go now? 'Cause if I get comfortable, I won't get back up."

About fifteen minutes later, we were headed towards the entrance of my building when I recognized two very familiar faces trying to call up at the door. "Maya!" I cried, racing up to throw my arms around her as I smiled up at Alec. "What are you doing here?"

"I wanted to see you. I've been so worried. Alec assured me that you were doing well, and now I know it's true. I feel the joy and love in your heart."

"Oh, Maya, it's so wonderful to be back here. I have to catch you up. Are you staying?"

"No, I have to be in Vancouver tonight. But we have a couple of hours."

"Wipe off that frown," Alec teased as he walked up, brushing the hair back from my forehead and kissing my temple. "You look good . . . happy."

"I am. I can't thank you and Joseph enough for making this happen."

"Seeing your face this happy again is thanks enough." Alec then seem to completely shift his attention to the woman standing quietly back from him. His crooked grin flashed at me for a moment and he waggled his brows just before turning to saunter towards Gemma. She appeared as if she were bracing herself for battle, planting her hands on her small hips. "So has the fiery redhead lost her bite today?"

"Don't you ever give up?"

"No," he laughed, as if that should be quite obvious. He then reached for one of her tightly planted hands and led her towards some flowered containers in front of the building . . . and she let him. "Here," he said, "let's give them a chance to catch up."

Maya and I sat down on a slat bench among the planter boxes. "I'm sorry I didn't get a chance to say goodbye. Have you been all right? Reese or Jude haven't given you any problems, have they?"

"I've been fine—great, in fact. Phinneas has been taking good care of me—making sure they don't come near me."

"So Reese hasn't sent Phin away as he threatened?"

Maya's eyes rolled with relief. "No, thank God. It seems Reese is trying to keep a low profile after his not-so-private run-in with Joseph. He and Lucas say 'hi'. I think they miss you. And Kane, of course, wanted me to remind you that his offer still stands if the vampire, quote, '*isn't getting it done for you.*'"

I couldn't help but laugh at that. It was so Kane.

"It's been kind of weird there since this whole thing with Reese went down. Most of it centers on the fact that Alec has left. Everyone there knows how important his future is to The Brethren and The Oracle."

"I've been worried for him, Maya," I whispered, making sure Alec wouldn't hear. "I think this whole thing with his uncle is much more difficult for him than he's letting on."

Maya glanced over my shoulder, an amused smile crossing her lips. "I don't think he's too concerned about it at the moment."

I turned to see him leaning over Gemma, who was relaxed against the building's brick facade. His lips were just above hers as he slowly brushed a purple flower he'd picked from the planter box across her collarbone. Although she appeared perfectly calm, I could hear her heavier breathing, her attention now completely focused on him. "Let's give this another try, shall we," he began. "Have dinner with me tonight. Or, better yet, may I cook for you? I happen to be a very good cook."

"Yes, how surprising that you think so. Confidence doesn't seem to be your problem." He laughed, his attention wholly absorbed on her now.

"He certainly does have a way about him that commands attention, doesn't he?" Maya suggested.

I blew out a hard breath. "He's going to get himself in big trouble."

Maya frowned. "What do you mean?"

"Jax! That's what I mean. He'll kill him for going near her."

"Jax—the vampire?" Maya blinked. "Oh, he's big . . . very big. That is a problem. Have you warned him?"

"Oh, I've warned him. But the fool just took it as a personal challenge." Then I sighed heavily. "I can't let him hurt her."

"I've never known Alec to hurt a woman intentionally. He's a good guy." Maya was right, but I stilled worried. "Oh, I almost forgot. I brought you a couple of personnel items you left in your room. I need to grab them from the car. I'll be right back."

While she was gone, I snuck another peek behind me. Alec was now running his fingertips down Gemma's sides as he pressed a slow kiss on her cheek. Her eyes were closed, her body relaxed, taking in his touch as his lips trailed towards hers. I gasped, not believing the spark that was getting ignited so quickly. *The boy must have a death wish!* Either that or he really was interested. "I want to get to know you, Gemma," he said with an enticing whisper. "It's just one little dinner."

"I'm watching Olivia tonight," she replied, her normally cheery voice sounding a bit strained.

Alec frowned at that. "Where's Caleb? Why's he not with her?"

"Not that it's any of your business, but he's preparing the house before bringing her up."

"So he's taking her back to the mountain?"

Gemma seemed to stiffen uncomfortably. "Yes. Is that why I have your attention? So you can keep tabs on him?"

Alec's crooked grin returned, and he purposefully moved his lips to her ear, his words whispered with challenge. "Have dinner with me and find out."

"Alec? Gemma?" I called.

They both turned their attention toward me right away. "What is it, Olivia?"

"Would you guys mind if I spent an hour or two here with Maya before it gets dark? It'll probably be the last time I see her for a while. I'm safe here at home, and the sun's out. I have my necklace, and she can drop me off at the condo on her way out of town."

Alec wrapped his arm behind Gemma's shoulders and gave her a quick squeeze. "I don't see a problem with it, but I doubt the spitfire here will agree with me on anything."

Gemma ignored the remark, stepping around him, and Alec just smiled. "OK, but be back to the condo before six. It gets dark earlier now."

"I will."

***

Around five, Maya dropped me off across the street from the building. She had to head out of town sooner than six, which had me returning earlier than I expected, but I figured Gemma would be pleased. I didn't want her to worry as the skies began to grow dark.

I so enjoyed my time with Maya. She told me how tensions were still high between my Guardians and Jude. They refused to even acknowledge him while continuing to try and discover the truth of what was really going on at The Oracle. Reese was also quite surly about the fact that his nephew had abandoned him to baby-sit me, someone who he saw as unworthy. I was just glad Alec was away from his uncle for a while.

Maya's best news, however, was that Phin had finally told her how much he cared for her, though she already had a pretty good idea because she could feel it. She literally beamed as she talked about how the Hunter doted on her every whim. I found it hard to believe that Maya would ever ask for very much. She wasn't the type.

As I crossed the street, I suddenly stopped. The feeling was back. My chest felt tight as I took in the energy shooting straight at me.

Vampire energy.

Chapter Twenty

It had been so long since I'd felt unknown vampire energy that I hesitated before responding. But soon I understood that I was not in any imminent danger. The sun was still above the horizon, and I was wearing my necklace. So I decided to use this as an opportunity to assess the situation, as Alec and Lucas had taught me in defense class.

The energy was foreign and faint, which meant the vampire was on the outskirts of my sensing abilities, a few blocks away. I was aware that he was maintaining his distance, so I trusted that he wasn't coming any closer; he couldn't sense me because of my necklace. This was a situation of me crossing paths, which was bound to happen many times in my life. I just needed to be aware and move away from him.

Satisfied with my assessment, I continued forward into the lobby, pulling my elevator key from my purse. Pressing the button for the top floor, I felt the energy again. This time *it was* closer, but soon seemed to move away again. *See, no need to panic, Olivia.*

Then I was startled by the sound of Gemma's voice crying out. My Dhampir ears caught the sound a little less than half way up the thirty floors to the penthouse. My heart sped up to a wild beat; it sounded like something was very wrong. Maybe I hadn't assessed the danger correctly. My hand shot to my chest, which felt normal, the tightening now gone. She cried out again as I hit the button several more times, trying to get the cab upstairs faster to help her. That's when I heard another voice— a male voice—bellowing out in unison with hers. To my horror I realized that Gemma was not screaming out in pain, but in passion.

Oh my gosh! I was interrupting!

My hands flew to the elevator panel, trying to find any other button, any other floor to stop the car on, but the private elevator had none. There was only one stop—and I would soon be landing on it. My face flushed with wild embarrassment as the couple's cries grew louder and closer together. Gemma was moaning in intense pleasure as she called out the name of the man who was immersing her in it . . . and I was flabbergasted even more. *Alec?*

What was she doing? I thought she found him arrogant and insufferable.

Unavoidably, I heard the climatic sounds of the impassioned couple. Alec then released a loud, almost startled gasp as the elevator dinged, announcing my arrival. My heart was in my throat as I scrunched myself into the corner of the elevator, pleading to God that the door wasn't about to open to display them right in front of me. But to my relief, after poking my head out, the heated pair was nowhere to be found.

From her bedroom, Alec and Gemma's post-passion panting was audible as I reached for the button to take me back downstairs, hoping they were too wrapped up in their own bliss to notice I was there. "Hi, Olivia," Gemma called out as if nothing was out of the norm. "Make yourself at home. I'll be out in a minute." *So much for sneaking back out.*

I went to the kitchen island and perched myself on a stool, continuing hearing the pair's voices from inside her bedroom at the other end of the condo. "Well, that was something new," Alec said breathlessly. "I've never been levitated off the mattress while I came. Does that mean I pleased you?"

Levitation was Gemma's special Dhampir gift, and it seemed that she had put it to an unexpected use. Her breathing was still labored as she answered, "You maybe pleased me a little."

"A little?" he laughed. "I'll try to remember that next time."

"I haven't decided if there'll be a next time." Then I heard the rustling of sheets and a hard slap against bare skin. "Now, get dressed and come out and speak with Olivia."

"Yes, ma'am," he drawled.

Within seconds, Gemma was standing in front of me in a

soft, ivory colored robe. I sat stiffly on the stool, too embarrassed to think clearly. "How was your time with Maya?" she asked, her relaxed manner even more confusing.

"It . . . it . . . was good."

Gemma's brows crinkled. "What's wrong with you?"

I blinked back at her. "Nothing."

Opening the refrigerator, she asked, "Are you hungry?" just as a beaming Alec emerged from the hallway, fully clothed in the jeans and fitted tee from earlier in the day. He had a broad smile from ear to ear as he walked up and kissed me on the forehead. It was then that I noticed the two fang marks in his neck. Alec did indeed like the bite of a Dhampir, and he certainly didn't seem to be concerned about exceeding his toxin levels at the moment. "Any problems?" he asked, perching himself on the stool next to me.

"N—No." His eyes narrowed cautiously. "Well, I mean . . . I sensed a vampire in the area downstairs, but it was nothing."

"Did he come closer to you?"

"Only briefly, after the sun went behind the clouds, then he moved away. I practiced assessing the situation like you taught me. I was just crossing paths."

"Good," he said proudly. "Can you sense him now?"

I was shaking my head when Gemma answered, "No. He's gone." She pulled cheese, meat sauce, and precooked lasagna noodles from the fridge to the island countertop while Alec continued to talk with me as though nothing had just happened between them. I couldn't believe it.

"Caleb's taking you up to the . . . *tree house*, you call it?"

"Tree house?" Gemma laughed. "I suppose that fits."

"Is that a problem?"

Grabbing several slices of cheese from a plate Gemma had set on the counter, he waggled his brows at her as he ate them, obviously trying to flirt with her. "No," he replied. "But we do need to agree on a way that I can check in with you weekly—to make sure everything's going well." He winked. "I'm not on vacation here, you know."

The man was sure acting like he was on vacation—and getting himself into more and more trouble by the minute. "I understand. It's more difficult for you to get up the mountain this time of year."

He snorted at that. "Not just difficult. The pass is closed. Perhaps that's what Caleb's counting on to keep me at a distance. He can't stand the fact that The Brethren's having me watch you."

"You two . . . ," Gemma replied, shaking her head. "You need to figure it out. You both have Olivia's best interest at heart. At least that's one thing you testosterone-filled behemoths can agree on."

Alec grumbled, "Regardless, I still need to be able to do my job."

"You can drive up to Crystal Mountain and rent a snowmobile at the resort. Olivia can meet you at the meadow," she said, as if the solution were obvious.

"I can talk to Caleb about this when he comes to get me tomorrow."

Alec stood stiffly erect, his muscled stance announcing his refusal to back down an inch. "You can talk to him about it, but he *will* agree to this if he wants The Brethren to remain out of his hair."

"Alec!"

"I'm sorry, Olivia. But I'm not going to just tell Joseph that everything's fine because you want me to. I need to know that you're safe. That this is what's best for you."

"Fine! But he's not exactly the easiest person to tell that he has to agree to something."

Gemma stifled a laugh. "That's an understatement."

A pleased smirk crossed the Guardians face, his light eyes brightening at the thought of irritating the vampire. "Stop that," I scolded. "You're no better. You're both ridiculously stubborn."

"Comparing me to that grumpy vampire? That's my cue to go." Alec looked at Gemma, who was still busily preparing the lasagna dish. "Walk me down?" She nodded as Alec gave me a quick goodbye kiss on the forehead. "Stay safe, little Charmer. I'll see you in one week."

As the pair headed into the elevator, Gemma relaxed casually against the back cab wall, while Alec followed and leaned in above her. While the elevator doors were closing, his grinning lips were falling to the crook of her neck. "When can I see you again?" he asked, his words muffled against her skin.

"I told you," she began with slightly rougher breath, "I haven't decided yet whether to see you again."

"Why not?"

"I don't like your disregard for Caleb."

"For you, I'll try harder."

"Right. I don't think so."

Suddenly, Gemma exhaled a sharp breath, a tiny squeal escaping her as if the air had been thrown from her lungs by being jolted off her feet. Then there were several rumbled sounds against the cab wall. "Does the fiery redhead need some convincing?"

"Alec, I have to get back to—" Her voice was cut off by her own delighted gasp, followed by several low moans. "Alec, we can't . . . *oohh* . . ."

A hand slammed against the stop button in the elevator. "No," Alec breathed. "If the little spitfire needs convincing then we'll take our time." Gemma responded with a tiny, muffled cry, then several more soft moans that conveyed how much he was soothing her body at that moment. "That's it. Relax, Gemma," he whispered. "Nice and slow . . . Just relax." His low, slow groan rolled over his harder breaths. "Take me inside you —deep inside you."

My entire face felt flushed with heat. I jumped up from the stool, trying to fill my mind with any other random thoughts to block out the private exchange my Dhampir ears were invading. I knew that living in a house where all of its occupants had extra-sensitive hearing meant I would overhear some things, but I hadn't had a chance to get used to the idea yet. Gemma was obviously already used to it, overhearing Caleb's and my loud exchanges, which explained her casual indifference about interrupting her and Alec.

"Alec," she murmured.

"You feel so good . . . so good."

Meanwhile, I fumbled with the controls for the IPOD dock in the kitchen. "No, I don't want to go back to featured artist!" I blurted at the stupid player as I struggled to just get any song to play.

"*Alec!*"

At last, success! Music finally began blaring through the speakers, just as the sounds coming from the elevator seemed to reach a climactic peak. I tried to ignore it by finishing up the lasagna noodles Gemma had started, but as I worked I couldn't help but think of Jax. He loved Gemma. I believed it with all of my heart. But he'd pushed her away while trying to find me, and now I feared his whole world was about to change drastically—and he didn't even know it. He was losing her, and possibly to a man who belonged to an organization he despised.

I loved Alec and wanted him to be happy. If Gemma was the special person who could help him heal from the pain of his uncle's betrayal, then I would support them both. Only time would tell now how serious Alec's pursuit of Gemma really was, but if he hurt my friend in any way, I would be furious with him., I did agree with Maya, though, that he wouldn't do it intentionally. Alec was a warrior in his own right, confident and secure in himself. I had seen the tender side of him. He would give his life to protect someone he cared for, and he always eased away the pain caused by others. A Guardian by nature, he would always be a protector of souls.

The elevator was quiet for a long while until I heard it moving down again. "Well?" Alec asked expectantly.

"Day after tomorrow—dinner," Gemma replied, trying to calm her hard-working lungs.

Alec laughed. "I don't know if I can wait that long."

"You're gonna have to, 'cause Caleb will kill you if he finds you here."

When Gemma returned a few minutes later, she had a

radiant smile on her face. Though her hair was a bit ruffled and a fine sheen of perspiration marred her forehead, her cheeks were flushed with happiness. As she neared, I stared at her in complete bewilderment. "What is it, Olivia?"

"How . . ." was all I could think to say.

She waved a dismissive hand. "Oh, come on. You said he's a good man."

"Yes . . . but what happened? How?"

Gemma checked the lasagna I had placed in the oven while she was . . . busy, and then turned to me. Throwing her arms up, she said, a bit flustered, "I don't know. He needed a ride back because Maya stayed with you, and next thing I knew we were going at it in the front seat of my car . . ." As my jaw dropped, she added, " . . . which isn't easy, by the way, there's not a lot of room in there."

"Y—You were together in your car . . . before the bedroom . . . then the elevator?" She shrugged her shoulders in reply. "But . . . but I thought you found him arrogant!"

She splayed her hands out in front of her. "Oh, he's completely arrogant. But if there's one place it really works for him, it's in there," she said, motioning with her thumb toward the bedroom. "I've no complaints. Of course, I'm not telling him that. His head's big enough as it is."

"Gemma," I began much more seriously, "if Alec makes you happy, then I support that, but what about your feelings for Jax? I saw how much it was hurting you to talk about him today at lunch. That has to means something."

Gemma's smile disappeared. "I told you, he doesn't feel that way about me. Isabeau was the love of Jax's life—his soulmate. No one will ever compare to her in his eyes, and I'd be a fool to try. I need to move on."

I had a lot of trouble believing that was true. I'd never heard Jax talk about my grandmother. Reaching over with a gentle hand, I touched her arm. "Just be careful," I said. "I don't think Alec would ever hurt you, but I'm worried that you may be hurting yourself."

"Don't be silly, Olivia. I would hardly call a little rumbling around in an elevator painful." She then rubbed her hand gently along her side. "Except that the stupid grab bar is hard on one's hip."

I wasn't really sure how to answer that.

***

Late the next day, after another long marathon of shopping, the sun was beginning to set. I was focused on getting back to the condo and dropping the half-dozen plus bags in my hands to the floor and collapsing on the sofa. But about a block away from the building I felt it—felt him. Caleb had returned.

"Gemma!" I squealed.

"I know," she sighed, "come on."

Suddenly, I was renewed. The weight of the bags in my arms was now like air. Waiting at the elevator, Gemma followed behind more casually. I, on the other hand, was bouncing around as if the laws of gravity didn't apply to me. So when the elevator door finally opened, my heart surely lurched right out of my chest. Caleb was drop-dead sexy, leaning against the back wall, his arms and feet crossed casually in front of him. Dropping all of my bags, I launched myself into his arms.

A shocked laugh escaped him as he wrapped his arms around me. "I guess this means you missed me," he said silkily beneath my smothering of kisses along his neck. Without effort, he lifted me off my feet until my lips were slanting over his. Taking me against his mouth, he swept the air right out of my lungs as he caressed and massaged until I parted my lips to him fully, my body falling pliant against him.

"Mmm, you know I missed you."

"Well, I hope it was worth it," he smiled. "Did you get everything you needed?"

I nodded in quick response. "And more."

"Silk?" he questioned, nuzzling his cheek against my neck. "Did you buy lots and lots of silk? I so do like your silky underthings."

"All right, all right," Gemma said with an exasperated tone

as she picked up the bags I dropped. "Can you two at least wait till we get upstairs?"

When we reached the top, Caleb moved all of the bags Gemma and I were carrying into the second bedroom, the one I was using. When he returned, his expression was much more serious. Leaning back on the wide arm of one of the lounge chairs, he stretched his long legs out in front of him, crossing his ankles. "You two have anything you want to tell me?"

Confused, I glanced over at Gemma. By the guarded look on her face I could tell she knew exactly where he was going with this, but she kept her expression smooth. "No," I answered with a shrug.

"Olivia!" he growled. "Alec's been here. His scent's all over the place."

Full awareness hit me about as subtly as a Mack truck. I hadn't thought about the fact that Caleb would pick up on Alec's scent. Apparently, neither had Gemma, which surprised me, since she had been used to living with Caleb's and Jax's super senses. Although . . . to be fair . . . that probably wasn't on her mind when she was with Alec.

Throwing another glance back at Gemma, I noted that her eyes refused to give anything away. I wanted to help her, even though I knew that Caleb would be furious. Gemma at least needed enough time to discover if Alec was worth the rift it would cause in their coven. "He was just checking to see how I was doing," I replied into the awkward silence.

"You're home now with me. It's not his concern."

I anchored my hands on my hips. "You know as well as I do, he has a job to do here. You need to let him do it."

Caleb's impatient expression showed he wasn't going to argue the point with me; instead, he turned to Gemma. "And how could you let this happen? Let him in here? Jax would be furious if he knew someone from The Brethren was in our home. I don't want to lie to him."

"Well, then, don't," she snapped right back. "Jax will just have to deal with it."

"What the devil's the matter with you, Gemma May?"

Oh this wasn't good. Caleb used her full name. Standing up from the chair, he walked directly to her, his six foot four frame towering over the small woman. "Jax and I discussed it last night. We've had enough of this *mood* you've been in. We've tried to give you space, but now it's time for you to come home."

Oh, not good at all. Caleb wasn't going to get very far with this heavy-handed approach. I felt sorry for him, though. He and Jax were doing it out of concern, out of love. Gemma just wouldn't see it that way.

Her face flashed with anger. "I'm staying right here! Jax can just kiss my—"

"Stop it!" Caleb barked. "You're acting like a child. Why are you so angry with him? He hasn't done anything to you."

I slapped my hand against my forehead. Men could be so daft. Caleb simply couldn't see the problem. Jax needed to *do* something, say something, or he was going to lose Gemma.

"Ooohhh," Gemma sounded furiously. "I'm not going back with you—and you both can just deal with it!" She then marched off towards her bedroom, slamming the door behind her.

It took a minute for Caleb to recover from the shock of having her walk out on him. "That doesn't work, you know," he called after her, finally. "I know you can still hear me. It's not safe for you to be here by yourself. Not with The Brethren so close by."

"Caleb," I replied with surprise. "Alec would never hurt her."

He muttered several angry curse words then headed to my room at the opposite end of the condo. I followed him, closing the door behind us once we were inside. He sat on the edge of the bed, staring out across the city skyline, his concern for Gemma plainly reflected in his strained features. Kneeling behind him on the bed, I smoothed my fingertips over his wide shoulders before sliding my arms around him and resting my cheek against his back shoulder. "That could've gone a little better."

He lowered his head, shaking it back and forth and heaving a long, hard sigh. "I don't understand what's wrong with her.

She's done this before, but it's never been this bad."

"Why isn't Jax down here saying these things to her? Telling her he's concerned?"

He snorted, throwing his arm out in an emphasized gesture. "Because she blows up even more at him. He can't seem to say anything right."

I slinked around Caleb's body until I rested on his thighs, curling my legs around his hips. His arms pulled me closer to him as he leaned his forehead against mine. "Tell me what you feel, Caleb. *Feel* her." I hoped somehow I could get the two men to realize what was going on without having to betray Gemma's confidence.

As he focused, his face became pained. "She's crying. She never cries."

"Yes, I can hear that. But what do *you* feel?"

"I feel confusion, and anger, and pain." He pulled me tight against him until my cheek slid up to caress the cool skin of his neck. "You know what's wrong with her, don't you?"

"Yes," I replied, simply.

"Tell me," he pleaded. "I want to help her. I can't stand to feel her in this much pain."

"I promised her I wouldn't say anything."

Caleb drew back with surprise. "Olivia!"

"What I can tell you," I began, smoothing the stress lines in his brow with my thumbs, "is that this isn't something *you* can fix. But what you *can* do is go in there and apologize. She needs your support right now, Caleb, not the over-protective sod."

His eyes were soft with emotion as he kissed me on the lips. "On one condition."

"And that is . . ."

A boyish smile slid over his features. "By the time I return, you'll already be naked under those bed covers."

"You have a deal," I replied. "But can we try something new tonight?"

His smile widened. "What did you have in mind?"

"That we make love silently," I said, lifting my chin to meet his tickling little nibbles. Gemma's had a hard enough day without having to listen to us scream and moan through the night."

"That'll be a challenge," he breathed. "Are you sure you're up for it?"

"Mmm-hmm," I sighed dreamily. "And just think how much more powerful it'll be tomorrow night when we don't have to be quiet."

Chapter Twenty-One

The next morning I stood in awe beneath a cottony sheet of gray clouds as I stared at the surrounding peaks from the parking lot of Crystal Mountain Ski Resort. It was early November, and for as far as one could see, the landscape was flocked with snow-capped evergreens. The familiar scents of pine and fir brought an instant smile to my face. How I had missed this place!

Caleb and I watched as the diehard early morning skiers took advantage of fresh powder on the slopes. "It's beautiful here this time of year, isn't it?"

"No, not beautiful—*magical*," I replied, enveloped in slow amazement. "I've missed these mountains. I've missed your home."

Caleb wrapped his arms around me and squeezed. "It's your home too, Olivia. Don't ever doubt it. Your home now is with me."

A home, a place to belong, a man to share it with. It was everything my heart wanted in this life, and I would fight to hold onto every piece of it. "Are you ready to start our trek up the mountain?" he asked as he buttoned up my new wool coat, red, his favorite color.

I nodded, with a smile.

"Good. I'll come down tonight after the resort is closed to gather the rest of your things."

"Are you sure? That's a lot of bags."

He responded with a soft laugh. "Well, maybe we'll recruit Grandpa Jax to help." We walked beyond the edge of the parking lot until we were out of sight of others, then he surprised me by sweeping me up into his arms. I blinked back at him. "You don't have to carry me. I can run pretty fast now. I can follow you."

"Oh, OK," he said, releasing my legs back down to the plowed surface and then pointing ahead of him. "We need to head that direction."

"Just try to keep up," I challenged, which wasn't a very good idea. I made it only a few steps before my feet dropped from under me as if I were falling victim to quicksand. Before I knew it, I was knee deep in snow and Caleb was throwing his head back in a deep laughter that shook his shoulders, still standing in the plowed area I had left him.

Embarrassed, I put my hands on my hips and tilted my head accusingly. "Very funny."

Still laughing, he said, "*What?* The Brethren didn't teach you to run over snow?"

"No smart-ass, they didn't. But I'm glad you're finding this so amusing. Are you going to stand there and laugh at me all day, or can I get a little help?"

Within a single breath, Caleb was beside me, his legs sinking into the snow just as mine had, but in light of his enormous height, he didn't look nearly as ridiculous as I did. "What are you laughing at? You're stuck, just like me."

"Sorry to disappoint you, but I can't fly. In order to stay above the snow your feet must skim above it so they don't have time to sink in."

"Show me."

He picked me up and moved me back to the plowed area so I could start on packed ground. "Once you start, keep your legs moving fast. Let the force of your forward movement carry you above the ground."

I frowned at him. "That sounds an awful lot like flying."

He smiled. "Just give it a try."

After a couple false starts, I was doing pretty well until I took a tumble, face first, into the snow, which caused Caleb to howl again with laughter. My resounding reply was a snowball to his backside, to which he swung around and responded with a truly evil grin. "That was a bad idea," he warned, then scooped up an entire armful of snow.

"No!" I yelped, but the fear of him drowning me in more snow turned out to be the eventual catalyst for keeping my feet skimming over ground permanently, except for a few more pitfalls and stumbles. By the time we reached the tree house I was soaking wet and more than a little cold, but as I stared up at the amazing structure nestled high in the trees above us I didn't care. The small dwelling was supported by round, concrete columns that were textured and stained to resembled tree trunks. Clustered among the real trees, the house became nearly invisible. "What's wrong?" Caleb asked, seeming to be concerned by my sudden silence.

"This will probably make no sense . . . but it's just that I've been away for so long, I had begun to think that this place couldn't be as beautiful as my memory of it—like I had imagined it differently. But it is. It really is." He smiled at hearing my reverence for the home his architectural mind had created.

From above us the familiar sound of several glass panes swinging open all at once invited us up. "Are you able to make this jump?" Caleb asked, referring to the nearly thirty feet it was up to the tree house doors.

"No," I responded with a frown. "Only about fifteen feet at most, and that's with a lot of effort."

He reached for my hand just then. "Then we'll do this together."

I smiled at him as he secured his arm around my waist. With one powerful push-off from the ground, Caleb sprung us upward amongst the evergreens, and before I knew it we had landed inside the glass doors, where one very imposing figure was waiting for us. "Jax!" I cried, throwing my arms around him, practically strangling him at his neck. "My Grandpa!"

He released one of his deep-throated chuckles at my ear. "It is good to finally have my granddaughter home where she belongs." He pulled back from me, his warm, amber eyes soft like spicy rum in the light—and filled with concern. "Are you all right?"

By his tone it was apparent that he was asking about more than just my time at The Oracle, and I suspected Caleb had confided in him to some degree about what had happened with Jude. I was OK with that, both because Jax was family and he was the one person who could help Caleb deal with his own anger over it. That was something *I* really needed because I didn't want him going back to The Oracle. "I'm much better now that I'm here," I replied, "and anxious to hear the story of my family."

"We will get to that. But let us first get you settled and out of these wet clothes. Caleb has something he would like to show you."

Jax's gaze then lifted over my shoulder to Caleb, the liquid warmth that had been in his eyes changing instantly then to a quiet stillness. "She did not come with you?"

No clarification was needed as to who *she* was.

"No," Caleb replied evenly. "She's being pretty stubborn about it. I don't believe this is just one of her moods."

A fierce, but controlled growl rumbled inside Jax's chest. Swinging his muscled frame away from us, he held that steely control even as his hands balled into white-knuckled fists at his sides. "What the devil is wrong with her? She has always confided in me about everything . . . and now she will not even come home."

Caleb looked to me with an almost pleading expression. He was silently asking me to reveal what I knew, but I couldn't. I couldn't break Gemma's trust. But I could try to get them going the right direction. "Maybe you should go see her, Jax—talk to her. Tell her that you miss her."

Jax's stared absently out into the distance. "Perhaps you are right," he replied, but I could see his hesitation. His reaction made it obvious that his emotions regarding Gemma were a little too close to the surface for him just then. I wondered if that was the reason he had Caleb confront her on the issue of coming home—instead of doing it himself.

"Come," Caleb said, retreating into that soft, velvety timbre of his. "I worked on a little project while you were away that I'd like to show you."

"A project?" I smiled. "Well, I loved your last project." His last project had been the amazing glass atrium he built on my terrace to house the grand piano. Incredibly gifted in architecture and engineering, I could only imagine what his creative mind would come up with next. Together we leapt up to the second level (the hastily built stairs I had used the first time I stayed in the tree house were now gone) where Caleb led us the short distance to his study. Both he and Jax had studies instead of bedrooms, because the need for a bedroom was pointless. They rarely slept. That was unique to them as Daywalkers. Nightwalkers, like Davin, came out only at night and had to sleep during the day to restore their energy.

A broad smile tugged at the corners of my lips as I remembered the makeshift bed I had made for us in the corner of his study, which consisted of a mattress on the floor and some nice bedding. Though certainly not grand by any means, there was so much love shared there—to me, it was perfect.

However, my happy expression soon faded when we entered the room and our bed was gone. I guess I shouldn't have expected that he would have kept it all this time. I tried to hide my disappointment at realizing we would probably be using Gemma's room again, the only true bedroom in the house. It just didn't feel right to me to use her room, even if she was away right now and not using it. "You're looking the wrong direction," Caleb said, pointing to the other corner of the room, or at least what used to be a corner. Now there was an open staircase that led to another level above, a level that hadn't been there before.

"What's this?" I blinked back at him.

A sly smile crossed his lips. "I guess you're going to have to walk up there to find out."

I didn't walk, but instead flew up the stairs in my excitement. Once I reached the landing I halted, utterly flabbergasted. Before me was a beautiful and cozy master suite, with thick trees nestling virtually against the glass beyond. A king-sized bed, with no headboard or footboard, handsomely dressed in silky ivory and taupe linens, floated on a platform at the center of the room. Dozens of unscented candles made the room sparkle, and in the corner was a brand new upright piano, its finish sleek and black. The instrument was just the right size to fit the cozy room, and I loved the thought of being able to play for Caleb as we would lounge the day away. "I . . . I . . ."

"You're speechless," Caleb smiled. "Is that good?"

"This is amazing. But you didn't have to do this. I would've been happy sharing the mattress with you on the floor."

He moved very close to me, his gray eyes shimmering with happiness as his thumb traced over the rise of my cheekbone. "This was the only thing that kept me sane while you were gone —the thought of this moment—to be able to offer you a real home when you returned. Not some hard mattress on the floor."

I wrapped my arms around him, standing on my tippy-toes to press my cheek against his neck. "Make love to me, Caleb— here, in our new room."

Smoothing his hand over my cheek to bring my head back to face him, he stared down at me and said, "We'll take our time. And I'll be gentle and slow. So slow you'll be begging, my sweet. Tonight, you *will* scream for me."

***

The next day I unpacked and organized all of my purchases in my new closet—no, in *our* new closet. It still felt a little strange, and I rather feared that if I said it out loud it might all disappear. But the full extent of the damage Gemma and I had done shopping was there in front of me as I tried to fit everything on my half of the closet. I really needed about half of Caleb's side, too, and he had the space to spare, but I didn't want him to feel overcrowded by me just as we were beginning our life together.

Gently, I traced my fingers down the sleeves of one of his favorite hand-tailored shirts, inhaling the earthy scent of him that permeated the fibers. The best part of all this was getting to share the space with him, just as I was now sharing my life with him. It seemed almost too good to be true. I thought back to that awful day on Vancouver Island when I inhaled the scent of his shirt for what I thought would be the last time. I had felt so utterly defeated in that moment, but now I had all of this. I had him. "You don't have to smell the clothes," his husky voice said from behind me. "You've the real thing right here."

Turning to him, his strong presence seemed to reach out in pulses like little electric shocks as he approached me. "What were you thinking about just now?" he asked. "You seemed so lost in thought."

"Your shirt—the one I'd left on Vancouver Island," I replied as I ran my fingertips over the sleeve of the shirt he was wearing.

"Mmm," he purred, wrapping his arms around me. "Do you think about that day often?"

"No," I replied, leaning my head against his shoulder. "Not anymore."

He sighed, a deep exhale that sounded like a cross between frustration and regret. "I'm sorry you went through that. You wouldn't have, if I'd refused to let you leave with Alec."

I blinked up at him. "Caleb, you couldn't have changed that day. You know Alec and The Brethren weren't about to let me stay here with you—"

"He wouldn't have had a choice in the matter," Caleb growled.

"—and I wasn't going to let either one of you get hurt over me," I finished. "Davin was already coming for me. He was the one who sent the Rogue that attacked Gemma and me here."

A low, incensed growl briefly rumbled inside his chest. "Jax and I need to find—"

"No!" I cut in. "It's too dangerous. He's a new Nightwalker, but he's gaining strength fast."

Caleb just scowled, "All the more reason to find him now before he gets more powerful." I started to protest further, but he silenced me with his fingers over my lips. "I'll not sit back and wait for him to come for you again. You know this, so don't ask me to."

Stubbornly, I pushed from his arms. "It's not just that he's getting more powerful. It's his gift to persuade others—it's incredibly strong. That's how he's been able to unite all those covens so quickly. He's dangerous, Caleb. You and Jax can't take on his entire army alone."

Caleb stared into my eyes, his face almost expressionless, which made it difficult for me to know what he was thinking just then. "I don't want you to worry about this. Jax and I aren't about to jump into anything without thinking it through. Is there anything else that I should know?"

I stepped away from him just then, turning my back to him. He was admitting that no matter how much I pleaded, he was still determined to go after Davin. It worried me. Davin was the one vampire I feared could blow apart all of the happiness I had found with Caleb. "I believe he's responsible for the tattoo on my neck," I continued, somewhat reluctantly. "The mark is the symbol for The Brethren. Davin knew to tell Isaac to look for it the night of the train crash, which means he knew it was there."

"The Brethren branded you?"

"I don't know if it was The Brethren as a whole. It may have just been Davin. I believe there are good people with them—those who want to do the right thing, like Alec. But there are also bad people . . . like Jude."

Caleb released a heavy sigh. "I wish you'd talk to me about Jude. You're keeping your feelings about that day to yourself."

"There's no need to talk about it. It's in the past, and now I'm here with you and happier than I've ever been. I'm all right —really. You haven't noticed it affecting me when we make love, have you?"

"No. I haven't," Caleb replied, a sly smile creeping onto his face—but minimized by his now more contemplative mood.

I didn't want to spend time dwelling on Jude and things that couldn't be changed when I had my life with Caleb to look forward to. "Can we go see Jax? I really want to hear about my mother and grandmother."

Caleb returned a half-hearted smile. "He's waiting for us downstairs."

My mood lifted, my eyes searching through my things until I spotted the precious wood box Gideon had given me at The Oracle. Grabbing it, I turned to Caleb and smiled, "Just try to keep up." Taking off at my fastest Dhampir speed, I rushed downstairs to the living room, where I sensed Jax. But to my surprise, Caleb was already sitting across from him in one of the leather lounge chairs, a huge smirk lighting up his face.

"You were saying . . . ?"

"I'll beat you, eventually," I grumbled, moving to join him in the oversized chair.

I sat between his legs and nestled back against his chest, placing the box on my lap as Caleb brushed my hair aside and placed a soft kiss on my neck. "I look forward to it," he murmured, then said to Jax. "You don't mind that I'm here for this, do you?"

Jax shook his head. "This is something I should have discussed with you long before now. If I had, we might have been better prepared to defend Olivia against The Brethren when they came for her."

"I'm not sure I understand," Caleb replied.

Jax rubbed his fingers along his chin line, his mind clearly accessing memories from the past. "This was not my first encounter with The Brethren. But to explain, I must start with Olivia's grandmother, Isabeau." He then looked straight at me and smiled as he said, "She was the most exquisite and charming creature I had ever met. Every man who encountered her was enchanted by her beauty, her grace . . . and I was no different. I had struggled for over a century to try and break my need for fresh human blood—with limited success that lasted only for short stretches of time. But her love changed me. She gave me the strength to change for good because I wanted to deserve that love." His eyes lifted to me then, with heart-rending sincerity and emotion. "I believe that you and Eve inherited your Charmer gifts from Isabeau—even though she was only human. If there was ever a time for human characteristics to transcend to the supernatural world, it was then, and the characteristics were hers. No one who knew

Isabeau could resist her natural charm."

Opening the wood box on my lap, I pulled out the photograph of her and Jax and handed it to him. "She was beautiful, Jax. I wish I could have met her." Jax then surprised me by handing the photo back to me. "You don't wish to keep it?" I asked him.

He shook his head and tapped his finger against his temple. "I have the images here. That is all I need."

"May I?" Caleb asked and I held the photo up for him to see. "She looks just like you."

"Yes, she does," Jax agreed. "Caleb, I am afraid I owe you an apology. My motives were purely selfish when I insisted that you return Olivia to her world that first time you brought her here. From the first moment I set eyes on her, all I could see was Isabeau. Olivia stirred memories inside me that I believed were long buried. It was even more evident when she returned with all of her changes. She became the spitting image of Isabeau. But I had no right to cause you so much pain simply because I could not deal with my own. For that I am truly sorry."

"I forgive you," Caleb replied. "We were all trying to figure out a lot of things back then. But Jax, you must've had some idea when you saw Olivia that she might be related to you?"

Jax shook his head. "I did not even know I had a daughter until just before Eve died. I had no reason to suspect that I had a granddaughter."

"What?" Caleb questioned. "How is that possible?"

Jax relaxed back in his chair, his elbow propped on the wide arms as his index finger and thumb strummed back and forth over his chin. "About seventy years ago, Isabeau and I were living peacefully in Maine. We were committed to each other by the laws of the human world—we were married. She was a religious woman—which was all the more ironic, considering what I was—and am. But she wanted very much for our union to be recognized by her God."

Just then I reached for Caleb's hand, interlacing my small fingers with his larger ones. I wondered if he had ever thought about recognizing our union in the human world. He squeezed my hand as if he knew what I was thinking at that moment, but he said nothing.

"When Isabeau became pregnant with Eve," Jax continued, "I feared greatly for her life, knowing how difficult the birth would be. But I kept my concerns to myself—not wanting to give her any reason to be scared. That was my first mistake . . . of many . . . but I tried to prepare us as best I could. I had made arrangements for a close Daywalker friend of mine, Chay, who knew a lot about human anatomy and birthing, to help deliver our baby. Isabeau seemed relieved by that, so I started reading medical journals on my own to learn even more. About a month before the baby was due, I had to go out of town overnight. There were disruptions with Chay's coven in the north. While I was there I felt Isabeau going into labor. Her pain was excruciating. It killed me to feel it. I rushed back as quickly as I could . . ." he said with a fading tone, "but I was too late. I had tracked her scent to a local hospital, where she had already been pronounced dead."

The agony in Jax's expression as he spoke was haunting. I had little doubt that what he was describing was the worst moment in his two-hundred and twenty-three years of life.

"I'm sorry, Jax," Caleb offered, with great emotion in his voice. "I've never heard you talk about that day."

"I could not. It is still painful—even to this day. I was taken to see her body in the morgue and was told by the staff that she and the baby were left on the steps of the hospital, already dead. They offered to show me the child, but I was in so much pain I told them did not want to see it. I just stayed with Isabeau, trying not to let the anger—the hate I felt toward her God and the whole world—swallow me up inside."

Images of what my grandmother must have gone through that night were flashing through my mind, and I couldn't help but squirm in my chair at the sheer misery of it. Caleb noticed and tightened his arms around me. "Hey? Is this too much?"

"I can stop, Olivia," Jax offered quickly.

"No," I replied. "I want to hear this. I want to know everything."

"I am afraid, even after all these years, that I still do not have all of the answers regarding what happened that night. After a severe bout of self-induced gluttony, I spent the next ten years trying to discover the truth. It was not until I was going back through some old boxes of hers that I discovered her journal. That led me to the truth."

"The truth?" Caleb questioned.

"Yes," Jax responded in a much harder tone. "The truth that *The Brethren* was responsible for Isabeau's death. And that they had stolen my daughter from me—Eve, who was still very much alive."

"*What?*" I said in a stunned whisper. *Oh God!* I couldn't believe it, and now I feared the complete fury Jax would feel when he learned that Gemma was seeing a future Elder of the group who had stolen his only daughter.

"Isabeau had still been going to church services on Sundays. Her journal revealed that she had confessed to her priest that she was pregnant with the child of a vampire and that she feared her own death was imminent during labor." Jax dropped his head, his eyes closing tight with the obvious misery he was feeling all over again. "How it pained me to learn years later that she lived with the burden of those fears and did not share them with me! I could have done something. I could have helped her . . . listened . . ."

Jax's voice sounded wounded and angry. I felt Caleb squeeze his arms around me again. I knew he was silently trying to tell me that he had the same fears for me about Jude.

"The priest she confessed to—a Father Daunay—told her he knew of an organization who could help her deliver the baby safely."

"The Brethren," Caleb answered.

"Yes. But at the time, I did not know their name. Isabeau had not written it in the journal. I am also not sure if she actually intended to seek their help, but when she began going into labor while I was gone, I believe she went back to the church."

"So this Father Daunay contacted The Brethren, who took Isabeau and the baby when she went into labor?" Caleb theorized. "And when she didn't survive the labor they left her at the hospital and stole your child?"

Jax nodded stiffly, as if hearing the words again physically hurt him. "I do not know who the child was that they left with Isabeau's body. And I tried to go back to the church to speak with Father Daunay—to get the truth about what happened that day—but he had already passed on. I did not get my next clue until 1992. I was staying with Chay's coven when they were attacked by The Brethren. That is the day I came face to face with my daughter in battle."

I leapt forward in my chair. "Eve? What happened, Jax? How did you know it was her?"

"Your mother mirrored me," he replied—and, I swear, I stopped blinking and my breathing became so shallow I could scarcely feel it. "You can imagine how shocked she was to discover that her gift had no effect on me. But we could both sense that we were blood related, and it was then that I knew the truth—she was my daughter. I could see Isabeau in her just as clearly as I see her in you."

"Were either of you hurt?" I asked, my voice sounding strangled from my lack of oxygen.

"Olivia?" Caleb questioned worriedly.

I recovered my breathing reflex at that point and inhaled enough to say, "I'm all right. I promise. Please, Jax, go on." But Jax seemed to wait for some sort of signal from Caleb before he continued.

"We both survived the battle unharmed, but my life had new hope. I had Chay tell me everything he knew of The Brethren—then tracked Eve to a Brethren support site outside of Boston, waiting weeks for the right opportunity to approach her. When I was finally able to make contact, Eve confessed to me that The Brethren told her Isabeau had been raped by a vampire." Jax said the words with such disgust. "That she sought the church's protection to take the baby safely away after she gave birth."

I simply couldn't sit still in the chair any longer. I freed myself from Caleb's arms and leapt to my feet. It all made sense now. "That's why Eve stayed with The Brethren. That's how they convinced her to use her gift against vampires. That's why she was hunting for you!"

"Yes," Jax replied in a somber voice. "I gave Eve that picture of your grandmother and me to prove to her that we were married and loved each other very much. I think she trusted I was telling her the truth, but I just wish I had put the pieces together sooner. I had heard of The Brethren almost since their inception, but I did not make the connection between them and Eve until it was far too late. By then, I had already lost my daughter."

"Why does this group feel so damned entitled to Dhampirs?" Caleb demanded.

I reached back for his hand, squeezing it gently. "They take in the children who have been abandoned by their vampire fathers. And there are a lot of them, trust me. My friend Maya was one of them."

Caleb snorted. "And, no doubt, their anger over being abandoned by their father helps the group manipulate the children against all of us."

"I did not abandon my child!" Jax snapped. "They stole her from me. I wanted to know my little girl. I wanted to raise her. She was created from the love Isabeau and I shared. And they robbed me of that."

"They'll pay for what they've done, Jax," Caleb assured him.

Jax's hand fisted against the chair arm, demonstrating that some of the emotions he was working so hard to keep hidden were seeping out. "Eve died in battle only a few days after I met her. The pain of losing her, after just getting to meet her, was as acute as it was with Isabeau. I had no idea that Eve had a daughter—that I had a granddaughter. They must have been keeping you on sacred ground, where I could not sense you."

I walked over to the windows, silent for a long while as I tried to control my own resentment. "How could they do this? How could they be so cruel? If . . . if the Greysons had not stolen me away I would've been raised under Davin . . . in that world of The Brethren. My life would've been the same as Eve's."

"But that's not what happened," Caleb replied emphatically. "You're here with us—your family—and you never have to return to The Brethren." I stared at him, appreciating his words but now fearing more than ever that somehow The Brethren was not done with me. Not after they would go to such lengths to get me back, no matter what Joseph had done for me.

"Jax, why did you never tell Gemma or me about Eve?" Caleb asked. "I had no idea about any of this."

"I have not spoken of Eve since her death. It was too painful. I felt as if I failed my daughter—failed my Isabeau. That day in the meadow, when I realized that Olivia was Eve's daughter . . . I was stunned. The only thing my mind could process was that I had another chance to be with Eve's child—my granddaughter."

"Jax!" Caleb cried out in frustration. "If you knew that day she was your granddaughter—and what The Brethren was capable of—how could you let her leave with them? How could you just stand there and watch Alec take her?"

Jax faced Caleb with an unflinching and sincere gaze. "I am sorry. I know this is hard for you to understand—"

"You're damn right it's hard!" Caleb exploded, rising to his feet in challenge. "Look at what they did to her. She won't even talk about the day Jude almost raped her!"

"Caleb," I gasped, his words catching me completely by surprise. To hear them said aloud like that hurt. But it was even harder to see how much that day was still bothering him.

Jax got up from his chair and moved behind me, placing his hand on my shoulder. "I am sorry, Granddaughter. When I discovered the truth that day there was no question that I wanted you here with me. I had planned to come get you as soon as I figured out how to make it work. At the time I did not know that Caleb would also be immune to your gifts. And it did not occur to me that someone like Jude would—"

I swung around, hugging Jax in a fierce grip. "What happened to me wasn't your fault."

"How it has pained me," he continued, "knowing what he almost did to you. I will never forgive myself for letting you leave that day."

I stepped back from him, walking over to grab Eve's journal from the wood box along with the picture of her and James. Then I returned to Jax, noticing Caleb's tense gaze following me the whole time. "I want you to have this," I said, handing him the photo of his daughter. "You don't have her in here," I added, tapping my finger against his temple. Then I handed him the journal. "This was Eve's. I think you should read it. She talks about you in the last few pages. In the end, she forgave you. She believed that you were good and that she wanted to know her father."

Jax appeared shocked and stood stock still for a moment. I could see on his face how much it meant to him to know that before she died his daughter saw him for the good man that he was. Placing my hand over Jax's forearm, I asked, "Does Gemma know of any of this?"

Jax shook his head. "She knows only some things. I have not had a chance to explain any of this to her yet. I was a little focused on trying to find—" He stopped suddenly, as if something important just occurred to him.

Bingo!

"Maybe you should tell her," I suggested.

A smile crossed his lips. "She will be here next week to help you prepare for your mating ceremony. I will speak with her then."

"Good," I replied, then turned my attention back to a very somber Caleb.

Jax walked over to him, facing him straight on with no hesitation. "I know you disagree with the decision I made that day . . . so do I. But I did what I thought was best for you at the time. You are also my family, Caleb, and you were shattered that day. How was I supposed to say to you that what you were going through did not matter? That she was coming home with us no matter what?"

"It's all right, Jax," Caleb replied in a 'barely there' voice. "I'm just angry at myself. *I* didn't have enough faith in what Olivia and I had. *I* let her leave with Alec. It was my place to stop her, not yours."

"Stop it! Both of you," I cried. "There was no way Alec was going to let me stay. It would've meant war between you and him that day in the meadow. I left with him to prevent that from happening. I would do the same thing again and go through ten attacks from Jude rather than see either of you or Alec killed over this."

"Olivia!" Caleb snapped, his response sharp and quick.

"It's the truth!"

Caleb cast a hard look at Jax, who immediately responded by saying, "I will give you two some time. I have a few things to take care of. Olivia, we will talk more later?" Within seconds, the glass doors closed behind him.

Slowly, I returned to Caleb, who had slumped back in the chair. I crawled onto his lap and wrapped my arms around him, lowering my head to rest against his shoulder. I didn't say anything, and after a few minutes I could feel him start to relax. He leaned farther back in the soft chair and pulled me with him. A few deep breaths later I said, "I know you're worried about me. But I'll be all right."

"You know I hate when you say that."

"Yes, but I mean it."

Despite my assurances, Caleb's somber mood continued as he held me there in his arms. I knew that deep down he just wanted to help me, so I decided to make a request, something that I thought *would* help me. "Caleb? You've already done so much for me that I hate to ask—"

"Ask me," he interjected.

I ran my fingertips over the buttons of his shirt. "Now that I'm to be part of the family, I . . . I want to contribute."

He kissed me on my forehead. "Bringing music into this house is your contribution."

I raised my head, smiling at him. "Yes, and I will play until you and Jax—and hopefully Gemma, soon—get sick of hearing it."

He laughed lightly and it was good to hear. "That's not

possible."

"But I want to contribute more."

Curled there in his arms, his finger traced my bottom lip. "What do you have in mind?"

"I'd like to grow some of my own food. But it's so cold up here I would need a greenhouse to do it, with a little power for heaters to keep the temperature just right." I glanced back up to see a new expression blossoming on his face: joy. He was clearly trying to restrain the happiness he felt from my request. I was hoping he might react this way. He was so talented and loved to build things, but it would also keep his mind creatively busy so he wouldn't be worried about me. "I don't need anything very big, just enough room for some herbs, vegetables, and a couple of berry plants. When Gemma comes home, the food can be for her—"

He stopped me mid-sentence, his mouth gently settling over mine, his lips heavenly as I relaxed against his body. Smiling against the cool rim of his mouth, I wanted more. Every time he touched me, my body responded completely to him and my heart pounded so loud I was sure it was like a thundering drum in his ear. I squeezed him as I finally pulled my lips away. "Does this mean you are saying yes to my request?"

"My sweet girl will have her greenhouse within a week," he said.

Chapter Twenty-Two

A week had passed and Caleb had completed the design and construction of the small rooftop greenhouse. He had even added a glass pane in our bedroom to open like the front doors of the tree house so I could slip outside from our room to my new garden anytime I wanted. It was wonderful, and everything in my world seemed right—except for my worry over Jax. His mood had grown somber over the past couple of days, and I was betting it had something to do with a stubborn redhead's refusal to come home. I had faith, though, that once they talked, some of the distance that had grown between them could be erased.

That faith and my happy days with Caleb was what made my current restless night of sleep so puzzling. All night I rolled around endlessly, sensing that Caleb was not there beside me. Usually that meant he was downstairs in his chilled sleeping room, but tonight my mind was telling me something different. I was worried for him, and that worry invaded my dreams.

I was back on the rolling grassy plains at The Oracle, where I watched in horror as Davin flew at Caleb as if gravity had no effect on him, the loud roar as he smashed into Caleb echoing off the mountain peaks around us. I cried out to Caleb that I was coming, but my voice had no sound. Then I crashed against the invisible wall of sacred ground, and it blew me back off my feet and firmly onto my rump. This time, I was the one who couldn't pass over the line.

Crawling back to the wall, I slammed my palms against the transparent field, trying to get Caleb's attention, but he was focused on fighting Davin.

"Ohhh, Olivia?" A playfully menacing voice called from behind me. I swung around to see Jude practically on top of me, his dark eyes flat and lifeless, his skin still grayish in the light,

and his curled smile showing nothing but contempt. And I realized just then that none of this made sense. Why could I hear him? Only him?

"No!" I tried again to cry out but the sound was lost in my throat. Jude swiped my legs out from under me and I landed hard on my back, his body dropping over mine until his heavy weight was suffocating me underneath him. I fought wildly, but my arm suddenly throbbed from being pulled against the chain I was shackled to, cuts forming as he pulled my arm harder against the chain.

"Stop!" But it was no use; the word was stuck in my head. Jude ripped at my clothes, his mouth smothering on mine as I fought to turn away from him. Then I saw Caleb again. Davin was charging him, and this time he held a silver-tipped lance that went right through Caleb's heart, dropping him to his knees where he stood.

I screamed until my throat was raw, but my cries still went unheard. Davin's cold, black eyes sent a chill through me as a truly evil smile crossed his lips and he watched Jude continue to force his body between my legs. "No! No!"

"Olivia!" Suddenly, I was being shaken, and a familiar male voice was calling me from above. My eyes popped open and I saw Jax staring down at me, his normally fearless face looking white as a sheet. That was saying something, considering he was already a vampire. "Olivia! You are having a night terror. It is not real."

"Jax?" Confused for a moment as to where I was, I struggled to catch my breath. Jax pulled me against his shoulder and tried to calm my shaking. "It is all right, Granddaughter," he said with obvious worry in his voice. "Jude will not hurt you anymore."

My grip around Jax's shoulders was tenacious, and from what he said I figured I must have cried out Jude's name from my dream. "Where's Caleb? Something's wrong, isn't it?"

Jax drew me back from him, holding me at my shoulders as he stared straight into my eyes. "Listen to me. He sensed a Rogue nearby and left to check into it. That is all."

I was shaking my head wildly back at him, sure that something was wrong. "Jax, you've to go find him. You have to make sure it's not a trap."

"Olivia, he is fine. The Rogue has moved on. I can sense it and him. He is already racing back here after feeling your terror."

I couldn't stop shaking my head. "He can't feel me at a distance while I have this necklace on. Please, don't tell him about this. He will worry."

"No, Granddaughter!" he replied sharply. "I will not keep this from him. But I will not have to. You two are connected. He has felt this and is almost here."

"I don't want to—"

A wave of cold air blew past me and there he was—Caleb was suddenly there beside the bed, his gray eyes wide with panic. His shortness of breath demonstrated both his exertion and his concern. Wrapping his arms around me in an effort to stop my shaking, he spoke through his panic: "What happened?"

"She had a night terror," Jax answered. "When I came into the room she was screaming and tossing around on the bed, asleep but plainly frightened . . . terrified."

"You're all right," I whispered in relief against his throat.

"Of course I'm all right. Olivia, what's this about?" When I didn't respond, he pulled back from me, holding my face in his hands. "Hey. Answer me. What was your nightmare about?"

"In . . . in my dream, Davin was fighting you." My voice was becoming so high and thready at that moment, I almost didn't recognize it. "I—I tried to help you, but Jude . . ."

Jax growled, his teeth clenching and hardening his jaw. "She was screaming for him to let her go."

Caleb stroked my hair, his gaze so intense it appeared he'd stopped breathing. "Tell me. What was Jude doing in your dream?"

Shaking my head, I was trying to figure out how to get off this subject. I didn't want to talk about Jude. I needed to know that Caleb would not be lured into a trap by Davin. "It doesn't matter. What matters is—"

Caleb shook me just enough to ensure he had my attention. "No, Olivia, listen to me. It *does* matter. Your nightmare is proof enough. Tell me!"

I buried my face in his shoulder, my arms constricting around him. "He wouldn't let me help you. He . . . he had me pinned underneath him and . . . and he was . . ."

Caleb tightened his hold around me. "Go on."

"My hand was chained. I wasn't strong enough to break free. I needed to be stronger." I realized then I was no longer seeing my dream, but re-living that awful day.

"Shhh, it's over now," Caleb whispered in such a gentle voice it seemed possible for him to erase the bad memory in just those few words. "Jude's not going to hurt you. Not ever again," he said as he rocked me back and forth in his arms.

"I don't want to lose you, Caleb. I don't want to lose anyone else."

"You won't lose me. I promise you, my sweet girl. I promise you."

✳✳✳

For the rest of the day, both Caleb and Jax moved through the house as if they were afraid of setting off a time bomb that would shatter me like glass. It was starting to drive me crazy, but I knew I wasn't being fair. My nightmare had scared these two normally fearless men, and I could no longer pretend that what Jude had done was insignificant, nor was it all in the past. No matter how much I just wanted to move on, my feelings of helplessness and fear from that day were somehow still with me. So I had asked them to give me a little space to think. Caleb didn't like it, but at this point he would agree to just about anything if he thought it would help.

Standing in front of the glass exit doors, I stared out into the winter wonderland and the snow cover that had deepened overnight. It was so beautiful here this time of year, so peaceful;

it was as though we were the only people in the world. Caleb and Jax were upstairs in their separate studies, anxiously listening to my sock-covered feet crossing back and forth over the wood-planked floor.

As I paced, I thought back to my time at The Oracle. Near the end, life was hard, but before Jude attacked me I was getting stronger. My fun little defensive challenges with Alec, the kickboxing Phin had turned me onto, and even my success in breaking out of the chain on the day of the attack, were helping me to find myself, discover my potential, and that was exciting. But then Jude took away all that I had accomplished, stripping my self-confidence from me and reducing my emotional spectrum to nothing more than fears and self doubts. The more I thought about it, the more I realized that the answer to stopping the nightmares depended upon my taking back control of my body, my mind, and my life—to a point at which I would absolutely *know* that I was strong enough to defend myself in any situation.

Grabbing a couple of chairs, I set them in the middle of the empty entry hall, facing them out towards the forested views. I was sure my vampire companions were eavesdropping on my peculiar movements, and probably they were becoming even more worried, but I believed that now I understood what I must do. Walking over to the control panel for the glass doors, I turned the handle. Immediately, the panes of glass opened ninety degrees, coming to rest in their locked position. Not even a half-second had gone by before I heard Caleb's deep voice behind me. "What are you doing?"

Standing there at the window controls and staring down at the forest floor below, the thirty foot drop seemed just as steep as the first time I had seen it, but I knew with absolute confidence that I could make the jump down on my own as I had the day I jumped in front of Gemma. Doing it successfully had be another sign of how I had gotten stronger since first coming here. But in the wake of Jude's attack I had allowed myself to forget it. Today, I would rectify that. I would not let those small but vitally important steps be forgotten any longer. I turned back to Caleb. "I'd like to speak with both of you."

Caleb's gray eyes sparked with hope, while Jax appeared beside him the next moment, obviously having been listening in from upstairs. I gestured to the two chairs in the middle of the space as I shut the glass doors once again. Both men glanced at me with an almost perfectly matching set of furrowed brows before cautiously taking their seats. As I moved to stand in front of them, I couldn't believe how they appeared just as towering and strong even when seated. I felt like a child trying to explain something to my disapproving fathers. "First, I want to say that I'm sorry. I know I scared both of you this morning. I didn't mean to."

Caleb tried to speak right away. "Olivia—"

I silenced him with my upraised hand, palm facing him like a barrier. "Please let me finish."

I began pacing back and forth across the floor as their baffled gazes followed my every step. "That day with Jude affected me. I know it did. But not all of my time at The Oracle was bad. I was getting stronger, and I had started to see what I was capable of—how to use my gifts."

The formation of a word began on Caleb's lips, but I stopped my pacing and warned him once again, this time with my eyes. He remained quiet, though, I could tell he didn't like it.

"My trainers had a hard time instructing me because they were drawn to me. But you both would be able to teach me without that being an issue."

Caleb would not be silenced this time. "Olivia, I don't want you fighting anyone—with humans or vampires."

"I'm not talking about fighting. I'm talking about getting stronger—*here*," I said, tapping my fingers at my temple. "I want that again. I don't want to live my life in fear."

"I will help you, Granddaughter," Jax answered without hesitation.

"Jax!" Caleb snapped, obviously caught off guard at how easily his friend and mentor had agreed to this.

Jax displayed no doubt in his expression as he turned to Caleb. "You should want this for her, too," he intoned, raising one hand and pointing at Caleb with an extended index finger, "especially if it helps prevent another night terror."

"I don't want her to have more nightmares," Caleb defended, "but I don't want her injured, either."

"I'll be all right," I insisted. "And this will help me conquer my fears. Please, Caleb. This is what I need."

My lover responded by dropping his head and shaking it back and forth as he released a frustrated sigh. He didn't respond verbally for the longest time. I feared he was going to fight me on this, but finally he said, "I'll agree to this only as long as you remain unharmed. If you are injured in any way— and I mean even if you need a band-aid bigger than one to wrap around your finger," he mimicked Jax's gesture exactly, even to the extended index finger—it ends."

"I agree," Jax added, seeming to relax within himself.

I blinked back at both of them. "You can't be serious! Injuries happen when you train. I was injured several—"

"No!" Caleb growled. "You can train without being injured. I won't agree to do this any other way!"

I raised both my hands in a kind of surrender signal. I needed to concede this minor point because I was already aware that I needed to ask something else, something that might set off a whole new round of resistance. I had to pick and choose my battles carefully because, unbeknownst to them, I had that one more request . . . and it was a doozy. "All right, then," I said, "I agree to your terms."

Caleb popped up from his chair. "OK. Meeting adjourned."

"Not quite," I said. "I have something else to ask."

Caleb's eyes narrowed on me suspiciously as he dropped back down onto his seat and haltingly said, " . . . and that would be . . . ?"

I knew this was not going to be easy. His brows continued to pull hard as he caught the agitated twisting of my hands before sliding his eyes back to mine. He was *feeling* my nervousness just then. "I need to go down to the meadow tomorrow to meet with Alec."

Caleb instantly leapt back to his feet, his answer flatly

predictable. "*No!*"

"What do you mean, *no?* I have to check in with him once a week or he'll have an entire army of Brethren fighters up here on our doorstep."

"It's none of his damn business now. You're with me. He needs to get that through his thick Brethren head."

"Stop sounding jealous. I've given you no reason to be."

"This isn't jealousy. I trust you. I just don't trust him."

"What do you mean you don't trust him? He's doing his job. Do you want him to tell Joseph that we haven't been cooperating? The Brethren will never leave us alone."

Like a stubborn bull, Caleb refused to back down. "Let them come!"

Jax, the much cooler head, decided to step in at this point. "You need to be reasonable here, Caleb. You know I do not want The Brethren anywhere near my granddaughter or Gemma, but if Olivia has to have a few meetings with this man to get them out of our lives for good, then that is what needs to happen."

"Since when are you such a coward, Jax?"

The normally restrained Jax shot to his feet and let out a fierce growl aimed directly at the younger vampire. "You are letting your personal dislike for this man control what you really know—deep inside yourself—is right. How would you feel if The Brethren came for Gemma while she was in the city by herself? We cannot protect her there."

"Precisely. That's why she needs to come home," Caleb argued.

"I am working on it," Jax grumbled. "She will be here day after tomorrow. Until then, you need to let Olivia meet with Alec."

"Jax—"

"I am still head of this coven, Caleb, and you will do what is best for all of us—not just for you."

"I want what's best for everyone. But I don't trust The Brethren or their favorite lackey."

"Do you trust Olivia's judgment?" Jax questioned hard, surprising the younger vampire. "She trusts Alec. And it was her idea that got her out of The Oracle without war between us."

"Of course I do." He turned to me, and from the startled look on his face I guessed the hurt that was pulling at my heart showed on mine. Gemma was right. Both Caleb and Alec had my best interest at heart, but they were too stubborn to see it.

Caleb's entire body seemed to tighten as his hands curled into half-fists at his sides and his expression twisted in knots right in front of me. "*Fine*. You can meet with him, but *I* want to take you down. Is that acceptable?"

I nodded quickly. "Yes."

Although he had conceded on the point, Caleb's snarly expression did not ease. His combative and penetrating gaze signified a veiled warning. "Olivia, . . . darling," he said with mock affection. "You'd better not have any other requests. I think I've had my fill for today."

"I don't," I assured him.

Caleb then headed back toward his study, the rigid carriage of his back and shoulders only accentuating the tense, corded working of the muscles beneath his clothing. I licked my lips, certain that unless I found something extremely silky, sexy and red to wear later that evening it was going to be a very lonely night for me in our new bed.

***

The next afternoon I found myself in our bedroom, on the cell phone with Alec, confirming final plans for our three o'clock meeting. Meanwhile, downstairs, a still very moody Caleb was announcing his discontent all the way from the kitchen. His irritated grumbles and cursed mutterings were so loud that Alec could hear him from the other end of the phone. I rolled my eyes as I continued to speak with my Guardian. And it didn't ruffle Alec one bit that Caleb was bothered. "I told you he was grumpy."

"Alec, stop. You enjoy pushing his buttons too much."

"Yes, I do," he said, without hesitation. "Is he going to be there today?"

"He's bringing me down, but he's not staying."

"OK. I'll see you at three, then," he said before hanging up.

Putting the phone down, I said—not really to myself—"You really are going to be difficult about this, aren't you?" My tone of voice was as if Caleb were right beside me. "Even though it's in our best interest."

Another irritated growl. Yes, he heard me perfectly.

I was surprised, actually, at his continuing mood. I had worn a perfect little red silk teddy to bed the night before, and Caleb had resisted for all of five seconds before tearing the garment away to devour me in blissful passion all night long. This morning, when I awoke, he was laughing and happy, so I thought we had arrived at an understanding. But all it took was a two-minute phone call from Alec to sour Caleb's mood once again.

I decided not to give in to his rather childish behavior, so I focused instead on the task ahead of me. After showering, I dressed in some black pants and an ivory sweater with a hint of a soft pink tee worn underneath and showing at the bottom across my hips. Once I added some warm boots, gloves, my dark wool coat, and a ski cap, I was ready for the winter conditions.

Downstairs, Caleb was relaxed on one of the counter stools at the kitchen island. He was facing away from the counter, toward me, his knees angled wide apart as he casually leaned back against the granite countertop, resting on his elbows. Despite his relaxed appearance, the temperature of the room seemed to skyrocket as he sat there confidently. My eyes scanned the inviting posture of his body, remembering the feel of his skin against mine the night before as he made love to me.

A knowing smile crept onto his lips as he watched me. Somehow, he knew exactly what I was thinking at that moment. He scanned my new outfit, slowly, from my head to my toes, and then he surprised me with a small snarl that curled up his lips as he offered, "You look nice."

Translation—you look *too* nice for a meeting with Alec.

I sighed. "Are you ready to head down?"

He didn't answer. Instead, I was hauled off my feet, his hands gripping the back of my thighs as I found myself suddenly straddled over his legs. One strong arm cinched around my low back, the other firmly gripping my thigh as he began kissing my neck. I wanted to refuse him for so obviously trying to take advantage of my amorous mood, but my body wouldn't cooperate. I moaned shamelessly as his mouth teased over the thrumming pulse in my neck and his large hands dug into the curve of my thighs. He nibbled, then licked, then sucked over the sweet spot on my throat, causing me to inhale sharply with pleasure. "Caleb," I breathed, "we need to go."

But I didn't want to go anywhere at that moment. My internal body temperature felt combustible as my limbs tingled. When Caleb finally eased up, he lifted his chin for a moment, taking a couple of deep breaths before lowering his lips to nuzzle right at my ear. "Why doesn't my sweet girl stay right here? I want to hear more of the screaming joy I heard from her last night."

Without a doubt, I could have easily surrendered to him right there . . . on a kitchen stool. Where had I lost my self-control? God only knew, but now it was time to get it back. I moved my mouth to nibble sweetly on his bottom lip. His throaty groan signaled his delight at my kisses, his apparent victory in getting me to stay here with him. Then I lowered to bite down over his throat. A loud, approving growl exploded from him just before I jumped off his lap. "Nice try," I said, with much more composure than I actually felt at that instant. I was just trying to get my internal temperature back in a normal range. "Now, let's go."

Caleb muttered his discontent all the way down to the snowmobile he had bought for me to allow me freedom of movement on the mountain in winter. It was a splashy red color with more than adequate power in its engine, and it was a blast to ride. Frankly, I needed no excuse to ride it. It was fun!

"I'll show you the most direct route to the meadow," Caleb began. "Follow your tracks back when you're done with . . . *him*. I will meet up with you on the way back." His hard inflection on the word *him* was the last straw.

"Caleb, what's all this brooding about?"

"I'm a vampire . . . we brood," he answered, a bit too dryly.

"No, you're a Daywalker. You're better than that." I sighed, realizing the words came out more snippy and clipped than I had intended. "But I truly want to understand you. Why do you distrust Alec so much?"

He hitched his hands at his jean pockets and mustered a firm scowl. "Are you seriously asking me that? The first time you went with him, Davin captured you in less than two hours. The second time you went with him, he hauled you off to someplace where I couldn't sense you for over three months. While there, you were wounded while training and nearly raped by one of his own men . . . all while under *his protection.* So are you seriously asking me why I don't trust him?"

I reached for his hands then, holding them within mine as I stared at him. "I get how it looks—I do. But from day one, Alec has been willing to sacrifice his own life to keep me safe, even though his future is ultimately even more important to The Brethren. Is it impossible for you to see that you both want the same thing?"

A sound comparable to a short grunt left his lips. "He better *not* want the same thing."

"*My God,* vampires are stubborn; that's *not* what I meant," I complained, throwing up my hands in resignation.

"I thought I was a Daywalker," he smirked.

"Don't push it. We're going to be late."

"I've no problem with that," he grinned, seeming ever-so-slightly less tense. Ignoring him, I took off, racing over the deep snow, refusing to be sucked into any more of his stall tactics. About twenty minutes later, we reached the meadow. Alec was already waiting, but when he saw Caleb, his casual expression cooled to an icy stare. "Have you kept her safe, vampire?" he asked pointedly, even though he already knew I was fine.

Caleb snorted, crossing his arms over his broad chest. Lord, it was like watching two gorillas fight for a place to piss. "She's always safe with me. Perhaps you should take notes."

Alec stepped forward, ready to blast back a scathing remark when I stepped in. "All right, that's enough, both of you."

I turned and kissed Caleb on the lips, letting him know it was time for him to go.

Caleb narrowed his gaze in warning at Alec before turning his attention back to me. "I'm going to circle the perimeter. When you're finished, I'll be waiting for you a little way up the mountain." Then he was gone, his fast feet skimming like magic over the snow.

Mine, however, were buried to my knees.

"Here," Alec said, reaching his hands out to help me take a seat beside him on his silver snowmobile. Once I was situated, he pulled a thermos from his side. Unscrewing the cap, he poured the contents into a cup. I could smell immediately what it was. "Hot chocolate?" I said with surprise. "I love hot chocolate."

"Yes, I know. You're a chocoholic," he teased, pouring another cup for himself. "So tell me, how are things going?"

I took a sip of the delicious, steaming liquid. "Mmm, perfect."

Alec's light brow arched. "Are you talking about the cocoa?"

I smiled. "That's perfect, too."

Rolling his eyes, he asked, "Have you crossed paths with any more vampires?"

I shook my head. "Caleb sensed a Rogue in the area the other day, but he was too far out to show up in my sensing range."

"Sounds like things are going pretty smoothly."

"They are. Caleb and Jax have even agreed to help me finish my training."

Alec blinked back at me. "I must say, I wasn't expecting that. I thought Caleb was against you learning how to fight?"

"Believe me—it wasn't easy to convince him. But I think that deep down he knows it's the best thing for me."

Alec scanned the tree line around us. "So, is he listening?"

"No. He's too far away."

"Good. I don't want him to hear me say this, but it sounds like he's taking good care of you."

"He always does," I smiled. "So, what's been going on with you? You seem happy."

"I am. Do I look older to you?"

"No. Why?" I then clued in. "Oh my gosh, it's your birthday?"

"Tomorrow. I'll be a very mature thirty-one. Although it's amazing to me how I still look older than thirty-five-year-old Gemma. But the little spitfire is keeping me highly entertained."

"You care for her, then?"

Alec's blond brows wrinkled at his frown. "Yes, very much. Do you doubt that?"

"I just wasn't sure. Are you sure you're not just using her to anger Jax and Caleb?"

His expression hardened into a scowl. "Do you think so little of me that you believe I'd do that? I'd never want to hurt Gemma like that. I know how much they mean to her. Even if Caleb—"

"Don't say it." I then took his hand in mine, realizing that my pointed question had been rude. "Of course, I don't think you'd ever intentionally hurt her. It's just that when Gemma finally does decide to tell them it's going to cause a rift within the coven. I just want to make sure it's worth it for her. Jax has been her whole family since she was a teenage girl."

"You know I don't give a damn about the vampire. But I do care for her. She has such spirit—such passion." He looked away then and smiled, as if accessing a fond memory. "She mentioned she was coming to see you tomorrow—some mysterious coven event?"

I swallowed hard, knowing he wasn't going to like this. "Caleb and I are going to be mated tomorrow."

"Mated?" he cried, spitting out his current sip of cocoa.

"It's when—"

"I know what mated means. I've been in the vampire world a lot longer than you. Olivia, are you sure you want to do this?

Are you sure he's the right one?"

"Yes, Alec. You know how much I love him. How hard I fought to get back to him."

"I know," he began, shaking his head. "But you need to understand this isn't going to affect my final decision with Joseph. If Caleb can't keep you safe, mated or not . . ."

"It won't come to that. He'll keep me safe."

After a long pause, he seemed to relax a bit. "Reese was here to see me the day before yesterday. He came to apologize."

"Really? Is that a good thing?"

"I don't know. He's obviously trying to make amends, but I still don't trust him. Neither does Gemma."

Alarm ran through me as I sat up straight on the edge of the snowmobile seat. "Reese didn't see Gemma, did he?"

A puzzled cast came over his expression, making me realize that I needed to tread carefully. Reese was still Alec's family. "Just as she was leaving. Don't worry. I didn't tell him who she was. He just thinks she's a woman I met here in Seattle."

"Alec, please don't let him get near her," I pleaded, squeezing his hand for emphasis. "Please! He was way too interested in her on that last day at The Oracle."

"And if you remember, I was the one who lied to my uncle to keep her a secret."

"I'm sorry. Gemma just means so much to me—to all of us. I just want her to be safe."

"Safe? You mean like how I didn't keep *you safe* from Jude."

"Stop it!" I snapped. "You know that's not what I meant."

He mumbled something under his breath that I couldn't quite hear and then asked, "Are you still having nightmares?"

"I'm fine, really. You don't have to worry." I didn't want to admit to Alec that I was still having flashbacks. He already felt responsible enough as it was.

"I do worry. But you hang in there, little Charmer. You're going to be OK."

Chapter Twenty-Three

The day was finally here. Today I would be mated to Caleb.

I rolled over in bed with a smile on my face, remembering Caleb's tender kiss before he whispered he was leaving with Jax to make some last minute preparations for tonight's ceremony. That's why I was so startled to hear hard, slamming noises downstairs, accompanied by Jax's clipped voice. "Not now."

"But we need to talk about this," Gemma answered in a very unsettled response. "Jax, please stop. I've been seeing—"

"I know you have been seeing someone," he answered, his voice firm but controlled, just as it always was when he was upset. "I have felt it. You had to know I would feel it."

"And you had to know this would eventually happen," Gemma countered, with some bite in her tone. "I couldn't just live here with you forever. I'm not that teenage girl you saved anymore. I'm a grown woman."

"I know that. I do not treat you like a teenager."

Gemma exhaled sharply. "Yes, you do! You won't . . ."

She stopped herself just then and I felt my own breath pause with her.

"*Won't* what?" he challenged. "I did not ask you to leave, Gemma. You left . . . ," He quickly cleared his throat. "You left us, your family." Jax was nearly growling out his words now, fighting to control emotions that were obviously too close to the surface. "Caleb is expecting me. I cannot do this with you right now. This is his and Olivia's day." "Please, Jax, I . . ." Gemma's voice fell away as she sniffed, clearly holding back tears. Then there was a long silence between them, and even though no words were being spoken, it felt to me that a thousand things were being said.

"You care for this man?" Jax asked in a much calmer tone. "He makes you happy?"

Gemma paused for a long while before she finally answered, "Yes."

"Is he human?"

"Yes. I know you may not approve, but he's a good man."

Another long silence. One didn't need the gift to *feel* to understand how much pain both Jax and Gemma were in at that moment. Part of me wondered if Gemma was hoping that by pushing Jax it would force him to say he wasn't OK with it; that *he* desired her as a woman. That *he* needed her. But Jax was a proud man, troubled by a sense of responsibility to this once teenage girl who had matured into a beautiful woman right before his eyes.

"I want you to be happy," he finally said. "It is what I have always wanted for you. If this man makes you happy, then there will be no interference from me. You are welcome to stay at the condo as long as you like."

"Jax?" she questioned, her voice no more than a whisper, just a breath. The vampire was letting her go, giving her the freedom to move forward with her life as she wanted, which is what she had asked him for. So why did she sound as though she were absorbing a hard blow to her stomach? "I won't stay long. It's your home. It belongs to you. Give me a couple months to find my own place."

Suddenly, the steel edge returned to Jax's words. "Can he protect you?"

There was a long silence before Gemma answered. "Yes. I don't need your over-protection anymore."

"I need to go," Jax growled. "Just do me the courtesy of waiting to tell Caleb you are leaving until after his ceremony with Olivia. This is their day."

"I'll come back for the rest of my things in a week. I'll tell him then."

An unnatural silence fell over the house after I heard the whooshing sound from the glass doors, indicating that Jax had left, and two additional sniffs from Gemma. I was getting up to go to her when a wave of fast-moving air hit me. I looked up to see Gemma sitting on the bed beside me. Trying to sound as cheerful as she could she said, "It's your big day, sweetie. Are you excited?"

I threw my arms around her, nearly strangling her in my arms. "Gemma, you can't leave us. It just won't be right around here without you."

She returned the force of my hug, her shaking eventually breaking down into tears. "I don't know what to do. I think I might be falling for Alec, but I'm losing my family."

"Oh Gemma, do you love Alec?"

"I think so. But I don't know . . . I'm so confused. I didn't think Jax would . . ."

Wiping the tears from her cheeks, I tried to comfort her the best I could. "You have to tell Jax how you feel about him. He needs and deserves to know the truth."

"You heard him," she half sniffed, half snorted in reply. "He as much as gave me his blessing to move out. He didn't even try to stop me."

"Did you want him to stop you? Because that's not really fair, to expect that kind of commitment from him when he has no idea how *you* feel."

"Why does he have to hear me say it?" Gemma burst out in response. "Why can't he just be a man and reach out to me . . . respond . . . to something . . . show some emotion—any emotion."

My soul went out to her empathetically as I hugged her again. "If I had to guess? Because he thinks it's wrong to care about you in any other way than as your guardian."

She moved out of my embrace and lay back on the bed, her red eyes staring up at the ceiling. "He still sees me as a teenager. And, let's face it—as Dhampirs, we don't look much older than teenagers. I'm not a woman to him—like Isabeau was." She wiped more tears from her eyes and then added, "I have to move on and focus on being happy with Alec."

I watched her with deep sadness in my heart. I felt completely powerless to help either one of them, but as her friend I knew I needed to support her choices, and her choice seemed to be Alec. I already knew how wonderful he could be, so I did believe he could make her happy. I just hoped that happiness was enough to make up for the rift it would cause within the coven. Including Caleb, who, no doubt, would have to be pulled back down from the stratosphere when he found out it was Alec—a man he despised.

Gemma wiped the remaining tears from her eyes and tried to return a smile to her face. "I'm sorry for dumping this on you today. This is your big day. Come on, we should get started," she said, but I stopped her.

"I won't say anything to Caleb. It's your place to tell him. But you need to tell him soon. I think that in this case, to stay silent is the same as telling a lie. And promise me you'll at least think about this more before you make a final decision to move out permanently."

"I will," she nodded. But I could tell she didn't really mean it.

***

Later that night, as it grew dark, I was finishing up with Gemma in her room. Caleb had returned and was getting ready in our bedroom. I had worked hard all day to hide my worry over Gemma and Jax, but now, as our ceremony drew closer, I was finding myself just a bundle of nerves about tonight, and I wasn't sure why. I knew I loved Caleb and without a doubt wanted to be mated to him . . . but what if our mating didn't take?

"You look absolutely perfect!" Gemma cheered in a high-pitched squeal as she clapped her hands in girlish glee.

I felt beautiful—and sexy. A mating gown was actually not a dress, it was more like bridal lingerie. The full length gown I had selected was a soft, blush color with an intricate lace halter top. Soft-flowing chiffon fell to my ankles, while a long slit ran along each leg, and the whole effect of the gown had me feeling slightly naughty. There was no matching coverlet, but the dress was so elegant, it didn't need one. "Do you think he'll be pleased?"

"Pleased?" Gemma snorted, tossing her hand through the air. "He's gonna have you out of that thing before you can blink."

"Gemma!"

We both laughed for a moment, but then her smile was replaced with one of sadness, followed by a soft sigh. "It's time for me to go."

Jax had not returned with Caleb earlier, probably wanting to keep some distance so Caleb wouldn't get suspicious that there was something wrong. But his staying away it seemed to cut Gemma even deeper, reminding her how Jax had pulled away from her the first time. "Please think about what I said," I reminded her.

"Don't worry about me and Jax. We have argued before, and I'm sure we'll argue again. But we always work it out sooner or later. Right now you need to focus on the fact that one of the most deserving vampires I have ever known is waiting to start the life he has wanted since the day you came back into his life."

"Gemma, you're going to make me cry."

"No more crying," she declared, although she herself looked as if she might shed a few more tears—some for me, some for herself. "Now, get going."

Taking a deep breath, I silently crossed the hall, looking down at my perfectly polished toes, noticing that my heart was beating wildly as I climbed the stairs to our room. When I reached the top I was greeted by the warm, aromatic scent of burning rose petals and the small flicker of dozens of unscented candles that were sparkling and reflecting off the glass and glossy black surfaces of the piano. The dim room felt like a romantic dream. White rose petals sprayed across the ivory-toned silk sheets and the rich, ruby red comforter that had been turned down to the foot of the bed.

"*There's* my beauty," he murmured from behind, his fingertips lightly tracing along both of my arms while his cool breath tickled over my neck. "How I have missed you today."

Slowly, I turned to face him. He looked like a gift from the heavens, standing before me dressed only in a pair of smoke colored silk lounging pants. The firm lines and planes of his body were accentuated by the flickering light around us. He took in every detail of my mating gown, his eyes following every curve along the snug-fitted bodice and down to the line of my leg, which was peeking through the floor-to-hip slit in my skirt. "Sweetheart, you're stunning." His one hand flattened out as he moved it over the stretch of delicate lace at my waist as the other found my hair and traced a loose curl at my cheek. "I can't destroy this. You're a vision."

My heart leapt—literally leapt, with a distinct bump-ditty-bump "I love you, Caleb," I said. "I want so much to please you, tonight and forever."

Carefully, he lifted me into his arms, his thorough gaze never letting go of mine as he carried me toward the bed, setting me down among hundreds of white rose petals. "You already please me, sweet." His hand barely held my cheek as his lips made several playful brushes over mine before taking me fully in a kiss that sent tingles shooting down my spine. When he pulled back, his eyes were alight with emotion. "Tonight I'm committing myself to you and only you. I want no other woman. But before you commit yourself to me, I want you to fully understand what it means to be mated in my world."

I ran my tongue nervously over my lips and swallowed once, trying to lubricate my mouth and throat, which were suddenly dry. "Is it like being married in the human world?"

"In many ways," he replied. "You are mine to protect, mine to care for, my soul's mate, my partner. I pledge to keep you safe, happy, and cherished every day of your life. All of you. Your heart, your soul, your mind—and most especially this beautiful body."

"That all sounds good," I blinked back at him with a smile.

"And," he continued, "in return, you acknowledge that I am the only man who may fulfill these needs for you. I am the only man who may touch you."

"I want no one else, Caleb."

He smiled. "I love you, Olivia. I've never loved any woman—

never wanted any woman—the way I want you. Never doubt that."

I returned my lips to his, my kisses tender and slow. But as he slanted over me and I tasted his cool tongue drawing me deeper into his kiss, my body sparked to life just that fast; all the nervousness had dissolved in his kisses. "Caleb," I whispered as my hands began to draw a possessive line down his abdomen, and then lower, till he finally pulled away with a groan.

"We'll get to that, my sweet. I promise."

Caleb then brought a tray from a side table near the wall and set it in front of me. The ornate serving piece carried a large, lavishly decorated pewter chalice and an equally decorative dagger. "A mating between two vampires," he began, "is very much instinctual, need-driven. It's the body's and mind's recognition of finding their sexual counterpart. Many times, the male will simply showcase his strength and conquer the female of his choosing—rather like matings in the animal kingdom. But I want this night to mean more than that for both of us."

He then held my face in his hands and stared at me with such emotion I was finding it difficult—no, impossible—to breathe normally. "You saved me, Olivia Ann Greyson, at a time when I believed I didn't deserve any happiness in this vampire life. You loved the demon inside me that even *I* couldn't face— and you've made me a better man and vampire because of that love. When we are mated here tonight, there will be no going back, and I want you to know that I don't want to go back— ever. I want to move forward with you at my side."

"Honestly, I . . . I don't know what to say. I swear I am always at a loss for words at the most inopportune times."

He laughed and kissed my cheek. "It's one of the many things I love about you. Just tell me you're ready for this."

"I'm ready," I replied without hesitation, squeezing his hand. "I'm so ready!"

Caleb's gaze then fell to the ornate pewter cup on the tray. It looked antique, hand crafted, sculpted in fine crafted metal detailing with angels weaved into its celestial design, and displaying several sapphires around its top. Inside the cup, the words *'Amor est vitae essentia'* were inscribed in an unbroken circle. "The chalice is beautiful. Where did you get it?"

A warm smile curved his lips. "This chalice is a gift to us from Jax. He and Isabeau used this cup to share wine at their wedding ceremony." I pressed my hand over my heart, absolutely touched that Jax would offer such a gesture with something that obviously held fond memories and deep significance for him.

Caleb then smoothed his hand over the knife beside the cup, his eyes watching me carefully for a reaction as his fingers traced their way along the sharp blade. Once he was comfortable that there was no hesitation from me he lifted the knife into his right hand. "Vampires exchange their blood by bite. Since I cannot bite you without turning you, ours will be more ceremonial, using this chalice—but the connection will be just as powerful.

"How will you be able to control your thirst during this?"

"Jax and I fed on fresh blood this morning. That will allow me to keep my thirst under control. You don't have to be worried."

"You know I trust you," I replied simply, and he seemed pleased with that answer.

"After our blood is mixed inside the cup we'll drink. This sharing of our blood will create a bond between us, and that bond will be our commitment to each other—a commitment no one can ever break."

My breath drew in sharply as I watched Caleb drag his fingernail over his forearm, slicing a deep cut into the skin. His vampire blood, the color of the darkest rose, poured into the cup for several seconds before the wound closed again as if it was never cut in the first place. "Vampire blood is very intoxicating for humans," he continued. "Once inside your body, the blood energy will affect you quickly—relaxing your inhibitions and arousing your deepest desires. It will warm you and help prepare your body for the connection that will be sealed between us."

As I watched him I could see he had complete faith that a connection would happen with our mating. I wished I could feel as certain as he did. Still nagging at me, deep inside, was the question: what would the future hold for us if it didn't? I didn't want to stop long enough to think about that possibility because all of my dreams for the future might be wiped out in an instant.

Caleb noticed my hesitancy immediately. "Are you afraid of the blood, my sweet?" Caleb asked, and as his voice penetrated the depths of my thoughts I realized that I was wringing my hands. "I've noticed you've been drinking blood daily since you've been home, so I had not considered that you might be uncomfortable with this."

I blinked up at him, thoroughly confused. "No, it's not that. I mean . . . *you know that I have been drinking?*"

He frowned at me gently. "Of course. I can smell the scent on your tongue after you drink." His thumb and index finger nudged my chin back up until my gaze met his. "Why are you trying to keep this from me?"

I sighed, lowering my eyes away from him. "Even though my body craves the blood, I feel less human. At The Oracle I drank to increase my strength . . . but now I'm having trouble controlling it. That scares me. I don't want to lose the human side of me—the side you love."

"Olivia, it doesn't matter to me how often you drink. You're still the same amazing woman I fell in love with. Feeding your Dhampir thirst changes nothing for me. Please tell me you know that." I shuddered, exhaling with my relief. The change in me then, the relaxation I felt in just an instant, was obvious to him as he continued to caress my face with his fingers. "What am I going to do with you? Surely you know how much I love you, don't you? If how often you're drinking is bothering you, I will help you."

Suddenly, I found myself throwing my arms around him. "Oh Caleb . . . What're we going to do if this mating doesn't happen?"

Carefully he drew me back from him and picked up the

knife with an expression that held no doubt. "It *is* going to happen." He then brought the sharp tip of the knife to touch my right arm just at the elbow, where there was a prominent vein.

"Wait," I said and moved my left hand, palm up, under the blade.

He flashed me a knowing smile. "That's the hand you cut the day we met at the lake."

I nodded. "This hand was our very first connection. It seems fitting."

His thumb caressed the heel of my palm just before he pulled the blade back and cut into my skin. At first I felt no pain at all, but then a slight hiss escaped me as a fiery pain followed within seconds and the blood pooled in my cupped hand. I made a fist and let the blood spill freely from the heel of my hand into the chalice, mixing with his. When Caleb was satisfied there was enough, he wrapped my hand with a cloth, raised the cup and recited the words *"Amor est vitae essentia."* Smiling, he said, "It is Latin for *'love is the essence of life.'* I can think of no more perfect sentiment for us."

He inhaled the scent within the cup, and his luminescent eyes instantly sparkled, showing a lot more blue as he was drawn towards the warm, salty liquid. Pouring the contents into his open mouth, his lips and lethal saliva never touching the edge, he closed his eyes and savored the taste as it flowed over his tongue. I felt entranced watching him surrender to his powerful thirst. As he drank, his muscles shook with the need for it. Yet Caleb Wolfe had never been more beautiful to me than at that very moment—and it seemed an odd thing to me.

Next, he pushed the chalice away, focused on maintaining his tight thread of control. Eagerly, I took the cup in both hands, surprising him by lifting it once again over *his* lips, and poured freely into his mouth. "More, Caleb. I want our connection to be as strong as possible."

He didn't try to grab for the cup, but his fingers wrapped around my hands and held them like a precious gift. His breathing roughened as the startling sapphire blue of his eyes appeared fully, along with his sharp fangs. I inhaled excitedly as

I tilted the chalice higher, watching the strained muscles work along his throat as he continued to swallow. Then he forcibly pushed the cup away and would not allow me to bring it back. "I have to stop," he said.

"Amor est vitae essentia," I smiled and raised the chalice in my hands. "You're an easy man to love, Caleb Wolfe. And I choose to give you all my love freely. It is now yours to guard and take care of."

Vampires don't cry. Their brains just do not respond the same way to emotion as when they were human. But at that moment, the emotions there in Caleb's eyes made it seem possible that he could. Bringing the cup to my lips, I drank all that was left in the chalice without hesitation. Immediately, my body began to heat and spark, just as it had the first time I drank vampire blood. Only this time I knew it was right as it pumped through my system. Caleb took the chalice from my hands and I inhaled several deep breaths, massaging my fingers down sensually over my throat and collarbone. A slight pressure pushed against my lips then, and I knew my incisors had lengthened.

Quickly I turned away, but Caleb brought my chin back around, his fingers caressing the under surface of my jaw. "Let me see them." I remained still, but he continued to reassure me with light strokes of his thumb over my bottom lip. "Please share this fear with me." It was one of the most romantic things a man had ever said to me.

Reluctantly, I parted my lips. He leaned forward until his forehead rested against mine and said, "You are so beautiful. And right now I want you more than I ever believed was possible to want a woman."

The truth of his words was evident from the hard erection straining against his silk pants. Slowly he traced down my arms, my skin sparking behind the trail of his fingertips. He then curled a long arm around my waist to bring me against him. "Caleb," I breathed across his cheek. "Please . . . I want more."

He tilted my head forward until my fangs were right above

the hard pumping veins in his throat. "Drink from me, my sweet." I tried to push back from him; I was sure I had not heard right, as both fear and excitement pulsed through me at the thought of drinking directly from him. But he continued to hold me against his body, letting me know he wanted this for me, and my breath became hard against his skin. "It's all right," he said, squeezing his arm around my waist. "You won't hurt me—and I can feel how much you want this."

Slowly, I began rolling my tongue over his slightly salty skin as the scent of the precious fluid in his veins seemed to spike my senses. "That's it," he whispered. "Let yourself want it."

I did want it. I wanted to suck from him, to feel his energy on my tongue. He groaned, continuing to hold me tight against him, his hand massaging over the chiffon and lace of my gown. "Let me feel those sharp little teeth sink into me."

Unable to believe how much I wanted to drink from him, I was now fighting a war within myself. What I wanted was natural to what I was, but at the same time it frightened me. What I wanted, *what I needed,* was very inhumane, and I would expose myself to this man I loved in a way I had never imagined. "Drink, my sweet," his deep voice urged me again.

My body shook with want. Opening my mouth wide, I snapped my head down and sank my fangs into his throat, the action feeling completely natural as I latched onto him. He sucked in a sharp breath, his chin lifting high as low growls let me know he was receiving pleasure from my bite. He began to rock me gently in his arms as I grasped onto his shoulders, my fingers digging into his skin as I buried my fangs deeper into his throat. The blood sent a huge charge of erotic energy into my system. My mind became more alert, my pounding heart beat even louder than before, and my body became ultra-sensitive— as if the slightest touch between my thighs would propel me into release.

"Yes, my sweet. The more you drink from me, the stronger our connection will be." Caleb relaxed his body, his hands releasing me to begin piling the chiffon skirt up into his hands. His groans were deeper, breathy, his hands possessive over my hips just before he tore away the lacy scrap of thong I wore underneath.

Finally releasing the hold over his throat, I was nearly panting over his shoulder. Erotic energy stronger than anything I had ever felt before threatened to consume my entire body in flames. The sensations were ten times more powerful than the first time I drank vampire blood, the connection with Caleb sharp, instinctive—as if the possibility existed for us to share the same thoughts, the same breaths. And now my mind could only focus on one thing.

How much I wanted him.

With a need I couldn't begin to explain, I came around his lips, trying to take his mouth hard against mine. I had to taste his mouth, to feel his lips moving against mine, feel his tongue searching, his teeth nibbling. At that moment I wanted his fangs to sink into me. But before I could make contact Caleb responded, his hands flying to both side of my face, holding me just off his lips. "Easy, my sweet."

I protested with soft cries, my almost painful desire for him consuming me as I tried to force myself forward over his lips. Within a hairsbreadth of his lips, Caleb held me still, staring back at me with concern. "Caleb," I pleaded. "I need to taste your mouth."

"I'm sorry my beautiful girl. You can't have my kiss right now." But my need seemed to only become stronger as the erotic energy continued to burn through my bloodstream. Again, I tried to push myself closer, but he wouldn't allow it. He gave me a gentle shake, asking for my attention. "I'm here, Olivia. I'm right here. Take what you need from me."

"Caleb!" The desperation to crush his mouth with deep kisses was all-consuming.

He shook me again. "Olivia, take what you need." I began pulling my gown up over my shoulders. "No," Caleb replied. "Leave the gown. I want you just like this." His one hand clasped my chin to make sure I didn't try to seal another kiss over him as the other reached down to prop his hips from the mattress, lifting his weight and mine so I could tug down his silk bottoms. Beneath the billowing chiffon, he caressed my skin, then wrapped his arms around my low back to pull me high against his chest. "Take me inside you," he breathed.

My fingers reached between us, encircling the long, thick length of him in my hand as I positioned the wide head at my entrance. I slid down on him just a couple of inches and my breath hitched at the insane pleasure of it all. Instinctively, my inner muscles clamped around him and he growled as he continued to impale me. Inch by slow inch, my walls continued to flex and stretched until I was filled with him, so filled I couldn't breathe for it. Then, unbelievably, the first quakes, the first tremors of release washed over me. I clutched at his shoulders to hold me upright, staring into his hot blue eyes with wonder. *My God*, I was coming around him. "Caleb!"

"*Christ*—that feels good," he hissed. "*. . . Oh . . . Damn!*"

When the tremors of my release finally subsided, he opened his eyes and stared straight at me. "Now, again. Take what you need."

Caleb continued to hold my face with both hands as I began to move on him. His rugged jaw clenched and his head dropped back as each movement of my hips plunged him deeper inside me. The erotic blood was not only heightening my need, my sensations, but also fortifying me with increased strength. My nails dug deep, forming crescent shapes into the back of his shoulders, and I continued to push him backward on the bed until he was lying flat against the silk sheets. Gripping my hands against the silk beneath us, I rode his body, feeling his hips thrusting to meet mine as if we both could never have enough.

Staring into his sapphire eyes, I recognized the piercing blue as a hot-cool glaze that burned me from the inside. He rolled us on the mattress till I was flat on my back, his hard length still buried deep inside me as he rose slightly. My breath caught in my throat while he reached for my thighs and curled my legs around his hips. I was mindless, lost in pleasure. He lowered onto his elbows, putting his lips right above mine, obviously no longer concerned about me trying to kiss him in my overwhelmed state.

He closed his eyes, the muscles flexing in his shoulders, his jaw tight as he slowly reared back from the deep depths, nearly withdrawing from my body completely before plunging back in to the hilt. "Caleb!"

He reared back again and thrust forward hard, then repeated, faster and faster. My hips worked in unison with his to meet each penetrating stroke. I begged and pleaded for release, until finally a sharp gasp froze me and my entire body began to tighten around him. There was no stopping the implosion that would surely destroy me. My back arched and my hips pulled. "That's it, my sweet," Caleb's strained voice rasped, "come for me."

I couldn't speak, couldn't breathe, the air swept from my lungs in a silent scream the very moment my vision went to black and I came around him a second time. But this time it was all new—earth-shatteringly new. My orgasm ripped through me not a second before Caleb followed, blasting his seed inside me with incredible force. We were climaxing together, and it felt as if a door was opening between us that had been locked before. His energy was crossing through the darkness, finding me, expanding within me until we seemed to dissolve into one another. Something was happening. I could now *feel* him, feel every detail of his body, every ragged breath in his lungs, every tingle on his cool skin, every single sensation he was currently experiencing under his mind-boggling release . . . and my body was responding.

Clawing over his impenetrable skin, my screams finally erupted like a volcano as the incredible power of his release shattered me beneath him for a third time. My walls clamped down on him so hard, a fierce guttural roar shot from his throat just before his breath caught and he came inside me once again. We were floating together, coming together. There was no past, not even a future—just this one, perfect moment.

Absolutely spent, Caleb's exhausted body rested its entire weight on me as he continued to pulse inside my snug depths. Moments passed before he could regain presence enough to roll over so I was out from underneath him and relaxing, virtually weightless, atop his chest. Our breaths rose and fell in harmony while we slowly drifted back into a normal state. "Something happened, Caleb," I said in a stunned voice. "I . . . I don't think I can move."

His deep, satisfied chuckle filled me with warmth as he curled his arms around me. "You know what happened. You are a part of me now. Mine forever."

"It really did happen, didn't it? I could feel it. We are mated."

He slid me up on his chest so my eyes were right above his. "Yes, my sweet, we are." His hands slid my disheveled gown up on my sweat-covered body, keeping the garment undamaged as he slid it over my head and tossed it to the floor. "Mercy . . . If I'd known my blood would have this kind of effect on you, I would've given it to you sooner."

He laughed, the sound low, relaxed, sated. "Oh we've only gotten started. We have all night, my beautiful mate, and I will need you again soon." Bringing his hand behind my neck, he pulled my head forward once again to his throat. "Drink my sweet. Satisfy your beautiful thirst."

Without hesitation, I sank my teeth into his neck, my body feeling less human and more like a vampire with each passing moment . . . and I loved it!

Chapter Twenty-Four

Standing in our closet, I stared absently at the wall of new clothing before me. I'm sure would have appeared rather odd to anyone looking on. The house was too quiet this morning, yet the stillness seemed to fit comfortably into my deeply reflective mood. Two weeks had passed since my ceremonial mating with Caleb, and each day since had been better than the last one . . . except for today.

Making the most of my fickle mood, I had tried on at least four different outfits before deciding on a pair of thick leggings and a toasty-warm woolen sweater to battle the chill. By the time I decided to venture downstairs it was nearly noon, very unusual for me.

Jax was sitting alone in the living room, his muscled body impressive even in repose as he leaned back into a lounge chair he had swung around to face out toward the forested views from the tree house. It was the first time since I had been in this place that any piece of the furniture had been out of its ordinary placement, so I knew something was wrong. "Good morning, Granddaughter," his deep voice spoke, his quiet, introspective gaze never leaving the view to look at me. "I was wondering how long you were going to stew up there today."

Stewing? I certainly wasn't stewing. "I don't know what you mean."

His humorless laugh was telling of his mood. "You insult me," he replied. "You forget. Caleb is not the only one in this house with the gift to *feel*. Your worry is unwarranted. Caleb has not gone to see Celeste today."

Now I was confused. That was exactly what Caleb had said he was going to do when he woke me at a pre-dawn hour. "He left early this morning . . ."

"He is just scouting the perimeter. I told him I would take care of warning Celeste."

"Why are you . . . ? Never mind. I don't want to talk about it."

Moving one of the other lounge chairs to a space beside his, I joined him while he ran his fingers back and forth over his jaw. Even though he was supposedly conversing with me, his mind was clearly somewhere else. I watched him play with a small, torn piece of paper, sliding it between his fingers—back and forth, back and forth. "Yes. You do tend to keep things inside," he said, finally turning his gaze to me. "It's curious where you get that from."

He wasn't serious was he? At the moment, observing him in his quiet, pensive little universe, it seemed rather obvious where I got it from.

"Caleb will be back soon, and he will be as devoted to you as he was when he walked out the door this morning."

Jax was a strong, handsome, intelligent man who kept too many of his thoughts to himself. He had taken care of Gemma and Caleb for so many years; I wondered who took care of him. Then I realized I already knew the answer . . . no one. This warrior of steel did not let anyone stand with him against any of his own demons. I now understood why Gemma, after beginning to care for him so deeply, felt a wall growing between them. It was there. He had built it. A remnant, of sorts, of a very painful past it seemed he couldn't completely let go of. "You found another one of Gemma's poems."

He held out the tiny bit of paper, staring at it for a long while before returning it to the safety of his palm. Gemma had been writing down her 'little thoughts' as she like to call them, for several years, leaving them in secret places all around the house. As Jax and Caleb found them, Jax collected and saved every single one of them, which Gemma seemed unaware of. "I do not find them much anymore. I believe this may be the last one. Would you like to read it?"

"No," I replied. "I believe they are all meant for you. They're all the thoughts she feels but does not say. They're love notes."

A quick frown moved across his dark brow like a thundercloud. "You do not leave love notes for a man who has raised you since you were a fifteen-year-old girl."

"Normally I would agree with you. But you and Gemma aren't like most people. *You* are not aging—you are the same strong, handsome, fiercely protective man she admired as a teenager. While *she* has grown into a confident, beautiful woman—far removed from the homeless girl you found abandoned."

"Hmm . . . ," he sounded.

Wanting to understand this man who was my family, a precursor of myself, I knew the best way to begin was to hear him speak of those things that were dear to him, specifically the one woman who was most dear—Isabeau. "Will you tell me about my grandmother?"

Stroking his chin again, he smiled—involuntarily, it seemed —against his knuckles. "You do so remind me of her sometimes," he began. "I had never met a woman more beautiful than Isabeau. But that was because I had never met a woman whose stunning physical beauty matched her inner loveliness. She was soft, refined, the definition of elegance and grace. And her charm . . . she had the ability to draw all the attention within a room with a simple smile."

He seemed to get lost for a moment in his memories, while a small ache pulled at my heart. In his eyes, Isabeau was the most amazing creature that had ever lived. I now understood the tremendous shadow Gemma feared she would never be free of if she opened her heart to Jax. In fact, Gemma seemed to be the complete opposite of Isabeau in almost every way. Quick-witted, spirited, and a fighter, she was stubborn when she got something in her head, and her temper could be as fiery as her ginger locks. But even on her worst day, I believed Gemma could rival any woman for her beauty. She was stunning in her own right.

"Isabeau was your soulmate, then?"

Returning his gaze to the outside view, he paused before answering. "At the time she was my whole world—my reason for breathing. Like you are to Caleb."

"I'm sorry, Jax. It must have been very painful to lose her."

"It was. I was in a very dark place for a long, long time. If only I had gotten a chance to say goodbye to her. It is my biggest regret."

It was amazing how Jax's love for Isabeau showed up in every word he spoke in remembrance of her. That kind of love was truly special. "I kept my promise to her, though," he continued. "I never fed my thirst by taking another human life . . . but I remained a Rogue for decades, falling in with a coven here and there. It was just easier to keep my promise when I was on my own, less temptation. That—and, I guess, my spirit—was too restless."

"Like Caleb," I replied.

"Yes," he said, flashing an affectionate smile that this time reached all the way to his eyes. "Until he met you. You have changed him. He is happy—at peace. He deserves that peace. He is a good and honorable man. Has been, since the day I met him."

I reached my hand over to take his larger one, squeezing it lightly. "So how did you finally conquer your own restless spirit, Jax?"

He laughed. "I found a sassy boatload of trouble disguised as a fifteen-year-old girl."

"I can picture that," I giggled in reply.

Jax's smile widened. "You should have seen her then. She was just a bundle of energy, and bossy as hell. But that was more about being abandoned by her father than anything else. She wanted to control her situation instead of having it happen to her. I just had to be patient with her—give her time to feel confident that I would not leave her as her father had."

I sighed with happiness. I loved hearing him talk about Gemma. It was almost as if he took pride in the strong woman she had become. I only wished she were here to hear it.

"The first ten years with her, I do not even think I realized how she affected me. I just focused on protecting her so that I could think about something else—someone else besides myself. It was during the second ten years that I knew she was changing me. There is a lightness about her, an easy acceptance of people. It is amazing, considering she had been abandoned."

It was interesting hearing Jax speak of both Isabeau and Gemma. Although the two women were very different, they each touched Jax deeply in their own ways. Gemma was right in that she was not Isabeau. But she was the woman that Jax cherished in his life today. I suddenly realized something I had been completely unable to comprehend before: when you're over two hundred years old you must adapt and change with the society around you, accept the personal demons that have brought you to that point. The woman Jax wanted seventy years ago was different from the woman he needed today. Gemma, in all her joy and feistiness, offered a renewal to his heavily damaged spirit. "And now you fear you've lost Gemma?"

The protective wall that had sustained Jax through all the difficult moments of his life immediately went up around him again. I could see the switch in his eyes. "If she loves this man, then I will support her. I want her to be happy."

"But what about what *you* want?" I asked, hoping to crack through a bit of the stone surrounding him. "Gemma has been a huge part of your life for twenty years. You can't just let her go. Not without telling her what she has meant to you."

"That is exactly what I will do." I stared back at him in disbelief. "I love, Gemma," he said. "When you love someone, you love them enough to let them go when it is someone else they wish to be with."

"Someone else?" I slapped my hand against the arm of the chair before rising to my feet, ready to tell him exactly what I thought. "Jax! What if this is only what she *thinks* she wants because she doesn't believe there's any future with *you?*" He stared up at me, surprised that I was challenging him like this. "You hold on to her poems—her love notes *to you*—as if they were the most precious gift in the world, and yet you won't even try to hold onto the woman herself."

"Do not belittle my actions, Granddaughter. You have given

up just as much for Caleb."

"No, I haven't," I returned quickly. "I *lied* to him. I tried to hold onto him even though I believed he was only under my illusion. I was as selfish as any person could get."

Jax rose from his chair, his brawny frame so large when he stood in front of me that I suddenly felt totally dwarfed. "You were not selfish. That day in the meadow—when it mattered most—you sacrificed your own freedom because it was what you believed was best for him. And when you were injured and in terrible pain from your battle with Davin, you told him you would rather he find real love with another instead of being trapped under your illusion. You did this because you loved him. Caleb being happy was more important to you than your own happiness!" His hands held me at my shoulders, as if pleading for his words to sink in. "Why do you think he has been struggling so hard with what happened with Jude? He carries the guilt of how much you sacrificed for him—and what it has cost you."

Flabbergasted, I quietly replied, "I—I didn't know . . . he never . . ."

Jax raked his hand through his long hair. "I am sorry, Granddaughter. I am letting my emotions get the better of me today."

He turned to walk away, but I followed him. "I understand what you're saying about sacrificing for those you love. But there was one major difference with Caleb and me." Jax swung around, openly curious about what I was going to say. "When I made those choices, I knew how Caleb felt about me. He had told me that he loved me, and I had told him. Gemma doesn't know how you feel. Out of respect for the joy she has given you over the last twenty years, you owe it to her to tell her the truth —whatever that truth may be. She can then be free to choose for herself—choose the life she wants. If you are not her choice, *then* you can sacrifice for her."

Jax's soft, amber gaze stared at me in amazement. He encircled his giant arms around me, his large frame swallowing mine in a hug as the glass doors opened beyond us. "My wise granddaughter fills me with pride. After all the pain of losing Isabeau and Eve, to have you here with me—a part of them— means everything. I will give great consideration to your points."

"What's this?" Caleb asked as he sauntered in, a wide smile tugging at his cheeks. "A family bonding moment?"

A proud grin came to Jax's lips as he placed a firm hand over Caleb's shoulder. "I was just telling my granddaughter how wise she is for her young years."

"*Caleb!*" I choked as he came forward and hoisted me off my feet, encircling my legs around his hips as he held me above him. "I agree whole-heartedly, Jax. I'm a lucky vampire."

"Well, if you want to remain *lucky,*" Jax began, "you will reassure your new mate here that she has nothing to fear regarding your old one."

I scowled at Jax for betraying me like that, but Caleb only laughed. "Don't worry, Jax. Olivia knows in her heart there's only one woman that I love. And she's a Charmer." I smiled, teasing my fingers through his hair as he winked playfully back at me. "Excuse us, Jax. I left so early this morning I didn't give my *mate* a proper ravishing."

"Caleb!" I said, embarrassed by his brazen announcement, as he began to haul me away.

"It's all right," Jax chuckled. "When I was with Isabeau, I was just as passionate, and just as proud."

***

Later that afternoon, dressed only in one of Caleb's white button down shirts, I was seated at the piano playing some new music I'd composed. Caleb was relaxed on the bed in only his low-rise jeans, his hands interlinked behind his head as his long body stretched out lazily over the disheveled bedcovers. His eyes were closed while listening to the last few bars float off my fingertips. "Hmm, that was nice, my sweet," he said, rolling to his side.

"You liked it?"

He nodded. "Very much."

"Do you think every day could be like this?" I asked, using my wistful voice. "Sometimes I still can't believe I'm actually here with you, living with you like this."

Caleb got up from the bed and crossed the room, surprising me when he tossed me up high in his arms, then wrapped my legs around his waist before sitting back down on the piano bench. "Each day can be whatever we want it to be, my sweet," he said, kissing my forehead. "I'm not going anywhere."

"When I was at The Oracle, I dreamed of days just like this. It was what kept me going."

Caleb stroked his hand over my hair from my forehead to the nape of my neck. "I wish there was some way I could take that pain away."

"You've already taken it away." His lack of response indicated he didn't believe that. "What about your pain?" I asked. "That last night when I played for you on the terrace? Did you believe you were under my illusion?"

"Yes," he sighed. "I believed I was. But I just couldn't let you go. That's why I came to you that night. I just didn't realize that would be the last time I saw you for months."

"I didn't want to leave you, but it was the right thing for me to do for you—"

"It wasn't the right thing for *me*," Caleb interjected sharply. "I wanted you to stay. The second I knew our love was real I wanted to bring you back here with me. If that had happened then Jude never would've—"

"Don't, Caleb. It's just not that simple. Even though Alec always insisted that going to The Brethren was my choice, I don't believe The Elders ever intended for me live outside of The Oracle. They would've come for me eventually."

"Then why do you trust that The Brethren will leave us alone now, even if we agree to these meetings with Alec?"

"I trust Joseph." Caleb was shaking his head, bewildered over how I could trust the son of the man hunting me. "I know he's Luther's son, but he knew and respected my mother. He knows she wouldn't have wanted me kept like a prisoner behind an invisible wall. He wants to give me that—if I can show him I can be safe."

Caleb frowned. "How can one Elder change the minds of an entire organization? Does he have that much power?"

"No. But he's a good leader. Good will find a way. Not all of the people associated with The Brethren are bad. But Alec's Uncle Reese and Jude—"

I quieted, not sure if I wanted to continue, but I could see in Caleb's eyes he wanted me to stop trying to hide my feelings from him. "Jude is evil. I could see it the first day I met him. I tried to mirror him so he could see his own evil nature, but my gift had no effect on him. That's why the blade went into my leg."

Caleb spat out a fierce growl at mention of the blade. "Fucking bastard!" But after a moment he calmed, sincerely wanting to continue this discussion without his anger getting in the way. "Why did your gift have no effect on him?"

"I don't know. But when I had my nightmare I felt as though my mind was trying to tell me there was a connection between Jude and Luther Davin. It probably sounds silly, but . . ."

"That's not silly. They already have The Brethren in common."

I sighed and laid my head on his shoulder. "I just don't understand what I ever did to Jude that he should have hurt me as he did, almost right from the start. It really seemed he hated me. And I hate how I let him turn me back into a fearful person."

Caleb's concern was evident in the reassuring kisses he was delivering to my ear, but there was also something else. *Relief.* This was what he wanted from me, to talk to him. "You didn't do anything wrong. And my beautiful girl has such strength. You just need to grab onto it again. *God,* I wish I could take this pain away. I wish I could've been there."

"So you could have fought him?" I asked in a somber tone.

He blew out sharply. "Well, yes, I would've beaten him to an inch of his life." Shaking his head, he added, "Probably more than that. But I meant so I could've been there for you—been there to hold you until you felt safe again."

"You're here now and I feel safe in your arms. Thank you for giving me that, for listening to me."

"I will always be here. I want you to talk to me when you're in pain. I don't want you to try and hide it from me anymore."

"I can't anyway. You can just *feel* it."

He chuckled. "That's true, but it never seems to stop you from trying."

"Maybe we can both do better. You've never talked about the hurt I caused you that last day in the meadow, with Alec, when you learned the truth of who I was."

He was silent for a long while; I feared I'd hit a nerve. "When I watched you leave with him I was so angry."

I lowered my head to his shoulder once again. "I'm sorry. I didn't mean—"

"Shhh," he whispered gently. "I didn't mean with you. I was angry at the world—at my circumstance. After I had finally accepted my fate in this life, you came in like a breath of fresh air and changed it. Suddenly, it was as though this amazing future was being dangled in front of me, and then, just like that, it was ripped away. It was as if someone were telling me I hadn't sacrificed enough to have that life—to have you."

I pulled my arms tight around him. "You do deserve this. All of it."

"Look at me," he whispered. When I did, his eyes were sincere, full of warmth. "I am immortal, Olivia. Dead . . . soulless —"

"No, that's not true!" I replied emphatically, surprising him. "Let me ask you something. After Celeste bit you, do you remember dying?"

"Olivia, what . . . ?"

My fingers were digging into his arms as I spoke—not that they were getting anywhere with all his lean muscle. "When you told me about that day, you said you could sense Celeste was following you almost right away."

"That's right. But where are you going with this?"

"Your hair grows," I pointed out as I brushed over his short beard. "You have an inherent scent to your skin, it's like fir trees. And twice now, when I've been resting on your chest, I have heard the faintest little beat, more like a murmur, in your heart—"

"Olivia, stop—"

"I don't believe you're soulless, Caleb. You still have a soul. I've felt it."

"Don't be ridiculous. I've no soul. No vampire does."

I paused, trying to think of the right way to open his mind to this subject. "But you at least agree that if you still had a soul, then you couldn't have died?"

"It doesn't matter what I believe—"

"It does to me. Let me show you. *Please.*"

"Proving whether or not someone has a soul is not exactly something you *show.*"

I smiled, raising my hands to his temples. "We can. Just relax, and when I tell you, I want you to focus on *feeling me.*"

His doubtful expression showed he was only humoring me, but I didn't care. I just needed him to follow along. Interlocked on the bench, my bare legs dangled over his hips as my fingers immobilized his face and held it motionless at his temples. Closing my eyes, I focused all my energy on him. After a few moments I saw flashes of images: the night Celeste changed him, the lives he fed from early on as a full vampire, then a collage of images of the countless human lives he'd saved. I felt the hope inside of him, a hope that was winning the war against the darkness, still trying to strengthen within him.

He began to breathe a bit more slowly and deeply from my touch as his muscles relaxed. "Ok, Caleb. *Feel* me. Feel what I'm seeing." For several heartbeats, he was utterly still while *his* gift wrapped around me, holding me secure. Then I felt the slightest movement—the slightest hitch in his breath. "There," I said. "Can you feel *that?*" He didn't reply, his face grimacing as if he were in pain, then he pulled my hands away from him.

"Was I hurting you?" I asked worriedly. Shaking his head, he said nothing. "You *felt* it, didn't you? You could feel the light inside you?"

"I don't know what I felt."

"I *do* know," I said, turning his chin to face me. "The light that you feel? That is a part of your soul that is fighting to free itself from the darkness. I've felt that darkness in Davin and Isaac. Isaac had *only* darkness. I don't believe you die when you are turned. I believe the virus that changes you creates this darkness that wipes out all traces of your humanity over time. Isaac's soul was lost, Davin's is dying. But you and Jax are fighting that darkness, and as long as you do, I believe you still have a soul and can access it."

"Your gifts are truly remarkable," he murmured, but his tone was still unconvinced. "I'm just not sure you fully understand —"

"*Don't,*" I said. "Don't do that. I know you felt it, too. Just promise me that until you prove me wrong, you and Jax will keep on fighting—that you won't ever give up. I don't believe you have to be perfect. Humans with good hearts aren't perfect, either. But you've got to want to fight for it. Please tell me you'll fight for it."

He wrapped his arms around me then, pulling me close as he rested his head on my shoulder. "Don't worry, my sweet. I've fought the darkness inside me since the day I was turned. Now that I have everything in this world that I want, I have no intention of letting it win."

Chapter Twenty-Five

Several more weeks passed, and my blissful days with Caleb seemed to only get better. I was thrilled to be in this home and sharing my life with my family, but there was one exception—Gemma. I still missed her terribly, and I knew I wasn't the only one. She still had not returned to pick up the rest of her things, which could mean she was giving more thought to her decision to move out permanently—or perhaps she just didn't want to face Jax.

Given our conversation about telling Gemma how he felt, I was surprised that Jax had not gone to the city to see her. His mood seemed to be getting grimmer by the day. I wondered if he could *feel* her deepening bond with Alec.

Since Gemma hadn't returned, Caleb was still unaware that she was moving out permanently, or that she'd been seeing a human—one he detested. But he knew something was very wrong with Jax. He tried to get his mentor to talk to him about what was going on, but the older vampire wouldn't, choosing to live in a silent pain. It broke my heart.

Though I still believed it wasn't my place to interfere, I began to question my decision to keep Gemma's secret. I didn't like keeping this from Caleb, and maybe if I had said something earlier—told Jax the truth—he would have fought harder to keep her with him. Now I was only counting time until the inevitable train wreck would happen when Gemma finally told Jax and Caleb she was seeing Alec. *That would not be a good day.*

However, one thing that had been coming along well was my training. Jax and Caleb were right. I *could* train without being injured. And as my skills improved, my nightmares stopped and I enjoyed a new-found confidence from knowing how well I could defend myself. Caleb had even worked with me on the high jump up to the tree house entry. I was still not strong enough to jump that high without his help, but he built a perch halfway up an adjacent tree so I could jump there first, then finish up at the glass doors. I rather enjoyed springing around in the trees like a wild monkey. But Caleb still preferred to just wrap an arm around me and have me come up with him . . . which I didn't mind, either.

Today, while Jax was out, Caleb and I were in the great hall, working on my quickness and agility rather than my strength. Caleb and Jax both believed the key to my training was that I learn to defend against strikes and position myself in such a way that I could use my gift of touch against my attacker. It was, after all, my greatest advantage, and it was getting stronger every day. Considering my lack of physical strength relative to other Dhampirs, it made sense.

"I can tell my sweet girl's confident she's going to take me down today," Caleb smirked as we circled each other on the temporary mat he had put down for us.

"You bet I am."

He then made a quick move towards me—although at a much more human speed than he was actually capable of—while I ducked under his arm. Coming back up, I pushed my forearm against his low back, sending him forward, while my leg tripped him, crashing his long frame against the mat. He rolled over to face me as I dropped on top of him, my arm pinning his midsection. A mischievous smile spread over his lips as he lay there, flat on his back, looking completely comfortable, like he was right where he wanted to be. "Congratulations," he offered.

"You let me bring you down," I complained. "That was too easy."

His smile widened as his arm snuck across my low back to snare me securely against his body. Before I knew it, I was squealing in laughter as he rolled our bodies on the mat and curled my legs around him. "I admit there are some other things I'd rather practice today."

"Really?" I replied, feigning casual indifference. And what

would those be?"

I screeched as his fingers speared into my sides to tickle me. I tried to curl away from him, but it was no use. Then our raucous laughter was interrupted then by the whirring of the window mechanism and the sound of a very wet Jax landing through the half-open glass doors. A wave of cold, snowy air swept in with him, causing me to shiver.

Caleb pushed from me at feeling my shudder, but I dragged him back. "No, stay with me."

"I see you two are still at it," Jax replied with a neutral smile.

Caleb wriggled against me, nibbling playfully at my chin. "She still thinks she's going to take me down."

"As fast as my granddaughter is learning," Jax began, "she may just do that. And I hope I am here to witness it when it happens."

I was about to cheer my wholehearted agreement when Caleb's body suddenly went rigid against me, his gaze now focused somewhere in the distance. Jax, too, was suddenly distracted. Both men were sensing something. I tried to sense it, too, but I couldn't. Their detection abilities were much more acute than mine. "Were they following you?" Caleb asked Jax.

"No. I just noticed them now."

"They?" I asked, glancing out into the cloudy skies. "Dhampirs? Are there more than one?"

Caleb nodded, releasing his hold of me. Standing back to his feet, he offered his hand to pull me up, and then turned to Jax. "I'm going to go check it out. Will you stay here with her?"

"Of course. Go."

Before I had a chance to voice my objections, he was gone. Staring out at the spot where he'd left, I wrung my hands in frustration. I hated it when Caleb went after other vampires, or even Dhampirs. They could be equally as dangerous. "Relax, Granddaughter. He will only be gone for a little while."

I brushed my hand over his cold forearm. "If there are two, shouldn't you go with him?" I asked quietly. "I can bring up the security."

"He will be fine. Trust me." Trying to conceal my worry, I nodded agreeably, but knew I wasn't fooling him.

"I'm going to take a shower," I said. "I'm sure he'll be back by the time I'm done." Jax said nothing, but his gaze followed me as I jumped to the second floor. After my shower, while drying my hair, my sensing abilities lost track of Caleb, which meant he had gone somewhere outside my range. I tried to not let my unease get the better of me so Caleb could focus on the current situation, but it seemed nearly impossible. I had been so happy these last few weeks. My greatest fear these days was that someone would come and take it all away.

Yet, even in my worry—and the loud whistling of my blow dryer—my attention was drawn to the low-level sounds of an argument coming from the first floor. Jax and Gemma were going at it again, and my heart broke when I realized that she had returned to pick up the rest of her things, which also meant she was here to tell Caleb the truth.

Wanting to give them some privacy, I quickly finished, leaving my hair still damp. Throwing on some jeans, a warm sweater, and a pair of winter snow boots, I slipped out through the glass panel Caleb had installed in our room and headed for the warmth of the greenhouse.

Taking in the magnificence of the snowy day, I lifted my face to the sky. Large, fluffy flakes tickled my skin as they landed on it and melted, bringing a smile to my face. There was nothing more beautiful than the mountains in winter, as long as one got used to the frigid temperatures. Once inside the greenhouse, I tossed my winter gloves onto the table and began working with the soil in the small herb boxes. I hated the idea of Gemma and Jax fighting, and I restlessly wished there was something I could do. "Shoot," I murmured to myself, remembering I'd left my watering bucket outside by the faucet the last time I used it, so its contents were probably one giant icicle by now.

Heading back out into the snow, I couldn't ignore the raised voices below. The argument was getting worse, and I debated the wisdom of interceding. Bucket in hand I walked forward a few steps and looked down into the living room through its huge skylight. Jax, dressed all in black, was an intimidating figure, literally towering over Gemma, whose flushed face betrayed the emotions she was trying to keep hidden. "This is ridiculous," Jax snapped. "Caleb is checking out two more Dhampirs as we speak. There have been too many lately crossing into this territory. You should be here with us so we can keep you safe. Not hours away, downtown."

"That's precisely why I'm safer in the city than here," she replied, not giving any ground.

"No, you are not! We cannot protect you when you are so far away."

"I have protection. You don't need to concern yourself."

Jax raked his hand through his long hair, working hard to keep himself in check, but the anger seemed to be bubbling over his normally high wall of restraint. He was thirsty, and his emotions regarding Gemma were just more than he could control at the moment. "A human cannot protect you!" he growled.

"*He* can protect me!" Gemma snapped back. I now had that terrible feeling; the train wreck I had been waiting for was about to happen. In one long step, Jax closed the distance between them. "Who is he?" he asked in a voice so low it warned not to trifle with him.

"It doesn't matter—"

"*Who is he!*"

I thought I could hear Gemma's heart pounding out loud, and I watched as her face filled with panic as she realized she was trapped. Jax's eyes widened; he knew he had hit on something important.

"Alec," she replied, her voice now timid and cracking from the knowledge of how she was hurting the man she was addressing.

For a long moment, Jax didn't respond, and I risked the thought that everything might calm down. But oh, was I wrong!

"*Alec!*" Jax roared. Every strained muscle in his neck was visible as he clenched his teeth against his jaw. For the first time since I'd known Gemma, she took a step back from Jax in fear. "*Olivia's Brethren Guardian? No! I forbid this!*"

"You can't forbid me," Gemma replied, somehow finding strength in her voice. "I'm a grown woman."

"Yes, I can! I will not allow The Brethren anywhere near you. I *will not* let them destroy you as they did Isabeau—as they did Eve."

"I'm not Isabeau!" Gemma cried. "*A fact you've made me all too aware of.*"

"What the hell is that supposed to mean?"

Gemma seemed to lose her fight in that moment. Instead, she fought to hold back her tears. The normally unaffected, happy woman Jax had known had probably cried more the last few weeks than she had all the years she had been with him. "Nothing! It means nothing." Her voice was again soft, not angry or confident.

She swung on her heels to leave, but Jax caught her arm, yanking her back to him until she was pressed firmly against his body. Her sharp, indrawn breath matched the shock in her eyes as Jax's other arm wrapped around her low back, immobilizing her completely. For a long moment they both seemed to be caught in their own surprise. Then Jax let go of her arm and raised his hand, cupping it behind her head, cradling her in it just before he brought his lips down to hers and crushed her with the force of a deep kiss. She squealed, her hands trying to push off from his chest, but her tiny frame didn't even get an inch from his steel grip. Jax slanted her head back by pulling on her hair, moving his lips against hers with such thoroughness that within seconds he seemed to be stealing the very breath from her lungs. Her wide eyes began to relax, and then fluttered closed as her stunned squeal gave way to the power of what was happening and turned into soft moans.

No longer resisting, her body became pliant in his arms. Jax's kisses softened, too, and lengthened, caressing her mouth with a tender mix of reverence and longing. He released the restraining hand from behind her neck, and began, with amazing gentleness, to thread his fingers through her hair at her temple. Jax was a strong man, but at this point he needed no physical strength to demand and achieve her complete surrender beneath his kisses. And surrender she did.

Her hands wrapped around his neck as he pulled her off her feet, smiling now as he began trailing soft kisses down her throat. "You are wrong, Gemma," he breathed. "I see you not as a teenage girl, but as a grown woman, a woman that I desire very much."

"Jax . . . ?" Gemma's breathing was rough as she moaned in response to his touch, her slight curves molded against him by the tenacious grip he retained around her waist. She dropped her head back so he could move lower, into the hollow of her throat, where he licked and teased her skin until she was literally breathless.

"Ah, my angel has a sweet spot," he breathed as he locked over her pulsing throat. In response, she released a soft, high-pitched cry as she clung to him, but in no way did she try to stop him.

I stepped back from the skylight, chanting a silent cheer as the large flakes continued to fall over my now *very* wet clothing. I no longer needed or wanted to keep watching this scene, but I couldn't help hearing what was going on.

"This has been a long time coming," Jax whispered through his heavy breathing. "So we will do this right."

"No," she whimpered, her voice laced with confusion, as if she just realized what was about to happen between them. "We can't do this. It's not fair to Al—"

Her words were cut off by more kisses, but I could hear her struggling against him. "Do not do this," he pleaded. "Do not push away from me. I can *feel* how much you want this—how much you want me."

"No," she replied breathily. "This isn't real. You're not doing this because you love me. You're doing this so I'll stop seeing Alec. Let me go. Now!"

After more rumbling, I heard Gemma scrambling for the glass door exit. From my high perch on top of the roof, I watched as she raced down the mountain in a shadowy blur.

Jax's bellowing voice resounded through the snow-covered forest as he followed close behind her. "Gemma, stop!" he shouted, over and over again until they were both gone from view and out of my range of hearing.

My heart was racing out of control. Gemma never should have taken off like that without protection. Not while Caleb was still . . . *Caleb?* Where on earth was he? Why hadn't he returned yet?

Cold and wet, I returned to the warm shelter of the greenhouse, trying to calm the uneasiness that was starting rise within me. Inhaling and then letting out a deep sigh, I decided to release my excess energy on my poor herb plantings, and I plunged into their fertile dirt with much more force than was necessary. I kept busy with this chore for quite a while, but it was never far from my mind that none of them had returned. My instincts screamed at me that something was very wrong. I needed to return to the safety of the house and wait for them.

Then I felt it. The energy of two unfamiliar Dhampirs headed straight towards me. Were these the same two Dhampirs Caleb had left to check on a while ago?

Feeling as though my heart were in my throat, I grabbed at where my shield of protection normally rested, but to my horror the gemstone necklace was gone. When I dressed after showering I had forgotten to put the necklace back on. No wonder they were headed straight for me! I was no longer blurred to them!

Turning back towards the house, I didn't make it more than a few steps before I was stopped in my tracks by two male Dhampirs. One appeared almost as brawny as Jax, with dark eyes that were cold and a Mohawk cut that ran from front to back over the center of his scalp. The other male was very young. No more than a teenager, and of less-than-average height. But as he tossed one of the nearby tables in the greenhouse out of his way with one hand, it was evident he had just as much strength. "You're coming with us, Charmer," the large Dhampir ordered.

"Oh, no, I'm not," I replied, knowing these soldiers had been sent by Davin. They knew exactly who I was and had probably been patrolling during the day, just waiting for me to make a mistake . . . like stupidly leaving the necklace on the counter in the bathroom.

The young male charged at me first. His speed was shocking, but I managed to swing both my arms out with force, breaking his attempt to pin them at my sides. I could then slip away from him. But he was on me again in an instant. This time, however, I was able to reach for his face. As my fingers clamped on, he cried out in agonizing pain and it startled me. Even though he was a Dhampir and his face seemed so innocent, his nature was not. His dark past and the thirst for human blood rivaled that of any vampire. My touch was now flashing those images back at him with the force of a thunderbolt.

"Take that," I shouted, but then I cringed away as a wash of horrific images flooded through my own mind. The absolute darkness inside him was filtering through to me. I had never encountered this much evil in a Dhampir before.

He stumbled several steps away from me just as the other Dhampir hit me like a Sherman tank, sending me crashing back through the greenhouse and onto—and over—a wooden table filled with planter boxes. The boxes crashed to the floor, and I hit the back wall with such force I feared that the thick glass would shatter over me.

Momentarily stunned, it took a second for me to feel the pain that hit my side. I had been cut by a sharp table edge or the pewter of a planting pot. I was hurt and bleeding, but I knew I couldn't stay down for long. Within two pounding heartbeats, the larger Dhampir was over me again, his dark gaze filled with fury as he pinned my arms to my sides and hauled me to my feet. His nostrils flared wide as he inhaled the blood scent coming from the fresh wound just under my ribcage. I used the momentary distraction to slam my forehead against his. The force of it was painful for me, but the contact with my skin caused him to release me from his grip. My powers were working.

Relentlessly, I kept on him, clasping my fingers over his temples, causing him agonizing torment as he spouted curse words and his incisors lengthened into pointed fangs. Though part human—and I sensed it was a very small part—he was every bit as dangerous as a vampire.

He was disabled for the moment, but before I had time to regroup, the young Dhampir appeared again. He had recovered, and he attacked fiercely, kicking me off his accomplice and back out the greenhouse door into the snow. I was shaking from the pain shooting through my side as he came at me once again. As I tried to stand up, his next blow came, and the force of it sent me tumbling over the edge of the roofline of the house itself. My fingers clawed at the edge in a desperate grip, but in the slick, snowy mess there wasn't enough to hold onto. I slipped over the side of the house to the steep drop below. Concentrating on trying to get my feet underneath me, I tried to control my flaying arms, but it was of no use. I was falling too fast, too wildly out of control. I grunted as I slammed against several tree limbs on the way down, glancing back up to see the smaller male drop over the edge of the house and propel straight towards me. The pounding in my heart seemed to beat right through my chest as I realized he would soon have me in his grasp. Closing my eyes, I prepared for either contact with him or the forest floor.

What I hadn't been prepared for was the jolt from a strong arm snagging around me from beneath and propelling me back upward. It was such a shock to my system that the air was whooshed from my lungs.

The smaller male Dhampir reached out for me but was brutally redirected toward the trunk of a tree by a hard fist to his face. "I've got you," Caleb's determined voice reassured.

Before I realized what had happened, we landed back on the rooftop. He set me down by the entry to the house and jumped back, the scent of the blood seeping from my wound threatening to overcome him in an instant. "Get into the house!" he ordered before swinging around to challenge the larger male Dhampir, who was active once again and nearly on him.

Stunned and shaken, I couldn't move. I stood there watching the surreal scene play out while snow continued to fall in buckets around me. Meanwhile, the smaller male had propelled himself back to the rooftop and decided to charge toward me with ruthless determination.

Just as he had me in his grasp, Jax came barreling over the edge of the roof, his piercing blue eyes full of rage as he slammed against my attacker. The impact sent the Dhampir back over the side of the house. Jax whirled around on me, his nostrils inhaling the scent dripping down my side. "Get inside —now!" The sound of his angry voice seemed to snap me out of my trance, and at the same time, Gemma latched on to my arm, yanking me back through the glass door.

She closed the door, turned without letting me go, and virtually dragged me to her room. After sitting me on her bed and warning me with one word—"Stay!"—she disappeared in a blur, and I could hear the low hum of the security lasers sounding within seconds. When she returned, her eyes were wide with concern. "*God, Olivia*, I smell a lot of blood. Let me see," she said, pulling up my stained and ripped sweater. After inspecting the cut, she drew in a quick, sharp breath. "This is deep."

Gemma wasted no time getting me out of my wet clothing, leaving me only in my bra and panties, then she draped a blanket over my shivering legs and more closely examined my sides and back. There were red welts where the younger vampire had kicked me, and a few more from my clashes with tree branches, as well as that deep gash on my side from being thrown over the table in the greenhouse. The large cut and the accumulating blood from it held her attention as she pressed around it to staunch the flow.

"I'm OK," I declared, but I found myself shaking uncontrollably; my blood was running cold in my veins.

"Stay right here, don't move!" she ordered. She wadded up my sweater, gave it to me, and told me to press it firmly against the wound, then disappeared into the bathroom. Above us, the fierce battle was still raging. The loud crashes and roaring growls made me cringe with worry. "Do you think they're all right?" I called out toward the bathroom. No answer.

But a moment later, Gemma returned. She had an alcohol

bottle and surgical tape in her hands and some clean hand towels draped over her arm.

"Don't worry about them—just focus here. This is going to hurt, but I have to get this blood flow stopped and the mess cleaned up as much as I can before Caleb gets here." She began pouring the alcohol over the open gash. It felt like fire.

I cried out in a high-pitched wail at the same moment Caleb shot out a furious roar above me, the battle sounding more violent than ever. "I guess I'm not nearly as brave as you when it comes to pain," I said amidst my series of hard breaths, remembering how she had remained completely silent while I pulled dozens of glass shards from her skin in this very room not long ago.

"Unlike you, I've known I was a Dhampir practically since birth. I've had a chance to build up a tolerance for pain. But even so, this is a deep cut. You're doing fine, Olivia." Gemma then gently wiped away the excess blood on my skin as I held my body rigid, refusing to breathe. "We're almost done." Using surgical tape, she pulled the separated skin together. "There. That should stop the bleeding and give your body a chance to heal. But we still need to get this other blood cleaned up."

As she continued to clean more blood from my skin, the noisy battle above us began to quiet. Gemma glanced up. "Shoot, they'll be here soon. Here, hold this to your side and lie down," she instructed as she balled up all the bloody cloths and discarded clothing and ran them downstairs to the metal, chilled room where the blood supply was kept. When she returned, she used the remaining towels to clean up the rest of the blood as best she could.

Within seconds, the light, buzzing sound of the lasers stopped and Caleb was throwing open the door to Gemma's room. His sapphire eyes were wide with panic and his breathing wild as Jax followed him into the bedroom and pinned him against the wall. "Jax!" Caleb growled, sniffing the blood scent in the air. "Let me see her."

"Stay back, Caleb!" Gemma ordered. "I've almost got her cleaned up."

"You heard her," Jax bit out. "Just wait until she has the blood under control."

Caleb's frantic gaze was locked on me as I tried to calm my shaking. "I'll be all right, Caleb," I assured him—just before biting back another cry as Gemma unexpectedly poured alcohol over a second cut she found on my hip.

"Olivia!" Caleb growled through clenched teeth, "Don't you dare tell me you're all right! I *feel* your pain." Finished with my hip, Gemma raced the last of the bloody towels downstairs, which was fortunate and timely because Jax couldn't hold Caleb back any longer. "Let go! I'm fine." Flying to my side, he took my shaking hands in his, his worried lungs working as hard as my own. "How badly are you injured?" he asked, smoothing his hand over the side of my face.

"I'll be—"

His sharp hiss of warning cut me off, a reminder that he didn't want to hear my standard response. I placed my hand over his. "It's just cuts and bruises. They will heal," I said between deep breaths. After a few moments and when his breathing was more normal, he relaxed enough so that his features morphed back to those of the gray-eyed man I loved. He planted several kisses on my forehead and cheeks before lifting the towel Gemma placed over my side. His hand moved carefully over the swollen red marks while examining the gash on my side. "I was able to defend myself against both of them," I said shakily. "That's good."

He stared at me with a mix of bewilderment and anger. "Olivia! You were thrown off the side of the house! I saw the damage to the greenhouse. Don't try to make me feel better by pointing out that you were able to absorb a beating by two Dhampirs until we got here."

"Davin sent them. I know it. They knew I was the Charmer, and they said they were going to take me with them."

Caleb let out a booming growl as he spun around on Jax and Gemma. "God*damm*it! Why was she having to defend herself against two of Davin's soldiers *alone?* Where were you two?"

"The blame is mine," Jax said without hesitation. "I left

Olivia alone to speak with Gemma in private."

Caleb stalked forward towards them as Gemma shook her head at his enraged face. "No, it's my fault. I was fighting with Jax and took off down the mountain," she explained, but Caleb stopped her by pulling a small pine branch out of her hair.

"What the hell is this? What, Jax—did you chase her into a tree?"

Neither of them answered. Jax, as usual, gave nothing away, but Gemma's face crumbled in guilt while Caleb continued his verbal assault, frustrated by their silence. "What's the matter with both of you? Gemma, when are you going to stop this childish behavior? Olivia has been injured because of your moody tantrums." Gemma blinked back at him in shock. She was obviously in more pain than I thought she could—or should—handle.

"Caleb!" I cried, "This was my fault. I forgot to put my necklace on after I showered." But Caleb remained focused on the Dhampir woman before him.

"I'm . . . I'm sorry," Gemma whispered before racing out of the room. Jax was right behind her, stopping her before she reached the glass doors. "Gemma, do not leave. It is not safe for you to go down the mountain by yourself with Davin's soldiers out there."

"I can't stay," she cried, her words sounded muffled, as though he must have been drawing her into an embrace and burying her face in his clothing.

"Please . . . Just remain here where I can protect you."

Caleb was hearing all of this and shaking his head, his two fingers pinching the bridge of his nose. He knew he had lost control of his temper and was now working hard to get it back. I always felt for him most in moments like this because I knew he tried so hard to keep control of a vampire side that was constantly working against him. "Caleb, just go talk to them," I pleaded. "They didn't mean any harm."

His concerned gaze was pained as he leaned down to kiss me gently. "I want you to close your eyes and get some rest. I'll be back in a few minutes." Of course, I couldn't rest.

Downstairs, the family's continued infighting was breaking my heart. They were trying to talk more calmly, but it was not working; there was too much emotion in all of their voices. "I'm sorry," Caleb began. "I know neither of you intended for this to happen. But we can't afford to be caught off guard like this again. Gemma, I need to understand what's going on with you. Your actions are now affecting other people."

"Caleb," Jax interjected, "Gemma has something she needs to tell you."

Gemma remained silent at first. I couldn't imagine how terrified she was to work up the courage to tell Caleb the truth. Already disappointed in her, he certainly wasn't going to want to hear the rest of it. "Caleb, I've been seeing someone—a human. I care for him very much and have decided to move my things out of the house."

"*What?*" Caleb's stunned voice replied. "How long has this been going on?"

"For about two months."

"Two months? That's the same amount of time Olivia's been —"

Caleb stopped.

It was like listening to his mind clicking the puzzle pieces together—and it didn't take long, especially when he probably remembered the scent of the man who had been in the downtown condo. "Who is it?"

Gemma didn't answer. "Tell him," Jax ordered.

"A—Alec."

As soon as she said his name, Caleb let out a bellowed growl that literally sent a shiver down my spine. To hear that this man, whom he once saw as his human rival for my affections, was now intimately involved with the woman as close to him as a sister, was too much. "God*damm*it! I want that insufferable Brethren lackey out of our lives." My stomach sank as I heard his words. I wanted Alec, the man who was like a brother to me, to stay a part of my life. But now that was never going to happen. "And you knew about this?" Caleb shot at Jax. "How could you accept this after everything that happened with

Isabeau?"

"Do not ever speak to me that way about Isabeau! Do you understand?" Jax warned. "I am not accepting this. A Brethren Guardian puts Gemma's life in danger. That is unacceptable."

"And you both don't?" Gemma snapped.

A low, warning growl ripped from Caleb. "Gemma, if you think we're just going to let you waltz out of here back into the arms of the man responsible for taking Olivia from us—his Brethren responsible for hurting her—then you're out of your mind."

"He is right," Jax added. "I will not stand by and watch him hurt you."

"He would never hurt me! He's been nothing but kind and protective—"

"*No!*" Caleb snapped. "I don't want to hear it. This isn't going to happen."

"Stop it!" Gemma cried. "This is my life—my choice. I understand that you don't want anything to do with him. That's why I'm leaving. And I'm leaving now!"

"No!" Jax commanded and had Gemma stopping in her tracks. "Stay right here. Caleb—a word outside. Now!"

After I detected several muttered curses from Caleb, overheard by all of us, I'm sure, as he was leaving, I next heard the glass doors open and Caleb was gone. "I will speak with him," Jax said, trying to soothe an upset Gemma. "But do not go. There is too much I need to say to you."

"Jax, I—" But her words were cut off by another kiss. Once again, her soft sounds signaled her surrender until she pushed away from him again. "Jax, I can't. I'm very confused. Why are you doing this now? After all this time?"

"Just give me some time to speak with Caleb. Then I will be back to explain."

It was silent after that, until the glass door exits closed again. Gemma immediately returned to my bedside. As I stared up into her torn face, I wanted to cry for her. She was shaken, confused, and in a lot of pain. "I'm sorry, Olivia."

"This wasn't your fault, Gemma. I forgot the necklace." Just then I noticed another sprig of evergreen in her hair. Slowly, I pulled it out, and her face flushed in embarrassment. Another passionate exchange had happened between her and Jax while they were out there on the mountain. I squeezed her hand. "He's trying to tell you how much he cares for you."

"Oh, Olivia . . . I thought my knees were going to give out from under me when he kissed me. There was such passion, such intensity. My stomach's still buzzing. But I'm so shocked. I had finally made the decision to move on, to let him go, and now he tells me he cares for me. I can't do this to Alec." I sat up on the bed, and Gemma blinked back at me in startled surprise. "Lie back down or Caleb will have my head!"

"I'm all right. Gemma, this isn't about Alec or Jax anymore. You have to decide what *you* want. Just give yourself a chance to breathe, and listen to what your heart's telling you."

She shook her head miserably. "But what if I make the wrong choice?"

"You won't."

"How can you be so sure?"

I smiled at her. "Because they're *both* wonderful men."

"Thank you," she said, hugging me gently, and then shaking her head. "But I can't stay here. I need a place to think."

"Don't run away from him, Gemma. At least let him tell you how he feels, what's in his heart."

Gemma just kept shaking her head. "What if he's saying this now just to stop me from seeing Alec?"

"You don't really believe he would do that, do you?"

"When it comes to The Brethren, all bets are off. Even if he believes he cares for me, he'll change his mind once he starts comparing me to Isabeau. I can't compete with her memory. Maybe I'm being selfish, but I want someone to love me—me alone. I don't want to just be the woman after Isabeau."

"You have every right to want that. But you're never going to know the truth unless you allow him the chance to tell you how he feels."

She bolted to her feet, appearing to have reached some sort of decision. "No. This is all too sudden. Jax doesn't change his mind like this. He's doing this because I told him about Alec." Gemma truly looked confused as she turned and raced from the room.

"Gemma!" I sprung from the bed to chase after her. "Jax will sense that you're leaving!" I followed her over the edge, but when I landed on the main floor, the force jarred against my side. I fell to my knees, hissing in pain as blood began again to pour from the wound.

"Way to go, Olivia." I couldn't stop Gemma, and now my blood was dripping onto the hardwood floors. I had to get it cleaned up before Caleb and Jax returned. Limping slowly to the kitchen, I grabbed some dishcloths and returned to wipe up the drops, only to notice that I had created an entire trail of blood to the kitchen. That's when I sensed Caleb and Jax returning, and they were moving fast.

"*Dammit!*" I said with frustration, hurriedly moving over the floor, wiping up several spots, but I saw I was only making new ones. I threw the towel down as the glass doors opened and both men were suddenly before me with bewildered expressions on their faces. "Olivia!" Caleb blinked. "Why are you out of bed?"

I couldn't answer him without getting him upset at Gemma again, so I remained silent, protectively covering my side. Jax hissed in anger, already sensing that Gemma had not waited as he had asked. Caleb moved towards me, but the sapphire returned to his eyes and he began to shake as he got closer. "Caleb, you are thirsty," Jax warned. "You cannot control it right now. Follow Gemma down the mountain and make sure she is not attacked by Davin's soldiers. Feed your thirst at the vehicles on the way back. I will tend to Olivia."

Caleb didn't even challenge the coven leader. He knew, as upset as he was, he couldn't control his thirst. His torn expression conveyed how much that bothered him. He hated that his life was so controlled by thirst and anger. "Take care of her, Jax," he growled, then left.

Jax lifted me off the floor into his arms just as Caleb turned on the security lasers from below. He carried me up towards Caleb's study. I felt bad for Jax. He was having what could only be called *a terrible day,* yet he still put others first. "I can walk. I know the blood is hard to smell."

"I am fine with the scent. Let me help you with your wounds." Setting me down on the bed, he pulled the bloodied towel away from my waist. "You have lost a lot of blood. I will get some clean towels and fresh blood for you to drink. It will help you heal faster." He stood to leave, then looked back at me. "I do not want you leaving this bed. Is that understood?" From his tone, it wasn't hard to figure out that some of his frustration with Gemma not staying put as he'd asked was bubbling over.

"Jax, she's confused, and in a lot of pain. She blames herself for what happened."

His expression tightened, then ended with a long blink. "I will go to the city tomorrow to speak with her."

"Good. She'll have a night to calm down then. That'll be better."

***

An hour had passed and Caleb still had not returned. Even though I knew he would be worried about my injuries, I feared he was upset with me for not saying anything to him about Gemma and Alec. I wasn't sure how I was going to explain that it just wasn't my place to tell him. It was Gemma's.

When Caleb finally entered the room he sat on the bed beside me, sighing inwardly as he stroked my hair. "Jax said he had to give you some blood." I nodded as he pulled the covers off me to examine my side. His lips pressed into a hard frown as he scanned my injuries.

"I'll be all right," I reassured him. "You don't need to worry."

His hand fisted in front of him and his jaw went tense. "Olivia, I was almost too late. You were falling from the house." Suddenly, he raced into the bathroom and was back at my side, the sapphire necklace that I had carelessly forgotten there in his hands. "Here," he said, placing it back around my neck. "I *felt* you weren't wearing this. That's how I knew to return. When I felt your pain after they attacked you—"

"I'm sorry if I scared you. It was my fault for forgetting the necklace."

"You shouldn't be in a position where your life depends on a necklace in the first place," he replied with frustration. "Just get some rest."

Caleb moved a chair beside the bed, holding onto my hand, but he was quiet for a long while. He was thinking. "Olivia, did you know about Alec?"

After a long pause I finally answered, "Yes."

He turned his head away from me. It was probably just as well. I didn't want to see the disappointment in his eyes. I wasn't sure I could handle it right then.

"You were hoping to hear a different answer from me?"

"Yes."

Chapter Twenty-Six

I was awakened during the night from a sound sleep by Caleb's cool hand brushing the side of my face. My lashes fluttered, my eyes opened, and I found myself looking directly into his worried gaze. Something was wrong. He pulled the covers low on my hip, examining the cuts and swelling over my midsection. "Can you move?" he asked.

"What's wrong?"

He kept his expression calm, neutral, but I could still tell he was worried. "I need to know if you're well enough to travel. We need to go."

I sat up in bed. The pain was still there, but lessening. "Tell me what's happened."

"Gemma's missing."

"Missing?" I gasped. "Are you sure?" He nodded. "Jax felt her struggle briefly, then she vanished from his senses. He's already left for the condo. I told him we'd be right behind."

I bolted from the bed so fast that dizziness came over me as I landed on my feet. Caleb grabbed my shoulders and leaned me back against his body to steady me. "Easy," he whispered, holding me still. "I don't like moving you so soon, but Jax and I discussed it. We think Davin could be setting all of this in motion, hoping we'll leave you here unprotected. I want you to stay with us until we have a better handle on what's happened to her."

"Yes," I nodded. "I want to stay with you. I want to help."

"I'll help you get changed and we'll head down."

✱✱✱

Moving at breakneck speed on foot down the mountain

and then in the car for what remained of the pre-dawn hours, we arrived at the Walker condo in a little under two hours. We were only about twenty minutes behind Jax, but he had already surveyed the condo and the surrounding streets by the time we got there. "I picked up Davin's scent about a block from here," he told Caleb. "He was here recently. I knew better than to leave her here unprotected."

"We'll find her," Caleb assured him.

"I don't understand," I said. "Why would Davin take Gemma? What does he possibly have to gain?"

Caleb turned to me, frowning as he noticed I was favoring my injured side with my hand. "He's using her to divert our attention away from you," he responded, placing his hand over mine. "Are your cuts bothering you?"

Shaking my head, I replied, "I'm fine, but I realize I'm not at full speed. I don't want to slow you or Jax down in tracking her."

Caleb leaned in to brush his lips across my forehead. The gesture was so tender that for a moment it felt like everything was normal between us . . . which, of course, it wasn't. "You need rest, and I need you to stay someplace where I know Davin can't reach you. That's either your home or sacred ground."

Jax's reply was absolute. "Not the church."

"Very well. Your condo, then." Caleb took my face in both of his hands. "I want you to stay there until we return. Do you understand?" Touching the sapphire necklace around my neck, he added, "Davin can't enter unless you invite him, and the necklace will keep you blurred from his Dhampirs."

"I understand. But, Caleb . . . something about this just doesn't feel right. Please, can we stop for a minute and think about this."

He kissed me gently, then pulled back so his gaze would meet mine. "There's no time. I know you're worried, but we'll be fine. I'll be back for you as soon as I can. Just keep the necklace on and stay inside."

"Caleb, please. I can't explain it, but—"

"We have to go, Olivia," he cut me off. "Gem's life's at stake."

I realized he was absolutely on target. We couldn't afford to waste time talking. I turned to Jax, moving to rest my head on his shoulder, my arms encircling his waist. "Please be careful—and bring her back safe."

He wrapped his arms around me, making sure not to put pressure on my wounds. "Do not worry, Granddaughter. We will return soon, safe and sound, with Gemma."

***

Back at my condo I paced back and forth until I almost wore a path into the floor. I knew I should be resting, but my mind was still nagging at me. The pieces just weren't falling into place. It didn't make sense for Davin to take Gemma, but there *was* one person who had showed way too much interest in her —Reese Lambert. The thought of Reese having anything to do with Gemma's disappearance worried me. He was an Elder with too much power who had been put down, forcefully, by another Elder . . . and he didn't like it.

Grabbing the overnight bag I had hastily thrown together, I dug around for my cell phone, hitting the first speed dial on the address list. Alec answered in two rings. "Olivia? Is everything all right?" he asked in a dazed voice, obviously not fully awake.

"No, it's not. I need your help."

"Where are you?" Just that quick, he was in full alert.

"At my condo."

"Be there in fifteen. Are you in any immediate danger?"

"No. But please hurry."

Less than fifteen minutes later, there was a hard knock at my door. When I opened to let Alec inside, his forehead was already wrinkled with disapproval. "You should always ask who it is before you open the door."

I rolled my eyes, grabbing his arm to drag him in the room. "I knew it was you. I recognize your energy." That brought just a hint of a smile to his lips, more evidence of how he loved seeing my skills come along.

"Tell me what's happened?"

"It's Gemma. When did you last see her?"

His light brows arched in surprise. "Night before last. I was with her before she returned to the tree house to collect her things."

"You've not seen her since?"

"Enough with the twenty questions, Olivia. What the hell's going on?"

"She's missing, Alec."

His body visibly stiffened as his mind clearly shifted into Guardian mode. "Missing? For how long? When was the last time someone saw her?"

"Just a few hours," I replied, squeezing his arm reassuringly. "We all saw her at the tree house, but Jax felt her struggling after she returned home, then she dropped out from his senses. He and Caleb are tracking Davin right now. They picked up his scent near the condo."

Alec's facial expression hardened to steel. "Davin!" he growled. "Son of a bitch—if he touches one hair on her head . . ." He turned away from me and marched toward the door, proclaiming, "I want you to stay here. And don't answer the door—"

"Alec, wait!" I ran to him, grabbed his arm and pulled him back around.

"Olivia, I need to go search for her!"

"That's why I called you to come *here*. I don't believe it was Davin who took her. I think something else is going on."

"Who . . . ?" He hesitated, obviously confused, thinking hard and getting nowhere. His eyes closed and his head shook back and forth for a second or two, until he blurted out, "You think The Brethren has something to do with this?" Hearing no denial from me, he stepped around me and faced out toward the terrace, so I could no longer see his expression. But I didn't need to. I knew he didn't like it. "What possible reason would they have to kidnap an adult Dhampir? That's *ridiculous*."

"Please, just hear me out."

"Look, Olivia. I know my uncle has done some inexcusable things the past few weeks, but he wouldn't do this." When he finally turned back to me, I could see in his soured expression that my accusation had cut deep, and the pain and doubt he felt the day we left The Oracle was now back in his consciousness. I suddenly realized that his hard pursuit of Gemma had been distracting him from confronting the reason why he left there in the first place: to decide his future.

Gently I reached out and stroked his arm. "I don't mean to hurt you, Alec. I may have this all wrong. But isn't Gemma's life worth the trip out there to know for sure?"

He rejected my gesture of sympathy and swung around on his heels, wide-eyed, determination on his face. "I'm not taking you back to The Oracle. Have you forgotten why you left in the first place?"

"No, I haven't forgotten. And I'm not looking forward to going back, believe me. But this is Gemma were talking about. She needs our help."

Alec threw up his arms in frustration. "OK. But before we jump in a car and head to Canada, let's think about this rationally. If The Brethren were behind her disappearance, then how would you explain Davin's scent around the condo?"

"That's a good question."

Alec snorted at that. "Yeah, because Davin's the likely culprit here—*not* The Brethren."

I began to pace the room again, recalling everything we knew up to this point . . . which wasn't a whole lot. Then, aloud, I began reviewing so Alec could follow my reasoning. "Jax said he found the scent a block away. He didn't say he found it in the building."

"And your point is . . . ?"

"What if Davin's scent was there *not* because of Gemma but because of *you?*"

Alec's whole expression stilled just then, and I could tell his mind was going to the same place as mine. "That day . . . at The Oracle . . . by the chapel . . . Davin said he knew to find me there because my Guardian was there—you. His exact words were that '*you'd always keep me near you.*"

"You're suggesting he's been following *my* scent trying to find you, since you are blurred to him by the power of your necklace?"

I nodded quickly. "It probably took him a while to figure out we were no longer at The Oracle. He's tracked your scent here and is hoping you'll lead him to me . . . which could mean it's just a coincidence that Gemma's nearby."

Without warning, Alec was suddenly right behind me, holding my arms. "Concentrate!" he said, almost in a whisper. "Do you sense him or any other vampire's nearby? Did I lead him here to you?"

"No. It's OK, Alec. I don't sense anything. And if he was anywhere near here, Caleb and Jax would've sensed him earlier."

Alec sighed in relief and then stepped around me, rubbing his fingers over his chin. "Well, then, here's the plan. You stay here. I'll go back to The Oracle and search for Gemma."

Before he even finished I was shaking my head. "No good. You take me with you or I'll just follow you."

"*Jesus Christ*, Olivia! Now's *not* the time for one of your stubborn streaks."

"I think it's the perfect time. And on our way back there we'll discuss how it's possible that your cursing has gotten even worse since you've been away from Lucas."

"*Dammit!*" he snapped. "I'm not taking you back there until I check a couple of things out." He whipped out his cell phone.

"Who are you calling?"

"Gideon."

While Alec made several phone calls, I freshened up, still feeling sore and tired from the battle with Davin's soldiers and my predawn start. Inspecting the cuts and bruises around my midsection, I was relieved to see they were healing nicely. The bruising was almost gone, and the cuts, though still ugly, would probably be completely healed in the next twenty-four hours. This time, 'freshening up' meant a careful shower, after which I dressed a little more slowly than usual because there was still some pain present where I was bruised. I put on a clean, red tee shirt and pulled my hair back in a clip, letting loose tendrils fall against my face. About an hour later, actually feeling much more refreshed, I went back to Alec, who had finally finished with Gideon. "Well? What did he have to say?"

"Joseph and the other Elders are returning to The Oracle to meet in chambers tomorrow night. Evidently, they're going to discuss what's been going on under my uncle's watch. Gideon's going to let Joseph know what's happened here. I told him you suspect they might be connected."

"But you still don't agree," I sighed. "Does Reese know about the meeting?"

Alec walked towards the terrace doors, where he stood very still, staring out at the rain that had started falling as if his thoughts were a million miles away. After a few long seconds of silence, he responded, "I'm sure he does."

"Alec, whatever secrets your uncle's been keeping—don't you think it's logical he would act now to protect himself?"

His head tipped down and he was quiet for another long moment. "I don't believe my uncle would take her. I don't believe he'd do that to me. He knows I care for her." Turning back to face me, he said, "I think you're wrong . . . but I need to know the truth."

"Does that mean you'll take us back to The Oracle?"

"I can't believe I'm saying this, but . . . grab your coat. We've already lost most of the morning."

I just started to reach for my things when I felt him take hold of my arm and turn me back to him. "You do know how angry Caleb's going to be once he discovers you went back? How much danger you're putting yourself in?"

I exhaled a hard, almost theatrical breath. "Hello!—I'm mated to the man!"

Alec rolled his eyes. "God, don't remind me."

"Besides, if I'm right . . ."

"If you're right, you'll be in even more danger. And he'll like it even less."

***

It was still dark outside when Alec woke me. I had been sleeping in the passenger seat of his SUV. We'd been taking turns driving through the rest of the day and into the night, with Alec having the final leg. The trip was excruciatingly long because of snowy driving conditions and multiple coffee stops. "Are we almost there?" I asked, showing him an exaggerated yawn.

"Yeah. We're about to cross the border. Your passport's in the bag in back." As I turned to reach onto the back seat Alec's sharp voice startled me. "What the hell is this?" he asked, pointing to my waist. My tee shirt had pulled up as I stretched, allowing him to see and focus on the cuts in my side, which he could see even in the dim lighting within the cab of our vehicle. "What happened?"

Grabbing my passport, I turned back stiffly, pulling my shirt down to conceal the last of my wounds. "Olivia, you better start talking in the next five seconds. I'm not asking again."

"Calm down, Alec. I just had a skirmish with a couple of Davin's soldiers."

"A *skirmish?* A skirmish?" he repeated in disbelief. "*Aaahh . . .*"

The sound Alec made was so eerily strangulated that for a second or two I was worried that he was having a stroke.

" . . . and you weren't going to tell me about this, were you?"

That was true. I had no plans to tell him anything about the attack. "Now, before you jump to any conclusions you need to know it was my fault."

Frustrated, he slapped his hand against the steering wheel. "I already jumped to conclusions when you called it a fucking '*skirmish.*"

Terrified that knowing about the attack would affect his decisions with Joseph, I knew I needed to downplay the incident as best I could. "I forgot to put the necklace on after I showered. It was an accident."

"And when did this happen?"

"Day before yesterday."

"Olivia! Those cuts had to be pretty deep to still be healing. How badly were you hurt?"

"I was fine. And you would've been proud of me. I defended myself against two of Davin's Dhampir soldiers. My training has come along well."

He rolled his eyes upward as if he were praying to the heavens for strength. "Don't try to sidetrack me with a search for praise. Where were Caleb and Jax?"

"Jax wasn't far away, and Davin tried to lure Caleb from the house with a couple of other soldiers. But they both showed up to help me, and together we defeated Davin's men. No big deal."

Proud at how simple the whole incident sounded in my retelling, I thought things were about to calm down, but Alec's expression turned suddenly furious, and it startled me. "Olivia! Where's your necklace?"

Oops. "Don't be angry," I began. "I took it off a few hours outside of Seattle, while you were sleeping."

Alec steered the car off the road, slamming on the brakes, his breathing hard and forced as he huddled over the steering column. The possibility of a stroke *did* seem very likely at that moment. Quietly, he said, "Why did you do that?" And then his voice erupted and he yelled, "The *last* thing we need is a couple of irate vampires pounding at the border to sacred ground while all of The Elders are in council and we're trying to search for Gemma."

"I'm sorry, Alec, but I think we're going to need their help." In response, Alec shoved open his car door, exited the cab, and began pacing along the side of the road, his hands flying into the air, then raking through his hair at his temples. I had never seen him so angry. At that moment he was giving Caleb's thirsty temper a run for its money.

I got out of the car, as well, and watched him as he continued to pace furiously back and forth in front of the vehicle, spotlighted by the headlights. "How exactly are they supposed to help us from behind sacred ground?"

"I don't know, but my gut's telling me that we're going to need them."

Alec threw his arms up again. "Of course! Your gut! Is that the same gut that's so sure Gemma's here?" He didn't give me a chance to answer. "Let me ask you something, Olivia. What if you're wrong? What if Davin really does have Gemma? If so, then you will have just pulled Caleb and Jax off of tracking *her* and now have them racing to come here to get *you*. What if something happens to Gemma because you're wrong?"

"I don't think I'm wrong, Alec. Your uncle was too interested in Gemma."

Alec stopped his pacing and turned his back on me. I could tell he was practically shaking with anger, but his voice was deadly calm. "He wouldn't do this. My family wouldn't do this."

Wow! Now I realized why Alec had been fighting me so hard. It wasn't about The Brethren at all. He had already lost his father, and Reese was the only family he had left. He didn't want to believe that his uncle was capable of doing something like this.

Walking over to him, I gently placed my hand on his back. "I'm sorry," I murmured. "You're right. I could be jumping to conclusions. I'll put the necklace back on."

"It doesn't matter," he said, shaking his head. "By now, Caleb realizes that you're on your way back to The Oracle. He'll be tearing this way . . . he's probably not far behind us. We have to keep going."

"He'll be farther behind than that. I waited a few hours before I removed the necklace."

Alec laughed, but without humor. "You forget. I was with him the last time he tracked over land and water to find you. He'll be right behind us. And fuming mad, I would guess. Whatever we find there, I wouldn't want to be in your shoes when you have to explain all this to him."

***

After arriving at The Oracle, we tried to make as low key an entrance as possible, though Gideon was there to greet us. "Gideon!" I leapt into his arms, not realizing until that very moment how much I had missed the quirky Englishmen.

"Olivia, it's good to see you," Gideon smiled. My hug became more of a choke hold before I finally let him go. Gideon then offered his hand to Alec. "And it's good to see you back here, my friend. Your presence has been sorely missed."

"I didn't want to come back under these circumstances," Alec said, offering up only a neutral smile.

"No, I understand. You picked a heck of a day to return, though. There's a lot of buzz around here, what with tonight's special session and all." He then turned back to me. "So, Olivia —you think the Dhampir that belongs with the vampire coven guarding you is here?"

"I do."

"Why would she be here?"

"I'm not sure. I just know Reese was much too interested in her the day we left, and he has since been to Seattle and seen her." Alec remained quiet as Gideon watched him.

"No offense, but I think Reese might have more than enough to worry about with tonight's council session than to be out kidnapping Dhampirs," he suggested gently. "Do you agree with her, Alec?"

Alec shook his head. "No." His answer was honest, as always. "But do you think you can get us in to see Joseph? If there's any truth to this, then Reese will have Gemma someplace only accessible to a few."

"You're quite right. I'll see if I can speak with him. I believe he'll make time for you, Alec. He's been concerned how you've been handling everything . . . what decisions you may have made?"

Alec's expression remained unaffected as he replied, "I've not made any decisions yet."

Mmm," Gideon sounded. "Follow me. Let's see if we can get

up there."

Alec and I waited by the elevator that had access to the twelfth floor while Gideon went up to see Joseph. It certainly didn't take long for people to notice that Alec was back. While we were standing there, several people came over to speak with him, their admiration and respect evident.

Trying to remain in the background, I was caught off guard when I felt a light tickle on the back of my neck. Swinging around, I saw the men I had missed—Lucas, Phin and Kane. Since I had not had a chance to say goodbye when I left before, I was so happy to see them that I greeted each of them by throwing my arms around one, then the other, and then the next, all the time squeezing tight. "Oh, I'm so happy to see all of you. I've missed you."

As I hugged Kane, he, predictably, held on longer than was proper. "Ready to take me up on my offer yet?" he whispered in my ear.

I stepped back and smiled at him in amusement. Sometimes Kane was just flat-out entertaining. "I think my *mate* would have something to say about that."

He waved his hand dismissively through the air. "No worries, mates are never a problem."

"You wouldn't say that if you'd met him," Alec snorted as he walked up to Lucas and gave him a quick hug and pat on the back. "Good to see you again, my friend." It was clear by the deep affection in his tone that Alec saw Lucas as a brother. After they exchanged a few words he then turned his attention back to Kane. "Kane, haven't you found someone else to sexually harass yet?"

He replied with a wicked smile. "Several, in fact."

"Any problems?" Lucas asked, ignoring Kane altogether.

Alec's expression was guarded. "We'll see," he answered. "Have you been able to figure out what's been going on around here?"

Lucas shook his head just as my attention was diverted by the sound of a familiar voice. "Olivia!"

"Maya!" I cried, rushing up to give her a big hug.

"Phinneas told me you were coming. I'm surprised to see you back here."

"I'm surprised, too. But Gemma's missing. We're trying to find her."

Maya batted her clear, blue eyes in a long blink. "Here? Why would she be here?"

"Then I take it you've not seen her."

"No." I was starting to worry that Alec might be right—maybe I had jumped to conclusions and Davin really did have Gemma. I hoped I had not pulled Caleb and Jax away from the search for Davin on a wild goose chase.

"It's just that Reese was so interested in knowing about her. Too interested—you know what I mean. My instincts are telling me she's here."

"Well, after everything we've seen from Reese lately, it wouldn't shock me. But if none of us have seen her, where would he be keeping her? It's hard to hide someone among all of us."

"You're right. She would have to be someplace where no one would see her or suspect anything."

"And they would have to get her there without anyone noticing," Maya added. "That's hard to do here."

"True. Someone would definitely be aware if she were brought inside the hotel—" Cutting off my own words as I stared back at Maya with a moment of déjà vu and asked, "Maya, this may not make a lot of sense . . . but what about the chapel? When Reese and Jude came in that day, they were headed straight towards the front."

"Yes," Maya agreed. "As if they knew exactly where they were going. We need to check it out."

"Check out what?" Alec asked, his tone filled with suspicion as he brought himself back into our conversation. "What are you two up to?" Swallowing hard, I didn't answer him right away. If my hunch about Gemma being here was correct, Alec would be devastated. If there was a way for me to discover the truth first, then let him know, he could be more prepared for it.

"Maya and I just have something we want to check out. No worries," I said breezily. "We won't be gone long."

We didn't make it two steps before Alec grabbed my arm to stop me. "Uh-uh. You have five seconds to tell me what's going on." Lucas, Phin and Kane were now right there with him.

"Why is everything five seconds with you today?" I grumbled. "Look, it's just a hunch I have. If there turns out to be something to it, then I'll come get you. Besides, someone has to wait here for Joseph."

Alec stood there with his hands on his hips, completely befuddled. "I swear to God, Olivia, you are going to drive me to some serious drinking. I'm not going to let you wander around here unprotected when we don't know what's going on. So you better start talking. Five—"

"—Seconds. I got it," I sighed. "We were talking about the day in the chapel when Reese and Jude interrupted us. They waltzed right in as if they knew exactly where they were going —heading straight for the front."

"Well, we certainly know they weren't there to pray," Kane smiled, those amazing silver eyes of his twinkling with his amusement.

Alec's gaze swept to Lucas. "We should check it out." Lucas nodded in silent agreement, while Alec nodded to Phin and Kane. "Stay here with them while Lucas and I go take a look."

"Wait a minute," I complained. "This was my idea. I'm going with you."

"This could be dangerous. You need to stay here."

Locking my hands on my hips and bringing myself up to my full height, I replied, "No way!"

"Olivia, don't be so stubborn. Just stay—"

I took off towards the chapel at top speed before he even finished. "Olivia!" he barked, but I kept going.

"Women," I heard Lucas mutter behind me.

"I know," Alec grumbled.

When I reached the empty chapel, I headed straight for the

front altar. There were two doors. One led to a utility/storage room, the other was locked. "This is what we're looking for," I whispered to myself. Grabbing the door handle, I pushed my shoulder into it until the door swung right open. *Maybe I'm not as weak as I thought.*

Peeking inside the dim space, I saw a set of concrete stairs leading downward to another level below. Knowing Alec would be furious with me if I continued on without him, I waited patiently but put the time to good use. Closing my eyes and taking a slow, relaxed breath, I focused on reaching out to Caleb. As I suspected, now that we were mated the connection was easier to make. I could see him clearly. His focused eyes were just as determined as the day he came for me at the prison. My chest swelled with relief just knowing he was on his way as I saw in my mind the long muscles of his legs continuing to fly over the surrounding landscape.

Then his brows softened in recognition. My connection had reached him, but it didn't stop him; in fact, he began pushing himself even harder and faster toward The Oracle. He was close. Relief seemed to wash over his expression; he was *feeling* that I was all right. "That's it, Caleb, keep coming," I whispered. He was now speaking to someone, and I was guessing he was updating Jax.

I really hoped I wasn't wrong about this.

The image of him suddenly dissolved as my focus was interrupted by Alec's voice. "Olivia?" he said, shaking me out of my trance.

I fluttered my lashes at his worried face. "It's OK, Alec. I just saw Caleb. He's close."

The Guardian's wide-eyed expression announced his amazement. "You can see him in your mind?"

I nodded back at him as he grasped my shoulders. "My mother could see James, as well. She talked about it in her journal. I believe our connection is stronger, though, because Caleb can connect to me on the other side with his gift to feel."

"That's just fucking great," Lucas grumbled. "The vampires are on their way here—with all The Elders in the house tonight.

Why don't we just invite Davin and some Lycans and have a damn block party outside?"

"Believe me, she's already heard this from me," Alec replied, moving around me through the broken door.

"This is what we're looking for," I said, moving forward, but his arm blocked me.

"Stay behind me," he ordered as he started down the stairs. Lucas motioned for me to go next so I'd be in between them. When we reached the bottom, we faced another door. This one was steel, fortress-strong—secured-access only—and there was no way we'd be able to break through to see what lay beyond.

"This looks newly constructed," Lucas said, with surprise in his voice as he focused on Alec. "How do *you* not know about this? You're a future Elder."

"That's a good question," Alec replied, distractedly, as he scanned the adjacent concrete and steel surroundings. "My uncle has never mentioned anything about this."

My eyes swept the little room in which we all stood. "There," I said, pointing to an air duct about eight or nine feet up in the high ceiling space. "We can get inside through there."

"Olivia, stop," Alec warned. "We don't know what's on the other side."

"That's kind of the point of getting in there, isn't it?" I replied, my sarcasm intended. "Now, stand against the wall under the vent, Alec . . . and Lucas, bend over to your knees in front of him."

"I don't think so," Lucas shot back.

"Oh for Pete's sake—don't be such a guy."

"I am a fucking guy," he defended sourly.

"You know what I mean. Now come on, I need a step up onto Alec's shoulders."

"Just do it, Lucas," Alec said. After a couple of minutes of rather comical stair-stepping, I rattled the vent cover off and handed it down to Lucas. "Be careful," Alec called back.

Following the confining tunnel in the direction of the door, I popped off another cover when I reached another hallway and jumped down, vent cover in hand, and headed immediately back toward the entry door, which I could see, dimly, a few yards ahead of me. I twirled the security wheel mounted on the door and pushed it open. Alec was waiting on the other side with his hands propped over his jean pockets. "Not bad," he said.

Lucas grabbed both metal vent covers and used them to keep the door propped open. "Just in case Phin and Kane come looking for us," he observed.

Alec gave a single, approving nod. "Good thinking."

Together we walked through a wide, unadorned corridor lit dimly from above. Soon we came upon several glass-fronted medical labs. "What's all this?" Lucas asked.

Alec's expression was hard. "I don't know. But I don't like it."

As we came to the next lab, I gasped. "Gemma!"

Chapter Twenty-Seven

None of us could believe what we were seeing. Gemma was unconscious, stripped down to her bra and panties and strapped to a metal gurney inside a medical lab. "What the fuck?" Lucas said in stunned amazement.

Alec didn't speak, his bewildered expression saying it all. The Brethren—his uncle—was somehow responsible for taking Gemma from her home and bringing her here, where it looked like they intended to use her as some sort of lab rat.

I rattled my hand back and forth against the metal handle on the heavy door. It moved, but the door did not open. "It's locked."

"Not for long," a furious Alec replied as he threw his whole body into the door, shoulder first, but it didn't budge. Alec cursed under his breath as he reached over his shoulder, his fingers bloodless as his hand curled deeply into the muscle.

"Alec, you're going to hurt yourself. That door is steel. We'll do this together."

"You think the three of us can get through that door?" Lucas questioned.

I shook my head at him in reply. "No. But I think we can come up with enough force to break the door at its hinge." I gazed at Alec and his somber expression just then, realizing he and Gemma needed me to be strong in this moment. They needed me to use every ounce of Dhampir strength I could muster inside me.

"Let's do this," Alec replied, and he and Lucas lined up on each side of me a few feet back from the door, but I moved around him to take the spot closest to the door jamb.

"I have the most strength." Alec didn't argue with me, which actually surprised me a bit. On the count of three, we burst towards the door. On impact, I could feel the door break away at its jamb, and all three of us crashed to the floor on the other side.

"Fuck, there are days I hate being human," Lucas growled.

Alec helped me back to my feet. "Are you OK?" I nodded, then ran to Gemma's side.

"Gemma!" I called, while Alec removed his jacket and covered her with it. "Gemma, can you hear me?"

Alec brushed the back of his hand over her cheek as his gaze thoroughly scanned the equipment and medical supplies on a cart next to her. "She's been given anesthesia," he said a moment before he ripped a ruby-red gemstone necklace from her throat. "This explains why Jax couldn't sense her. *Dammit!* How could I be so blind?"

"Alec," Lucas called.

"Not now, Lucas. We need to focus on getting her out of here."

But Lucas's tone was firm. "You need to see this." Alec glanced up to meet the Guardian's hard gaze, realizing something was very wrong. He tossed the necklace onto the medical cart and rushed to the adjacent doorway. I followed right behind him. In the next room there were three metal gurneys with the same monitoring equipment and IV carts that had been next to Gemma. And on two of the gurneys men lay unconscious, also anesthetized and strapped down, while blood was being transfused into him.

"Aiden? Zane?" Alec's stunned voice whispered. "What is this? Who did this to them?"

"You know them?" I asked him.

"Yes—they're Guardians. Damn good Guardians, at that. Aiden is Kane's closest friend."

"Yeah, and it gets worse," Lucas said as he held one of the blood bags in his hand. "This is vampire blood. They're being transfused with it."

"What the hell's going on here?" Alec questioned. "That

could kill—"

"Alec!"

A sharp voice snapped at my Guardian. Swinging around, I gasped at seeing Reese Lambert and Callum Maberey at the door of the lab, their gazes almost seething as they glared back at me. "What're you doing in here?"

Alec responded quickly, pulling me behind him and away from the two Elders who now stood between us and Gemma. "What is all of this?" he demanded. "What have you done to them? These are good men."

There was no mistaking the pure fury in Reese's eyes at hearing the nephew he cared for speak to him with such contempt. Both Reese and Callum stepped inside the room toward us. "As a future Elder, all this would've been shown to you in due time—when you were ready," Callum replied, a somber, threatening coolness in his tone.

"Well, then, perhaps as a *current* Elder—you could explain this to me," came a strong voice from behind them. Reese and Callum swung around to see Joseph standing there with Gideon, Phin and Maya, and fellow Elder Nathaniel Hawking. It appeared that Lucas's call to leave the door propped open had been a good one.

Rage continued to build in Reese's eyes. This man of secrets had been caught in his struggle for power and was being called out on it by the younger Elder. And he didn't like it one bit.

"What is this?" Alec growled again. "It looks as if you're transfusing vampire blood into—"

"—Into Guardians," Reese replied without apology. "You're so naive, nephew. We're losing this war. The Immortals are stronger and have few weaknesses. If we are to win, we must find new ways to fight them. You know this cause is worth the sacrifice of a few men."

Alec stood there, looking completely stunned—as if he were staring into the face of a pure stranger, someone he didn't know, not his uncle.

Learning the truth of what his uncle had been up to was breaking him inside, and it worried me.

"Are you completely mad?" said Alec, almost shrieking. "You're taking human men and turning them into something . . . something not human."

"Jude," Lucas snarled. "That's what's wrong with him! He's been transfused. That's why he's not acting like the Jude we all know."

"Jude's a Super-soldier, right, Reese," Joseph began as he stepped closer to his fellow Elders. "That is what you're trying to create here? Humans with the strength of a vampire by blood."

"Not trying—succeeding," Callum snarled, sounding triumphant. "We've been able to cross-match human blood with the cells of vampire blood. Jude's strength is ten times that of any Guardian here. Don't you realize what that means, Joseph? Eventually we can create an entire army—one that can stand toe to toe in battle against the Immortals."

As I stood there, equally shocked, I repeated Callum's words *ten times stronger* in my head. Suddenly I realized how Jude had overpowered me that day in class, and I also knew why he was so emotionless about the whole thing. The human part of him was lost, and in a strange way I almost felt sorry for him— or at least the man the rest of The Brethren seemed to care about.

"What I see are two Elders exercising a reckless abuse of power," Joseph hissed. "This isn't what our forefathers would've wanted. They valued human life—wanted to protect it, not to use it by converting good men into something not human."

"Are we to rely on your leadership to defeat the Immortals?" Callum snarled. "You're such a coward, Joseph. You refuse to do what's necessary to win this war."

"I *will not* allow you to try to win it at the expense of the very human lives we have taken an oath to protect," Joseph bit back.

Reese stepped closer to Joseph in warning just then, and Phin reacted right away, putting himself between Joseph and the two Elders. "Don't get all high and mighty with us, Joseph. Who do you think built all of this?"

Joseph stiffened as if he'd been slapped in the face. "My father?"

My heart suddenly went out to this man. What must it be like for Joseph to learn that his father, Davin—the man he loved —had become twisted by darkness, possibly even before he became a vampire? And there just seemed to be more and more of Luther's secrets unraveling in front of him.

"Yes, Joseph," Reese smiled, splaying his hands out. "He's the architect of all of this."

I looked to Alec. He already understood the pain of having someone you loved—your family—betray you in a way that would leave scars on you for the rest of your life. I hated Reese for hurting him this way. "And what were you going to do with Gemma?" Alec asked. "The Dhampir you *kidnapped?*"

"We merely wanted samples of her blood," Reese replied. "Completely harmless."

"We're not fucking idiots," Lucas growled. "You could've taken her blood in Seattle. There was no need to bring her here."

Alec's gaze bore into Reese. "For once *Uncle*, tell the truth."

Reese didn't respond, but Nathaniel did it for him. "Let me guess. You wanted to impregnate her?" Alec's lips pressed tight in anger as his eyes slowly returned to his uncle. "It would be the next logical step—a child between a Dhampir and a Super-soldier."

"Why Gemma?" Alec asked dryly. "Because you knew I cared for her?"

Reese remained silent. It was clear that he felt far above having to answer these questions. "For that exact reason, Alec," Nathaniel continued. "She could be impregnated without her knowledge and tracked in the outside world. My guess is they were hoping you'd believe the baby was yours and bring her and the child back to The Oracle. They would insist on it."

Unable to hold back his rage, Alec lunged at Reese, throwing The Elder back against the wall. "You bastard! You make me sick! Did you impregnate her? *Did you?*"

Lucas dragged Alec back, but my Guardian continued to go after him verbally. "Answer me, you son of a bitch!"

"The girl's fine," Reese snarled. "Nathaniel's jumping to conclusions."

Alec's hard, raspy voice seemed to scrape in his throat, the fury behind his words lethal. "You're a disgrace to the title of Elder."

"Never speak to me that way again, nephew," Reese hissed, then turned his mad glare on me.

I was really wishing I had listened to Caleb and stayed put in Seattle. I didn't care how furious he would be with me. I just wanted to be back safe in his arms.

"This is all because of you, you miserable little tease. You enjoy the power you have to make men lose their minds over you!"

As Alec pulled me farther behind him, I caught just the barest hint of a flicker of awareness that had flashed through Joseph's eyes. "Stay away from her, Uncle," Alec snarled. "That's the only warning you'll get."

In a tone that commanded attention from everyone in the room, Joseph then said, "This Dhampir wasn't the one you wanted to impregnate, was it, Reese?" Joseph said this more as a statement than a question, and then he looked to me. I was startled as I began to realize his meaning, and I found myself grabbing Alec's hand, squeezing it tight. "You wanted a *Charmer* in the family."

"*What?*" Alec barked, swinging his body around to face his uncle directly. "That's why Jude tried to rape her? Because you ordered him to impregnate her?"

"I think you're missing Joseph's point, Alec," Nathaniel pointed out. "He's suggesting that Reese wanted *you* to impregnate Olivia. Then he'd have a direct claim—and control —of the next line of Charmers."

"You're just making this stuff up as you go," Reese growled at him. "You've no proof of any of this!"

"The blood?" a stunned Gideon finally spoke. "The vampire

blood that was "*mistakenly*" given to Olivia. It wasn't an accident, was it? You both knew how it would affect her—weaken her resistance. And you knew Alec, as her primary Guardian, was already struggling with her illusion—his attraction to her. I'd told you of this. You were hoping the two factors would result in him impregnating her."

"Yes they were," Joseph answered for them. "Then, when that didn't work, you ordered Jude to get the job done. But your Super-soldier's been out of control. And you realized it once he tried to rape Olivia. Then you both had to start covering your tracks. That's why you worked so hard to persuade the others in council."

My gaze dropped to my feet while I focused on remembering just to breathe in and out. It was all becoming so clear to me. Even though there were many people here I cared about, I recalled now why I fought so hard to leave, not realizing but somehow knowing that somewhere along the line The Elders had lost their way. Overtaken by greed and power, they had lost sight of their original mission, to help humans. Or, at least, some of them had.

"Well, shit," Lucas laughed humorously. "That explains why Kane was assigned to our team." Then, as if right on cue, Kane burst through the door and moved to Joseph, but his eyes went straight to Aiden, his friend, lying there on the gurney, unmoving, and you could plainly see the confusion and concern transforming his expression, emotions the overconfident shifter rarely displayed. But—dutifully—he said to Joseph, "The complex continues underground to another section. From there it extends beyond sacred ground."

"Yes, they would need an area in which to draw the vampire blood without being noticed," Joseph replied. He then turned to Reese. "Where is Jude now? No one's seen him for days."

Reese just stood there, defiant, refusing to say a single word.

Joseph shook his head in disgust. "He's having trouble staying on sacred ground, isn't he? The Jude we all know—the human—is gone."

"How could you do this?" Alec yelled. "How could you be a

part of this?"

"Oh, shut up, Alec," Reese snarled. "We wouldn't be in this mess if you'd just done you're your job when the girl was throwing herself at you."

I gasped at exactly the same moment as Alec's arm flew back and then whipped forward, his fist connecting with a loud crack against Reese's jaw. Reese went crashing back against the wall of the lab and slid down, uncontrollably limp, to the floor. Lucas dragged Alec away from him, and Kane and Phin hauled Reese to his feet. But Alec couldn't stop his anger—his newfound hatred for his uncle—from exploding. "You're such a fool. Both of you are such fools! You did all of this for nothing!"

He then looked at me, his eyes asking a silent question, and I knew what he wanted to say. He just needed my permission to do it. I nodded at him and he turned back to his uncle.

"Olivia can't have a child!"

Both Reese's and Callum's faces froze in shock. Maya glanced over at me, her heart absorbing in all the pain welling inside me. "The Greysons had a procedure done on her when she was a teenager. She can't get pregnant."

"God*dammi*t!" Reese cursed loudly. "Why did Luther ever trust those people? The girl would've been raised here if it weren't for their meddling."

Joseph stilled us all with a raised hand. "What did you just say . . .? My father was working with the Greysons?" When neither Reese or Callum answered him, he demanded one. "Speak!"

"Indeed, Joseph," Callum began with aristocratic disdain. "You look at us with such contempt. It's laughable. Your own father made arrangements for the Greysons to be offered before The Elders as her surrogates. He could then remain in control of the girl. He marked her with our symbol so it would always be known whom she belonged to."

"She doesn't belong to The Brethren!" Alec shouted. "*My God*, the vampires were right. Olivia isn't a free person in your eyes. She's an object to possess to further your own agenda."

Alec then turned to me, his expression apologizing a

thousand times over as he reached his hand toward me and smoothed it over the side of my face. "That's why they did it, Olivia. That's why the Greysons ran off with you. That's why they had the procedure done. They realized what kind of man Luther really was. They must have somehow figured out he planned to impregnate you as soon as you were old enough. They were trying to protect you, to give you a normal life. However misguided their intentions, they did it out of love."

Alec pulled me into his arms and hugged me tight, trying to ease some of the pain that suddenly seemed to be swallowing me.

This was just too much. I couldn't take it all at one time like this. Closing my eyes, I yearned desperately to connect with Caleb at that moment . . . and I did. His handsome face was full of worry as my connection reached him. He closed his eyes, his respiration deepening while his mind took in the firestorm of emotions now swirling through me. When his eyes flew back open, he furiously beat his fists against the impenetrable wall just outside. I raised my head and turned back to Alec. "They're here—waiting outside."

"The Daywalkers are here?" Joseph questioned, and then turned to a still unconscious Gemma. "Does this Dhampir belong to their coven?"

"Yes," I replied. "And they want her back."

Joseph sighed as if at a loss about where to begin. "What a mess you two have made."

Reese took another threatening step forward, but Phin held him back. "What do we care of their coven? We're not in the business of negotiating with vampires."

The normally calm and controlled Joseph snapped his head up with fire in his eyes. "And you wonder why we're losing this war! If you truly respected this cause, you would be out there trying to build a bridge with the vampires who want to live in peace with humans, encouraging the idea so they'd spread it among their community. Instead, you're building Super-soldiers and destroying the good men who are fighting for our cause. Jude doesn't even resemble the human he once was. The Jude we knew would never have tried to rape a woman. That's on your head."

Joseph then turned to Maya. "The woman's clothes are over there. Will you dress her, please . . . quickly?"

"I can't believe you're our Brethren leader," Reese growled. "You're now catering to the wishes of vampires? Who cares if they want the girl—or her," he added, pointing to me.

"Well, you're free to bring the issue up of my leadership tonight in chambers. We'll let the group decide."

When Maya had Gemma dressed and was carrying the unconscious girl in her arms, Joseph looked at Alec and me. "Alec, return the Dhampir and Olivia to the vampires, then I want you to come and find me." He then turned to Lucas. "I want you, Phin and Kane to escort Reese and Callum back to their rooms. I'll have guards dispatched to relieve you soon until the matter of their actions can be addressed tonight in council."

Alec grabbed my hand and pulled me past Reese and Callum without another moment's hesitation. Taking Gemma from Maya's arms, he nodded for me to follow. After a quick hug for Maya and motioning goodbye to all of my Guardians, I didn't hesitate to leave. I was ready to return home—to the vampire waiting for me outside with zero patience. Just thinking of being back in his arms made me breathe a little easier.

But Reese's anger continued to thunder behind us. "Nathaniel, do something!"

"Don't look at me, Reese. I think he's being generous to send you to your suite. You deserve a lot less."

Once we hit the cool blanket of early morning air, I scanned the grassy field until I spotted Caleb and Jax about a hundred yards ahead of us, waiting. *No*, more like challenging the laws of vampire physics by trying to bully their way across sacred ground. At seeing me, Caleb's brute bashing of the invisible wall seemed to slow, but the exaggerated rise and fall of his chest didn't. *Oh, man*, Alec was right, Caleb didn't look happy with me at all. I could see it in the rigid stance of his body and hard glare of his eyes. Until my butt was firmly planted back on that side of sacred ground, the hard scowl stamped on his face would remain.

Jax appeared just as angry until he saw Gemma's slim figure lying limp in Alec's arms. The hard line of his brows seemed to soften as his expression shifted to worry in an instant. "Gemma!" he called.

Anxious and excited, I now raced towards Caleb. I didn't care if he was upset with me for taking off and trying to handle this on my own. Right now I just wanted to feel his strong arms around me and beg for forgiveness later.

"Ohhh, Aaaalec!" a familiar, dark voice called from behind us. I swung around just in time to see a silver-tipped arrow brush within a hairsbreadth of Gemma's cradled body and drive straight into Alec's chest. The instant loss of breath dropped Alec to his knees as Gemma fell from his arms.

Jude raised his curled lip just above the trigger of his crossbow and said, "My Charmer's not going anywhere."

"*Alec!*"

Chapter Twenty-Eight

I raced towards Alec as his body lay there, motionless, legs and arms splayed awkwardly on the ground. My mind feared the worst as I dropped to my knees beside him. His eyes already appeared heavy, as if he had to fight to keep them open. His breathing was weak and his face was ghostly pale. Blood poured from the wound the arrow had created in his chest. It looked to be dangerously close to his heart. "Alec?" My tears fell onto his face as my hands soothed over his temples. "Just stay still. You're going to be all right."

"Go to Caleb," he said weakly just before his eyes fell closed and he went still against the wet grass.

"Olivia!" Caleb called from behind me. "You heard him. Come to me—now." Though he tried to remain calm, I could hear the icy tension in his words. His breathing was hard, primal, growling, and I knew something was very wrong.

I glanced up to see Jude stalking towards me, but there was no way I could leave Alec lying there alone. "Alec, please hold on," I begged.

"Olivia!" Caleb bellowed again. "Get over here!" I felt for Alec's pulse at his throat. It was still there, but it was too faint, his breathing too shallow. I knew he was dying right in front of me, and my heart just couldn't take it. "No, not again," I said tearfully as I dropped my head to his shoulder. "I can't lose anyone else, Alec. I can't lose my Guardian."

"Olivia . . . ?" Caleb's voice sounded as if it were all breath as he spoke. "It's going to be all right. But I need you to come to me—now. Gemma needs you. Please, bring her to us."

I couldn't focus on what he was saying. Alec was dying!

Then suddenly Caleb's low, fierce growl snapped, "You touch one *fucking* hair on her head and you're a dead man!"

"Olivia, come," Jax ordered, but I couldn't move. *Alec was really dying!* Now a new emotion was overtaking my fear—*anger*. The more I thought about how I could do nothing to stop this from happening the more it seemed to seethe from every pore in my skin. I hated Jude more than I had ever hated another human being. He had to pay for what he had done to Alec.

Rising slowly to my feet, I must've appeared like a serial killer, standing there with all that blood staining my clothes—Alec's blood. I challenged Jude's merciless grin and took a step towards him, while Caleb sounded as if he were going ballistic behind sacred ground. "Olivia, don't you dare!"

Jude seemed to love the challenge, throwing his crossbow to the ground without so much as a break in his hard strides towards me. "Welcome back, Olivia. I've been waiting for you." His features were too manic and his forehead beaded with too much sweat over the gray cast of his skin. He appeared sick, but he moved forward as if he were invincible. Being on sacred ground was hurting him. The immortal blood pumping in his veins was blackening his soul, eating away all traces of the human man and leaving only unspeakable evil.

"Olivia! Get over here, *now!*" Caleb thundered, while Jax released an animal-like snarl, the sounds of both of their primal voices telling me the men were now gone . . . the warriors were here.

"You and I have unfinished business, Charmer. The vampires can't help you . . . but I'll let them watch."

"You'll pay for what you did to him, Jude."

"*Jude!*" Caleb pounded his fists on the invisible wall. "*Do not touch her!*" His voice was rough, nothing more than a rough scratch against his throat.

I backed away from Alec and Gemma so they would be out of harm's way, but Jude took that as a sign of weakness. He removed his jacket, tossing it to the ground and looking as if he were preparing himself for battle. "Oh, we're gonna have fun. And we're gonna do a lot more than touch." He took the first swing at me, jamming a hard fist into my side. I gasped beneath the power of his strike before finding the strength to block his second punch. He then raised his eyes to Caleb. "And you've got a front row seat."

"You fucking bastard!" Caleb roared. "You're dead!"

Twice my size, Jude came at me with every ounce of force within his hybrid body. I ducked under his next punch just in time when it occurred to me that there was a flaw in the training plan where Jude was concerned. It didn't matter if I defended his blows and got myself into position to use my gift. My gift didn't work on him.

"Keep letting her hear your voice," I heard Jax say. "You must keep trying to break through."

"Dammit, Jax! She's full of nothing but rage."

"I know. I feel it. But she hears you. Keep trying."

Jude swung at me again and then dropped to try and sweep me to the ground with his leg, but I was able to maintain my focus and countered with a hard kick to his jaw. His head snapped back. "That was for Alec," I said. "And this is for me." I landed a second blow to his hip that shoved him backwards. I never felt so strong in my life! "Olivia," Caleb tried to speak in a calm, assuring tone. "Come to me. I know you're angry. I can help you. *Let me* help you."

"He can't help you," Jude warned. "Just like he couldn't help you that day in class. Do you remember that day, Olivia? I think you do. You loved fighting me. Your sweet, helpless girl routine is just a cry to be dominated by a real man."

"Is that the only way you can get a woman, Jude—by forcing her? Rather pathetic." Enraged by my words, Jude came at me hard. I managed to block a second shot at my hip, but he followed immediately with two punches across my middle that threw me breathlessly back against the ground. He then dropped over me like a conquering force, covering me with his large body.

"*Goddammit!*" came from behind me. All rational thought had evaporated from Caleb. The warrior, with his steel edged voice, roared in blind fury as he was made to watch helplessly while Jude crawled over me. Though the Guardian's big body felt suffocating, I refused to let fear take over. I waited for the right moment, conserving my energy and watching him carefully for a weakness in his defenses, even as he began pulling at my jeans. He straddled over me, and I let him believe he had all the power so he would lose focus for just a moment. "You're right, Jude," I murmured softly. "I do want you . . ." Then I yelled, "I *want you* to get the fuck off me!" I swung my knee dead center into his groin so hard he crumbled over onto his side with a guttural groan.

Using the opportunity to roll away from him, I came to my feet and could hear Caleb's hard, uncontrolled rasps. "Olivia, please. Get over here!"

Meanwhile, Jude was already getting back to his feet, his gaze burning with hate, as I positioned myself carefully on the field. Reaching a hand behind my back, I signaled to Caleb and Jax behind me. But Caleb was now breathing as if he were strangling in his own breaths. He was so livid that I worried he missed the signal I gave him.

Jude swung at me again but I ducked just in time, coming up behind him and hitting him in his low back. But this time he succeeded in swiping my legs from underneath me, sending me crashing to the ground on my back. My head hit against the hard, rocky ground, momentarily stunning me.

Jude considered me weak just then, and for some reason my instincts told me I needed to use my gift. As he tried once again to pin me to the ground, my fingers latched onto his temples. Instantly, I could feel the shift in his weight. He cursed, rolling off of me. My touch now affected not the man who had been transitioning, but the dark creature who had replaced him. That's why my gift hadn't worked before. It couldn't recognize the soul that was lost in the in-between.

Staggering to my feet and taking several steps back, I realized that my limbs had little strength left. I would need to rely on my gift, not my strength from this point forward. Jude followed me, step for step, his flat eyes glancing beyond my shoulder to locate the vampires pounding furiously against the invisible wall. "Your fighting skills have improved, Charmer."

"Can't you see what they've done to you, Jude? Reese and Callum have turned you into something not human. The vampire blood they transfused into you is destroying the man all your friends here care about." I wasn't saying any of this for Jude's benefit. I needed Caleb and Jax to understand what we were up against—a hybrid with no human feeling or emotion left inside him. "Joseph can still help you if you let him."

Jude snorted with contempt. "Joseph and the others are weak-minded fools. They can't see how I'm now better than a human. But Reese and Callum can. And you, my little Charmer, are my reward."

"I don't think so."

He laughed with a truly evil laugh as he continued to march closer. "Getting tired, little Charmer? Let's see if we can put you out of your misery."

Jude charged once again, and I knew I wouldn't be able to absorb many more of his punishing blows. As his fist descended I threw my arms up to block him, wrapping my hands around his bare forearms. His motion was halted as his mind was injected with torturous images, and the pain was acute. I knew, because the images were shooting back at me, scraping like nails over an open wound. Flashes of his attack on me that day in class were replaying through my head, causing both of us to tumble back to the ground. "Olivia, what's happening?" Caleb demanded.

I didn't get a chance to answer him because Jude's booming voice shouted, "You bitch!" His hands were clinging to his temples. "You'll suffer for that."

Shaky on my legs as I arose once more, I stepped back as he came at me, this time with such force he shoved me back several feet before I hit the ground. I cried out as more images flashed through my mind, my hands flying to my temples that were throbbing in pain. I no longer had the strength to defend myself.

But I didn't have to.

Caleb dropped in front of me, his powerful body imposing a steel barrier between me and Jude as his warning growl rumbled so low in his chest it shivered through me. "You should pay more attention to where you're standing," he said.

Jude's eyes widened in recognition that I had lured him off sacred ground, but like the trained soldier that he was, he brushed it off quickly and focused on the current task of destroying the vampire blocking him from what he was obsessed with having—me.

Caleb threw a quick glance over his shoulder at me. "I've got this. Stay with Jax." Marching forward with menacing strides, he jutted a sharp finger at Jude. "You like hitting women?" he thundered just before launching himself in the air to smash into Jude, sending him the opposite direction, assuring he couldn't return to sacred ground. "You like raping women?" he continued, his voice thick with rage as he kept coming. "Well, you messed with the *wrong* woman."

Jude returned quickly to his feet, showing no fear of his challenger. "And I'll fucking mess with her again as soon as I'm through with you." The two met in the middle of the field with titanic force. The vampire blood pumping through Jude's system did, indeed, make him strong, but as Caleb smashed into him the newer, less experienced hybrid grunted at the hard impact. Caleb was dangerous on any given day, but when he was enraged from seeing someone he loved attacked, dangerous was an understatement. He was my invincible blue-eyed warrior.

But that didn't stop me from worrying. "Jax, shouldn't you help him?"

"And take this away from him? Not a chance. He has wanted this since that first moment you told him Jude attacked you." As Jax came to stand beside me I clutched onto his arm and tried to steady myself. "Easy, Granddaughter," he said gently. "Let me take a look at your injuries."

But all I could focus on was the fact that Jude had pulled out a silver-tipped blade and was twirling it between his fingers in front of Caleb, showing his proficiency with the weapon. Caleb's lips tilted into a crooked smile. "You think that blade is going to save you? I warned you not to touch her . . ."

"I think it's going to be pretty damn painful for you." Jude launched at Caleb with the knife in hand. My breath stilled as I watched Caleb become no more than a shadowed blur, twisting away from Jude's strike and countering with a hard elbow to his ribs. Caleb was too quick, too strong and too angry. His powerful body slammed Jude back against the earth. The force sent Jude down on all fours, and in another blink Caleb reached him and snapped his head between his hands, breaking his neck instantly. Jude fell, lifeless, to the ground as my heart pounded like a drum in my ear.

"Granddaughter, we need to get you somewhere I can tend to these injuries," Jax said. I nodded, and with his help I stood back to my feet, but I surprised him when I darted back onto sacred ground. "What are you doing?" he growled.

Nodding to a still unmoving Gemma I said, "I'm the only one who can get her."

His worried gaze scanned over her unmoving form as he nodded, "Get her quickly—and then we need to go." But Caleb's loud roar as he tossed Jude's lifeless body on a now burning pile and then turned to find me standing on the wrong side of sacred ground was letting me know he wasn't happy. He flew back to the invisible wall, his eyes storming with a mix of anger and worry as he held out his hand for me to take. "Olivia, come."

Just then I heard the faintest sound. "Alec!" I cried, swinging around to see his fingers curl slightly against the grass. "*Oh, God.*"

"Olivia!" I heard Caleb cry again behind me as I raced to Alec's side. My Guardian was so pale and had lost so much blood I feared he didn't have much time. I cursed myself for wasting precious minutes to get him help in my fight with Jude. "Alec? Don't you dare stop fighting. I'll get help."

He barely opened his eyes, his breathing weak as the faintest smile pursed his lips. "You're going to be OK, little Charmer," he whispered, then fell silent again.

"*No!*" My body fell protectively over his as unrelenting sobs tore from someplace so deep inside me. I knew I was helpless to stop it. "I need my Guardian. I can't lose you, too. Please! Please, not you, too!"

"Olivia?" Caleb questioned, his voice now sounding weak, fragile.

"Caleb, please," I begged. "He can't die. He can't!"

"Listen to me," Caleb replied. "I can help him. I need you to check his vest pockets. See if you can find any kind of empty vial or container." I tried to focus on Caleb's words so they would sink in. *He could help him?* "Olivia, do you hear me? Do it now."

"Caleb, are you sure?" Jax asked, while I searched frantically through his pockets.

"Yes," Caleb answered simply, and I wasn't sure what that was all about. But after pulling out first aid supplies, a kit of needle and thread, and some silver chains, I located a small plastic container filled with some holy water. Pouring the contents out, I held it up towards Caleb. His expression stalled at seeing all the fresh blood covering me. Nodding, he waved for me to come to him.

I jumped to my feet and ran over to him, his concerned gaze following me the entire way. I reached out and moved the container over the line. Caleb grabbed my bloody wrist, and I feared he would pull me off the sacred ground again. His breathing was labored as he tried to control the blood scent that was reaching him as he squeezed my hand. I stared up at him, never before feeling so desperate. "Please help me, Caleb. Help me help him!"

He sliced his fingernail across his wrist, catching the blood in the container he held before placing it back in my hand. "Give this to him. Make sure he drinks all of it. Hurry."

Back at Alec's side, I raised his head up and patted his cheek. "Alec! Alec!" After what seemed like endless seconds, he finally opened his eyes, his breathing still faint. "You need to drink this." I placed the vial on his pale lips. As he took in the first sips he began choking, trying to spit the salty liquid back out, but I wouldn't let him. I tilted his head back so he was forced to swallow. In my mind, rejecting the blood was not an option if it would save his life. "More, Alec. Take all of it. Please."

I poured the rest of the contents into his mouth so fast he had no choice but to focus on swallowing it. Continuing to hold him in my arms, the silver-tipped arrow that had struck him down still pierced his chest as his chilled body began to tremble from the blood taking hold of his system.

"Olivia!" Caleb called. "Grab Gemma and come to us. Right now!"

Alec fell motionless in my arms again. Shaking my head, I cried, "I can't leave him, Caleb. I can't."

"Now, Olivia!" Hearing footsteps behind me, I turned to see Lucas, Phin, Maya and Gideon all rushing towards me. Caleb feared The Brethren would keep me out of his reach, so he was demanding that I leave Alec's side and return to them with Gemma. I understood his reaction, but there was no way I would leave my Guardian. If the situation were reversed he would never have left me.

"Alec!" Lucas called, dropping to his knees beside us. "How did this happen?"

"Olivia!" Maya gasped. "Look at you."

"It was Jude," I sobbed helplessly. "He shot him."

"That son of a bitch!" Lucas spat. "Where's he now?"

Shaking my head, I replied, "I fought him. I was so angry that he had hurt Alec."

"Are you hurt?" Gideon asked, worried by the sight of all the blood on me.

"I'll be OK. Caleb fought Jude beyond sacred ground when I couldn't anymore." I slid my gaze to the now roaring pile of flames behind Caleb and Jax. I couldn't tell if Lucas was upset or angry by the discovery. His neutral expression faded for a moment, as if he was considering the human man Jude had once been. But then his focus returned to the man who was like a brother to him. "Please help him, Lucas. I've done everything I could."

Gideon squeezed over my shoulder. "It's OK . . . you did good. It was smart to leave the arrow in his chest until we can get him to a doctor. It may end up saving his life."

"Tell Dr. Li I gave him vampire blood." Several pairs of eyes widened in shock around me, and I blinked back in my defense. "He was so close to death . . . I had to do something." Both Lucas and Gideon looked over at Caleb to see the dried blood drops on his already healed wrist.

"Lucas, Phin," Gideon began. "Get Alec up to Dr. Li right away. Lucas, I want you to stay with him and get the doctor whatever he needs. Understand?" Lucas nodded as Phin carefully lifted Alec's body into his arms. "Phin, I need you to bring me back some warm, wet cloths and a clean shirt for Olivia. Can you could grab something from Maya's things?"

"In my top dresser drawer," Maya added.

Once Phin and Lucas were gone, Gideon turned his attention to Maya. "Return the Dhampir back to them. If you're afraid in any way, remain on sacred ground. All right?"

"Yes," she said as she lifted Gemma into her small arms.

"Don't be afraid, Maya," I said in my now gravelly voice. "They won't hurt you."

Maya simply winked one of her blue eyes and headed toward them. A very anxious Jax waited as she stepped across the line unafraid. Jax made no sudden movements so Maya would know he had no intention of hurting her. Besides, his eyes were fixed on the woman in her arms. "Hello, my name is, Maya. I'm Olivia's friend." She presented Gemma to Jax as if she were a gift, and Jax wasted no time pulling the unconscious woman into his arms. "She'll be awake soon. I can feel it." Maya then pressed her hand on the forearm that was curled around Gemma's leg. Jax's gaze moved to Maya and watched her curiously. "You love her," Maya said simply, gazing directly into Jax's eyes.

"Yes," Jax replied without hesitation.

Maya smiled brightly. "Tell her."

Jax's brow arched high as he watched her move to Caleb. Reaching up on her tip-toes, she kissed the warrior on his jaw. Caleb's sapphire blue eyes shone back at her with surprise; he was not quite sure what to make of the situation. "I've wanted for some time to thank the man who safeguards my dear friend's heart."

"You're the woman who came to the clinic."

She nodded. "I was trying to help her."

"Maya, will you bring her to me? I need her."

Maya smiled and simply walked back towards Gideon and me. Even though I was exhausted I tried to stand back on my feet, but dizziness forced me back to my knees. Gideon was at my side, his arms keeping me propped up as I sat again on the cold ground.

"Olivia?" Caleb questioned.

"I want to go to him," I murmured at Gideon's shoulder.

"I know, but we need to get you cleaned up a bit first. You've too much blood on you."

Just then, a gust of air blew over me and the sound of Phin's voice spoke from above. "Here you go." He handed Gideon the damp towels and Maya the clothing. Gideon cleaned as much blood as he could from my face, hair and arms. Once he was finished, he looked at Maya. "Help change her out of these bloody clothes." Gideon and Phin turned away while Maya pulled the sticky clothing mess from my body, wiping down the last of the blood underneath.

"Very good, Maya. I'll take it from here," Gideon said, lifting me into his arms and walking towards Caleb. Stepping to the line, he didn't cross. I could literally feel Caleb's breathing stop. "I knew Olivia's mother and father," Gideon began. "All they ever wanted was for her to be happy. I believe she's happy with you. Please be worthy of my trust in you."

I blinked up at Gideon in surprise as he stepped over the line and passed me into Caleb's arms. I curled against him, literally wanting to crawl up on his body as he kissed me on my temple. "We need to get you out of here so we can tend to your wounds."

"I need to stay," I murmured against his shoulder. "Until I know Alec's all right. Please."

"Over there is an old Headmaster's quarters, just off the

property line," Gideon said, pointing toward the base of the mountains. "It's unoccupied, but it's a place to sleep and has running water. You can stay there if you wish. I'll have Maya bring you some food and blankets for Olivia and the Dhampir, and another necklace for Olivia so Davin doesn't sense her." Caleb nodded as Gideon glanced back towards The Oracle. "I must return. The gathering will begin in a few hours. There will be much to explain."

Chapter Twenty-Nine

The headmaster's quarters was a small house with very few windows and appeared to have been rarely used since The Brethren bought the hotel a century ago, though it was obvious that someone had been at least maintaining it. It was good enough for shelter and had a working fireplace for heat and a wood framed bed on the loft level. Caleb made that into a place for me to rest, using the blankets and pillows Maya had brought from The Oracle.

Gemma had finally awakened from her drug-induced sleep, and Jax had not left her side for a moment. He knelt beside her on the main floor as she lay across a bench padded with extra pillows and blankets. The heat from the fire warmed her as he gently stroked her hair, pulling a fresh blanket around her. "Did they hurt you, Gemma?"

"I don't think so," she blinked back at him, seeming still a bit dazed. "I don't remember much until I woke up here. Where are we, Jax?"

"We are at The Brethren stronghold in Alberta."

"The Brethren? Where's Alec?"

Jax peered off into the distance for a moment, and then proceeded to tell her everything I had explained to Jax and Caleb about how we ended up here. When he was finished, including telling her about Alec, Gemma's eyes were wide with worry and wet with unshed tears. "We will not leave here until we know how he is," Jax promised her. "Try to get some sleep. I will be right here."

There was a long silence between them. "Go ahead and say it, Jax. You warned me it was dangerous to be involved with someone from The Brethren. I didn't listen."

"I will not say I told you so. All that matters is that you are safe and unharmed. That is all that has ever mattered to me."

She brushed her hand over his cheek. "You're a good man, Jax Walker."

Shaking his head, he replied, "No. I am just a man who cannot lose you, Gemma. I want you to come home with me so I can take care of you for the rest of your days."

Surprise illuminated the woman's expression as he threaded his fingers through her hair, pulled her close and dropped his mouth over hers, moving his lips against hers in a deep, longing kiss until soon her eyes closed and her hands slid behind his neck as she relaxed into the moment.

When Jax finally drew back from the now heavily breathing Dhampir, a soft smile pulled over his lips, his gaze caressing her with such warmth. "I love you, Gemma. I have for a very long time. I have just been too stubborn to admit it. I wanted to be noble and let you go if that would make you happy . . . but I realize now I cannot. You make *me* happy, and you are second to no one. Just say you will give me a chance to prove that to you."

Gemma stared at him in stunned amazement, her torn whisper sounding almost desperate as she spoke. "Jax, I have waited so long . . ." Her words trailed off, as if unsure how to finish her thought. "I need to know you're not just saying this because of Alec."

He held her close, quiet for a long while as he watched her. "If you truly love Alec . . . If he is your choice . . . Then I will not stop you. But I will be damned if you go to him without knowing exactly how much I love you. Love you not as the teenage girl I saved, but as the woman who has bewitched every part of me that fights to be worthy of you."

I was watching all of this from the cramped loft space above them. Lying on top of several blankets, I was cheering inwardly at the scene below while resting my head on a pillow that was spread over Caleb's legs. Caleb, however, was not in such a jovial mood. In truth, he was a bit surly. Somewhat from thirst, but mostly over the fact that as I was watching the couple, he was examining a multitude of welts and bone-deep bruises on my body—residuals from my fight with Jude. He flattened his wintry palm over my stomach, his touch helping greatly to soothe the swelling, but he did nothing to calm the muttered curses beneath his breath. "I'll be all right, Caleb. You should go feed. You're grumpy from your thirst."

Shaking his head, he shot me a hard scowl. "I'm not leaving you. I'll feed later while you sleep. You'll just have to deal with a little grumpiness—which, by the way, was caused by your stupid decision to fight Jude on your own."

I rolled over carefully onto my back so that I could gaze at him fully. "I'm sorry. I didn't mean to scare you."

His brows lifted high, staring at me with an incredulous expression. "Scare me? Olivia, I've never felt so helpless in my life. I could do nothing except stand there and watch him beat on you. You can't—no, *you won't*—ever do that to me again." I covered the bone soft hand that was tending to my bruises with my own, watching his features twist painfully. He was recalling those recent moments. "And then, when I watched him drag you under him . . ."

"Forgive me," I said. "I was just so angry. All I could think about was revenge. Revenge for what he did to Alec. Revenge for what he did to me."

"I understand that. But Olivia, you are my mate—my other half. I know you want to be able to defend yourself, but you have to let me help you. Don't ask me to be a bystander. I won't do it."

Slowly, I lifted to a seated position and wrapped my arms around him, settling my head into his neck as I nodded my silent reply. "Hey, look at me," he said, stroking his hand across my cheek from my ear to the tip of my nose. "What happened to you when you were fighting him? I felt you in tremendous pain. From your wounds, yes, but also in here," he said, touching his index finger to his temple.

"It's my gift. As it becomes stronger I'm beginning to take in the evil images of those I mirror. I'm trying to not let it distract me when I'm fighting, but with Jude . . . I saw the images of the day he attacked me."

Caleb pulled me close. "Jude's not ever going to hurt you again."

"I know. But about Alec," I began, then stopped, the words stuck in my throat. " . . . I know you don't like him, but he's my friend. I can't lose him." I just couldn't allow myself to think that he might be dying inside that building and I was not there to help him, to say goodbye.

"It doesn't matter what I feel for him," Caleb replied. "I *never* want to see you in that much pain. If you need him in your life, then I want him to survive."

I wrapped my arms around his broad shoulders, my bruised body protesting as I pressed against him, but I didn't care. "I do need him. But please tell me you understand it is very different from how I need *you*—how I want *you*? You are my life."

He laughed silkily, his breathing soft over my ear. "It had better be."

***

"How can they do this?" I cried, slapping my hands against my bath water while several small ripples splashed over the side of the old, cast iron tub. "How can they not know I need to hear something? Anything!"

"Easy, sweet," Caleb murmured as he smoothed the soap filled rag he was washing me with over my shoulder. It had been two days since the battle with Jude and there had been no word on Alec's condition, leaving me only to hope that no news was good news. It would be unfair of me to insist on staying much longer, though I knew Gemma wanted to stay, as well. Caleb and Jax had used up the blood supplies they had brought with them and would have to find more soon.

Caleb rose to his feet, reaching for the bath towel, which he draped in front of him. He stared down into my pouting face and didn't even crack a smile. *My pouting face always made him smile.* Something was not right with him. He had been too quiet, too helpful for two days now. I stood up and he wrapped the thick towel around me as he lifted me into his arms, carrying me through the empty first floor before jumping us up to the loft.

Jax had taken Gemma out to stretch her muscles, and it was the first chance Caleb and I had had for any privacy in two days. He set me down on the edge of the bed and knelt before me as he rubbed the towel slowly over my shoulders, then my arms, his gaze following the soft strokes of the cotton material. When he was finished, he let the towel drop to the bed, leaving me completely exposed while his fingers explored the skin where the bruising had nearly healed. "It doesn't hurt anymore," I told him.

Caleb's fingers stopped as his eyes lifted to meet mine. "Good," was all he said, giving me nothing to work with to figure out if his introspective mood was because he was thirsty and just trying to hold back the sharp edges of his temper, or if something else was bothering him.

His hands slid up along my sides as he inhaled a slow, deep breath, and then seemed to pause as he held me just below the hollows of each underarm. My tongue moistened over my lips as I watched the heat flowing into his gray eyes, darkening them until they smoked. This was a different kind of hunger, no doubt, but I stilled worried what might be beneath it. Then his gaze lowered and stilled over my breasts as his thumbs brushed over the soft swells, massaging the blushing peaks with slow, circular strokes until they hardened beneath the pads of his thumbs. I sighed at the pleasure as my back arched away from him, rounding my breasts even more and making me feel confident I would soon feel his cool tongue drawing them hungrily into his mouth.

"Caleb," I gasped roughly at the unexpected trail his mouth burned down over my stomach while his dexterous thumbs continued to work the sensitive tips of my breasts. His hands guided me back to lie on the mattress, then he proceeded to kiss and lick around my navel, and then lower. I moaned and shivered at the cool, spiky tingles happening beneath his tongue. His breathing roughened as he lower himself into the dark curls between my thighs, the warm, feminine scent eliciting low rolling growls from somewhere deep in his central being. "Caleb, are you sure this is a good idea?" I asked with nothing but breath. "What if your fangs . . . ?"

His gaze lifted to me for a moment, his eyes tense, hungry. "I'll be careful. I'll control it. Just lie back and hold still." *Hold still?* Was he crazy? My skin already felt ten degrees warmer as my hips tried to arch right out of his hold on them.

"Caleb, I . . . *Oh!*" His tongue parted my flesh with such slow reverence I nearly screamed as my hands squeezed the blankets between my fingers. He hooked my legs over his shoulders and slid me to the very edge of the mattress. Wrapping his hands around my thighs, he locked me in place before proceeding to suck the sweet, rosy skin between his lips, like candy. I squealed at the sensation, my breathing becoming not just hard but choked, my hips begging to move violently with these overwhelming sensations.

Soon I was totally breathless, helpless, feeling the low rumbles continue to build through his chest and vibrate on his lips as he held me locked within his grip, his tongue swirling faster, his lips sucking harder. The warrior inside him was clawing to take control, and the sensations he was producing inside me were incredible. My body was on fire! I was panting now, and my skin felt as if it were literally buzzing with a total body electricity. I was so close to letting go, so close to the world exploding before my eyes, that I gasped and reflexively tightened every muscle in my body when he suddenly jarred back, lifting his chin high as his eyes swirled from their human gray to the brightest blue and the warrior took full control of him.

His breathing was fast and shallow, too, as we stared at each other unblinkingly for several moments. I felt like I had been left dangling at the edge of a cliff and I begged him with my eyes to continue even when I knew he couldn't do that without hurting me.

"I feel how close you are, sweetheart. You're right at the edge," he whispered. I blinked at him, wondering if he was torturing me on purpose.

He forced my hands above my head, clasping both my wrists in one of his large, strong hands.

My breath then caught as he flipped me onto my stomach, propping my hips high on a couple of stacked pillows. I lifted onto my elbows while he opened his jeans and positioned himself behind me. Grabbing my hips, he spread my legs with his knee and then braced himself on his hands just before I felt the smooth and silky thickness of him push through the soft tissue of my entrance. My head came up off the mattress and I gasped as he stretched my inner muscles at a snail's pace, driving deeper and deeper. When he was halfway in, I pushed my hips back, forcing him deeper. He growled and thrust forward in two powerful movements that fully seated him inside me, taking full control of my pleasure. Lowering on his elbows, his body caged me, his wide shoulders curling around me as his hands covered my fists, which were grasping at the blankets below me. He nestled his chin at the crook of my neck, his breathing slower, deeper, but louder and lined with a hard rasp, while he held his body still. "You feel so good," he breathed just before he groaned and began to move inside me. I couldn't even speak. He had me in such a frozen state of pleasure I thought I was seeing stars. A broken whimper left my lips as his deep, penetrating thrust moved in an almost lazy rhythm. He was building that fire again, but to a roar from a single flame. *Damn him!*

I could feel it, feel how close I was to release, but he stilled. "No, please" I whimpered. "Please don't stop."

He flexed his hips, stretching himself deeper. "Is that better, sweet?"

"No!" I bit out, squeezing over his length from hilt to tip in an effort to encourage him to finish what he started. He fell forward with a harsh growl, his hands curling over mine just before his hips began to pump harder, faster, more directly aimed at the very center of me. There was nothing lazy about these thrusts; they were possessive, unrestrained and urgent. "Are you ready to fly with me, sweet?"

My hips rose in answer and my back arched, my neck stretching to curl with his. I just needed him to be entwined with me when the explosion burst. And as the warning ripples began to strengthen and pull him deeper inside me, I was incapable of giving voice to the mind-blowing sensations. A silent scream held me locked in breath-holding silence then escaped as a series of deep moans as he continued to thrust inside me until he was sure he had wrung every ounce of release out of my body before he stiffened then shuddered behind me, roaring through his own release as his hands squeezed tightly over mine, then relaxed and opened as he came down from it.

Still locked together there, panting, forming one giant heap, we stayed together like that for several minutes. His broad shoulders arched around me as he rubbed his bristled cheek against mine. The contact was loving, the emotion of the moment raw, and the ongoing silence more meaningful than I first realized. "Don't you dare scare me like that again," he finally said. "Never again. I can't lose you."

I snuggled closer to him as he kissed every inch of my temples and cheeks. Somehow I knew then that everything was going to be all right. The frustration and fear of feeling completely helpless while being forced to watch Jude fight me had finally been released from his memory. He finally felt that I, too, was all right . . . and so did I. For some strange reason, I felt stronger than I ever had in my life, and I would continue to build on that strength as I moved forward to build my life with him. "I love you, Caleb Wolfe."

He squeezed his arms around me. "And . . ." he prompted.

"And next time, I'll come to you. No questions asked."

Caleb took hold of my lips, caressing them with a soft kiss that revealed all of his loving emotions at once. "I love you too, my sweet. Always."

I smiled at him. "So, are we going to stay in this position all morning?"

His low chuckle tingled over the shell of my ear. "Nope. Just long enough for me to have you one more time."

"Mmm, sounds good to me. Who knew a dusty old cabin could be such a—"

Suddenly, we both froze. We could feel Jax and Gemma heading back towards us at warp speed. I had never in my life dressed so fast. I had time only to throw my half-dry hair up into a clip, creating a loose tendril mess, while Caleb refastened his jeans and shirt. He rushed downstairs to greet them as they burst through the door, giving me a precious few more seconds to finish. "They're coming!" Gemma yelled.

"What!" I jumped down from the balcony and rushed right past all of them and out through the door of the cabin. Caleb, Jax and Gemma were right behind me as I ran through the thick and clinging fall morning mist that made it hard to see much of anything until it was practically right in front of you. I stopped right at the line of sacred ground, knowing Caleb would *kill me* if I crossed over it. As figures approached through the mist, we could soon see there were more than just a few. At least two dozen Guardians and Hunters appeared, advancing on us with full weaponry in hand. Unsure of what was happening, Caleb and Jax pulled Gemma and me behind them.

Lucas, Phin and Kane were all part of the triangle formation that headed towards us. Lucas was at the point, with Maya walking unarmed beside Phin just to Lucas's left. They all slowed, stopping several yards from us, and I backed up a bit to stand at Caleb's side, his arm holding me close. "I don't see him," I said anxiously. "What if Alec didn't make it."

Caleb took my hand and squeezed it gently. "It's all right. I feel it's all right."

I blinked up at him in surprise. "You feel it?"

He nodded just as my attention was diverted to a long line of men approaching in some sort of formation. They walked side by side, an equal distance apart, their identities becoming known as they cleared the mist. The twelve Elders, dressed in full-length velvet robes, regal in their deep, eggplant color and marked with the Celtic symbol proudly displayed on their chests. My breath drew in sharply when I saw them all together like this. "What is it, Olivia?" Gemma asked.

"Those are the twelve Elders. You don't understand. They assemble together only in council, in the inner chamber. They've never gathered out in the open like this."

Joseph was at his rightful place at the center of the group, and to his right, in the position usually held by Reese Lambert, was Alec! Tears welled in my eyes as I watched my Guardian approach with his eleven peers. He looked a bit slow in his movements, but there was much more color in his cheeks than I had seen the last time we were together. He looked from me to Caleb. There was something meaningful in their visual exchange . . . and for once, it wasn't anger.

"Alec and I are now linked by blood," Caleb said.

"Caleb?" I stared up at him in slow amazement. "You still helped him, even though you knew it would connect you?"

He placed a quick kiss on my forehead, then returned his stare to the small army in front of us. "I did it for you."

Lucas raised his arm just then, motioning to the group just before the protective advance force split into two groups, each group moving away from the center to allow The Elders to continue forward until they stopped about ten yards from us. To Joseph's left, in the position formerly held by Callum, now stood another young man, not much older than Alec. I didn't recognize him at all. "Olivia," Joseph began, stepping forward, "As you can see, Alec is healing quickly and will make a full recovery, thanks to Caleb's blood offering. For that we are very grateful and want to acknowledge it openly and freely." Joseph then nodded in a motion of respect towards Caleb, while I moved even closer alongside him. Caleb didn't try to stop me as he nodded his head in return, but his expression was still guarded. "Alec Lambert and Owen Maberey have now ascended to their rightful place among this group."

At Joseph's words I was caught off guard by the pride swelling inside me that Alec had chosen to accept his destiny. The conflict inside him about his duty and the direction of The Brethren must have been resolved, at least in part. As I smiled at him through watery eyes, he winked at me and then shifted his gaze to Gemma. She had the same prideful smile on her lips and the same glint of tears in her eyes.

Without warning, she ran to him on sacred ground. Jax watched in silent stillness as she left his side. He was setting her free. He had done all he could to tell her how he felt, and now the decision was in her hands.

Unlike Jax, however, the vampire standing beside me had no intention of letting me cross back over that line. His grip tightened on my waist to make sure I was clear on that point. He still didn't trust The Brethren, and I couldn't really blame him.

Alec took several steps forward and motioned with his hand to the men standing on each side of them to stand down as Gemma approached. She gently placed her hands on his chest where he had been injured and reached up on her toes to kiss him softly on his lips. "Thank you for helping me," she said.

His hand traced the slope of her jaw. "I'm sorry my uncle hurt you. I'll never be able to make up for his actions. But I promise he'll never hurt you again."

"It's not your fault, Alec. You're *not* your uncle. I know that. You'd never hurt me." Alec smiled, and I could see the love in his eyes. He truly cared for Gemma.

His gaze swept to the men and women around him before he added, "I need to do this. I need to make things right here again. But in choosing this, I have accepted that my life is here, at The Oracle. Seeing your beautiful face, though . . . I fear the consequences of this choice."

Gemma's voice broke with tears. "I'm so proud of you for doing this. You are a good man, the best of men, and I know you can handle this responsibility. But this isn't my home, Alec." She glanced back to Jax, whom I was almost sure hadn't taken a breath since she left his side. Outwardly, he projected the image of a man of steel, but I knew better. Inside he was pure, emotional liquid, frozen with the fear of loss.

Gemma smiled at Jax and in that moment, something changed within him. She returned her gaze to Alec. "I think I'm where I'm supposed to be."

Alec gave a meaningful look to Jax. Gemma had made her choice. Disappointment filled his eyes, along with the reluctant acceptance of the rightness of her choice. The spirited woman who had been raised in the vampire world didn't belong at The Oracle. She wasn't one of the Dhampirs who had been abandoned. She was free and wanted . . . and very much loved.

He kissed her one last time, brushing his hand over her cheek. "I will miss you, Gemma May. If you ever need me . . ."

Gemma's bottom lip quivered as she nodded her reply. Releasing his hold, Alec watched her as she crossed back over the boundary of sacred ground and returned to Jax's side, taking his hand. He said nothing, but I could have sworn that his wide chest visibly swelled with pride.

Joseph moved forward, motioning for Alec to follow. They stopped just in front of us, and I looked up at Caleb, silently pleading. He closed his eyes and flexed his hard jaw as he let go of my hand. I took the few steps forward that brought me face to face with my Guardian, the man who had become as important to me as any friend, any brother. "You're going to be all right?" I asked, really needing to hear him say it.

He nodded. "Yes, but I'm afraid I can't be your Guardian any longer, Olivia."

I laughed, tears falling freely over my cheeks. "That's OK. You've more important things to do now."

He shook his head. "Not *more* important. Important."

"Are you sure this is what you want?"

The man of truth didn't hesitate to answer. "It is. There's good here and there is still evil in this world. The Brethren can once again be what it was intended to be, a protector of the innocent. I need to be a part of that."

"Will you be here at The Oracle? Can I come see you once in a while?"

"I'll always be here for you, Olivia. As will Lucas, Phin and Kane. I have assigned Lucas to be your primary Guardian from now on. I trust him—"

"—like a brother," I finished for him.

He smiled. "Yes. Like a brother. He'll check in with you from time to time and report to me. If you need anything, you can always reach him and he'll know how to contact me." I glanced over at Lucas, who was standing beside Kane. He nodded, giving me the same smirking wink that reminded me of Alec. The two were so similar.

"Alec?" Joseph began, "What do you say to Olivia remaining with this coven? Can they protect her?" I turned to Joseph, biting my bottom lip, forgetting that in their minds a decision had not been made yet to allow me to stay with Caleb.

"They can protect her," he replied as my relieved smile met his. "As long as she's happy and it's what she wants, she should be allowed to stay without interference from us."

I hugged Alec gently around his middle. "Thank you."

Joseph turned back to the row of Elders standing behind him. "Are my ten brothers in full agreement with Alec's assessment?" Ten unanimous responses of "Aye" rang out, and I wanted to add my voice to the chorus, but I respectfully held it in.

Joseph turned to Jax. "Very well. Olivia is now your responsibility. Keep her happy and safe. I think Eve would've been pleased to know that her daughter's with you."

"Eve should have been with me, too," Jax replied sharply. "This group denied me that right—the right to know my own daughter."

Caleb went rigid, not happy at all with Jax that he picked that moment to fail to keep his emotions in check because I was still standing on the other side of the line. But could anyone possibly understand the pain Jax went through losing his wife and daughter to this group?

"I can't speak to that," Joseph offered sincerely. "It seems that under the reign of my grandfather and father this group forgot its purpose. Alec, Owen, and I are part of a new generation committed to restoring the original intent that The Brethren was born out of. But I believe we can learn something from your coven. Are there more Daywalkers out there like you? Vampires who want to live in peace with humans?"

Jax's nod was curt. "Yes. But I will not tell you where they are."

"No, I wouldn't expect that you would. But I'm hoping that in time you'll see that this new knowledge changes things for us. We no longer have a single mission. We want to defend the innocent from evil in whatever form it comes—vampire, demon,

Lycan, or another human. But we'll no longer take action against any coven such as yours as long as they are living in peace among humans." Joseph then stepped closer, as if to express sincerity with his words. "As I said, I can't change the past, and I can't give you back your daughter. But this Assembly of all twelve of us standing together before you, and the gesture of returning your granddaughter to you, is our offer of good faith."

Jax stared at each Elder as if memorizing their individual faces before returning his gaze to Joseph. "I accept the gesture."

Joseph turned to me. "Olivia, you will always be welcome here at The Oracle. And you have my word that The Brethren will continue to hunt for Luther and his soldiers until they're destroyed and no longer a threat to you." There was no conflict in Joseph's eyes. He understood his father was lost. Only memories remained of the man he knew. I mouthed the words "*thank you*" to him. He smiled and nodded before turning back to the group. "Let us return, Alec. We have much work to do."

Staring at my former Guardian, my bottom lip began to quiver. I was saying goodbye to him for a while, and knew I would miss him. He offered his arm to escort me back over the line of sacred ground, right to Caleb. "Be good to her," he said, offering his hand to him. "She's truly one of a kind."

As they stared at each other, it was as if both men accepted they would be forever linked. That link brought a small truce between them . . . at least for now. "Yes she is," Caleb replied, taking his hand.

Alec kissed me tenderly on my forehead for the last time before I watched him return to take his rightful place among The Elders. The twelve dignified men turned and began walking back towards The Oracle until they disappeared into the mist, the Guardians and Hunters following.

Maya ran up and gave me a quick hug and kiss before returning to Phin's side.

Caleb took my hand as we turned to see Jax wrapped around Gemma, kissing her as if he feared he might not ever get the chance to kiss her again. Gemma laughed as she finally pulled herself from Jax's grasp and lip-locked caress. "Now what was that you were saying . . . ? You wanted the chance to prove your love for me?"

Jax smiled. "Every. Single. Day."

Caleb turned to me with a knowing smirk. "So, that's what was wrong with them? You know, it would be nice if my *mate* would fill me in on these things once in a while."

"Yes, it would," I smiled. "But you're stuck with me, regardless."

As Caleb started to walk forward, I reached for his arm again. "What if Davin's waiting for us when we return?"

His fingertips brushed my cheek as his softly liquid gray gaze smiled at me from his heart, producing in me a warmth I felt to my toes. "Then we'll deal with him together. And once he's taken care of, the only thing you and I will have to worry about is being happy." He leaned in and kissed me, his body relaxed as I melted into his arms. "Are you ready to go home, mate?"

"Hmm, yes. Let's go home."

Epilogue

A long, slender hand with snowy skin and perfect, pink-tipped nails glided over the sleeve of one of his favorite sport shirts. As she leaned forward and inhaled the earthy infusion of fir, sage and leather that wafted from the fibers, she searched for a deeper scent. The scent she hungered for was more subtle, natural—a musky, masculine scent that was the unique identifying marker of the masterpiece she had created . . . but it had somehow changed. She had felt it, feared it, sometimes even over a great physical distance between them, and now it was confirmed by his scent. The same scent she smelled on the clothes of the female who shared his space.

In one quick motion she tore off her own shirt, leaving her bountiful, pale breasts exposed to the air. Tearing his shirt from the hanger, she rubbed the fabric against her skin, making sure her natural markers were unquestionably left behind in the fibers for him to find. Then she dropped the garment, almost carelessly, to the floor.

She smiled. It was a wicked smile. He would know she had been here. This shirt would be her subtle calling card. He would be warned.

"Re-mated?" Celeste spat out the word as her face took on a look of pure fury. "I don't fucking think so."

Acknowledgments

I have a wonderful team of people who, without their efforts, these books would not be possible.

For Robin Ryan, who has dedicated her life, and publishing career, to helping others succeed. Thank you for all of your guidance and counseling on this wacky world of publishing.

For Paul and Kevin, my editors, my second voice, who worked under a grueling pace to make sure this second book got out on time. Your commitment to its success is truly astounding.

For Sam, who came up with yet another amazing cover for *The Charmed Souls*. You have evoked the essence of these of books with imagery that's beautiful, haunting, and romantic.

Mom and Dad...thanks for just about everything else.

About the Author

Christine is a graduate of Washington State University where she received a BA in Interior Design. And true to form of using mostly her *'right brain'*, she splits her time between her commercial design career and her imaginary world of writing. She lives in the scenic Pacific Northwest where she enjoys hiking, camping and photographing many of the wonderful places that serve as inspiration for her Charmed Trilogy. Her biggest reward in life is any given day when one of books connects with a reader, because she herself is such a lover of reading.

Made in the USA
San Bernardino, CA
02 August 2013